RAVEN'S REDEMPTION

A CYBERTECH THRILLER

JOHN D TRUDEL

Raven's Redemption is a work of fiction. Names, characters, places, and incidents either are products of the author's imagination or are used fictitiously. Any resemblance to actual events or locales or persons, living or dead, is entirely coincidental.

Author: John D Trudel
Cover Design and Art: Bruce DeRoos
Raven's Redemption is available on Amazon.com, through major book distributors (e.g. Ingram, Amazon, etc.), in paper and all major eBook platforms.

ISBN: 0983588678
ISBN 13: 9780983588672

DEDICATION

I dedicate this book to our Veterans, Christians, and Local Law Enforcement. May God bless them all, and may God Bless America.

Our Vets are being treated shamefully. At present, they make up 40% of the homeless. One third of those waiting for VA care have died, and this at a time when we give free healthcare to illegals. *Every day 22 of our Vets commit suicide – one every 65 minutes.*

Obama's "Arab Spring" resulted in an Islamic Winter. The barbarous radical Islam of 1,000 years ago is back. Migration *jihad* – *"Hijrah"* – has flooded the world with more refugees than any time in history.

Largely unnoticed in this bloodbath is that what started as oppression of Christians has gone from persecution to slaughter. It is now approaching genocide, with world and religious leaders as silent about it as they were in the 1930s. It is here too, in America. From Roseburg to San Bernardino, *jihadists* are targeting Christians.

Progressives and Communists (see http://revcom.us) now target police, the Thin Blue Line that protects us. "Kill the Pigs" from the Bill Ayers 1960s is back, and this time with the DOJ assisting.

I also dedicate this book to my wife Pat. Without her patience and understanding, this book would not exist. She is a saint.

The **Raven's** series has been a wild ride. The harsh reality of the shameful "Iran deal" – which prevails, though **opposed** by most of Congress and 71% of the public – crashed into my novels and disrupted our lives.

ACKNOWLEDGEMENTS

Ernest Hemingway said, "There is no such thing as writing, only rewriting." He also said, "You never finish a book, you just let it go." He was right.

I could not write at the level I do without my critical readers, content experts, and editors who take the time to scan my drafts with eagle eyes, amazing insight, and brutally honest criticism. Each time they touch my words, my novels get better. Kay Jewett deserves special credit.

My novels bring me into contact with exceptional people who have sacrificed to keep America safe from our enemies both foreign and domestic. You know who you are. I honor your service and I am inspired by your personal stories.

The story line of my *Raven's* novels is coming true: *terrorists with nukes and long-range missiles.* The world is forever changed. I hope Americans are waking up.

Finally, you, my readers, are most important of all. **Thank you for your support.**

"To imagine a nuclear deal with Iran working is to imagine the Islamic Republic is without its revolutionary faith. So Mr. Obama's deal making is in effect setting the necessary conditions for military action after January 2017.

Above all, the clerical regime cannot be understood without appreciating the centrality of anti-Americanism to its religious identity."

Wall Street Journal
July 9, 2015, pg. A11

"No stronger retrograde force exists in the world. Far from being moribund, Mohammedanism is a militant and proselytizing faith. It has already spread throughout Central Africa, raising fearless warriors at every step; and were it not that Christianity is sheltered in the strong arms of science, the science against which it had vainly struggled, the civilization of modern Europe might fall, as fell the civilization of ancient Rome."

Sir Winston Churchill, 1899

"The astonishing spread of Islam in its first century was due to the sword. There was a hiatus after the defeat at Vienna when Western technology made battle inadvisable. The nuclear weapon will be the great Equalizer, and allow *jihad* to proceed. The only option the West has to derail this juggernaut is to demonstrate that the Allah of Islam is powerless. That will be very difficult, since Islam has had so many successes in the recent decades."

Private Source, 2015

"[Obama's deal] doesn't block Iran's path to the bomb; it paves Iran's path to the bomb."

Israeli Prime Minister Benjamin Netanyahu

CHAPTER ONE
STORMS AND INTRUDERS

Present Day, Private Estate near Mendocino, California

The storm front arrived about six. Clouds rolled in, first purple, and then becoming inky black, roiling, whipped into tormented shapes, with edges as sharp as if carved by invisible knives. Wind howled, rain pounded down in torrents, thunder rolled, and jagged streamers of lightning strobed the sky. Raven huddled on the deck, sheltered by the overhang, watching huge waves pounding the rocks and shore, throwing spray and foam high over the cliffs.

Blinding flashes of actinic light were followed by deafening crashes of thunder. Lightning strikes were close and all around, coming so fast he could not count them. The thunderclaps merged into a constant roar. The flashes were too bright to look at directly.

Raven smelled ozone. He could taste it on the air, metallic and acrid on his tongue. A big fir exploded about fifty yards from the cabins. It did not burn. It shattered into hundreds of pieces, the debris instantly swept away by the winds. Ribbons of blue-white fire lashed the sea like laser beams.

There was no way he was going to walk the few hundred yards to the restaurant. Even if he made it, the power was out. *No hot food tonight.*

Raven struggled to his feet to go inside, leaning into the wind. He turned his gaze back towards the sea, only to catch a blast that would have humbled a thousand flashbulbs.

He closed his eyes tight and dropped to his knees, fingers interlaced, with his arms sheltering his head and covering his ears, backing into the most sheltered location he could find, the upwind corner formed by the building and the privacy wall that edged the deck.

He felt the rolling thunder through his entire body, and did his best to curl himself into a ball. Time passed. When the afterimages faded from his vision, Raven crawled inside on his hands and knees. The sound diminished only slightly when he latched the double-glazed sliding door.

Wow. He leaned against the couch for a time taking deep breaths, thankful for the shelter. When his heart stopped pounding, food and a cold beer came to mind.

Using his flashlight with the red lens, he prowled the kitchenette, coming up with a tin of sardines, Tillamook cheese, a box of crackers, and a six-pack of cold IPA. Raven settled down on the couch facing the slider to the deck, watched the storm, and remembered.

The IPA brought back memories. On his last mission, the Brits had introduced him to India Pale Ale. They said it dated back to the 19th century and Queen Victoria. He sat there pondering his last mission, sipping the hoppy, slightly bitter brew, thinking of a small, gentle woman with soft eyes and long brown hair. She had been a casualty and it was his fault.

Josie was a national treasure, a woman with unique talents. In a different time, long ago, she had been a pagan high priestess. The few in Washington who knew of her existence called her a remote viewer, a paranormal, but that was if they spoke of her at all, a rare event which could occur only at the highest security levels, in hushed tones, and on a need-to-know basis.

At the beginning that was all he and Josie had in common. Neither officially existed, neither could share their inner secrets, neither dared develop close relationships. Beyond that, they came from different worlds, lived in different universes.

Josie lived on a higher plane, a land of radiance and bright spirits. Raven prowled the deep dark of midnight. There he hunted monsters, part of a thin black line that sought to protect more peaceful souls.

They were forced together by necessity, both national and personal. Josie was tasked with providing high-value intelligence. Raven was to protect her so she could do the work. It grew to be more than that. Alone against the world, the two bonded, first as associates, then as a team, then as friends, and finally as lovers and mates.

For Raven, it was the closest thing to living he had ever known. Sharing. Trust. He always woke up thinking about Josie, her gentle spirit, love, and paranormal powers of perception.

And of how he'd almost destroyed her. Mostly, he thought of that.

When terrorist assassins came, he had been badly wounded, and she had been forced to kill. It had damaged her mind. That he was responsible, even if by accident, broke his heart.

He kept missing Josie, revisiting what went wrong and how much of it was his fault. They said she was catatonic, being tended in some high-security medical unit. He was not allowed to see her, but the experts assured him she would be fine… in time.

Raven had doubts.

He remembered the old Spielberg movie. Experts said the same about ET, the funny-looking little alien with psychic powers who was rescued by children who took it home. Shit happened, government came to help, and ET wound up in a plastic bubble, tended by clueless technicians in NASA space suits – who were unknowingly killing him.

That was the part of the movie that grabbed him, death by ignorance. ET far from home, dying accidentally because those treating him were acting in a realm beyond their limits of knowledge.

Raven did not like the movie and now Josie was living it. "Trust us," they said. The more sincerely they said it, the more Raven was convinced they didn't have a freaking clue.

ET was resurrected by being who he was. Not by the government.

Raven opened the last bottle of IPA. He took a few sips. It didn't even taste good any more. He pushed the bottle away.

Raven drew the thick curtains and rolled into bed. He put a pillow over his head, trying to silence the crashes of thunder. Time passed and the storm continued to rage. The incandescent flashes penetrating the gaps around the curtains were subliminally disturbing, even with his eyes shut.

He could feel his body tense with each flash; it reminded him of incoming artillery. The wind was shrieking and the entire building trembled in the heavy gusts.

He finally got up and duct-taped the curtains to the wall, stuffing towels in the gaps for good measure. It helped.

In addition to the pillow, Raven put a towel over his eyes. He rolled over facing the wall. That helped too. Eventually the thunder grew more distant and the room darkened. The gloom outside merged with the darkness in his soul, and sleep came.

When Raven woke, the first thing he noticed was the silence. He ripped the tape off, opened the curtains, and saw stars. He slid open the deck door, taking deep breaths. The air tasted clean, and, looking around, the buildings were missing shingles but remarkably intact.

There was debris strewn all over the lawn. Nothing was moving. The wildlife was still hunkered down, but there were a few lights showing. The power was back.

Raven tried to think positive. The shrinks wanted him to do that. *A new day. Life returns to normal.* That would be nice. The problem was he wasn't sure what normal was anymore. Whatever or wherever it was, he had not seen it for a long time.

Raven washed down two aspirin and started fixing a pot of coffee. He would have a cup with an energy bar, and start his workout when his head stopped throbbing.

Job #1 was to get well, be released, and go see Josie himself.

The small resident staff called it "the Ranch." It was remote and rustic in the 1960s California style, nestled on the coast near the big Redwoods.

The siding was straight-grain Cedar, the roof of low pitch, covered with shakes, and the construction solid with massive roof beams. His unit was one story, tucked into the steep hillside, with most of its west wall consisting of the large sliding glass door leading to a sheltered deck overlooking the ocean and sweeping lawns far below.

In summer, you could leave the slider open to the cool breezes with full privacy. Hell, the lawn was over thirty feet down. Unless an assailant had special equipment, the only good approach was through the front door. It was solid wood with a pickproof latch and a bolt. It might not stop an intruder, but it sure as hell would slow him down.

The unit had been upgraded with a flat-screen TV fed by a satellite dish, a small bar, and a big soaking tub with ornate silver handles, but it lacked phone or Internet connections. The emphasis was on privacy, simplicity, comfort, and functional design. The Ranch was secure enough to be calming to recovering agents with ragged nerves, but without looking like a fortress and attracting undesirable attention.

From the soaking tub, you could open a screen and watch the ocean while still being shielded from the view of anyone on the grounds. The king-sized bed took up most of the main room, but there was a small couch in front of the river-rock, wood-burning fireplace next to the TV. Out on the deck, there were two wooden chairs and a small table to put drinks on, still there and intact even after the storm. The deck had a partial roof overhang and a waist-high privacy wall instead of an open railing.

The sliding door had two sets of window coverings: translucent blinds for privacy, and opaque blinds for darkness. Raven preferred leaving them open during daylight hours. He liked being able to see what was coming, and there was a telescope he could set up on the deck to watch passing fishing boats and ships.

The problem with doors and walls was that you didn't know what was on the other side.

The setting reminded Raven of the early James Bond movies. Once an elegant private resort at the dead end of a 2-lane road in disrepair, it had fallen on hard times and gone bankrupt during one of America's financial meltdowns. Somewhere along the way, it had come into government hands, probably through a series of shell companies.

The grounds were getting a bit overgrown – it helped conceal the sensors and security cameras, but the old resort still looked good. The 800 number still worked, but you got a recording saying the estate was in receivership and hoped to reopen next year. It took a five-digit code to interrupt it and leave a message for a callback. In reality, the Ranch was now used as a rehab facility for recovering deep-black operatives.

That is why Raven was there. Two 9-millimeter slugs in the chest, a bad attitude, and the need for seclusion to get his shit together made it the perfect place.

He was slouched in a chair on the deck of his cottage with his feet up on the small wooden table, sipping coffee, when he heard footsteps coming down the front walk. The path was steep down to his front door, alternating between wood planks, gravel, concrete, and steps. He had practiced identifying and locating the local sounds. Whoever it was had just come off the board planks, across the gravel, was now on the first concrete pad, and should be approaching the first set of steps.

A few seconds later, he heard the slight creak of the steps shifting under the load. If they turned left to his unit, a raised walkway gave hollow echoes. A right turn led to solid concrete that produced less sound.

The person – there was only one set of footsteps – turned left. Whoever it was, they were coming toward him, maybe for him.

Raven frowned, pulling the small pistol out of the pocket of his robe. He extracted the silencer from his other pocket, screwing it on by feel, his attention on the door.

He had been uneasy of late. It was not the storm, not really. Something wasn't right. He could sense it. His mission sense kept kicking in. The world seemed just a little tilted.

Raven took a few deep breaths. *Don't worry about what you can't control. Worry about what you can, and be ready for the unexpected. Adapt. When an attack comes, deflect it and use the power to your advantage.*

The little SIG .45 ACP was cocked and locked, with a full magazine and one up the pipe. He slipped off his sandals, and catlike, moving freely, dashed across the room and positioned himself so as to be behind the door when it opened.

His body was coming back. He felt strong.

Raven paused and focused, controlling his breathing, listening intently. *What was different?* It was not the sound of the nurses' rubber soled white shoes. The sound was leather shoes with heels. It was not his doctor. Wyden walked with a limp.

There was a distinctive creak from the loose board. *Probably a male, vigorous and not too heavy, maybe 180 pounds. Dr. Wyden was overweight and moved slowly.*

The intruder was coming down the last two steps, the footsteps slower and softer. There was no knock. A key turned in the lock, the latch moved, and the door slowly opened.

A man stepped silently into the room, bald, wearing glasses, and dark clothing. He was scanning the room, his back to Raven, his right hand on the doorknob, the other one empty.

He was an easy target. A hammer fist or an elbow slash, *Sok Tee*, to the side of the head would kill, a jump kick, *Gra-dode Teh*, to the kidneys would disable.

Instead, Raven took one long step forward and touched the gun barrel against the intruder's ear. The man stood totally still, frozen in place.

He's had training. This one is a pro. Raven reminded himself to be careful. He'd made enough mistakes for one lifetime.

"Hands up, slowly," Raven said. "Good. Now two steps forward, and face-down on the floor."

Without a sound, the man complied.

Raven kicked the door shut. The latch clicked. He leaned a chair against it, under the knob, and flipped on the lights.

"May I get up now? Or have you lost your fucking mind?"

Oh, Shit. Great way to get your boss' attention. Raven took a deep breath. He clicked the safety on and lowered his weapon. "Sorry."

He helped Goldfarb to his feet. "Why didn't you knock?"

Goldfarb glanced at the gun, now aimed at the floor.

Raven unscrewed the silencer. He pocketed it and the gun. "Predawn is a dangerous time. The last time I had intruders was not a happy one. People died."

"Most of them by your hand." Goldfarb was silent for a long moment. "You cause me concern. Your reactions are becoming unpredictable. Six weeks ago, I walked in here and you were unarmed, sitting with your back to the door, helpless as a kitten. I could have stuck an ice pick in the back of your head."

Raven looked Goldfarb up and down slowly. He smiled like a wolf. "Not this time...."

"True enough," Goldfarb said. "The doctors say you're recovering, but perhaps they're mistaken? There doesn't seem to be a lot of white space in your mind between sloppy and paranoid."

"I didn't like sloppy."

"That's encouraging. Why? "

"If someone is going to get hurt, I'd prefer it not be me or my friends."

"Quite right," Goldfarb said musingly. He seemed to make a decision. When he spoke again, his voice was crisp and held an edge of command. "Now that you've scared the shit out of me, perhaps I could get some coffee before we talk."

Raven led him out on the deck, gestured at the second chair, handed him a cup, and poured from the white carafe. "It should still be hot."

Goldfarb eased himself down, took a sip, and nodded appreciation.

It was starting to get light outside. Colors were becoming richer, less muted, and Raven could hear the sounds of gulls looking for breakfast. He situated himself with his back against the wall where he could keep eye contact with Goldfarb and watch the sunrise on the water.

"I expected a mission briefing," Raven said. "A month ago."

"You weren't ready."

"How the **hell** would you know if I'm ready or not?"

"You're out of line."

"When I'm in the field, you're my lifeline. When you stuck me here, you moved me off the board. You left me twisting in the wind. Are you my control or not?"

"I am. And you weren't ready for a mission."

"Exactly what gives you this divine insight?"

"My sources and methods are not your concern. Here's what is: I take care of my people."

"**Really?**" Raven did not try to keep the skepticism out of his voice.

"You're safe here, and recovering. The same goes for Josie. I'm doing my job."

Raven took a deep breath and let it out slowly. "Let's try this again, Doctor. What made you decide to drop in?"

"You beat Nai last week," Goldfarb said.

Raven blinked. "What?"

"*Muay Thai.* You beat Nai. Is that true?"

"So?"

"I've never had anyone beat Nai. That's why I hired him."

Raven smiled thinly. It was as close to a compliment as you got from Goldfarb. "Not even the young, macho studs without bullet holes?"

"No." Goldfarb seemed to relax slightly. "How is your rehabilitation going?"

"Good. It's going good."

It was. He needed to stay busy, to do positive things. Each day, he would go to the gym and work the machines and weights, followed by aerobics: a run along the cliffs, down to the beach, and back.

"Back" was a bitch. Nine hundred and thirty feet up a steep dirt path, followed by a mile run back across the grounds. When he started, he could barely walk that 930 vertical, having to look for rocks to lean on and branches to hang onto. He could do it at a run now, and each day he got stronger.

After that, Raven would enjoy his shower and have a solid, high-protein breakfast: three eggs, ham, and a fresh biscuit with the excellent local honey. Three days a week, he would go down to the dojo mat where they had provided instructors to refresh his unarmed combat skills. Raven was studying Muay Thai, an unusually lethal martial arts form.

Muay Thai had an arsenal of nine weapons – the head, fists, elbows, knees, and feet. Attacks could come from any direction, and with bewildering rapidity. Even defense was violent. Since one hit could put an opponent out of action, defense keyed on small, precise motion to return to the guard quickly with minimum energy expenditure. Advanced techniques were usually counters, used to damage the opponent to prevent another attack being made.

Raven's instructor, Nai, had competed in Thailand and was damned good. At 22, he had been invited to the Royal Household to teach Muay Thai to the King's private security staff.

Nai kicked like a mule and had the speed of a panther. Raven had never seen anyone with so much quick. Nai pulled his blows, but missing a block, redirection, or evasion was still bad news. Even with Thai pads and focus mitts, the impacts hurt like hell.

The brutal physical combat kept Raven's mind fully occupied. Each session ended with four intense five-minute rounds with short rest periods between. Raven was getting better – he was fighting to draws in the early rounds, and, yeah, he even won one last week – but Nai kept the pressure on. He said the pros sparred every day.

The regimen kept Raven from thinking about Josie and how he'd let her down. It was also helping to hone his senses. He welcomed the conflict.

"I take care of my people," Goldfarb said softly. "If you can't trust me, we shouldn't be working together."

"I'm sorry," Raven said.

Goldfarb's eyes widened slightly. "Excuse me?"

"I said I was sorry. I apologize."

"The last time I saw you, you were in bad shape. Right?"

"Yeah. I was."

"You wanted to run off half-cocked to avenge the girl."

"Maybe."

"That was stupid. I need you to focus on the mission and to be able to perform. I need you to act like a professional. The Agency called you Cowboy. That shit doesn't cut it with me."

"Can we move on now? I don't work for the Agency anymore."

"True. You work for me, and I need to know if you deem yourself to be mission capable. Are you up to another run?"

"What about Josie?"

"You'll see her."

Raven frowned.

"You're fit for a mission. I want you to bring her in. She's irreplaceable."

"She is that, Sir, but I don't understand. Why don't you just issue orders to have her released?"

"Do you want me to paint a target on her forehead? Our own bureaucracies would put her at extreme risk. The doctors will not release her without specific written orders to override their opinions and rules, which would then become a matter of record. The ObamaCare protocols will make these records available to our enemies, both foreign and domestic."

"How so?"

"The ObamaCare core is a shared database run by the IRS that contains everyone's medical, personal, financial, and tax records. The security of all this information is highly suspect. Even if these records are not hacked by enemy states, seven or eight Federal bureaucracies share them. Tens of thousands of people have access. It is beyond comprehension to imagine such a database would be secure. Would you like to have your records there?"

"Of course not."

"Me either, and Josie is more of a high value target than either of us. She is there under false name, a legend. If they tracked it, it would lead nowhere, but that in and of itself would raise red flags. You need to make a covert extraction without leaving any fingerprints on it that could lead back to the intelligence community or the office of the President.

"I want you in and out like a ghost. I need her to vanish without alerting anyone or leaving any paper trail."

"An interesting notion. Did you come to brief me about how we are going to do this?"

"I came to confer with you. It is not that simple. There are some problems."

There always were. "I'm listening."

CHAPTER TWO
OLD FRIENDS, ANCIENT ENEMIES

The Ranch, Mendocino, California

G oldfarb took his glasses off and wiped them carefully. "Langley has been asking inconvenient questions."

In a previous life, Raven had been dismissed with prejudice from the CIA. He had enemies in high places.

"About me?"

"Not specifically. About Durham."

Josie's safe house. Raven winced, remembering gunfire and burning buildings.

"I think it's a closed issue now." Goldfarb gave a thin smile. "A dead issue, actually... since you died from your wounds."

"The world will miss my charm and repartee."

"So we hope. I gave you a nice ceremony."

"They'll dig up...."

"The body was cremated. Investigations are winding down."

"You came here to tell me I was dead? Again."

"No, but I thought you'd find it comforting. There is no indication that anyone has discovered your new persona."

Raven shrugged. Blown covers were generally undetected beforehand. You did what you could. Worrying about it did not help. Catching leakers and enemy agents helped the next operative, not the one attacked.

"We don't need people probing around looking for connections and patterns. The Agency has a long memory. I didn't think you'd mind."

"I don't."

"It worked the first time," Goldfarb said. "Cowboy Lang, former CIA operative, was buried with honors. We used the same cover strategy for Durham, but deeper. This time for the legend of an operative who'd never actually existed."

"Langley believes it?"

"Remember *Noah's flood*?"

Under Obama, the Chinese hacked the records of everyone with a DOD clearance, addresses, social security numbers, photos, bank records and more. Thousands of American agents were compromised. The records of over twenty-one million citizens in sensitive jobs were taken. It was arguably the biggest theft of sensitive data since the Russians got America's atomic bomb secrets in the 50s. The government kept it covered up for over a year. Under orders not to discuss the debacle, insiders gave it a code word: Noah's Flood.

"I expect everyone does, Sir."

"Yes. Thousands of assets went under identity protection in the aftermath. There were hundreds of thousands of new legends created. We are drowning in cover IDs. I buried yours in that pile."

"Let our various agencies chase after ghosts?"

"And the Iranians, along with the other enemies you've made over the years. Don't forget them."

"I haven't."

Goldfarb smiled beatifically. "This gives the enforcement people something harmless to do. Those old identities do not connect to you at all, and neither of them connects to the other. I prefer that all possible paths of inquiry lead down blind alleys to dead ends. I assumed that would be acceptable to you."

"It's fine."

"It's better than fine. Our mythical fallen hero had death benefits. I put them into a private trust to cover Josie's medical care and future support. The government is not involved. It is not on their radar. There are no government funds to account for."

"What's your point?"

"No matter what happens to me, no matter what happens to you, no matter what the future policy of Washington becomes, Josie will be taken care of. She'll be provided for with private money."

Raven blinked. "Thank you. That's decent of you."

"Are you all right?"

"We all remember Benghazi, Sir. The government abandoned brave Americans for political reasons. We left them to die. For two hundred years, Americans who went in harm's way could trust that their backs were covered. Now we can't any longer. It sucks."

"I share your feelings. These disastrous and shameful precedents are wounds that will take a long time to heal. It will take years before political Washington is trusted again. That is part of why no one knows of this arrangement, save for you, me, and Josie if and when you choose to tell her. It's totally off the books."

"Is that what you came here to tell me?"

"As we have discussed, it is time to bring Josie in. That's why I came."

"That's all? Just an extraction, a rescue mission?"

"Do I look like Mother Teresa?"

There is an operative reason he wants such a deep cover for me and is sheltering Josie. I thought so. Raven looked at Goldfarb sharply. *What isn't he telling me?* "What?"

"I'm considering changes. As of yet, these do not concern you."

Something is going on. I knew it....

At least Goldfarb took care of his people. Those in the field, those at the tip of the spear, knew that in the end it got down to that. Governments did not have hearts; they had bureaucracies, rules, and politics. In the end, you had to look out for each other.

At Valley Forge, Washington's men lacked pay and shoes. Our troops coming home from Vietnam, many of whom were draftees serving involuntarily, were spat upon and vilified.

America's history was written in the blood of patriots.

America prevailed against the odds in World War II and survived the Cold War, but it had forgotten the lessons. Political leaders confused interludes between wars with peace. Avoiding action, hoping for "peace" and sending prayers that the wolves would pass them by. When they did act, the Western Democracies had generally resisted hanging their traitors, killing their enemies, and allowing total victory for their troops when they did fight. Hence, low-level counterinsurgency wars were constant.

The pattern seemed to be disasters and wars every generation, as memories faded and patterns repeated. So it was now, eerily reminiscent of the 1930s when the Western Democracies slept. A dark time where socialism was ascendant, at first promising Nirvana, but to be followed in short order by Tyranny, Fascism, Nazism, Communism, Holocaust, and World War.

America was currently waking up, but was greatly weakened. Its military was smaller than before World War I. Worse was the internal corruption and unaccountable bureaucracies. There had been too many betrayals and distrust was high.

Raven sighed and chose his words carefully. "I appreciate your looking after Josie. What made you change your mind about letting me see her?"

"Your arguments. Josie's problems are in her mind, somewhere far beyond our medical science. You and she are connected in ways the rest of us cannot hope to understand. You said the only way she can heal is by being herself. I've come to agree with you."

Raven was silent for a long moment thinking. "Neither of us can finish this mission alone. You need us both functional, don't you? That's what you care about."

Goldfarb shrugged.

"You told me the orders that prevent me from seeing Josie were approved by the President. Were you lying about that?"

"I wasn't lying."

"So my visit will require Presidential authorization."

"You will have to be resourceful. The situation has changed."

"Has the order blocking me been canceled?"

"No. The order remains, but you are not that person. That person no longer exists."

"Can you state that more clearly?"

"I can get you in to see Josie. It is your job to get her out. If you do it quickly and quietly, I can handle the blowback."

"How?"

"Her doctors have given up. They will be relieved not to have responsibility for her. Am I correct that you've never met her former boss, Doctor Lundgren, from Rhine?"

"Never."

"Good. He is in charge. He was delighted to be relieved as Josie's control. He'll go along with anything that gets her out of his hair."

"So you want me to stop by, shake his hand, pick Josie up, and vanish? That's all?"

"It's more like a vacation than an assignment. Lundgren goes back to do research, her doctors are blameless, and you get to see Josie. Just be sure you leave no trail."

"Why do I feel like I'm missing something?"

"Probably because it's too easy. It is what you wanted. Are you in or out?"

"I'm in."

"Good. There is one minor issue, something you will need to decide before you go for Josie."

Raven waited. *Here it comes....*

"The President needs a national hero."

Raven stared at him.

Durham was a disaster. Everyone on his team had been seriously wounded. Josie, a National Treasure because of her unique talents, was comatose.

Raven's primary mission was to have been the quiet, covert collection of historical information. They were doing research, collecting technical intelligence to support a sensitive but authorized offshore operation. It was supposed to be low-key, safe, and totally black. Josie was a non-combatant. No one was supposed to get hurt.

But one thing led to another, and, before it was over, an upscale neighborhood in a peaceful American city was burning, police officers were dead, and troops had been mobilized. Another terrorist attack on the homeland.

"You're kidding me, right?"

"I don't joke about Presidential orders. We have been running way off the reservation, without any official sanction or support. Borrowing support from other groups who cannot be briefed in and are badly overcommitted to begin with. We had no legal way to help you. Luckily we drew a savvy commander in Durham, Major Kincaid."

"He must have been the guy I ordered to come in hot. He gave me shit."

"But came in shooting?"

"Yes."

Durham seemed like a long time ago, as if weeks were years. The Iranians called their program STARFISH. Long-range missiles with advanced EMP warheads, an Antarctic base, and a plan that could have eliminated America as an advanced nation. While Raven's team was focused on the strategic threat half-a-world away, a kill team from an Islamic sleeper cell in the U.S. had come out of nowhere, blindsided them, targeted Josie, and almost succeeded.

It was his own damned fault. He should have been more alert. He was the pro. Raven knew Homeland Security was too politically correct to be effective and that America's borders were leaking sieves. His mistake was thinking his team was under the radar. Somewhere, somehow, someone had fingered them.

"So you need a hero to get support from Washington?"

"Correct. Our operation was successful. The President is grateful. He is seeking a hero so he can get more resources."

"I do not qualify."

"Tell me why."

"I don't exist. I'm not in the military or with any official agency."

"I told the President that. He needs an American hero to blunt criticism and gain support from the media and Congress. That's how our system works."

"Without any mention of the extreme measures and carnage necessary, or the need to kill acres of jihadists to end this. Not wipe their noses, read them Miranda, or lawyer them up — to summarily execute them when and as needed. Versus driving around building schools and getting blown up by IEDs."

"Yes."

"Do you want to expose what we do? What we fight?"

"God, no." Goldfarb said. "Of course not. The notion that a hundred million Americans might have died from a sneak attack could trigger a panic."

"Or a war…."

"Here's the thing. You were as deep black as it gets. Our enemies still knew enough about what you were doing to target you. Do you think they are going to give up?

"I do not."

"What will they do?"

Raven said, "Double down. Find us. Target us. Do their best to kill or abduct Josie. Like they just did, but with more resources and better intelligence."

"Agreed. That is why we are having this discussion. We were lucky this time."

"You have an odd notion of lucky, Doctor. Do you know that?"

"Here's what I know: We can't continue as we have. I cannot throw a tiny force in harm's way repeatedly with no way to support or extract them. No matter how desperate the need is, no matter how good you are, eventually you would be overwhelmed. Our military was gutted during Obama. It is too thin now to do the tasks it is assigned, much less the tasks it is unaware of. We need more resources."

Raven was watching Goldfarb intently.

"Do you agree with me? Working as we do, we would eventually be unable to give you timely support, you would die for nothing, and we would lose Josie. We almost did."

"You might be right, but schmoozing in Washington, even to get a support base, is a bad idea. This is madness."

"Tell me why."

"It would make things worse, not better. If we are tangled up with Washington's politics and bureaucracies, we would be unable to do our jobs. This is why you have been spending so much effort keeping us deep black. We can't be heroes. We don't even exist."

"What do you suggest?"

"Let Major Kincaid be your hero."

"We've already played that card. It took an award ceremony at the White House to keep his chain-of-command from crucifying him. Sorry. You are my only possible candidate, even if it blows your cover. What do you say?"

"I say, no."

"Last chance. Would you like some time to think about it?"

"I do not. No way. No how. Not only 'no' but 'Hell, no.' "

Surprisingly, Goldfarb smiled. "I'm glad you said that. It leads us to the next option. I'm making some changes that I want to run by you." He started talking....

CHAPTER THREE
A THIN BLACK LINE

The Ranch, Mendocino, California

Raven was staring at Goldfarb. "I'm still trying to understand the big picture. You want me to defy a Presidential order and kidnap Josie? Then develop agents in Iran? Followed by participating in an insurgency movement to set up an unaccountable paramilitary team clear of the government?"

"Working outside the box. An opportunity to improvise. That is pretty much your history. The first step is easy. Just get Josie and wait for the rest to come together. If we get greenlighted, you go to Iran, check things out, and see what develops. What's the problem?"

"I don't like the part about Josie. I would prefer the word 'rescue.' I'm not going to take her against her will."

Goldfarb shrugged.

"Box or no box, you need to give me some ground rules."

"We are simply going to be putting a bit more space between our operations and the government. Josie is one of us. To start, we need to get her back."

"Not against her will."

"She may not be conscious. Almost certainly, she'll be disoriented."

Raven said, "You have a point, but I need flexibility. I want it to be my call, at the time on the ground. At least she's safe where she is."

"Maybe not. What if the option of extracting her isn't available in the future?"

"You think we're compromised?"

"Of course we're compromised. Washington is infested with moles and leftovers from back when we were being politically sensitive to Islam and leading from behind. It is also full of ambitious politicians and bureaucrats who delight in leaking information for their own advantage.

"It's going to take decades to clean up all the damage. I have been doing my best to keep you and your team operationally clear, but that goes away every time we need to tap outside resources. If you need cover documents, Intel, backup, security, we have to negotiate, explain, and even beg, and work around blockages and constraints."

Raven nodded slowly. "Like Ollie North and the Contras. Or the reason it took ten years to get a kill order for bin Laden."

"Exactly. President Blager has had me working through committees. Every time we need support or Intel, there are dozens of people reporting to other organizations involved. Everything is too slow, too limited, and too damned public. We might as well publish our plans in the *New York Times*.

"It's going to get worse. After Durham, everyone is puckered. People are asking too many questions. Our operations are too provocative to be dependent on outside assistance. I told the President that we needed some changes."

"He agreed?"

"In concept."

"What does that mean?"

"It's complicated. Call it a reorg."

"Um." Raven frowned. "Who will I be working for?"

"That won't change. I will still be control for you, Josie, and a small support team. I have funding to cover that, and it's black and off the books. My small sums will be lost in the round off error."

"So what's the problem?"

"The Intel and Operational Security we need involves big money. Hundreds of millions of dollars a year. Remember Blackwater?"

"Legendary. Mostly they protected civilians."

"They did more than that. They covered Columbine, the USS Cole and 9/11. In 100,000 missions in Iraq and Afghanistan Blackwater contractors never lost a U.S. official under their protection. But the company gained a trigger-happy reputation, especially after the September 2007 shootout that left 17 civilians dead in Baghdad's Nisour Square."

Raven said, "Yeah, and they wound up facing criminal charges for killing our enemies in the middle of a war. Do you want to repeat that?"

"I do not. The real issues were visibility, collateral damage, insensitivity, and not being UN approved or politically correct. The guy that ran them, Eric Prince, was demonized. He gave up and left the U.S. We lost a good man, a patriot."

"And you want to bring him back?"

Goldfarb shook his head. "Absolutely not. He is radioactive. Every media outlet and politician left of center would be running after him with torches and pitchforks."

"Who then?"

"Ever hear of Mike Mickelson?"

Raven blinked. "I have. Twenty Mike. A kick ass Marine General. He did the Bukhari raid. Way deep into bad-guy country and back out without losing a man."

"That's the one. Before that he was Director of Intelligence for Marine HQ."

"I met him once when I was with the agency. Good man. He disappeared after Bukhari. Wasn't he invalided out or something?"

"He took retirement after President Hale termed out."

"What's he doing now?"

"If matters unfold as I desire, he'll be providing operational support for us and doing some of the heavy lifting when that extends into military matters. The man is a genius at small force interventions in hot zones.

"We set up a company. Transnational Services Group, TSG. You can look them up on the Internet. Offices in London and New York. They are a Security and Logistics Company focused on Global Economic Prosperity. Mike is the CEO."

"Why London?"

"Ever hear of Charles Proudfoot?"

"Negative."

"A Brit. SAS in his younger days, then MI-6, then private sector doing diplomatic security and a bit of this and that for Her Majesty's Government. His mom was American. He has dual citizenship with the U.S. He's VP of Operations for TSG, their second employee."

Raven raised an eyebrow. "Anything else?"

"You tell me. What's missing?"

"Geeks. Someone to play Q for James Bond. People to hack us in where we're not supposed to be."

"Correct. Ever hear of a company called Cybertech?"

Raven shook his head.

"Run by a PhD named William Giles. They do Cybersecurity and keep a low profile. Mr. Giles has a bit of a bug up his ass. His Dad is Special Ops. He was abducted a long time back. There was a lot of effort to find him, but no results. Giles has not given up."

"How is he involved with us?"

"He's not, yet. He will on the TSG board once we're fully operational."

"His Dad was abducted? Where?"

"They took him right here in the US of A. A *jihadi* team took him in Oregon. It was part of what led to the Bukhari OP. Will's sister is married to Twenty Mike. She used to be a program manager for NSA."

Raven said, "Impressive."

"But…."

"How are you going to pay for all that? We cannot fund our own military, let alone set up another intelligence agency. You are talking tens of millions of dollars a year. America can't afford that."

"Yes, big problem, and a total disconnect. The plan is to not spend a dime of taxpayer money, except for my small budget."

"You are going to turn straw into gold?"

Goldfarb smiled. "Close. Do you know how much money is sucked out of the world economy by the Global Warming scam, arms, oil, blood diamonds, and other forms of smuggling? Add to that UN boondoggles, drugs, human trafficking, and the like.

"A lot. Huge sums."

"Correct. It's in the trillions of dollars."

"What's that got to do with us?"

"We sometimes encounter such people when we're running OPs."

"We do."

"Why not take their goodies?"

"It's against the rules."

"TSG won't follow the old rules. As part of its normal OPs, TSG will keep the spoils. Once it is profitable, we can even find ways to funnel some back to the governments and groups that help us."

"We grab terrorist drugs, guns, or assets and get to sell them and keep the profits?"

"Why not? Local police and the Federal Government have been doing it for years."

"What's the catch?"

"None of this exists yet. This is a concept, a proposal, something that it is going to take years to bring into full operation."

"What does exist?"

"So far pretty much, just us, our team. Twenty Mike and Proudfoot are starting to recruit. Cybertech is a running company, and will pony up some of its R&D budget."

"So this is all?"

"For now. Like I said, TSG is staffing up."

"We're still on our own?"

"For now. But help is coming. We need access and significant funds to go operational. So far, just setting this up and putting in some infrastructure has cost over $50 million dollars."

Raven blinked. That was a lot of money. "What does the President say?"

"Officially, nothing. He is not involved. He does not want to touch it with a ten-foot pole politically. That is my problem, not yours. He has been helping us with access and lining up seed funding.

I am hoping he will help us get the pump primed so we can start the machine running. We need more funding. I'm hoping he can get us a loan against future revenues from some of the resources that you and Josie found in Antarctica."

"Truman blocked that, back in the day. Now there are treaties. Those resources can't legally be extracted."

"That didn't stop the Iranians, did it?"

"No."

"It need not stop TSG either. The United States was rich with uranium, but the deal the Clintons made with Russia has, ah, clouded our ownership rights. We are a bit short if we need to deploy more nuclear power, much less build new generations of weapons. That greatly limits our options."

"We could tell the Russians to stuff it."

"Perhaps. Still, a major new source would help. And TSG can move into oil and coal as well. An America with energy abundance gets us on the road back."

"What's the current status of this?"

"Speculative. The President has promised me a decision. Until something breaks, we are stuck. As I said, we are aware of the issues. I'm working on them and trying to get you some help."

Raven was quiet for a long moment. This was too big to wrap his mind around. The issues were way over his pay grade.

"Well?" Goldfarb's eyes were like laser beams. "What do you say?"

"I want to get Josie back. That's what I say."

"Good answer. One step at a time. Let's start there...."

Goldfarb started to say more when there was a strident beeping from his pocket, morphing into a raucous claxon.

"What...?"

Goldfarb waved his hand for silence and extracted a cell phone. The noise suddenly stopped. His eyes widened, and he stood up, his face turning ashen. "Jesus Christ."

"Jesus," he said again. The coffee cup fell from his other hand, shattering on the deck, splashing his pant legs. He did not even look down.

"**What?**"

"Turn on the television."

"The **television**...?"

"Damn it, do it **now**." Goldfarb put a snap in his voice, making it an order. "Check the news. There's been a disaster."

Raven ran inside and did so, quickly clicking through CNN, FOX, and the major channels. When he returned to the deck Goldfarb was still standing there holding the phone, white as a ghost, a stricken look on his face.

"Nothing," Raven said. "No disasters, but I've got a question."

"You're sure?" Goldfarb stared at him questioningly.

"Of course I'm sure." *He leaves me stuck here for months without a visit, won't let me see Josie, damned near gets his ass shot for not following protocols, and hits me with the ring tone from Hell. Now he second-guesses me about watching television?*

Raven took a deep breath, letting it out slowly. "Nothing. Zero. Nada. Zip. No disasters. Nothing unusual."

Goldfarb was staring at him with a puzzled look on his face

"You might want to try Hebrew," Raven said.

"Huh?"

"Hebrew. It might work better."

Goldfarb said, "I don't have a clue what you're talking about."

"You're Jewish. Don't you think '*Yahweh*' might be preferable to 'Jesus Christ?' "

"Christ was Jewish, and I'm coming to think the Agency was right. You really can be a pain in the ass."

He held his phone up for Raven to see. It was a text message, scrolling. **Brickbat-01, Brickbat-01, Brickbat-01...**

"What's a brickbat?"

"It's from the President. A codeword from the Cold War. It was once the ultimate priority for projects relating to national security. He's never used it before now."

"What does it mean?"

"It's a call to his side. This meeting is over." Goldfarb started for the door.

"What are my orders?"

"You can come with me, or wait for me to sort this out. I have to go. I have a plane waiting at the airport. It will have been alerted, fueled, and ready to go with a flight plan on file. My car is outside. Do you have a bug out bag?"

Raven nodded.

"Let's go."

CHAPTER FOUR
PRIVATE AND SAFE

A Lear Jet, running South, off the California Coast

G oldfarb had declined to reveal where they were going. "It's a short flight," was all he said. After they had rushed to the airport, they waited for an hour to take off.

Typical government, Raven thought. *An urgent call to the President's side, and then we sit around and wait.*

Raven looked up across the small conference table. The two of them were the only passengers, and the door to the flight deck was closed.

Goldfarb was reading a small report in a red binder. The cover said TOP SECRET, SPECIAL ACCESS, and NO FORN. It was serial numbered. Goldfarb's copy was # 3 of only five.

Raven kept thinking about Goldfarb's last visit to the Ranch, the one where he had tasked Raven with something that he had sworn never to do – return to Iran. Against his better judgement, Raven had agreed. For personal reasons.

Raven had been in and out of Iran several times, but each visit had been scripted, brief, and backed by the full weight of the US military. Once he went in to take out a QUDs force leader, and several times to extract assets or intelligence information. Just quick, pre-briefed snatch and grabs. It was not a place to linger.

Iran was what had caused his problems with the CIA. He was sent in to extract a valuable agent, a defector. Raven had come back without the asset, who had lost his life while in the process of destroying an Iranian nuclear weapons storage facility.

Some were pleased at the outcome, but his masters at the Agency had gotten their knickers thoroughly knotted over it. After words like "treason" were mentioned, he had changed employers. His new boss, Dr. Goldfarb, protected him and gave him a new identity, the Raven legend. Goldfarb wanted to target Iran's nuclear programs.

Raven's assignment had started off simple enough. Just a bit of research and intelligence collection using unconventional methods. Raven had been patched into Goldfarb's team to provide operational security. Goldfarb still wanted to know the specifics about where Iran's nukes were coming from, but then it turned out that a major attack code named STARFISH was imminent. The job of thwarting it had fallen to Raven and Josie, working outside the system with little planning or support.

They had succeeded and survived. Barely.

Along the line, an Iranian businessman named Akbar Safdari had put out a kill order on Josie. How that was even possible strained the mind unless you understood how Iran's government was organized.

Raven needed to learn more about Iran. He had studied Sun Tzu. "If you know your enemy and you know yourself, you need not fear the result of a hundred battles." He was part of a new team facing a poorly understood enemy. They had been lucky, talented, and had adapted in time, but it had been too close.

Goldfarb now wanted to send Raven to Iran to develop deep cover assets there. Raven had refused at first. Once he had agreed to go, he started doing his own homework.

The Iranians were a sophisticated people, Muslims but not Arabs. They used to be called Persians, an ancient Empire with roots back to the dawn of recorded history. It was a sophisticated but odd mix of Western modernity and primitive, barbaric fundamentalism.

Current day Iran had the most Byzantine government structure in the world, with multiple groups reporting to different entities responsible for the same jobs. It had several police and paramilitary groups, and even two separate, competing, military organizations, the Revolutionary Guards and Iran's conventional military, with the former by far the more powerful and better equipped of the two. Off the books, it controlled Hamas and Hezbollah. It was the world's largest sponsor of terrorism.

It was difficult to know who was in charge, much less to assess their intentions. Hell, once it got past "Death to America," even the Iranians did not know half the time.

Safdari worked for the business arm of Iran's Revolutionary Guard, the Khatam al-Anbiya Construction Company. His title was Director of Energy Projects. One of his projects, **STARFISH**, targeted America with nuclear-tipped EMP weapons. It came close to succeeding.

Raven's team, thanks to the talented remote viewer, Josie Lynch, had thwarted it. Barely and at high cost.

Raven never discovered how Safdari targeted Josie. Was there a leak? Had he missed something? There was a theory about what went wrong, but the truth was he did not know. He needed to know for sure, and he needed the threat to Josie removed.

That was why he had agreed to take Goldfarb's mission. The only reason. Raven wanted payback. A simple in-and-out, a few days or a week in hostile country, and he could wrap up all the loose ends. Snatch Safdari, interrogate him, discover his sources and methods, and discreetly eliminate him.

Now it was more complicated.

When **STARFISH** was thwarted, opportunities presented themselves. Success breeds success and attracts allies. Goldfarb gained access to funding and the President's support. Raven now had leverage and allies in Iran.

It was the first good news in years.

Goldfarb wanted to try for the brass ring. He wanted an agent in place close to the centers of power in Iran, a nation where America had lacked assets, sources, or even diplomatic contact, for decades. America needed eyes and ears on the ground. Lack of good Intel was a formula for disaster. No one presently serving in the US State Department or Intelligence had ever worked in Iran.

There was still an imperfect understanding of how much Valarie Jarrett, John Kerry, and other Obama Administration officials had compromised America's security. There were still tens of thousands of State Department emails and records from the Obama Administration missing.

During that time, Muslims with Iranian connections were granted high-level clearances. It was unknowable how much damage they had done. John Brennan, the head of the CIA and an alleged Muslim convert himself, had emphasized "diversity" over "fighting jihad" as an Agency focus. Hillary's Personal Assistant and State Department Deputy Chief-of-Staff, Huma Abedin, was a Muslim with close family connections at the highest levels of the Muslim Brotherhood.

During the Cold War, and despite the Iron Curtain, America had maintained embassies and diplomatic contact with the Soviets. However, not so with Iran, not since the hostage crisis on November 4, 1979, when fifty-three embassy workers were held hostage for 444 days and not released into US custody until a few minutes after President Reagan took office.

The hostage incident ripped a gaping hole in America's Mid East diplomacy and ability to influence events. Later, when Obama was negotiating to give Iran nuclear weapons, his administration's ignorance of reality was at an all-time high. Both teams were negotiating to give Iran what it wanted, not to protect America's interests and national security.

Obama gave a speech about how Iran would not pose a threat "because it was against their religion to use nuclear weapons." This at a time when their Ayatollah was saying otherwise, ridiculing the deal, and chanting "Death to America." Obama's handler, Chief-of-Staff Valarie Jarrett, was Iranian. The Secretary of State negotiating the deal, John Kerry, had an Iranian son-in-law. It was reported, but then denied, that the son of Iran's foreign minister had been best man at the Kerry wedding. And so it went....

Some compared the Kerry negotiations to those Chamberlin had with Hitler in Munich in 1938. The point had merit, but at least the Brits did not have Nazi sympathizers on their treaty team, not as far as history knows.

*No legally binding treaty resulted despite intense Obama Administration efforts. Congress was not **that** crazy. The Kerry agreements were not submitted for the Senate treaty approval that the Constitution required. Only after confrontation – and approval by the UN that lifted sanctions – was Congress allowed to see the "deal documents." It was never entirely clear that Congress had actually seen all that had been agreed upon in the deal and its attendant codicils and deals. Kerry himself admitted he had not seen all the agreements.*

*The main thing was that agreements and Executive Orders **were** signed that allowed Iran to proceed. They held force until Obama left office. Iran continued its work to get nuclear weapons, and the world was forever changed.*

Iran was a major enemy, jihad was ascendant, and America was weakened. The resultant status quo, the new normal after leftist "transformational change," was a dangerous place for America and the world. Goldfarb wanted to change the game.

He wanted Safdari flipped, tossed, recruited. He wanted better intelligence. He wanted a network of well-placed deep-cover agents inside Iran's regime, access to their oil, and a channel into their advanced weapons programs. He thought Raven could do it.

Raven had wanted no part of it.

To counter Raven's skepticism, Goldfarb offered him a sop. If Raven accepted the mission and Goldfarb's ambitious plan stalled, Safdari would no longer be useful. They would be back to square one. In that case, there would be no objection if Safdari met an untimely demise.

Raven could live with that. Everything he knew about the government made him confident that Washington would not make any major efforts to confront Iran. We were weak and war weary.

Raven would go and verify that the mission was impossible. Then he would terminate Safdari, and come home to Josie. They would ride off into the sunset with no enemies hunting them.

Assuming Josie recovered. And, if not, he would have avenged her death.

Now Goldfarb had revealed a plan to establish a covert organization to enforce America's interests without being accountable. It was crazy, and it changed everything.

Raven cleared his throat. "Can I ask you a question?"

Goldfarb looked up. He sighed, closed the red report binder, and nodded.

"You are taking me to meet the President?"

"I am."

"Are you sure you want to do that?"

"The man wants the mission. I want the mission."

"Getting Josie back. Trying to flip Safdari. That's the mission that I agreed to do."

"That's not why we are going to meet him. Those are details."

"Why, then?"

"Infiltrating and subverting Iran to remove it as a threat is a major strategic offensive operation. It would take a prolonged commitment and sustained operational independence to pull it off. It is the sort of operation that an intelligence agency would need to work covertly for years. For it to be worth the effort and risk, America would need to act appropriately – decisively, in a timely manner, and with the proper resources and force levels – on the intelligence provided."

"I wanted Safdari. You wanted strategic. We worked it out. What's changed?"

"My realization of massive opportunity."

"An interesting vision, but it seems to me that you're drawing to an inside straight. Very low odds. Do you really expect we're going to walk in to see the President, me a person who he's never met, and he's going to OK something like what you've proposed?"

"I'm coming to know you Raven. You were going to visit Safdari, convince yourself he is an asshole we cannot trust, dispatch him, and then come back to report. Right?"

"He **is** an asshole we can't trust….."

"The world is full of assholes, and some of them are more useful alive. We are going to meet with the President. I am going to introduce you as a patriot on a potentially suicidal one-way mission to Iran. You are then going to leave and go retrieve Josie."

"All I have to do is say, 'hello,' under a throwaway cover ID?"

"Correct. After you leave, I'm going to gently mention to him that this is all pointless unless he's willing to consider what he and I have been privately discussing – actions contingent on the reactivation of Josie and the success of your visit to Iran.

"He's not going to even discuss that in front of you, but he is honest enough he **won't** get you killed on a hopeless quest."

Raven blinked. "You play hardball, Doctor."

"It's the only country we have."

"So if the President says no, I just go get Josie, bring her in and keep her safe. If he goes with it, I get Josie back, and then I take a trip to Tehran and make the impossible happen?"

"Almost right."

"Help me get it straight, Doctor. I need it right all the way."

"After you bring Josie in, you go to Tehran and do your best to make the **improbable** happen. If you succeed, then Twenty Mike and I try to make the **impossible** happen. Josie is safe either way."

Raven nodded slowly. "She's still recovering. I want a few weeks alone with her after I bring her in. Enough time for her to become stable and functional. Somewhere private and safe."

"Agreed. What do you say?"

"I say we both may be crazy, but let's do it. God Bless America."

CHAPTER FIVE
DARKNESS AND LIGHT

OHSU Research Hospital, Portland, Oregon

Josie was drifting, floating in a soft gray fog. Occasional bright images appeared. She did not feel the catheters connecting her to the drips, the oxygen cannula, or the leads connecting her to various medical monitors.

The fog was gone.

She saw a strange land, an alien place. A dim and hazy yellow sun with a white center was setting directly under an enormous white crescent moon. The moon was easily fifty times larger and a hundred times brighter than the sun, and the arms of its crescent were turned up, cupped as if to hold water like a chalice, and very slender. The huge moon was sharp and clear, while the faded sun was vaguely ethereal, more of a suggestion than a physical object. Its reflection off the ice was brighter and more substantial than the object itself. The far horizon was edged with a soft golden glow that backlit distant mountains.

The scene was beautiful, but when she tried to open her eyes, she could not. She could not feel her body. Somehow, that was normal to her, not frightening.

The image shifted.

She was sitting on the deck behind a house, next to a man. It was warm, with bright sunlight, and big trees, oaks, to shield her from the heat. She could sense her body, but it was not her. She was seeing and sensing an image of herself. She felt sweat on skin, but out there in that place, not here where her body was.

There was a warm breeze there, but here the fog was coming back cool and still. There, she wore a yellow summer dress, loose, open, with no underwear. Here, she did not seem to have a body.

The man with her on the deck had steel-blue eyes. He wore his black hair in a military style buzz cut. His face and arms were tanned. He looked fit.

He was lounging in a deck chair like a big cat, appearing relaxed. But he wasn't. His eyes were moving, scanning the environment, constantly searching, except when they lingered on her. Only then did they soften before they slowly moved away, as if unwilling. The touch of his gaze was like a caress.

Something about him was comforting, secure. She sensed closeness. Somehow they were connected.

The image faded, and another appeared. It was a face, his face, the same man, now at her bedside in a hospital of some type. He was holding her hand, concern in his eyes.

She was somewhere high up, seeing every detail clearly. The room was stark white, even the floor, and there was a tube in her arm. He moved closer, put his arms around her, whispering softly in her ear, "Come back. Come back. Come back."

He was saving her from something. Somehow, that moment was important.

The view shifted. Now it was night, cold and bleak. She was standing behind a house, her back to a large stone barbecue grill. She saw a man in moonlight, crawling toward her across a body clad in black, a body lying face down and limp next to a large knife.

It was him, the same man. He was looking up at her. There was dark blood pooling on the stone patio. She was holding an empty gun, her finger still pressing the trigger.

Josie started screaming. The sound resonated through her. It continued after the vision faded. She could feel the silent scream in her bones, her mind, and in her soul. It was a cry of pain and loss, but she did not know why. She was afraid to know why. Something horrible....

There was a soft click in the distance. She felt it more than heard it. She could finally feel her body. Something warm was rushing through her veins and the world was slowing. She could feel each beat of her heart through her veins. *Thump, thump.* Slower and slower.

She could not scream any more. It was too much effort. She was trapped in darkness.

Who is he? Where am I? Everything faded into stillness.

Nurse Kristi Louisell ran marathons, but she burst into the room like a sprinter. "What are you doing in here?"

The man turned. He stepped away from the IV drip. It was not a modern pump, just a primitive drip tube dangling from a bottle hung from a stainless steel post. The bottle had masking tape stuck to it, with a scrawled label.

"Doctor," he snapped, glaring up at her, demanding respect.

He was wearing one of the hospital's white coats with the logo, but she did not recognize him. Kristie stared at him, puzzled.

"Why do you work with such primitive equipment in an ICU?"

Kristie ignored his question. She towered over the man, shifting her position to block his access to her patient and the drip. His nametag said Dr. Gates. He was frail looking and short, maybe five six or a bit less, thin with a high forehead, a receding hairline, mahogany skin and kinky black hair. "I repeat, what are you doing in this room?"

"Your protocols are as deficient as your equipment. Let's try that again. *What are you doing in here,* **Doctor.**" He put heavy emphasis on the last word.

"Doctor," she conceded grudgingly.

"My job," he said.

"You didn't come by the nurse's station, and you're not on the roster." She paused, and then finally added, "Doctor Gates."

"I'm new, on a sabbatical from Harvard Medical School."

Am I supposed to be impressed? Kristie bit back a response and waited, making an effort to smile politely.

"I'm doing postdoctoral research in molecular pharmacology. I was told this is an unusual case. I wanted to see the patient myself."

Kristie's eyes narrowed. "At one thirty AM?"

"Whenever I choose." The little man looked irritated. "I work unusual hours."

"I'm sorry," Kristie said. "This room is restricted access and you are not on the list."

"You have no...."

"Why was my patient screaming?" Kristie held up the small wand on the cord around her neck. "I'm responsible here. At night I push this button and guards come."

The man shook his head and took a step back. "I don't know. She started when I walked in...."

Kristie moved to the drip and checked it, keeping her eyes on the doctor. Something about this was wrong. "Did you adjust this?"

He shook his head.

She glanced at the monitors, now flashing orange, and the oxygen flow. "What were you doing?"

"Trying to calm the patient."

Kristie adjusted the drip level, watching the monitors turn to green. She looked back at the doctor. "This was set too high. My instructions are that this medication is to be administered precisely as directed, and to call and report any exceptions or problems to Doctor Lundgren. Should I call him?"

"No," the little man said. She could see beads of sweat on his face, though the room was cool. "That's not necessary."

"I think you should leave, Doctor Gates."

Gates stared at her, frowning. "I was just looking in on a patient...."

"Now," Kristie said, fingering the wand.

"I'll be forced to speak to your superior about your attitude."

"That's your right. You'd want Dr. Lundgren."

Gates looked pointedly at her nametag. Without a word, he nodded, turned, and departed.

What was that all about? Kristie wondered as the door closed softly behind him.

Whatever was going on, it was not urgent enough to wake Lundgren. She decided it was best just to put a note in her nightly report about the incident.

It was a decision that would cost her life.

CHAPTER SIX
EXECUTIVE ACCESS

Monterey Peninsula Airport, Monterey CA

T he Lear sliced down out of the clear blue sky into the top of the fog, just as the wheels thudded down into place. They were getting special handling and landing to the West, runway 28L, the pilot had announced.

Raven cinched his seat belt tighter. An odd thing about life on the dark side of American diplomacy was that often what killed people was stress, alien diseases – which seemed to be proliferating every year, most with new names and uncertain treatments – and accidents.

Being killed en route to a target had always seemed a useless way to go. It was the aspect of missions that operatives had the least control over. Special OPS was a tight-knit community, and the years since 9-11 had been brutal. He had lost several friends to accidents from vehicle rollovers or collisions, a few to friendly fire, and three to aircraft crashes.

One of them had been here at Monterey. East of the airport, there were mountains.

Skill did not matter in such situations, just cold statistics, odds that had a way of catching up with a person eventually. Raven did not like playing roulette.

This time the landing was fine. He glimpsed the runway, and they were down. The Lear kissed the ground with a chirp from its tires and slowed as the engines roared in reverse. Moisture condensed on the windows as they turned off the runway, groping through the fog. There was a click as the pilot, unseen behind the cockpit door, keyed the cabin speakers.

"We're going to shut down and get a tug into a hanger. Everyone sit tight."

Raven glanced over at Goldfarb. "They don't want anyone to see us?"

The only response was a shrug. The engines spooled down to silence and the cabin lights dimmed, switching to red emergency lighting. There was a slight lurch as the tug was connected.

A large blue building loomed through the fog, a hanger with its doors gaping open. Then they were inside. Raven glanced out and watched as the large doors closed behind them. As soon as they closed, banks of halogen overhead lights came on, harsh and intense.

Raven turned back to Goldfarb, blinking to clear his vision. "Who's meeting us?"

"Good question. You don't care. Pay close attention to this part: *Keep it simple.*"

"Okay...."

"Your cover name is Ron Browning." Goldfarb handed across a government ID that said Environmental Protection Agency, and a Virginia driver's license. The photos were good.

"Do EPA agents carry guns?"

"With their budgets and political clout, they carry whatever they choose."

Raven grinned. "Do I protect America from Global Warming or toxic sludge?"

"No one cares. Just show your creds and keep your mouth shut." Goldfarb said. He watched Raven put the cards in his wallet and held out his hand for Raven's old documents. He put them in his briefcase. "I'll hold these for you."

"I was just getting used to being George Raven...."

"For today you are Ron Browning, a senior EPA investigator. This identity is temporary. I want to distance you from the intelligence community as much as possible."

Raven frowned.

"What?"

"It seems like a thin cover."

"Thicker than needed, actually. You are in the databases. The EPA will verify your employment."

"What if I get busted by some FiBI or Secret Service type? I don't know shit about EPA."

"I repeat: Just show your creds and keep your mouth shut. The fix is in. The SS will not care and the FBI is not involved.

"You won't be interrogated today. Just hand them your badge, if asked, and let me handle it. The Browning identity is a Dixie cup. Got it?"

"Yes, Sir." Goldfarb was saying the Browning identity was a throwaway, a Dixie cup. It was to be used only once.

"The person we are meeting is Jordan Harrington. He is an assistant to the President's National Security Advisor. He has unlimited access to the President. He will get us in. Do you know how the National Security Council works?"

Raven shook his head. "I'm not even clear what it does."

"NSC is chaired by the President. Regular members are the Vice President, the Secretary of Defense, and the assistant to the President for National Security affairs, Jordan's boss. Specialists in the President's Cabinet attend by request."

"A gathering of political creatures...."

"Essentially, though they are not elected, with the two obvious exceptions. Each is presumed to have skills and experience commensurate with and appropriate to his title."

Raven smiled wryly. 'Presumed' was the operative word, and they both knew it, especially in intelligence and black OPs. "I used to have a tee shirt that said, 'Let's go water boarding....' "

Goldfarb scowled, apparently not amused. He continued after a long moment, "With Senate Approval in some cases, NSC members serve at the pleasure of the President."

"So where do you fit in?"

"The same place you do. *Nowhere*. You are not there, neither am I, and I assure you Jordan is fully aware of this constraint.

"Jordan will facilitate our meeting. He knows I was summoned, and it is not going to show up in any logs. You should not be asked any questions, but if you are, your name is 'Browning.' Until we are in the President's presence, and alone, you keep your mouth shut and defer to me. Is that clear?"

"Crystal," Raven said.

"I presume you are carrying weapons?"

"Sir?"

"It was a simple question. Are you armed?"

Raven blinked and stared at him. *Is the Pope Catholic?*

"Well?"

Raven nodded.

"You don't need weapons. Security will be provided."

"I've heard that before, Sir, and you said...."

"I have just given you a direct order. No weapons. I'll leave them in the airplane for you."

Raven carried the Sig in a belt clip holster so he could easily dispose of it if he was to be searched. His was the limited production custom model designed for the SAS. It was compact, eight inches long, five high, an inch and a half thick, and weighing only 31 ounces, but chambered for the big .45 ACP round. Its 185-grain hollow points packed over 600 foot-pounds of energy, enough to knock a man off his feet. He reached under his loose shirt, removed the gun and holster, and offered them to Goldfarb.

"Weapons in the President's presence would draw attention and be remembered. I do not want anything on you that looks like a weapon. Not even a nail clipper."

Raven smiled innocently. He pulled his spare magazine from a pocket and handed it over.

"Is that all?"

Raven sighed and produced a composite sheath knife from his pants leg.

"Thank you. Any questions before we get started?"

"Do you attend NSC meetings?"

"Never." Goldfarb's tone made it clear that this was not a topic for discussion.

Raven shrugged. He had never understood Goldfarb's position in the government. His only operational contact was Goldfarb. He was the cutout. Raven could live with that. Sometimes the less you knew, the safer you were.

CHAPTER SEVEN
MAGIC MUSHROOMS

Monterey Peninsula Airport, Monterey CA

R aven stood alone, watching as Goldfarb and Harrington talked. They showed good tradecraft, heads averted, standing between the limo and the Lear to prevent anyone from hearing or reading their lips. Harrington's people had chased everyone else, even the flight crew, out of the hanger bay. They had tried to remove Raven as well.

Goldfarb quashed that with a word and a wave of his hand. "He's with me." Harrington nodded, gestured at the exit door, and suddenly they were alone. Goldfarb flicked his eyes toward the exit. Raven took the hint and moved out of hearing range. He leaned against the wall and watched from a distance.

The two men looked as if they came from different planets. They were talking in low murmurs, leaning close, watching each other's backs, with their eyes darting around suspiciously.

Jordan Harrington was a towering presence, at least 6' 5" and thin as a rail, with gray eyes and a thatch of white hair. When he raised his voice, the Maine accent came through loud and clear. *"Ayuh...."*

Harrington was dressed in an expensive three-piece black suit, with a white shirt, gold cufflinks, and a navy blue tie. *Who wears a three-piece suit in California?* Raven wondered. The two were speaking so softly that he could only catch an occasional word.

In contrast, Goldfarb was a scruffy professor in his worn tweed jacket, with the elbow patches and the pipe he never smoked stuck in his vest pocket. Five foot seven and stocky, he looked like an unkempt dwarf next to the big man. He was bald, with a goatee, rimless glasses, intense blue eyes, and an odd look on his face.

Whatever he was being told, it was unexpected. Harrington was poker-faced. His expression revealed nothing. Goldfarb was trying to question him, but did not seem to be getting answers.

The two reached some type of an agreement. Goldfarb gestured for Raven to approach. "Get the driver. We're leaving now."

"No escorts?"

Harrington shook his head. "One cah only."

Raven presumed he meant *car*. He frowned and started to speak, but Goldfarb interrupted, "No questions. You will find out why when we get there. Get the driver."

"Yes, Sir."

Building 422, The Presidio of Monterey, California

Raven was surprised by the lack of security and the use of rote TSA procedures. There were armed guards at the gates who had obviously been expecting them, but he had expected security barriers and layers of skilled Secret Service Agents. There were only two, but they had a scanner and a metal detector, and also put them through the drill about checking shoes.

This was reactive nonsense made standard by bureaucratic process. *We look for metal, and the new explosives are made of plastic.* Given suicidal Islamic maniacs pouring liquid explosives on their underwear and tucking explosives in their shoes, security would eventually have us all traveling naked. Half the public accepted TSA gropes. *Sheep.*

Raven smiled to himself. He remembered the incident at Portland, back in 2012, when a high-tech worker and frequent-flyer named John Brennan – no relation to the Muslim CIA Director – refused a body scan. TSA ran him through a metal detector, patted him down, and said he tested positive for explosives.

Brennan stripped naked rather than submit to X-Rays. He was clean, if a bit overweight. TSA was not amused. They filed charges and harassed him for a year until a judge found in his favor, ruling that flying naked was part of free speech.

Flying naked might scare away some bombers, given Muslim culture and the shape some people were in. Groping and expensive scanners were okay, but Obama's obesity police had failed. Even liberal America preferred hamburgers.

Raven brushed the thought aside. Real security came from identifying and eliminating threats at a distance, which was not politically correct because it involved profiling and violence. Ironically, Raven's ID as an EPA agent passed muster with flying colors, while Goldfarb was stopped until Harrington made a phone call.

Raven's grin drew an irritated roll of the eyes from Goldfarb and a puzzled look from Harrington.

WTF? Was Raven's first reaction when they entered the building, but he did not say it. "This looks like a hospital."

"Not exactly," Harrington said.

A doctor in a white coat approached. The Secret Service agents looked uncomfortable, but kept their positions at the checkpoint.

The doctor obviously knew Harrington was in charge. "Are all three of you going in?"

Harrington said, "Yes. The President wants to speak with these men. I'll escort them personally…"

"No."

Harrington raised an eyebrow. "What?"

"Space is limited and you've already seen the President." The doctor's nametag said Shapiro and claimed he was Chief Physician. "I'll see them in. They can have twenty minutes."

Harrington paused for a long moment before he nodded. He stepped aside, and the doctor escorted the two of them through the large double door and down the hall to a room. A guard standing by the door had his attention focused on the doctor, not the visitors. He had a Colt 1911 on his belt in a military holster with a snapped-down flap.

Raven watched with professional interest. Drawing the big .45 was probably a bit easier than retrieving it from a locked safe, but not much.

Doctor Shapiro stopped and turned, blocking the door. "We've had to make some adjustments. This is normally a clinic, not a full hospital. I have been given instructions to let you have access. Only you."

Goldfarb said, "We need to speak with the President alone."

Shapiro said, "My primary responsibility is for the President's health. Until his private physician arrives from Washington, I'm in charge."

"This is a bad time to start a pissing war over turf, Doctor. We will be brief. Do make sure that our visit is not logged."

"You are not to raise his stress levels. If a medical alarm goes off, your meeting is over."

Goldfarb nodded. "Agreed."

"Wait here." Dr. Shapiro entered the room and closed the door softly behind him. In short order, three doctors in white coats and a nurse in a starched uniform came out.

Raven shifted to stand behind Goldfarb. The medical team, without saying a word, lined up on the other side of the hall, keeping their distance.

Shapiro appeared, his hand on the door. "He agrees. You have twenty minutes, and we'll be right here."

"Thank you," Goldfarb said.

Raven was surprised at the size of the room. It was crammed full of equipment, monitors, oxygen tanks, and other gear he did not recognize. There were thick yellow extension cords everywhere, some plugged into outlets, others reaching up into the ceiling. Some of the outlets were white, but others were painted a glaring shade of red.

A large machine in the corner was making a whirring sound with an undertone of gurgling noises. It was almost six feet high, stainless steel, and had two large wheels that were spinning. The clear tubes attached to it and the President seemed to be circulating blood. At least the color of the fluid going through them looked like it: dark red, almost brown, in one tube, and a lighter shade in the other.

President Blager was facing them, his bed cranked up. He had an oxygen cannula in his nose and sensors attached to both arms. Two of them were wired to the big machine in the corner, and another to a modular three-wide digital unit that was labeled A, B, and C. Each bay had its own small display with one large knob and a variety of push buttons. The largest buttons had up and down arrows. The unit itself was emblazoned with a purple plum for some reason.

Cables led to a computer with four plug-in modules. All its bays were occupied. A shelf above it had a small printer that was not in use, but which had a green light. The large color flat panel by the bed was covered with green traces crawling across the screen, the signs of life.

The President was pale, but his eyes were alert. The heavy door clicked shut behind Raven. Other than noises from the big machine, the room was quiet.

"My God." Goldfarb eased himself into one of the gray metal chairs next to the bed. "What have they done to you, Peter?"

Raven reached over and took the adjacent chair, positioning it to block the door before he seated himself. *We don't need interruptions*, he thought.

The President smiled faintly at Goldfarb. "They think it was the pasta...."

"Sir...?"

"Two days ago, we had a reception dinner at the Defense Language Institute Foreign Language Center here. Someone slipped *Amanita phalloides* into the pasta."

Goldfarb was staring at the President. He shook his head. "I don't understand."

The President's smile vanished, and there was regret in his voice. "Poisonous Mushrooms, Aaron. Extremely toxic. They tell me...."

"Save your strength, Sir. We can get a briefing from the doctors."

The President blinked and tried to raise one of his arms. "Let me finish." He took several deep breaths. "I think they've killed me, Aaron. There is no antidote. They have me on a dialysis machine and are giving me high-dose penicillin G and something called silibinin, but these are merely supportive, not curative."

The President's eyes flicked to Raven. "I know who you are."

Raven blinked. He remembered his briefing and said nothing.

"Thank you for coming. You've done well for America."

"Thank you, Sir." Raven felt a lump in his throat. *He is dying, and he is worried about recognizing me and what we did?*

Goldfarb said, "What can we do to help, Mr. President?"

"Nothing medical. It is past that. The delay before symptoms appear allows enough time for irreversible organ damage to the liver and kidneys. The end is normally by liver failure within three days. The doctors hope to stretch that timeline, but the only cure is a liver transplant, which is unlikely.

"They are looking for a donor match, but I will not trade my life for one of my children. I have to assume the worst. My primary responsibility is to the nation."

"Has the Vice President been made aware of your condition?"

"No. I explicitly do not want him informed. I do not want anyone informed. We are waiting to tell my wife. Is that clear?"

"Yes, Mr. President."

"I'm not incapacitated yet. For now, only the attendant medical staff, Harrington, and the Secret Service members here know. They are under my orders as Commander in Chief not to reveal anything. As are you."

When Goldfarb did not speak, the President said, "I need both of you to acknowledge my order."

"Yes, Sir," Goldfarb said, echoed a breath later by Raven.

The President exhaled slowly. In the background, monitors beeped softly, but the screens stayed green. "I don't have the time or strength to argue."

"Just tell me what you want me to do," Goldfarb said. "Anything."

"Does this man," the President glanced at Raven, "know what we've been discussing?"

"A little, Sir," Goldfarb said. "He'll be going in alone…."

The President glanced at Raven. "Do you think he's crazy?"

"A little, Sir. Look at the team he's put together…."

The President managed a wan smile. "Yes." He looked at Goldfarb. "People die, Ari. Look at me and know that. We don't want to, but we all do. If we're lucky, some of us get to choose how and perhaps even why…."

Goldfarb swallowed hard and closed his eyes.

"How long do we have together?" the President asked.

"Sixteen minutes more," Goldfarb said.

"That's sufficient," the President said.

"I'll wait outside." Raven left, closing the door behind him softly. He held up a hand, commanding silence.

"They need sixteen minutes without interruptions." Raven blocked the door with his body, standing at parade rest with a grim look on his face.

The medical team backed away. No one spoke.

CHAPTER EIGHT
BROKEN MIRROR

OHSU Research Hospital, Portland, Oregon

D r. Niles Lundgren was sitting on his patio under the awning sipping his morning coffee. Gazing out, he could see OHSU on the hill in the distance.

How did I get into this mess?

He was growing to dislike Oregon. He missed North Carolina's laid back southern politeness and climate.

Yes, the rose garden was beautiful, but Portland's obsession with being weird was tiresome. To go downtown was to be accosted by legions of panhandlers and having to step over people sleeping on the sidewalks. The rain was relentless.

Lundgren had to abandon his practice and classes at the Rhine Institute to babysit one of their remote viewers, an attractive but troubled young woman named Josie Lynch. Lundgren's career was on hold, but there was nothing he could do about it. He was stuck here until Josie either came out of her coma or died.

A national security matter they had said, reminding him of the contract he had signed. His lawyer warned him not to even *think* of getting out of it, and, so, he had been cooling his heels in Oregon for weeks waiting for something good to happen.

Nothing did. Nothing ever changed. The days were starting to blur together.

His portable phone rang. He glanced at the display. 7:03 AM. It was the hospital. The new shift would just be coming on. *What now?*

"Lundgren."

"I'm Sergeant Johansson. On the security team. You are needed at the hospital immediately."

"Is there a medical problem?"

"I can't say. You are on the contact list for the patient in 302. They told me to call you."

Josie's room. They had kept her name off the roster, listing her as a Jane Doe. "Is my patient all right?"

"So far as I know. Her night nurse did not make it home and it triggered an alarm procedure. There were instructions to put extra guards on that room and to call you. That is what I am doing. Do we have to send a car?"

"No. I'll be there in 15 minutes."

He set the phone down carefully, considering what he should do next. He remembered his instructions and the manner in which they were delivered.

His hands were shaking. He dialed the number he had committed to memory, hearing it ring five times before it clicked over to a recorder with a soft beep.

He took a deep breath, then spoke the code word he had been given. "***Broken Mirror.*** This is Doctor Niles Lundgren. We have a possible Broken Mirror. There is a problem at the hospital. So far as I know our patient remains...."

Lundgren paused, searching for the correct words, knowing a record would be kept and that powerful forces were over-watching. He did not know who he was calling, nor did he want to. That the computer he was talking to would forward his message was sufficient.

The day after the Durham disaster, Lundgren had arrived at his office to find a man sitting at his desk. Somehow, he was there despite the locked door and active security systems.

Lundgren had been ordered to take over Josie's recovery. He asked what that entailed, and the answer was chilling. "It would be excellent if she recovers fully. It would be unfortunate if she dies or fails to become fully functional. However, if you allow her to be abducted or removed from your care, that would be unforgivable. That outcome must not be allowed to happen under any circumstances.

"If Josie is taken by America's enemies, you will be held responsible. You'd do better to kill her yourself than to allow that to happen."

He was then given the phone number and code word.

The situation terrified him. Lundgren was a research psychiatrist with a specialty in paranormal psychology. When he had been Josie's superior, she had been doing remote viewing to support military operations in the Mideast, helping Special OPs teams target *jihadists*.

Josie abhorred violence. Her assignments for the military were not a good match for her peaceful sensibilities, but those viewings were what the government was paying the Rhine Institute to do.

The carnage on the ground was horrific. After months of viewing bombings and beheadings, Josie began to fall apart.

Lundgren shifted her to rescue missions, but that made it worse. She started losing focus and exhibiting bizarre behavior.

Finally, she threatened to quit, a decision that took matters out of his hands. That was not allowed. Josie knew too much. Her powers were too strong. The government deemed her irreplaceable, a national treasure.

After Lundgren passed the problem up his chain of command, she had been shifted to other duties. He was never told what, but she had seemed content and he was allowed to resume normal duties.

She seemed happy. She seemed less crazy. Lundgren had heaved a sigh of relief, happy that Josie was no longer his responsibility, and relieved to get on with his life, with his career.

Whatever they were doing, it went badly wrong. Durham was attacked. Terrorists came for her. After the violence, Josie was unconscious and on life support.

She did not have a scratch on her, but her mind had shut down. The doctors and paranormals were unsure what to do. He had been put in charge of her care because of his prior relationship with her, and there was nothing he could do to get out of it.

A firefight had destroyed the safe house he had rented for Josie in Durham. Those protecting her had launched a military assault that left an upscale neighborhood in flames. Then it all was covered up.

Whoever these people were, Lundgren did not want them as enemies. He needed to report accurately her current condition.

A vegetable. Comatose. None of the words that came to mind sounded reassuring, and admitting the naked truth – that he did not know her condition – was worse.

"Stable," he finally said. "Our patient is reportedly stable. As far as I know, this is not a medical issue involving the patient. I am told one of the hospital staff is missing, a night nurse. I can't recall her name. I am on my way there. I just got a call from a security guard named Johansson. That's all I know."

The computer at the answering center did its best, sorting down its decision tree in microseconds. A general security alert was premature, but immediate action was required. The first call was to a number that might have reached Goldfarb, but his phone was turned off. The computer left a call back code on the recorder. It clicked to itself as disks spun in remote locations, searching secure databases.

The project file had a red code on it. More action was required.

The computer dialed a second number with the same result. It left the same message. The third number rang in a room in Ohio. It was answered on the second ring, this time by a human.

"Black here," the voice said, triggering a different branch of computer code.

"Count to ten, please," the computer said in its mechanical voice. Matching the voiceprint, it gained the necessary authorization to leave a message and initiate action. Since the recipient was a fallible human brain with imperfect memory, it repeated Lundgren's message twice, before it said, "Acknowledge, please."

"John Black acknowledges receipt of a *Broken Mirror.* I will respond. End recording."

The computer was not able to frown. "Instructions please."

"I need the target location."

"Release of that information is not authorized."

"Bullshit," Black snapped. "Command override. Code 93 Alpha Zulu."

"Override is approved. Go to Portland, Oregon immediately. I will record and forward your request. Please speak after the beep."

"John Black is responding to a *Broken Mirror.* I know the general location is somewhere in or near Portland, Oregon. I will be in the air heading west as soon as I can get transport. If I do not have a fucking address, phone number, and contact name by the time I get there, I assure you there is going to be hell to pay. Support and a briefing is needed. Whisky Tango Foxtrot? Black out."

There was a click and the line went dead.

CHAPTER NINE
A FEW SURVIVED

Building 422, The Presidio of Monterey, California

Goldfarb and Raven were in Dr. Shapiro's office, sipping coffee. He had promised to return after he had attended to his duties.

"What now?" Raven said.

Goldfarb sighed. "You tell me. I have no idea what the President was doing here."

"Maybe Harrington knows."

"We're meeting later to discuss such things. Do you know anything about DLI?"

"The Defense Language Institute. I took courses here a few years back. It's where they train interpreters."

"They?"

"The military services consolidated their language programs here after Vietnam. In the 80s, DLI was granted academic accreditation. It claims to be the premier foreign language training institution in the world."

"Is it?"

"Hard to say. State Department doesn't use them."

"Did you attend DLI when you were in the Army?"

"Technically, no. I did not attend as an Army officer, and I was under a false ID. In Iraq, the Army mostly used natives, just like State did. I took the DLI program in a class of foreign nationals. The army paid for it, but I was working for CIA under cover."

"That's not in your records."

"My legend was as a minor official from a friendly country. I had bogus fingerprints, a bushy beard, thick glasses, and poor language skills." Raven shrugged. "I only had that identity for a few months."

"Tell me more about DLI."

"It's the top DOD center for Category IV languages, especially Arabic. Persian is ranked at only Category III – it is considered less difficult, like the Iraq dialect of Arabic. I personally found the way they taught it here, with the local dialects and slang, to be more challenging." Raven smiled. "I had a good Persian instructor. She grew up in Tehran."

"DLI has foreign nationals as students?"

"Sure. Instructors too."

There was a soft rap at the door and Shapiro entered. "I can spare you a few minutes. What was it you wanted?"

"We were just discussing DLI," Goldfarb said. "What can you tell us?"

"They teach languages. Claim to do well at it."

"What was the President doing here?"

"I'm not sure. He was poisoned at a DLI dinner. Right now, we have twenty-six students, three instructors, and a cook who were poisoned. Not counting the President and two of his staff."

"Poisoned by mushrooms," Raven said.

Shapiro nodded. "Only the President and his staff are my responsibility. The others have been evacuated to other facilities."

"Amita phallus?" Goldfarb said.

"The correct term is *amanita phalloides*," Shapiro said, "but, yes, the term does come from phallus. The common name is 'Death Cap,' coming from a poisonous basidiomycete fungus of the genius Amanita. Some say the mushroom resembles a circumcised human penis, though I personally don't see much resemblance."

"What color are they?" Raven asked.

Shapiro said, "There are toxicologists examining the remains of the pasta, but I'm told there are over 600 varieties that can come in a several colors. Most are toxic. The rare ones are white, others have yellow caps, and the most common have distinctive olive-green caps. Oddly, the rare ones are often found growing together with the green ones, the ones that prompted the name 'Death Caps' in the English vernacular. Some call the white ones 'Destroying Angels.' The main thing is that a tenth of a gram is enough to kill an adult human. All the victims here ingested more than that. There is no definitive antidote."

"Are these mushrooms common?"

"Not in the U.S. They are native to Europe and widespread there."

"Have you ever encountered a case of this poisoning?" Goldfarb asked.

"I've not personally seen a case, but the textbooks claim a 70% mortality rate."

"There's one chance in three of survival? The President seemed less hopeful."

"I told him the truth," Shapiro said. "He insisted. His prognosis is not good. The first cases were not detected until almost 24 hours after ingestion, after most of the damage was done."

"Have there been any deaths yet?"

"The head chef was found dead in his room. They are doing an autopsy. It seems too early, but he may have sampled his cooking early or had an unusually low tolerance."

"Where else?" Raven said.

"Pardon?"

"Where else are these mushrooms found?"

"Poland, Western Russia, Italy, and Spain, for sure. Perhaps Morocco and Algeria. I don't know."

"Any in the United States?"

"Not many, but there have been a few identified cases of *amanita* poisoning, four in Oregon a few years back. There are a small number of deaths all over the world every year."

"Any patterns?"

"Not really. Nothing statistically significant of which I am aware. There were seven deaths in Canberra, Australia, over the last decade, but the circumstances are scientifically uncertain."

Uncertain? Raven frowned. "They died, didn't they?"

"Most did. A few survived with liver transplants." Shapiro shrugged. "The cases in Oregon were all from one Korean family, and most of the Canberra victims were from Laos. These fringe cases often involve east and southeast-Asia immigrants falling victim."

"They must like mushrooms," Goldfarb said.

"Apparently…."

"They didn't buy them at the local supermarket," Raven said.

"No."

"So where did they get them?"

"No one knows. And no one much cares, given all the myriad of other health issues we face. Globalization is rampant and borders are porous."

Goldfarb said, "Swine flu, bird flu, AIDs…."

Shapiro said, "There were almost two and a half million deaths in the United States last year. *Amanita phalloides* is highly toxic, but it only causes a few deaths per year worldwide. There are other fungi that provoke more medical concern and attract more research funding, dozens that pose threats to humans and thousands that threaten agriculture or wildlife."

"Jock itch," Raven said. "Infected toenails."

Shapiro said, "The *Cryptococcus neoformans* fungus causes an estimated one million deaths each year worldwide. It's a horrendous disease, and even with therapy, you often can't get rid of it."

"If it's a disease, how do you catch it?"

"By breathing. *C. neoformans* typically enters the body through the lungs and can spread throughout the body, including the brain."

"Let's get back to the mushrooms," Goldfarb said. "Might they be local?"

"It's possible. There is speculation the species may have invasive potential."

Raven said, "How about Iran? Are they native there?"

Shapiro shrugged. "No idea."

"Have these mushrooms been used before for political assassinations?"

"Certainly. Roman Emperor Claudius, Pope Clement VII, Tsaritsa Natalia Naryshkina, Holy Roman Emperor Charles VI…."

Raven interrupted, "Have they been used *recently* for assassinations?"

"Other than on the President," Goldfarb said drily.

"Not that I'm aware of. Most of the cases in the literature are accidental poisonings of mushroom collectors. It is easy to confuse *amanita* with mushrooms that are safe to consume. The genus is responsible for some 95% of the fatalities resulting from mushroom poisoning."

"Wouldn't cooking tend to reduce the effects?" Goldfarb asked.

Shapiro said, "No. The toxicity is not reduced by cooking, freezing, or drying. Some authorities claim that even touching these mushrooms or putting them in the same basket with fungi collected for the table can be lethal."

Raven said, "So they would require special handling? Gloves, that sort of thing?"

"You'd have to ask a toxicologist. I think they probably would. I certainly wouldn't care to handle them myself."

"I need the bottom-line." Goldfarb looked Shapiro in the eyes. "Can you save the President?"

"We're trying. His personal physician should be here tonight. We're using the procedures that have been recommended."

"Would it help to move him to a better facility?"

"Transport isn't recommended. Most likely only a liver transplant can save him, and we can do that here."

"If you can find a donor," Raven said.

"Yes." Dr. Shapiro looked at his watch. "Is there anything else?"

"Not that I can think of," Goldfarb said.

"Can I have my office back now?"

"Give us ten minutes. We'll check our messages and I'll leave you a contact number."

"The President has directed that you be kept informed and given access. I passed that to the Secret Service."

"Thank you," Goldfarb said.

Shapiro nodded and made his exit.

Raven said, "We need to talk."

"Yes we do. Give me 30 minutes. I need to make a few calls, and then I want you out of here before you attract attention. Call the airport and tell them you'll be using the plane."

Raven nodded, pulling out his phone and turning it on.

Both their phones started beeping urgently. They exchanged worried looks, shaking their heads. Goldfarb was scowling darkly.

Raven thought, *What now?* He closed the door behind him.

CHAPTER TEN
SINCE THE EVENT....

Hillsboro, Oregon

Sergeant Johansson met Black at Hillsboro Airport. It had not been a good flight.

The only airplane he could borrow was an ancient T-33.

It was older than he was, designed during WW II and one of the first jets the military used. It was civilian registered, owned by the flying club at Wright Patterson who had restored it, no doubt for nostalgic reasons.

The aircraft was uncomfortable, cold, and slow. It sucked fuel like a hungry hog. The instruments were antiquated, the most useful one being a hand-held GPS jury-rigged into the panel and duct taped in place. Worst of all, it lacked an autopilot, so he'd had to hand fly it all the way, eight hours, not counting the fuel stops.

At that rate, you could take the airlines, security and all. Or walk. The only good thing was, he finally got there.

"Welcome to Portland," Johansson said.

"Are you sure?"

Johansson blinked.

"Portland," Black said. "The Airport data says we're in Hillsboro. KHIO."

"The hospital is close. The FAA gave us your flight plan. I was told to pick you up and brief you."

Johansson had the visage of a Viking, a shaved head, and the physique of a fireplug. He was maybe five nine, stocky, muscular, and sported a bushy blond mustache. He wore a blue windbreaker, zipped halfway down, with a lighter blue patch showing a stylized yellow, blue, and green flame, a logo of some type, and the letters "OHSU."

The jacket sure clashed with his bright yellow sweatshirt emblazoned with "Hood to Coast Run" in neon orange block letters, white and blue Nikes, faded blue jeans, and a wide brown leather belt that secured a Glock automatic in a black holster on his right hip. He would be hard to miss in a crowd, but it was probably less noticeable than wearing a tunic and one of those helmets with the horns.

Black frowned. "OHSU?"

"Yep. Oregon Health Sciences University."

"You don't look like a cop. Does everyone tote guns around the ramps out here?"

"Cops on campus are not loved. OHSU has its own security. It has adopted the "Portland is weird" culture in the cause of political correctness. They put out a memo not to wear uniforms, to dress naturally, so I did. We have concealed carry permits, but I like to show my weapon when I am on duty. It gets more respect. On campus, I wear my badge."

"May I see it?"

Johansson handed over a keycard. It showed a bust shot of a man in a guard uniform with the same patch wearing a hat. The back had a magnetic stripe, an RFID square, the flame logo, and a number to call.

Black studied the picture quizzically. "Is that really you?"

"My mother says so. Like I said, I am not a cop. Want to see my driver's license?"

"Never mind," Black said, handing it back. "You *were* a cop, before?"

Johansson shook his head. "Marines. My last job was security for the embassy in Kabul after they kicked the private contractors and their Gurkhas out. It sucked."

Roger that. At least he is professionally trained. "How'd you get here?"

"I like Portland and it's good duty. They pay better than the government, and you don't get shot at much."

"Who shoots at you?"

"Drug gangs do most of the shooting in Portland, but we make sure they don't deal on the grounds. The gangbangers stay close to the MAX lines, and the drive-bys are usually downtown or over in NE. The Portland cops handle that." Johansson shrugged. "We've had trouble with the animal rights people. The radical greenies tested us a few times, but mostly it's the animal rights whackos."

"Protests?"

"Sure, but those are usually stage-managed political events. They bring lawyers and media and provoke incidents to get publicity. We worry more about arson, and bombings."

"Huh?" *What planet is this?*

"OHSU is not just a hospital. The scientists do medical research using monkeys. It pisses the greenies off. There have been homes burned, cars trashed, that sort of thing...."

"Militants?"

"Wannabes." Johansson shrugged. "Activist political assholes. Mostly it is intimidation. They made death threats on one of our researchers and went to torch her house in the middle of the night."

"They threatened to kill her over *monkeys*?"

"Sure, why not? They got the neighbor's house by mistake. Killed his dog, but the family got out safe. Nobody hurt and nobody convicted, but they did extensive damage, the neighbor moved away, and our research staff was freaked. That was a year ago. It would be a media event if one of our big scientists was killed or a lab blown up.

"We put security cameras out, upgraded our security, and shot the next intruder eight times. It's been pretty quiet since...."

Compared to what? Black rubbed his eyes. "How's Josie?"

Johansson looked baffled.

"Your patient. I'm here to see her."

"Jane," Johansson said. "The patient involved is Jane Doe."

"Right. Jane. Sorry. It's been a long day."

Shit. I just screwed up. No one had told him Josie was under an alias.

Johansson said, "No problem."

"I wouldn't be here if there wasn't a problem, Sergeant Johansson. How about you give me the highlights for Jane Doe? For starters, convince me your patient is safe."

"We've increased the guards, 24/7. Three of my best people are there. Three more are on hot standby and could be at the hospital in ten minutes. Plus we got a SWAT team from the Portland Police assigned."

Black took a deep breath, then another. He relaxed slightly. "Okay, you've got security, but she's in a hospital. I assume that means there's a health problem?"

"Since the event, we're up to our ass in Doctors. Do you know Dr. Lundgren?"

"I know who he is."

"He's in charge. He spends days in the room next door to her. Seems nervous."

"You didn't answer my question."

"Ask the Docs," Johansson said. "The word they told me to use was 'stable.' Don't have a clue what it means, but no one seems worried."

"When do you get to tell me what the 'event' was?"

"You don't know?"

Black shook his head. "My orders were to get here. I am here. What are your instructions?"

"Like I said, pick you up and brief you."

"Well?"

"One of our nurses is missing. So is the log they keep at the nurse's station on the floor. We've had detectives and FBI all over the place."

"That's all?"

"Pretty much. It is under control. No problem."

"I haven't eaten anything except energy bars and coffee for fourteen hours. Unicom said there's a shower in the FBO." Black gestured at the building next to the gate. "Have I got time to clean up and get a burger or something on the way?"

"Sure." Johansson nodded.

"I'll be quick." Black grabbed his bag from the baggage bay and started towards the building.

CHAPTER ELEVEN
YOU CALL HIM....

Building 422, Dr. Shapiro's office, The Presidio of Monterey, California

Goldfarb looked up when Raven entered. "So who called you?"

"It was the kid."

"John Black? The pilot?"

Raven nodded. "He's on his way west, highly pissed off that he was alerted and can't contact me. He left me two messages to call him. Wants to know what's going down."

"Tell me about it. He got the alert computer into a loop somehow. It's been sending me urgent call backs every ten minutes."

Raven grinned, drawing a sharp look from Goldfarb. "The kid's learning...."

"Before my message box filled up, one of my calls was from Wright Patterson AFB. It appears your young lad stole one of their museum airplanes. They say I'm responsible..."

Raven's grin widened. "Are you?"

"Of course not."

"Stealing an aircraft is a Federal offense, isn't it?" Raven murmured.

"This was an emergency protocol. Black would have been called when they could not contact us. He will have been directed to Portland, Oregon by now. That is where Josie has been secluded. You got the auto response from the computer too, I presume?"

"**Broken mirror**," Raven said. "Josie's at risk. I have the plane on standby. Do I have this correct? Something about a missing nurse?"

"I got the same information you did. Lundgren called it in. Did you ever meet him?"

Raven shook his head.

"He was Josie's control before you."

"I know that. I am more interested in *now*. Since Durham, no one has told me shit."

Goldfarb shot Raven a look of disapproval. "The imperative has been...."

"We're running under new rules now," Raven said. "You heard what the President said. You agreed to bring Josie in. Let *me* go to her. And tell me what Lundgren's involvement is now. Is he a problem?"

"We'll get to that. First, I need to emphasize a few things. First off, no one is to get a whiff of the fact that the President has been poisoned."

Raven's eyes narrowed. "Of course not, I...."

"Let me continue. Harrington thinks this was likely an inside job. Whoever did this, we have enemies within at high levels. So when I say 'no one' that includes our own government. If questioned officially, you say nothing. If pressed, you will deny any knowledge."

"Yes, Sir. Understood."

"I need you to understand fully. The President has broad powers concerning investigations that touch the White House. Some have abused that power. Nixon lost, but subsequent Administrations were more, ah, heavy handed, starting with Clinton."

"The blue dress...?"

"That too, but the relevant precedent that fits best is the death of Vince Foster. Do you recall that one?"

Raven shook his head.

"Mr. Foster was a White House counselor and an associate of Hillary Clinton's at Little Rock's Rose Law Firm. He was a fixer who kept the lid on their scandals. He died in the park across from the White House by a single gunshot in the head. A small caliber gunshot that entered around the jawline on the right side of his neck, most likely a .22."

"That's an assassin's weapon. A .22 with subsonic rounds. I used to have a suppressed Walther. It just made a little 'poof' when you fired it."

"Correct. Foster's death was, however, ruled to be a suicide. You can look it up online."

"What does that have to do with the President's being poisoned?"

"Everything. Who do you think investigated Foster's death?"

"The DC police? The FBI?"

"The Park Service. By Presidential order. That sets a legal precedent. President Blager has signed an EO that assigns his own Secret Service detail to investigate his attempted assassination. Should they need any assistance and if a terrorist connection is suspected, they are instructed to consult with me as a liaison."

"Will that stick?"

"Only for a time. Do you know much about Vice President Dunbar?"

"No, Sir."

"Harrington told me Dunwood Duncan Dunbar III is the President's political baggage. He is a leftist. He has always been a leftist. He inherited his wealth. He's never had to run anything himself or make the tough decisions."

"I'm not much into politics, Sir…."

"Dunbar's operational preference has historically been appeasement and compromise. His focus is on his personal image and charisma. It always has been, and he is unlikely to change."

"He's a politician. Why do we care?"

"The President cares, Raven. He was worried that Duncan was never going to stand up to Iran. Harrington agrees. Our team just thwarted an Iranian sponsored nuclear attack. It was a major setback, and one we seek to exploit."

Raven was nodding slowly. "So?"

"What if they had a Plan B? It would be very useful for them if our top leadership suddenly changed and we reverted back to Carter-Obama policies."

"What do you want me to do about this? Take out Dunbar?"

"Absolutely not. This is all speculative. Such tactics would be abhorrent and likely counterproductive. I want you to continue just as we've discussed."

"Bring Josie in? Flip Safdari?"

Goldfarb nodded. "Yes. If you and Josie can get back to full operational status, this is more important than ever."

"So why are you briefing me in on this thing with the President?"

"You were already in. You know the President's condition and prognosis. And now you know why you must never reveal that to anyone."

"Josie will know about the President as soon as she regains her powers."

"Yes, of course she will. When we get to that point, you must persuade her not to reveal his condition to anyone. Agreed?"

"Yes, Sir. But if President Blager dies….."

"If Blager dies, we're screwed. I am working on that, and I will be staying right here until this crisis is past. At present, you are not involved. It is my problem. Understood?"

"Yes, Sir. Understood. What about Lundgren? You were going to brief me."

Goldfarb took a deep breath. "Doctor Niles Lundgren is a psychiatrist with a Top Secret SI clearance and a specialization in paranormal psychology. He is in charge of Josie's medical care. He is responsible for her health. He was not given a choice about the assignment. We can safely assume that he's not happy about his situation."

"So?"

"Get him to release her and get out. It's simple."

"What about her security?"

"She's at Oregon Health Science University. It is a research hospital, but they also do medical research with animals. It has excellent security for a commercial facility."

"What does that mean?"

"You know how some people kill doctors who are doing abortions?"

Raven shrugged. "Heard about it."

"Medical research using animals attracts animal rights activists with the same proclivities. OHSU is not Fort Knox or Langley, but they have armed guards, badged access, cameras…."

"You said an on-duty nurse disappeared. How is that?"

"Disturbing. She left at the end of her shift, but never made it home. That is not necessarily a security lapse. Maybe she has a boyfriend."

"Now who's getting sloppy? Maybe something happened on her shift that someone doesn't want discovered."

Goldfarb nodded slowly. "Yes. You are leaving to get Josie as soon as we finish this conversation. I presume you are motivated and capable of extracting her. It would be best to do so with a certain amount of urgency. Do you have any questions?"

"Just one. Will you give me operational control on the ground?"

"No more Durhams. I do not want to see burning buildings and dead cops on the news. And I damn sure don't want to have to explain it publicly."

"Of course not," Raven said. "Non-violent, like choir boys."

"What's your plan?"

"It's simple. Josie's location is compromised. Black is there, or will be soon. He picks her up, I arrive, and we get her out of there."

"What if she can't be moved?"

"She can. Probably the same way she got there in the first place. We put her into an ambulance and get her on a life flight, making sure the medical support she needs is provided."

"Taking her where?"

"How about here? We've got security and we'll soon be up to our asses in medical experts."

Goldfarb pursed his lips, frowned, and seemed to be concentrating. "It might work. How reliable is Black? I put him through a small arms class while you were recovering, but he's not had field training or experience."

"How'd he do?"

"He did fine on the range. Out in the field is different."

There's the rub, Raven thought. "He survived Durham. The kid's got balls."

That part was true. The problem was that Black had not proved himself to be lethal.

Goldfarb looked dubious. "I think you need backup."

"Sure," Raven said, mostly to buy time. He was thinking furiously. "This place where you stashed Josie, OHSU...?"

"Oregon Health Science University."

"Are they secure?"

"They claim to be." Goldfarb shrugged. "We don't know yet what happened with the nurse, but any facility can be penetrated if you put enough into it."

"I'll get their best man. Pay him a bonus. I prefer one who is ex-military, preferably one who has done convoy or embassy security duty and seen combat."

Goldfarb was nodding. "You run the OP. I'll handle support."

"Works for me," Raven said. "Fix it about Black's stolen airplane, and get a crew to wherever the hell he parked it to return it. I am taking your aircraft and having it converted for a medivac flight. If that doesn't work, I'm still taking it, and you can have someone meet me there."

"We're doing this here in the US of A." Goldfarb hesitated for a moment. "That suggests keeping a low profile."

Not like Durham, Raven thought. A subtle reprimand or perhaps a caution. Is he testing me? "Uh huh."

"We can get military support if needed, but..." Goldfarb let his voice trail off.

"I plan to get in and out, have it over, and be gone before anyone notices."

Goldfarb nodded. "Let's do it."

"Right," Raven said.

Both men started making calls.

CHAPTER TWELVE
MONKEYS AND MADRASSAS

Heathman Hotel, Portland, Oregon

D r. John Henry Gates, MD, PhD, Associate Dean for The Office for Diversity and Community Partnership at Harvard Medical School, a member of three boards for health care foundations, and an advisor to Public Health Council for the Commonwealth of Massachusetts had not slept well.

He was not used to criticism, not for a long time, not anymore.

Gates had come a great distance from the slums of the holy city, the place of Martyrdom. Mashhad was the second largest city in Iran, an old provincial capital on the Turkmenistan border. It was named after the martyrdom of Imam Reza in AD 823, a religious center, and very cold in the winter.

The saying was, "The rich go to Mecca, but the poor journey to Mashhad." Some of the poor did not need to journey. Already there, they lived in squalor with little hope, dependent on the largess of the State and the Mosques for survival.

The Revolutionary Guard discovered Gates in the madrassa and was interested to learn his father had been in the British Secret Service, and went missing, presumed dead, during the revolution that deposed the Shah. Gates' Western appearance, intelligence, and an aptitude for science spared him from duty as a martyr. The Guard saw his potential and Iran saw to his education and training.

When his mother proved troublesome, they took him away and limited her visits. Then they sent him out of the country and the visits stopped. She had died when he was a second year student. Gates put his studies first and did not return for the funeral.

Iran used Western grants to send him to Cambridge, then paid for his medical school and helped build his career. They groomed him well, and, with his medical credentials, it was no problem to arrange a sabbatical to Harvard, and, eventually, U.S. Citizenship.

Gates found that he was more interested in policy than the practice of medicine. He mostly gave speeches and political advice these days, but occasionally was tapped for special assignments to serve the needs of the Revolutionary Guard to pay back what they had invested in him.

This was one. His mission was to penetrate a secure hospital facility and kill a woman patient undergoing intensive care without attracting notice. It seemed insane, but he had no way to refuse the assignment. Disobedience would be punished.

Why were they risking him in the field? Was it a test? Was there something special about this target? Gates did not know. Nor dared he ask.

What he did know was it had not gone well, due to that cheeky nurse. He had panicked and let her push him around.

Gates needed time to get the right adjustment for the IV drips. He had failed to anticipate the primitive equipment in the ICU. It was crucial that his target's death occurred after enough time for him to be gone and without leaving evidence that might show up during an autopsy. It was something he needed to get right. There was no chance of that with the nurse watching.

The medications in the drip were unexpected, a combination of ketamine and valium. Whatever they had been doing to that patient, it was a major medical intervention. Ketamine has unusual psychoactive, paralysis and sedative properties. Valium is a barbiturate sometimes used in conjunction with ketamine to prevent side effects when coming out of it. It is tranquilizing but an overdose will stop respiration.

Both drugs were easily detectable after death. Gates had brought along sodium phenobarbital, still used for prolonged sedations but with a well-known low margin of safety. A death from an overdose would be unremarkable and easily attributed to error.

However, Phenobarbital was not being administered and Gates was reluctant to add it on top of the other drugs. The effects of such a combination were problematic. And even if he was lucky and the effects were delayed, it increased the risk of anomalies being detected by an autopsy.

Adding Valium could kill, but it would have taken a lot for a lethal dose, he did not have any with him, and the single drip was pre-mixed. Gates was left with adjusting the drip rate by trial and error. He tried running it up and down, watching the medical monitors. It was a tedious procedure and he dared not trip the alarms.

In the middle of this, the bitch nurse appeared. Gates snapped. The years rolled away and he was back to being a scared child in the slums of Mashhad. He fled.

Badly shaken, Gates walked back to his hotel. He stopped in one of the parks and had a few tokes to settle his nerves. He did not drink alcohol, but marijuana was everywhere in Portland and he had scored some nice local weed last night in one of the coffee houses.

Gates was glad to find his hotel lobby empty except for a bored desk clerk reading **Willamette Week**. *So far, so good.*

The clock on his nightstand said 4:32 when he entered his room. He decided to wait until 5:00 AM to check in. He knew his sponsor would be in his New York office by then.

When he called, he got no sympathy. Firouz cared nothing of medical technicalities or protocols. He was a hard man, old school, and it seemed as if he already knew something had gone wrong.

Before the Shah, the people of Persia did not use surnames. Firouz held to that custom. In English, his name meant "victorious" and it fit. All the man cared about was results.

Gates dialed the phone, and when his sponsor answered, said, "*Allahu akbar.*"

"Did you get the package?" Firouz demanded on the open line.

Gates had not. The girl was still alive. "There was a problem. The attendant wouldn't give it to me."

After a silence that seemed long, Firouz said, "You were given a simple task."

"I can go back tomorrow. This time I will succeed, *In sh'allah.*"

"Were you seen?"

"A nurse walked in…." He dared not lie to the man.

"You still have access?"

"Of course," Gates said. "I have a card key and a badge."

Firouz's demeanor changed. He brushed aside Gates' explanations and ordered him to get some sleep and stay in his room. "I'm getting you help. You will go back tonight."

Then he hung up.

Gates was awakened by the phone. He fumbled for it and mumbled, "Hello."

"You be John Henry Gates?"

"I'm Dr. Gates."

"Oliver's Bar at Six. Have your bags packed and bring what you need to get the package."

"Oliver's." He had seen it across the street. No windows and a sign with a stylized picture of the boy urchin holding up his porridge bowl. Gates loathed Dickens and his portrayals of archaic English criminals and their sordid lives. Workhouses, baby farms, and pickpockets. It was nonsense. In a Muslim country, they would lack hands.

"I'll be there, *In sh'allah.*"

"Don't dig Muslim jive, but we be on the same side. See you there."

"How do I recognize you?"

There was a short laugh. Then the line went dead.

Gates spotted him at once, in a booth in the back of the bar, holding a beer stein, nursing his drink. He was a big man, at least 250 pounds. He wore jeans, dark glasses, a black leather coat, and a chauffer's cap. He looked familiar. "Do I know you?"

The man shook his head. "Call me Tre. We do this tonight, then I going to help get you out of Portland."

"I've seen you somewhere."

The man smiled and removed his dark glasses and coat. Underneath he was wearing a black T-shirt. Gates saw amber eyes, dark skin, massively muscled arms, and a tattoo of a Polar Bear on his right biceps.

"You were on television a year or two back."

Tre nodded. "Stupid. STOO-PID. Made a bad move. I'm an Elf."

Gates shook his head, puzzled. Polar Bears and elves? It made no sense.

"We stop the exploitation of the environment and animals. Raise hell. Do good work. Met your Firouz at a conference in Quebec. Good Mon. Lots of common interests. We was taking the heat off you Muslims till 9-11."

"What's an Elf?"

"Earth Liberation Front."

Gates searched his memory, and then nodded as realization came. "You torch things. You burned the Vail ski resort a few years back."

Tre smiled and nodded. "Not me. I was hiding out in Canada then. We was doing fund raising up there, and I got dumb enough to give the newsies a TV interview. Came back too soon, and the pigs busted me. Fucking FBI targeted us. Operation Backfire. Lots of snitches, and I was set up. Messy trial, but we won the appeal. Free as a bird now."

"You burned a car dealership or something."

"SUVs. Pollution spewing, oil sucking, bastard machines. I hate them for sure, but I was acquitted. Politicians cut off the gas now. Time to move on. We have better ways now."

"What are you doing here?"

"Spreading the love. I gonna help you. You gonna help me. We make the world better."

"How are you going to help me?"

Tre grinned, winked, and took a sip of his beer. "Already did. Bros been watching. You had trouble with a little nurse woman. She be no more problem. Bad accident."

"She's dead?"

"Very sad. More sad is they locked down. Nobody getting in or out. You messed with something you didn't know. Now we gotta work together, Mon, or we both fucked."

"Do you have an interest in that patient?"

"No mon." Tre shook his head. "Monkeys."

CHAPTER THIRTEEN
BREAKDOWN....

Monterey Peninsula Airport, Monterey CA

Raven's cell phone was ringing. He fished it out and glanced at it, scowling. *No ID and a secure call. It had to be Goldfarb. Just what I need right now.* "City morgue," he said.

"Very funny." Goldfarb did not sound amused. "Are you in Portland?"

"Negative. I'm still at the airport."

There was a pause. "You should have been in Portland an hour ago."

"Tell me about it," Raven said. "They are still upgrading the airplane for medevac. Needed some equipment, but it's finally arrived. They're putting it in now."

A muttered curse came over the phone. The redundant encryption made Goldfarb's voice sound hollow. "You should have informed me."

He does not swear well, Raven thought. "I've been a bit busy."

"Doing what?"

"Dealing with shit. Spending your money. We will be underway shortly. How are things at your end? Or am I having all the fun?"

"No change locally."

The President is still alive, Raven thought. "How about with Josie?"

"The Bureau just gave me a briefing on that. I've been in phone conferences or on Shapiro's computer ever since you left."

"I'm sure the Presidio is thrilled about having you take over their offices...."

"I didn't ask permission. They have more pressing issues."

No shit. Raven smiled grimly. "Anything going down I need to know about?"

"Jordan Harrington chairs something we call 'the Working Group.' It reports to the NSC, with a dotted line to the President. It is a useful backchannel. The FBI has a seat at the table, and Jordan has been pressing them about Durham. He suggests the Portland incident is possibly related to the security lapse in Durham."

Someone messing with Josie in what is supposed to be a secure, safe environment damned well should be considered related. And the FBI does not yet know about The President's poisoning, Raven translated. "Any results?"

Goldfarb said, "The Portland incident is becoming clearer. The security there is being buttoned down. Black is onsite. He says our patient is stable."

"I've spoken with him. He is with a security guy, a Sergeant Johansson, who worked for the hospital there. Black has borrowed Johansson and some of his guards. Said we would pay, and I agreed. They have SWAT teams from the local police for backup. There is a guard on Jane Doe's door 24/7, that wing is restricted access, and they are screening anyone entering the facility. We seem to be covered for the time being."

"Is Johansson someone we can depend on?"

"He checks out good," Raven said. "It says MOS 8152 in his personnel file."

"Ex-Marine?"

"Yes, Marine Security. Won a Silver Star in Kabul. His last job was security duty at the embassy. They offered him a field commission trying to keep him, but he turned it down."

"Why?"

"I think he just wanted out. Can't blame him. Afghanistan sucks. He's been with OHSU for almost three years now."

"Does Johannson give a shit about our issues?"

Raven said, "You'd have to ask him. I have never met the man. His involvement with us is limited to assisting Black."

"I'm asking you."

"Black says he's needed."

"I'm still asking you."

"I think he's motivated to deal with the penetration of Josie's room."

"Why?"

"First off, he's pissed that they hit his facility. Sort of like I was when our safe house in Durham was blown, Sir."

"We do seem to have some leaks," Goldfarb said. "What else?"

"It's personal for him too. One of his guys was dating the nurse that disappeared."

"Kristi Louisell, twenty six years old. They found her."

"What did she say?"

"Nothing," Goldfarb said. "She's dead. Tucked into a dumpster behind her condo. Her neck was broken."

"Do you have any good news?"

"Actually, yes. That why the Bureau called me. Nurse Louisell did her job. Her notes said there was an intruder in the room tampering with the IV drips. Interestingly, that page is missing from the logs at the nurses' station. Someone on the inside must have removed it."

"How do you know?"

"She sent an electronic copy to Dr. Lundgren, which survived. The intruder was a Doctor and his nametag said 'Gates.' That checked. We got a match to the security cameras on the floor. Better yet, the room was smart wired and it triggered his RFID."

Raven frowned into the phone. "Say again?"

"OHSU has sophisticated security. It tagged him."

"How?"

"Gates was carrying his passport for some reason. As you know, U.S. Passports have imbedded microchips, RFID chips. The computers logged his biometrics."

"Do we have him?"

"Not yet, but we will. When interrogated by a radio signal, the RFID chips report. Radio Frequency Identification. We have Gates' description, finger prints, SS number, digital photo, employer, home address, and...."

"Any red flags?" Raven interrupted.

"Several. He is originally from Iran. In the past month his passport was stamped in London and Tehran."

"What is this, amateur hour?"

"I beg your pardon?" Goldfarb said.

"You told me our patient was safe. Now you are telling me we just let an Iranian assassin float like smoke through our security and into her room. What is this, a repeat of the PC cluster fuck in Texas with the *jihadist* Army Doctor a few years back?"

"The FBI doesn't think so. Gates was born in Iran, but he moved to England as a teenager. He is Western educated and has been a model US citizen for the past seventeen years. He is a high profile doctor from Harvard Medical School and is on several government panels. He lives in Cambridge and has a Secret Level clearance. They sent me a large file on him."

"Is he a Muslim?"

"His file doesn't say. Parts of it are redacted."

Raven took a deep breath and let it out slowly. "Where is Gates now?"

"We don't know. He arrived in Portland three days ago with an open return ticket."

"Marvelous." Raven saw the pilot coming across the ramp and gestured frantically, pointing at the sky. The pilot nodded and held up five fingers.

Goldfarb was still talking, but Raven cut him off. "The plane's fixed. We are ready to roll. I need support."

"Understood," Goldfarb said. "What do you need?"

"Get those SWAT teams deployed. We will use this aircraft for an air evac. I am getting Jane Doe the hell out of there. I want a total lock down at OHSU until we get her clear."

"Negative," Goldfarb said. "It's a working hospital and research facility. We can't shut it down."

"Well, do the best you can. Get law enforcement to put out a BOLO on Gates. Get Black and OHSU's security staff a copy of his description, photo, and fingerprints. Have them distributed to their guard stations, and to local law enforcement, including the FBI office there."

"Can do," Goldfarb said. "What are your intentions?"

"I'll bring her back myself. Any objections?"

"It's your call," Goldfarb said.

"You'll back me?"

"That's what I said. What else do you need?"

"Can you have the FBI pick Gates up and hold him?"

"Probably. They're looking for him now...."

"Escalate that please, and make sure I'm informed immediately when they have him in custody. Have them find some reason to hold him until I can get her clear. Is Lundgren is still in charge of Jane Doe's care?"

"Correct."

"I need her conscious so I can talk to her. If he can do it safely, Lundgren is to get her off whatever meds they are stuffing into her and ready to travel." Raven looked at his watch. "Pull some strings. Get this airplane a direct routing to Hillsboro, where Black landed. I want them – Black, Lundgren, and as much security as they can put together – to meet us there if possible, and if not, I want transport waiting to take me to OHSU. Tell Black I am coming and to bring me a copy of Gates' file. And get us some weapons and body armor if you can."

"Anything else?"

"Damned right. When they apprehend Gates, for Christ's sake do not let them turn him over to law enforcement and lawyers. He needs to be interrogated."

"I've not...."

"I've gotta go," Raven said, with the sound of engines spooling up in the background. "I'll call you from Portland."

CHAPTER FOURTEEN
A BLACK ROSE

OHSU Hospital, Portland OR

Josie was waking up. Keeping her eyes closed, she took deeper breaths. It felt good, and she sensed fragrances. *Roses, it was the scent of roses.*

Josie flexed, feeling her body around her. Her arms were unencumbered. She was free of the tubes that had been taped to her arms. She remembered feeling the drugs moving through her veins. Irresistibly slowing the world, calming her, and clouding her thoughts. That wasn't so bad.

Worse were the drugs that blacked her out, slamming her down into darkness, leaving memory gaps. Worst of all was the zombie juice that left her body working but took away conscious control. That spooked her. She would be awake and aware, but only as a spectator.

Josie begged them to stop. The doctors said they could not, that it was the only way to ensure adequate exercise. Each day a trainer would walk her to the gym, help her on the equipment, instruct her, and watch as she exercised every muscle group.

When she was exhausted and covered with sweat, the trainer would take her back to her room where a nurse would clean her up, give her one of those awful hospital gowns, put her back in bed, hook her up to the drips, and wait until she drifted off.

Josie did not even like to exercise, but she had no say in the matter. Nor could she get them to stop the drugs. Lundgren was evasive when she demanded answers. When she tried resisting, they just medicated her more.

Josie had nothing against soft drugs. She sometimes used them for recreation or to enhance her powers, but the drugs they gave her here were too strong.

Now they were gone. She was clean and her mind felt clear. It felt good. She flexed her fingers, her toes, wiggled her nose, and then reached out with her special senses. Testing herself. Everything worked, her heart rate was low, and her special talents felt stronger than ever. *Excellent.*

She sensed someone in the room. Not a threat, a friend.

Josie slowly opened her eyes. The first thing she saw was the flowers. Dozens of roses, on a long table down the right side of her bed.

Red roses for love, white roses for purity and spirituality, or, some said, as a sign of reverence and humility. And set aside, separate from all the rest, and standing alone in a central vase, there was a single black rose. It was a message without words, a message in the language of flowers. She remembered a poem from college.

In Eastern lands they talk in flow'rs
And they tell in a garland their loves and cares;
Each blossom that blooms in their garden bowr's,
On its leaves a mystic language bears....

Josie knew only one person who would leave such a message for her: A *black* rose. Like his name, Raven. He was a loving companion and partner, but a man who lived in darkness and fought his own ghosts. He had admitted it, once telling her that he could only feel safe in the deep dark of midnight.

The two of them were lovers, but they lived in the shadows fearing the light. That was their curse. It had almost destroyed her.

Josie studied the flowers. A single black rose, flanked on one side by white roses, on the other by red. She inhaled sharply, marveling at the centerpiece. She had never seen a black rose, but had read about them in her studies of symbolism.

A black rose means revenge to a foe or wanting to kill someone. However, because a black rose is virtually impossible to procure, it can also mean pure love. A black rose can also mean rebirth.

The voice came softly. "There are twice as many red ones as white. Raven said to tell you."

Josie turned her head and saw the man as he stood. Tall, thin, unshaven, and wearing a desert tan Nomex flight suit with no nametag or rank. He had thick brown hair and green eyes. "I know you."

"You saved my life."

Memories were coming back. "At my house in Durham…?"

"Un-huh."

"John Black," she said. "Right? We surveyed Antarctica together."

He nodded.

"Put the flowers together, please. Don't leave the black one isolated and alone…."

Black reached out and did as requested, carefully positioning the arrangement so Josie could see it without lifting her head. "It's not really black, you know. That is not possible in nature. The rose just looks black because it's such a deep red."

A symbol of love in the shadows, Josie thought. *How fitting.*

"I've never seen one before."

"I hadn't either except for pictures in books. They're rare." Josie raised her head and looked directly at Black. "No more drugs."

"Okay. No problem."

"Can you promise me that?"

Black nodded, produced a small pistol, and then slipped it back into a pocket. "I'm in charge until Raven arrives."

"How did I get here?"

"We were blown. There was a leak and you were targeted. Our mission was successful, but we were all wounded in one way or another."

"Where am I now?"

"Portland, Oregon." Black waved an arm dismissingly. "There's no need to talk about it now. The people who attacked us in Durham won't bother you again."

"I remember it all now. Raven saved you," she said softly. "He bound up your wounds and got us help."

"He tells it different. He says that at the end you were guarding me like a mother bear with a cub, with your back to the stone barbeque and an Uzi in your hands. He said it was awesome."

"I shot him…."

"It was an accident. He is fine. You did good."

Josie took a deep breath, then another. "Raven is okay?"

"He's fine." Black nodded. "I promise."

"Where is he?"

"Coming to get you. He'll be here soon."

"When?"

"Probably minutes, hours at most. He wanted me to cover for him, and for you to see the flowers when you woke up. He thought it might help. Do you like them?"

"They're beautiful….." Josie felt a surge of relief. She felt tears running down her cheeks. "So beautiful. And Raven's safe."

"Absolutely." Black looked concerned and handed her a handkerchief. "Do you want me to call the doctors?"

"No more doctors. Please."

"Whatever you say. I am not going anywhere until Raven arrives. We have guards outside. No one will bother you."

"Thank you," Josie said softly.

"We're going to get you out of here…."

"I'm tired."

"Rest," Black said gently. "It's safe."

"I must look awful. Don't I?"

"You look like a woman in a hospital."

"Will you do me a favor?"

"Sure, if I can," Black said. "Name it,"

"Before Raven arrives, can you get someone here to fix my hair and do my nails?"

Black grinned so wide it made his eyes twinkle. "I should be able to do that."

"Thank you." Josie relaxed, not into blackness, but into a healing sleep, trusting and believing that Raven would be there when she woke up. The last thing she remembered was the flowers.

CHAPTER FIFTEEN
MONKEY ABUSE

OHSU Bookstore, Portland OR, 10 AM

Gates sipped his latte slowly, savoring the taste. It was a smooth blend of Kona and Ethiopian coffee beans. He could not fault the local coffee.

The store had few customers. The morning rush was gone and students were in class.

Tre rolled in like an avalanche. The man radiated attitude. Two hundred and fifty pounds of jet black badass.

Tre approached and seated himself with his back to the wall where he could watch the door. He glanced at Gates' badge. "ID still good, Doctor Mon?"

"Of course." *Why wouldn't it be?*

"You be knowing dat for sure?"

"I used my badge an hour ago. I entered the hospital and went up to her floor."

"Not into her room?"

"Seemed unwise. There was a guard outside. Did you bring the package?"

Tre tapped his pocket. "Got two. One jab. Go home and chill. Bye bye later. No problem."

Two EpiPens loaded with undetectable slow poison, Gates translated. Tre was staring at him intensely. It was unnerving. His eyes were red under the bright lights of the bookstore.

"You see anything unusual?"

Gates said, "They're screening visitors using metal detectors."

"Saw them. TSA bullshit. Damn fool screeners not bother us."

TSA created jobs and made people feel safe, but it had little impact. They both knew that. Most everyone did, but it was not deemed polite to discuss it in public.

"Are we ready to go?"

Tre shook his head. "Got my ear flicked. Need to think on it."

"Think on what?"

"Live on the edge long time, and you pays attention. Don't want to be caught doing bad shit, so you take notice. Slightest thing sets it off. See a string of cars tapping their brakes for no reason on the same stretch of road, maybe there's a cop out there, just out of sight. I gets a feeling. It's like when my ear gets flicked. Says, 'Watch your ass.' I pays attention."

"Is there anything specific?"

"It don't work that way."

"I don't understand."

"Ever do guard shit?"

"No." *Of course not, I am a doctor*, Gates thought. But he did not say it aloud. Tre made him nervous. He just wanted to get this over.

"Boring. Nothing happens. You know why?"

Gates shook his head.

"Millions of sheep, and only a wolf or two. Maybe no wolf at all. Guards go to sleep, and it don't matter. Not till it does."

"I have no idea what you are talking about."

"These guards be on their game. They ready to rock and roll."

"How do you know?"

"Little things. Maybe cause they looked in my eyes and paid attention. Flicked my ear."

"Do you want to abort? I can go back to Boston." Gates did his best to hide his relief. "I was given specific orders, but….."

"No, Mon. We just hold off. I got help coming. We gonna create a diversion for you. Gonna get news, while you handle the lady."

"When?"

Tre looked at his watch. "News at six. We start early so they can get TV crews out."

"I don't want to be on the news."

"They be too busy for you. We are doing this for long time. Years. Gonna save the poor little monkeys from bad scientists. We get attention, raise money, and make the Man look nasty and dumb. It is what I do. They not pay notice, we burn something, throw bricks at the pigs, and lay down social justice.

"While we does that, you slip in, hit the woman, and walk out slow and easy. Then we watch the fun from a distance, ditch the evidence, and you go home."

"To Boston?"

Tre nodded and handed Gates a set of car keys. "Gray Ford in the patient parking. Slot ten. Hit the unlock button and the lights flash. Your luggage in the trunk and a plane ticket in the glove compartment. Leave the car in short term parking at the airport. It be taken care of."

"I'll handle the woman. It will look natural."

"Know dat." Tre bared his teeth. "I go along to make sure. No more screw ups."

The Presidio of Monterey, California

Harrington pushed open the door. "We need to talk. Now."

Goldfarb finished jotting some notes and looked up. "It's best to knock before you barge in, Jordan."

"You're the one who's a guest here."

Goldfarb took a deep breath and gestured politely at the chair in front of the desk. "Have you noticed too much time in Washington brings out bad manners?"

"I have." Harrington folded himself into the chair in front of the desk.

Harrington was not wearing a tie. His high thread count white shirt was wrinkled, and his two thousand dollar, custom-tailored suit looked like he had slept in it. He needed a shave and his eyes were tired.

"You look like shit. What's the problem?"

"It seems like you've settled in for the duration. Dr. Shapiro is complaining. He wants his office back. He says he needs space for the President's physician."

"I was summoned," Goldfarb said mildly.

"I need office space."

"I can share."

"Unfortunately, I can't. I doubt either of those doctors is cleared for whatever the hell you are doing. I'm not cleared for it myself."

"Do you have a need to know?"

"I don't even have a *desire* to know, Aaron. Whatever you are doing, it needs to be as distant from the President and me as possible. Maybe Pluto. Somewhere cold, dark, and far away.

I need you to get your ass out of here. We're starting to get calls from the White House staff that I can't handle."

"That shouldn't be unexpected. How *is* the President?"

"No change. It is not about that. I'm getting calls about *you*." Harrington was looking at him intensely, with narrowed eyes. "Are you running an operation on U.S. soil Aaron?"

Goldfarb shook his head. "No."

"The last thing we need is anything that draws attention to Monterey and an incapacitated President."

"I won't draw attention."

"You already have. Do you know a man called John Black?"

Goldfarb closed his eyes and groaned silently. He waited for follow-up questions about the "borrowed" airplane, but they did not come. When he opened them, Harrington was still staring at him. "Yes."

"Yes, what?"

"Yes, I know John Black. He and...." Goldfarb paused. The temporary identity Raven used was Browning. *Best not to go there.* "I have a scientist on our team who's been ill. She is being released. Black is picking her up. There were some transport problems...."

"We're talking about OHSU in Portland, Oregon, I presume."

Goldfarb nodded. "How did you know?"

"The Learjet that brought you in burned out of here pushing red line on a direct clearance into the Portland area. The FAA said it was riding its Mach limit when it passed Klamath Falls."

"They were in a hurry. So?"

"It got attention. The FAA was told it was a life flight, that a medical emergency was involved. They gave it a priority routing which caused airline flight delays at several major airports, including San Jose, San Francisco and PDX."

"Is there a problem?"

"I handled it, but there's more. Mr. Black commandeered OHSU security personnel and requested Portland Police SWAT teams with snipers and automatic weapons."

Oh, Goldfarb thought.

"Do you care to explain? He seems to be preparing for a war."

"My team is edgy after Durham. Black is authorized to request security and support."

"No, he's not. I have canceled the SWAT teams. They would be provocative."

Goldfarb's eyes narrowed. "How does this involve you?"

"Surely you don't plan to bother the President with a turf war?"

After a time, Goldfarb said, "No."

"Good. This was done on your authorization. Funds were disbursed and the money trail led back to the White House. Portland's mayor called the Governor, who called the White House staff liaison to Homeland Security, a young woman named Christie. When she was unable to reach the President, she called me."

Goldfarb nodded. No wonder Harrington had his knickers in a knot.

"I told them to stand down the SWAT teams."

"Without consulting me?"

"Damned right. Within the hour there will be several hundred demonstrators protesting in the streets outside OHSU, including an Oregon Congressman and several State Representatives. There will be news crews from all the networks, of course."

"Protesting what?"

"Does it matter?" Harrington shrugged. "Portland's Mayor thought it would be unwise to have all that firepower around, cocked, locked, and looking for trouble. She has a point, don't you think?"

"Perhaps I asked the wrong question. Who are the protestors?"

"Christie reeled off a list of names. A regular alphabet soup. I recognized a few of the heavy hitters. WWF, Greenpeace, Earth First, PETA….

"Why?"

"The Green movement is big. They hold protests. It's what they do."

"Why are they at OHSU, a hospital, bothering people, instead of out protecting trees or something?"

"I asked about that," Harrington said. "OHSU runs a research hospital. It does biomedical research."

"No endangered trees, spotted owls, or wolves?"

"Not to my knowledge."

"I don't get it."

"Monkeys. I just learned more about monkeys than I ever wanted to know."

"Do we even have monkeys in the United States?"

"These are imported."

Goldfarb said, "From China, like everything else?"

"Actually some of them do come from China."

"These groups are there to protest about *Chinese monkeys*?"

"Apparently so."

"Are they endangered or something?"

"Not at all. OHSU uses two types of monkeys in its research: both are 'LC' conservation status. LC means 'least concern.' Rhesus Monkeys from Southern China, and Japanese Snow Monkeys."

"So what's the big deal?"

Harrington shrugged. "It's like abusing children. At least that is how Christie explained it to me. If the office of the President is linked in any way to animal abuse, it could set off a political circus. White House staffers are very concerned about this."

"OHSU abuses monkeys? Surely you are shitting me."

"Among other things, OHSU does research on hormones. It is important. Women can get depressed, bipolar, or worse."

"I've noticed."

"We all have," Harrington said. "It's important research."

"They use monkeys in the research – instead of, say, chickens – because their reactions are similar to humans?"

"Exactly right."

"It's okay to use chickens but not monkeys?"

"Nobody claims it makes sense."

"A man's got to eat," Goldfarb said musingly. "They eat monkey brains in Asia and Indochina. Years ago, I had the dish in China. It was memorable."

"The researchers don't *eat* the monkeys."

"Perhaps they should. Eating monkey brains is claimed to enhance sexual prowess."

"You're damned lucky to be alive. Mad Cow disease. The researchers do not even touch their monkeys without gloves. Something like 40% of them are infected with hepatitis. There's a fear of AIDS too."

"There should be. Some say that's how AIDS got started."

"Fornicating with monkeys? That's *disgusting*."

Goldfarb laughed, delighted to get a rise out Harrington. "So no monkeying with the monkeys. The squalid beasts are safe. Why not ring up the protestors and ask them to call it off?"

"The monkeys are killed as a part of the research."

"Oh."

"Part of the protocol is to freeze monkey brains, saw them apart into thin slices, and examine them under microscopes. Can we get back to my point?"

"If you wish."

"I want you to call off your people. Get them the hell out of there."

"My people have nothing to do with monkeys. This has nothing to do with me."

"I need your cooperation."

"You're getting it," Goldfarb said. "I'm doing my best. First off, I am not running a mission. Secondly, my people are already doing what you want. They plan to get the hell out of there. They were sent to pick up a colleague and come right back, low profile. I'm waiting for call-backs when they egress."

Harrington was silent for a time.

"I need this office for now," Goldfarb said. "I give you my word that no offensive domestic operation is running. I am just trying to get a wounded asset back safely. We have valid reasons for concern."

Harrington grimaced, thought, and then nodded and made a gesture of surrender. "Okay, but not back *here*. We have enough problems already."

"I need access to the President. You know that."

"We're on the same side here. If you need face time with the President, you can come any time. You have access."

Goldfarb thought about it for a time. "That is acceptable. I'll stash my team somewhere safe and get out of your hair as soon as I'm satisfied that's been accomplished."

"Agreed. Thank you."

"Just take care of the President…."

"I'll do my best," Harrington said glumly.

CHAPTER SIXTEEN
NONLETHAL

Basement, OHSU Hospital, Portland OR, 4:10 PM

Gates' breathing was quick and his palms were sweaty. They had made it into the building with no problems just before the main doors locked down. Now was a time for waiting.

Outside the streets were full of protestors carrying signs. Bullhorns and sirens could be heard even deep in the bowels of the massive building.

Tre was silent. He reached in his pocket and pulled out a small knife. He flicked it open and held it up. The blade flashed in the overhead lights. He tested the edge, nodded, then closed it and put it back in his pocket.

"It's how we gets by. Kill the Man softly.

"Green Bros do heavy jail time before we got on the game. Best not tote guns, just a little blade. Legal. Clean as a baby if I get busted. We burn things and blow them up, but the courts soft on us. We saving the planet from evil Man. Everybody love us."

Saul Alinsky's **Rules for Radicals** *applied at the street level,* Gates thought.

"We the good guys. Learn dat from a Harvard lawyer. Big Mike got him a plaque in Ferguson when that pig shot his ass. He was guilty as hell, but the news made him a hero."

"Does that work when you kill people?"

"Killed a cop once. Best not get caught. You know how many people get killed or hurt in Portland every year?"

Gates shook his head.

"Whole bunch. Not many murders, maybe twenty, but 4,000 violent crimes. Shit happens. People disappear. Fires, accidents, overdoses, suicides, gang fights, drive-by shootings, lots of shit. My little blade get the job done. If I get busted, they let me go soon as I lawyer up."

"Smart," Gates said.

"We have good lawyers. If one of the Bros is busted, we blame the pigs for excessive force and get face time on TV. Greenie way is better, Mon. You *jihadis* still figuring it out, blowing your own asses up and getting everybody all pissed off…."

Before Gates could say anything, the lights flickered. He heard Tre's soft laugh and saw the white flash of his teeth. The lights went out. Then the backup generators came on line, along with emergency lighting.

"Right on time. We good. I be right behind you. Just keep moving, slow and easy. The scanners be down. They probably move the guards out front.

"She's in room 302," Gates said. "Just keep everyone out while I'm there. If I'm not outside in 5 minutes, you come back me up."

"Know dat," Tre said, his strange eyes reflecting red even in the dim light. "Ain't no picnic here. We got business. I give you two. No more."

The elevator buttons were dark. It must run on the main power.

"Take the stairs, Mon."

Gates moved down the hall and pulled the door open. No alarm and no one on the stairs. Just dim red emergency lighting in the stairway.

On the third floor, Gates eased the door open slowly. No one in the hall. He looked around trying to orient himself. The fire doors had closed automatically when power was lost. He could not see that end of the hall.

Gates was trying not to make noise. Every six rooms, he had to stop and struggle with a fire door. They were not locked, but they were heavy, and they made noise as he rolled them open. The rollers rumbled and there was a loud click when he secured them open.

The scanner station near the elevator was not manned and there was no one at the nurse's station. The rooms he passed were empty, the doors blocked open.

Maybe they evacuated the floor.

By the time he got to room 302, his shirt was soaked in sweat. Unlike the others, this door was shut. A sign said "no admittance."

Perhaps the orders were not to move that patient. He didn't know. *Only one way to find out.*

Gates looked back. Tre gestured impatiently with the blade. *Move your ass.*

He took a deep breath and put his hand on the knob.

Hillsboro Airport

Raven bounded down the jet stairs towards the white Ford sedan on the ramp. It was unmarked, but blue lights were flashing, the engine was running, and there was a driver behind the wheel. The passenger door popped open as he approached.

"Black sent me. My name is Roberts. They call me Rob."

Raven reached over and shook the driver's hand. "Never mind names, I won't be here long. What's the plan?"

"Buckle up. I will brief you on the way. I work part time for Sergeant Johansson, OHSU security. I'm a law student."

"I know who he is," Raven said. "What's going down? My boss is shitting bricks and leaving me voicemails. Something about monkeys."

Rob laughed. "Greenies protesting about our using monkeys for research. Happens a lot. The streets around the hospital are full of protestors and TV crews."

"They use monkeys in the hospital?"

"Hell, no. It is just a place to protest and get on TV. The primate center is outside of Portland, but the protests are usually at the hospital or the mayor's office. They also target some of the researchers' homes for intimidation. It scares the scientists and gets the newsies, mayor, and city council cranked up."

"How far away are we?"

"Fifteen, twenty minutes. Less if I use the lights and siren."

"Hit 'em and haul ass." Raven was slammed back in the seat as the car leapt forward with a chirp from its tires.

"This buggy has the interceptor engine and heavy suspension, like what the State Cops use. Always wanted to let it out." Rob blipped the siren, ran a red light, got a clear spot, and floored it, moving over into the oncoming lane as the traffic parted and cars on both sides scurried for the curbs.

Jesus, Raven thought, tightening his seat belt and grabbing for the overhead safety handle as Rob cut a corner, bouncing over the curb, sliding, and then regaining control. He looked across the seat, noting a Glock on the kid's hip. "I need a weapon. Can I borrow yours?"

"No way. I would lose my job for sure. We are on a short leash for the protests. Can't even draw it myself unless my life is threatened. The rules are restraint and nonlethal force."

"Don't tell me what you can't do. Tell me what you can. How close can you get me?"

"Real close. There is a door in back I can drive right up to." He flicked the wheel to dodge around a slow car, and then back into the lane. Without looking, Rob reached out and tapped the pump gun clamped to the dash. "You know how to use that?"

"I love the Remington 870. Nice weapon. What the hell is this? Some kind of toy?"

The gun was gaudy orange. The stock was emblazoned "Less Lethal" in large letters.

"It's nonlethal. Politically correct. We were issued them back in the 'hug a thug' days."

"What are you talking about?"

"Back when cops were not allowed to defend themselves. Too many thugs and crazies were being shot. Remember Ferguson? Same thing happened in Portland first. Some psycho attacked a cop with a knife. When he kept coming, the officer pulled a riot gun with beanbags. Problem was, he blew the guy away. Someone had loaded it with Double-Ought Buck."

"Gosh. Sounds like a real tragedy," Raven said drily.

"That came later. The Feds sued the city about Civil Rights, and now we have these."

"Stupid. Give me live rounds."

"I can't. The only loads they issue us are nonlethal. Six in the gun, that's all."

"I need a weapon." *The first rule of unarmed combat: Don't be unarmed.*

Rob was concentrating on his driving. After a moment he said, "That's all I can offer. I can't give you my gun, but no one said I can't loan you the car and get back to my post during a riot. Who can blame me if I forgot that it contained a weapon we never use anyway?"

"Nobody. I will leave the car at the airport when I leave. If there is any problem, blame it on me."

"Right." Rob tapped the siren and slid through another corner, tires squealing and the car fishtailing violently. He came out of the skid pointed the right way and floored it again.

The big sedan squatted back on its suspension, got traction, and launched itself down the straightway as if shot from a cannon, slamming Raven's skull back against the headrest. He tasted blood in his mouth.

"Hang on. We're getting close."

"I *am* hanging on." Raven blinked back tears. "Your shotgun is loaded with beanbags?"

"It is. Six rounds only."

"Thanks. Just get me there."

"Working on it." The big engine howled as the car became airborne, and then slammed down hard, bottoming out its suspension. Raven had his seat belt full tight and still hit the roof. "I'll have to slow down and go silent when we get closer."

"Do what you need to do, kid. Safety first."

The only answer was a laugh.

CHAPTER SEVENTEEN
APRIL FOOL

OHSU Hospital, Portland Oregon, Room 302

Gates pulled the door open, entered, and then stopped dead in his tracks, confronted by a stocky man in a white coat who moved to block him. Behind him, Gates heard the door close and latch with a click.

"What are you doing here?"

"I might ask you the same," Gates said, tapping his OHSU nametag.

The man moved closer and braced himself. "This room has restricted access. I'm Doctor Niles Lundgren, and I am responsible for the care of this patient."

Gates took a step back. Lundgren looked determined, was several inches taller, and outweighed him by at least 40 pounds. He remembered the name. Lundgren, the same one the nurse had mentioned.

He stuck out his hand, deciding on a softer approach. "John Henry Gates. Pleased to meet you, Doctor. I am from Harvard Medical School. We're doing an informal survey of your procedures."

"No one told me about any survey…."

"As I said, it's informal. I'm writing a paper on unusual pathologies and this patient…." Gates looked past Lundgren and paused. There was a curtain shielding the bed. "I just wanted a quick look. Is the patient still here?"

"It's not your concern. This room is off limits. I must ask you to leave."

Gates raised his hands in protest.

"Leave now," Lundgren pulled the door open, and gasped. He was looking up at Tre.

Before Lundgren could speak, Tre shoved him hard, pushing him back into the room. "Check the hall and latch this damn door open so it don't lock."

Gates could not see a way to set the latch, so he flipped the little brass door holder down with his toe, blocking it open.

Lundgren started to say something. Tre hit him in the stomach pulling his head forward. Then he calmly broke Lundgren's nose with a jab from his right hand.

"There's no one out there," Gates said.

Lundgren was gasping for breath. He had blood running down his face.

"Get it done," Tre said, pointing at the curtain concealing the bed. One big hand grabbed Lundgren by the scruff of his neck and stood him up straight.

Lundgren started sobbing. Tre cuffed him until he stopped.

Tre was unbelievably strong. Lundgren must weigh 200 or more. Tre was holding his deadweight vertical with one hand and no visible strain. "That wasn't necessary...."

"Ain't no game, Mon. Get it done. Use dat needle."

"I am," Gates yanked the curtain open and froze. The bed was rolled up to the sitting position. Instead of a middle-aged woman in a hospital gown, it held a young male with vivid green eyes wearing a tan flight suit. What he noticed most was the black automatic pistol centered on his face. He was looking down the bore of the weapon.

"April fool," the man said. "Put the needle down and back away."

"Don't shoot," Gates said. He did as instructed.

"You be da fool. Hand him the gun. Less'n you want the doctor man dead."

Gates took two careful steps to his right and looked back over his shoulder. Tre's left hand was now holding Lundgren straight up by the hair, stretching his neck, pulling him to his tiptoes, using him as a shield. The little knife was in Tre's other hand, pressed against the doctor's throat.

When he looked back at the bed, the weapon's aim had shifted away from him to Tre. The shot came immediately, the noise deafening in the small room. The gun kicked and then came back on target. Gates jerked his eyes back to the tableau by the door.

There was a hole in the wall behind Tre at head height. Tre was so massive that Lundgren, stretched out or not, did not make a good shield.

"Drop the knife and step over by your friend."

Tre laughed and shook his head.

"Drop it or I put the next one in your head."

"I see your finger tighten, and I cut his throat ear to ear. Ever see how quick a man dies that way?"

"You're dead too, if you do." He fired again. A streak of blood appeared on Tre's left ear, and another hole in the wall behind him.

"You be a cop?"

"My name's Black. That's all you need to know. Drop the knife."

"You never killed anyone, have you, boy? You a pussy. I can see it in your eyes."

"You can be the first." Black fired again.

Tre carefully drew his knife across Lundgren's throat. Lundgren gave a strangled whimper and slumped, bright red blood running down and soaking his lab coat.

"Drop the gun. We in a hospital, maybe they save him. Or hold it and watch him die. My next cut goes to the bone."

Black didn't reply.

Tre pressed the flat of his blade against Lundgren's neck. He smiled and added pressure. Lundgren's eyes rolled back, and he went limp.

Tre braced himself and shifted to using both hands to hold him erect. The left holding his hair and the flat of his blade under Lundgren's chin, the edge pressed against his throat, lifting his feet off the ground.

"Stop," Black said.

"The Man only hang me once. Already killed the nurse lady."

"There's no need to kill him…."

"He getting heavy. Up to you…."

"Don't do it. I'm putting my weapon down." Black placed his pistol on the bed.

"Get it," Tre ordered.

Gates picked the gun up, pointing it at the floor. "Where's the safety?"

"Don't make no never mind. Where da the woman?"

"I'm not going to tell you," Black said.

Tre smiled into his eyes, slashed Lundgren's throat, and stepped back, letting him fall. "You will. You jus don't know it yet."

Raven was breathing hard when he burst through the open door into the room. He'd come up three flights of stairs in time to hear the shots. He saw John Black in a flight suit sitting in the bed, and a man with a gun standing over him.

The shotgun in his hands roared, and the man, hit between the shoulder blades, jerked like a dog hit by a truck, the pistol flying high in the air.

"Get the weapon," he yelled at Black. "Shoot the son of a bitch."

Clearing the room to the left, Raven saw a dead body and a huge black man with tattoos and a knife starting to turn. He racked the gun and fired again, the beanbag hitting the man in the shoulder. It staggered him, but did not stop him. He kept turning.

Raven racked the pump gun, let him turn square, and fired twice, hitting him in the chest and face. That was the nice thing about a pump gun with a hot trigger. A skilled shooter could fire as fast as with an automatic, some said faster.

The big man stumbled back against the wall, hitting so hard the plaster cracked. He slapped it and bounced off, charging Raven, who put his next-to-last beanbag into his stomach, sidestepped, and clubbed him to the floor with the stock of the gun as he went past.

Tre hit in a judo roll and was coming to his feet. Raven went airborne and met him halfway up with a *Teh Trong* straight leg kick to the temple.

The big man went limp. The noise of his skull hitting the floor was like a melon hitting concrete.

Raven was on his feet, the gun level, scanning for a target. Black had the pistol. He stamped on Tre's wrist and kicked the knife away.

"I think you killed him," Black said, looking down at Tre.

"Not yet. He is still bleeding. That one is the muscle. What was the other one up to?"

"He had needles. I think they were intended for Josie."

"I'm sure he'll tell us about it if we ask him nicely." Raven jerked Gates to his feet and slammed him against the wall. "What's in the needles?"

"Poison."

"What kind?"

"They didn't tell me. Something slow but undetectable."

Raven stepped back and glanced around the room. His eyes lingered on Lundgren's body. "Who's he?"

"Josie's doctor," Black said. "He tried to stop them."

"We'll leave him there. Get me surgical gloves out of that supply box over the desk. Put on a pair yourself. Then bring me the needles."

Black did as instructed.

"Watch that one." Gates was on his feet. "Can you shoot him if he tries anything?"

"Yes."

"I'm not going to try anything."

Raven glanced at Black. "No warning, no chitchat. It is a gun, kid, not a magic wand to make people obey you. Aim high center mass and pull the trigger. Repeat as necessary until he drops."

"Yes, Sir." Black pointed the pistol at Gates. "I can do it."

"Good." Raven donned gloves and held one of the EpiPens up, examining it. "Cute."

He walked over, leaned down, and carefully stuck it in Tre's neck, making sure it hit an artery and discharged fully. He left it there. "Give me the other one."

Gates looked horrified. "Please don't use that on me."

"I don't plan to." Raven took the last EpiPen and jammed it in the other side of Tre's neck. He left it there too.

Black was staring at him, still pointing the gun at Gates. "You killed him in cold blood."

Raven walked over, and picked up the knife. "War involves killing the bad guys. Sometimes you have to do it up close and personal."

"What about him?" Black wiggled the gun at Gates.

"He's a problem. We have to leave a crime scene that doesn't make the investigators struggle too much to reach the right conclusions." Raven glanced around the room, noting the holes in the wall. "Who fired those shots?"

Black said, "I did."

"Is the pistol you used traceable?"

"No idea. I got it from Dr. Lundgren."

"Leave the brass, get my beanbags, and wipe down anything you touched, especially the gun and the shotgun. Stay clear of the blood."

"Yes, Sir."

Holding the knife, Raven approached Gates and gestured at Tre's body. "Get over by him. You're going to help us with the clean up."

"I'm not going to try anything."

"You work for a man named Firouz, a former Revolutionary Guard, now on the Iranian delegation at the UN with diplomatic immunity," Raven said.

"How do you know that?"

Raven ignored the question. "Firouz sent you here to kill Josie."

"I'm an American citizen. I have rights."

"I'm not here to arrest you. Yes or no?"

"You know what I say under duress without a lawyer present isn't admissible in court."

Raven nodded.

"I didn't know her name. He told me it was a woman who was dangerous to our cause. That she was probably going to die anyway."

"We all are," Raven said. Before Gates could react, Raven slashed his throat from ear to ear – *Halil* style, the way the Islamic extremists executed Theo van Gogh – and stepped away.

Slashing throats is a messy business.

The average human body has ten pints of blood, which is a lot. Blood makes up about 7% of body weight, and the carotid artery in the neck is the primary path to the brain. When the carotid is completely severed, as in this case, death takes less than a minute. When injured, the body automatically restricts flow to other organs, but not the brain. It gets the ultimate priority.

A gush of bright red blood spilled down Gates' white coat. He tried to speak, but only a gurgle came out. He swayed. Then the pressure to his brain went to zero and he went limp and collapsed across Tre's body, a puppet with the strings cut.

Tre was still breathing and the puddle of blood around him was not much larger. Raven jammed the knife in his right eye up to the hilt, careful to avoid the blood.

Gates lay across Tre's legs with one arm outreached, almost if he was pointing.

Raven stepped back. "Time to go, kid."

"Jesus. Was that necessary?"

"Seemed like. Loose lips sink ships. You spoke Josie's name and he heard you. *They came to kill her without even knowing who she was. Maybe the same for Durham.* We're at war, and we don't need security lapses to help them target her."

Black opened his mouth, but closed it without speaking.

"You wipe that gun good?"

Black nodded.

"Keep your gloves on and toss it over by Lundgren."

Black did so, gently, underhanded. The gun hit the body, bounced, and slid down into the pool of blood on the floor with a muted thud.

"I've only got egress for friendlies. A lot is going on. No witnesses and no comebacks. We're way off the reservation."

At the door, Raven paused. He checked the room and finally nodded to indicate satisfaction. "You moved Josie somewhere safe?"

"Yes, Sir. Sergeant Johansson is guarding her. They pulled my backup...."

"Later." Raven picked up the shotgun. "I've got a car. Let's get her and get the hell out of here. Keep your gloves and the wipe rags. We'll ditch them somewhere safe."

Black followed him down the hall at a fast trot.

CHAPTER EIGHTEEN
REUNION AND CONFUSION

The Ranch, Mendocino, California, Three Days Later

They had spent the first night holding each other, talking and healing, followed by the most exquisitely tender lovemaking Josie had ever enjoyed. It was a side of Raven she had not seen before.

The next day was one of passion, interspersed with showers, walks on the beach and excellent food. On the third day, Raven restarted his physical workouts. Josie turned to Yoga, meditation, and testing her powers.

She sensed guards at a distance, but no one bothered them. At Josie's request, the chef had fixed them a special dinner, local fare served up on their patio in private. Josie started with the cauliflower puree, but Raven insisted on Manhattan clam chowder.

"The cauliflower is excellent. Do you want to taste mine?"

"I need something red. A balanced meal."

Josie smiled. Raven usually ordered dead red meat, which she had omitted. He liked fresh game fish, but said the farm-raised variety came from sewage ponds in the third world.

He chose the grilled swordfish. She had the sea bass, paired with local wines, baby red beets, winter squash risotto, and fresh baked bread.

Everything was superb. She had to admit most of it was white, though.

"Want some of my beets? They're red."

Raven held up his wine glass, showing off the dark red color. "Cabernet. I'm good."

"You're better than good. That wine is a 2001 Beringer Private Reserve." Josie smiled coyly and plunked a beet down on his plate. "Take one anyway. I don't want you to be deprived."

"Depraved, maybe, but never deprived, not when I'm with you, Babe. The food is great. Tastier than armadillos, spotted owls, goats, or MREs."

"*Beast!*"

Raven stabbed the tiny beet with his fork, devoured it, nodded thoughtfully, and then leaned across and kissed her.

"My mother warned me...."

They chatted lightly, savoring each other's company, enjoying the low sun on the sparkling water. It was starting to cool down, but they were sheltered and there was little wind.

The fish and the setting sun on the water reminded her of Hawaii. The bread was as good as any she'd ever had, even in Paris.

Josie pushed the beeper left by the woman who had served them. Within minutes, a muscular young waiter in a black tuxedo appeared at the door to whisk away the remains, light the candles she had placed, and leave a tray of cheeses and fruits.

She appreciated the elegant touch, even though she knew the tuxedo was there to hide a shoulder holster. Strangely, the weapon did not bother Josie. It made her feel safe and helped Raven to relax.

Josie took a deep breath. Raven had been reluctant to discuss business and the outside world, but there were things she needed to know. She'd been isolated for too long. It was time.

She took a sip of her chilled California Chardonnay, folded her copy of The *Oregonian*, and glanced over at Raven. "The newspapers are calling Dr. Lundgren a hero for defending his patients. Did he, really?"

Raven was watching the sunset, his gaze fixed on the far horizon, sipping the last of his wine. "Does anyone believe the media?"

"Not me. The incident at OHSU is vanishing into history. But *you* were there...."

"You're the psychic."

"Whatever happened over the past few months, my powers are stronger than ever now." Josie sighed. "Even so, I don't choose to delve into that one closely. You know how disruptive violence is to my abilities. Please tell me."

"Lundgren died badly. Black said he did his best."

Josie was silent for a time. Lundgren had never been comfortable with the covert aspects of her work. Neither had she, but the thing was he did not trust her, and it made her nervous.

Raven was watching her closely. "Are you okay?"

"Working on it. Thank you for getting me out of there. Lundgren and I were not friends. The relationship was professional, and not close. To be honest, I'm more worried about your young man."

"Black hit a rough patch, for sure."

"He looked like he'd had a glimpse into Hell when he dropped us off at the airport."

"He did okay for a newbie. He did that run on his own, unsupported. He may have saved your life. He has balls."

You live in a scary world, my love. "What aren't you telling me?"

"It wasn't pretty." Raven sighed. "They sent another kill team for you, same as at Durham. I got there just short of too late. Black was lucky. Lundgren wasn't. Black got to watch him die."

"Who exactly is this 'they,' the ones we keep missing, the ones who persist in trying to kill me?"

"Iranians. I don't think it was Safdari this time."

"Why?"

"I don't know, not yet, but that's what I think. They used different sources and methods than the last group."

"You'll need to explain more."

"**They**," Raven put emphasis on the word, "this new group, made an earlier run at you in the hospital. Sloppy and unprofessional. It was as if the operation had been patched together.

"Their lead was a political operative, an Iranian doctor from Boston named Gates. The idiot was carrying a US passport with an RFID tag. He left his biometrics and identity all over the hospital's security systems. Black had his phone tapped, his room bugged, and his house staked out."

"Dr. Gates has been apprehended and questioned?"

"He's dead. I think he was getting to the end of his usefulness. They brought in contract muscle to tidy up, a Jamaican named Tre with dual US and Canadian citizenship. Not directly linked to Iran. An eco-terrorist."

"It's not getting any clearer. The 'they' part."

"Gates' control was a man named Firouz. We have that on tape. He has diplomatic cover as staff at the UN. I know it doesn't fit, but that's where we are...."

Josie frowned and shook her head. "Doesn't fit...?"

"These were high level assets. Gates served on several White House and Congressional advisory committees. Firouz is # 2 to the Iranian Ambassador for the UN. It doesn't make sense they'd risk Gates in the field or have someone like Firouz running a kill OP on American soil."

"Why not?"

"It doesn't work like that," Raven said. "It would be like using a Bengal Tiger to give kiddy rides in the park. State-sponsored terrorists don't operate that way, and neither does a state intelligence organization."

"Not even Muslims?"

"Especially not them. They have an endless supply of uneducated, hate-filled fanatics trained in weapons and eager to die for Allah, but are short of top talent. Muslims tend not to risk policy level talent. If we were allowed to kill a few dozen of the right people, and to keep doing it, it would cripple *jihad*."

"And...."

"I'm about done. There is a lot about this I do not understand. When you get to feeling more solid, there are some things I'd like you to view."

"Why did Lundgren keep me sedated? Why wouldn't he listen?"

"Excellent questions. I don't know."

"Do you think Lundgren was turned?"

"I think he was in way over his head and trying to cover his ass. We may never know. There are larger issues."

"You made some agreement to get me out of there."

It was not a question, and Raven did not bother to reply.

"How long do we have together?"

He smiled. "The rest of our lives, I hope...."

Josie refrained from using her powers. She waited to see what he would say. "How long do we have together **now**?"

"We can squeeze out a few weeks here. Maybe a month."

"Good. Can we just relax and heal?"

"Soon. I want you to look into a couple of things when you're up to it."

"We're in this together, right? No matter what happens."

"You have my word."

"Good." Whatever the future held, they could face it together. She would cling to that.

The UN, New York

Firouz switched off the big screen TV and started drumming his fingers on the desk. There had been extensive coverage of the protests in Portland. There were videos of tear gas, rocks and bottles thrown at police, angry protestors being clubbed and dragged away, and finally the National Guard firing rubber bullets. Almost a hundred people had been arrested. It was international news.

As a media event, it was bigger than the annual WTO protests, almost as big as the white-hot fury and Communist flags in the streets of Copenhagen, back when the first Climategate scandal broke during the Narnian Winter of 2009.

Copenhagen was Obama's first setback. It delayed decades of high-level plans for global energy taxes and rationing. It embarrassed world leaders and set back global warming alarmism. It even embarrassed the UN, which was hard to do.

None of which mattered to Firouz. The current media circus, now being called the "Monkey Day Protests," was pleasing to the Green groups and damaging to the Great Satan, but he had his own objectives.

And his own problems.

Gates was dead, as was the thug from the ELF.

Firouz winced as his secure phone rang. It could be only one person, the name never to be mentioned. *"Salam!"*

"Shoma chetur hastin?"

How am I? Firouz rolled his eyes and responded in English. "Good. Thanks be to Allah."

"Are we secure?"

"Electronically, Sir, we are," Firouz said, "and my staff doesn't speak English."

"Yes." There was a long pause. "English is better. Questions are being asked."

By the Supreme Leader, Firouz presumed. "Sir, you will recall that I advised against this mission."

"I reminded him of that. We were ordered to support Major General Razlivi and the Revolutionary Guards."

"Without compromising our primary mission....."

"Yes. What happened in Portland?"

"We provided the support requested. We lacked a suitable field asset. We secured one locally, a Green terrorist enforcer named Tre."

"He arranged the protests?"

"Yes. The man was a psychopath, but I was forced to use him. He was a street thug, perhaps a good suicide bomber, but a poor field agent."

"Sometimes a broken bottle makes a better weapon."

"Sometimes a broken tool is just a broken tool. In this case, Tre and my best asset seem to have killed each other. I presume you saw that on the news?"

"Yes. Did they accomplish their mission?"

"So far as I know, yes. The mission was to terminate a female patient, hardly a difficult task. Did the General ever reveal who she was and why this was so important?"

"He did not. The Revolutionary Guards had a failed mission that our leaders needed tidied up. They were cleaning up loose ends."

"You didn't ask?"

"No. Didn't Gates tell you?"

"He didn't know. The woman was listed as a 'Jane Doe,' a nameless person. Her attending doctor was a man named Lundgren who also died at the scene. The body of the night nurse, a female named Louisell, was found in a trash bin."

"Why was this Jane Doe being treated? How does it involve the Guards?"

"I have no idea. The only record the hospital has regarding her is a death certificate signed by Lundgren. If there was a file, he took it. The death certificate lists natural causes."

"That's all?"

"It's all my sources could find. Dr. Gates was on staff at another major US hospital. They made a formal inquiry and came up with nothing."

"Four people died, two of them yours. Who killed them?"

"Five, if you count the patient. Dozens more were injured in the riots outside the hospital, including twenty-three police, three of whom are critical. Why do we care?"

"I have a report to make. How did the nurse and Gates die?"

"Violent trauma in both cases. Gates had his throat cut, as did, incidentally, Dr. Lundgren. The nurse had her neck broken. Probably that was Tre. Gates was afraid of him and unhappy with this assignment."

"Probably?"

"That was how Tre worked. The news only said the Portland Police are investigating that possibility, but that would be my guess. The knife that killed them both was Tre's. It had his fingerprints on it."

"What are your recommendations?"

"To let the matter drop, Sir. I didn't think this important to begin with."

"What about Tre?"

"It's not our concern, Sir. Why not let Tre and his organization take the credit for Portland? He can be a hero. They are pleased with the protests. The Portland incident will help them intimidate the locals and advance their cause. Revolutions need martyrs."

"You want them to take the credit?"

"I'd prefer that we not be involved with this. We have more important issues."

"How did Tre die?"

"The FBI reported massive amounts of poison in his system. Most likely it was the same poison and delivery system we'd supplied to his organization at Gates' request."

"Do you think Gates killed him?"

"It would be reasonable to assume. Do we care? Let Tre be a martyr."

"In summary, your operation was successful, but marred by violence from a borrowed asset with known flaws. We should not depend on infidels."

"Yes, Sir. And if I might say one more thing, trusting in you to convey it diplomatically to our most holy leaders...."

"Go ahead."

"Cleaning up others' camel shit when we have important work for the Islamic Republic does not well serve Allah or the Revolution. I just lost a valuable asset."

"Do you want the Revolutionary Guards as enemies?"

"No, Sir. Of course not."

"I'll look for a way to communicate your thoughts at the appropriate time. Perhaps this would be best done when you return home as a hero."

"Yes, Sir."

Firouz's control cleared his throat, signaling the discussion was finished. "There has been nothing on the news about the American President lately."

"A hopeful sign. Allah is great. Several functions and events involving the President have been canceled or deferred."

"The Supreme Leader is, of course, highly interested …."

"*In sh'allah*. The situation is still developing. I'll report fully when we know."

"I'll tell him that. You may plan on returning to Tehran when you have results."

There was a click, and the line went dead.

CHAPTER NINETEEN
JAMES BOND WAS RIGHT

The Ranch, Mendocino, California, Next Day

Raven stood watching as the now-familiar blue and white Learjet turned off the runway. It looked awkward on the ground with the big flipped-up wingtips, taxiing slowly. He held his arms up to get the pilot's attention, and covered his ears as it rolled up and stopped in front of him. The door popped open even before the engines finished winding down.

Goldfarb pinned him with an intense look. "How's Josie?"

Your experts were wrong. "She's fine. Her powers are intact."

"Really?"

"Positive. She did a remote viewing."

"What about the rest of it?"

"There were problems...."

"I noticed. Riots in the streets. Dead bodies. The mayor and governor voicing concerns. Reporters and TV crews in a feeding frenzy."

"Animal rights protests. Crazies. We weren't involved in that."

"So why the body count in the hospital?"

"You know why. We encountered opposition."

"How did Black handle it?"

"He did fine, considering. He's flying your misplaced airplane back."

"The plane I had nothing to do with...."

"The Air Force is happy, and the record is being cleared. It was all a misunderstanding."

"Good." The ramp was empty but for a dozen or so tied-down light aircraft, and a tired looking DC-3 freighter with faded paint and puddles of oil under its engines. There was a small cluster of people, three, standing around a high-wing Cessna at the fuel pumps several hundred feet away.

"I'm tight on time. Where can we talk?"

"I have a car. There is great food in Mendocino. If you like French, there is Café Beaujolais. Famous bread and fresh catch seafood. It's about twenty minutes away if you want to grab some lunch."

"French food is usually slow. Anything closer and quicker?"

"A hippy-dippy eco-freaky place. Vegetarian, but you'll like the name." Goldfarb looked dubious.

"Tofu and tempeh. Stuffed eggplant cannoli too. You'll love it."

"What do they stuff it with?"

"No idea, but they call the place Ravens."

"You are shitting me."

When he looked over, Goldfarb was not smiling. He had his mission face on, his serious face.

"If you want quick and dirty, then it's the Bay View café. Fresh, tasty, American, cash only, and don't look in the kitchen."

Goldfarb shook his head. "I'll send the copilot to forage for food. We can talk in the plane. There's hot coffee, bagels, and privacy."

"Yes, Sir." Raven handed him the car keys. "It's the Blue Taurus by the gate."

Raven finished his report and waited, trying to read the expression on Goldfarb's face. Something was bothering Goldfarb, hopefully something other than the mission, but you never knew.

Goldfarb drummed his fingers on the small conference table, gazing out the window at the ramp. The plane was plugged in to outside power. The only sounds were the soft hush of the air vents.

Raven was starving. He took the opportunity to grab a bagel and refresh his coffee. He knew better than to interrupt.

Goldfarb looked up. "Not your fault. The whole thing was FUBAR. Did you know Portland is a sanctuary city?"

Raven shrugged. *Politics.*

"Oregon has 250,000 illegals, most of them in the Portland metro area, but the policy reflects an attitude. Portland is a throwback, like Berkeley in the radical 60s, but with roses and trees. Law enforcement is soft. If a homeowner defends his property and fires shots to prevent a theft, he is the one who is arrested. When the police use lethal force to defend themselves, they endure a trial by media."

"Oh," Raven said.

"There are restaurants in Portland that won't serve uniformed police."

"Do they still call them pigs, like in the 60s?"

"I don't think so."

"What do the Oregon politicians say?"

"Not much." Goldfarb laughed without humor.

"Portland doesn't prosecute crimes?"

"The policy is 'keeping the peace,' not enforcing the law. Half the City Council are leftist social activists, 'watermelons,' green on the outside, but red inside. Portland was a poor location for a safe house. Dr. Lundgren picked it."

"Marvelous." *Why am I not surprised?*

"Let's just say we can't go back there."

"It was a clean OP. We accomplished our objectives, got out, and didn't leave a trail."

"You left behind a hornet's nest."

"The hornets were there to begin with. There is a reason OHSU is guarded. There have been numerous riots, threats, and intrusion attempts."

"How did that affect your mission?"

"What affected my mission were **two** attempts to kill Josie. My team was thin on the ground and short of firepower and backup. I damned near lost Black. Again. Without his help, we would have lost Josie. This was in the crapper before I even arrived. Is it true you cancelled the SWAT teams he'd ordered?"

Goldfarb sighed. "No. That came from higher up."

"And you didn't bother to tell me. Do you want my resignation?"

Goldfarb was the first to look down. He shook his head.

"I love this country, Sir, but she's become a harsh mistress. I need to hear your answer, and I do not want to be blindsided again. I didn't want to go to Iran anyway."

"You may not have to."

Raven blinked.

"I don't want your resignation. The situation sucks. There is far too much naïveté and political correctness these days. Every time we get a leftist administration, it takes a World War and mega deaths to recover. The President is working to fix that."

"Last I saw the President he was working to fucking stay alive...."

"I withdraw any implied criticism of your methods."

"Thank you."

"Portland's attitudes may be a blessing. Oregon hates national publicity. They want this to fade away as much as we do. I doubt much effort will be spent investigating details so long as government involvement is not suspected.

"The smoke we're floating is that the eco thug, Tre, did the killings. It has the advantage of being largely true. Did you terminate Lundgren?"

Raven rolled his eyes. *Jesus.*

"Your doctors reported hostility towards him."

"Of course I was hostile. He was an asshole."

"Lundgren was fearful. You resented him keeping Josie locked up and doped up."

"Damned right. He was also afraid of Josie, afraid of her powers, and afraid of the responsibility of knowing what she did. He was in the wrong line of work."

"He was terrified of **you** after Durham. The man almost had a nervous breakdown."

"Before we had shrinks, society used witch doctors. I think they did better. Lundgren lost his mojo."

"But you didn't kill him?"

"No. If I went around killing people for being assholes, there'd be no end to it."

Goldfarb nodded slowly. "Good point."

"Like I reported, Tre killed him."

"Why?"

"Ask Black. It happened before I got there. Does anyone care?"

"I do."

"I'll let you know if I ever find out."

"Never mind. The media accepts Tre as the killer without any problems. Its coverage of him is sympathetic."

"All those years of saving Bambi and spotted owls made him crazy?"

"Something like that...."

"Jolly good for Bambi, I say. Can we wrap this up now?"

"I'd like to. Our cover is working, but there's a problem."

Raven waited. *If you can't stand the answer, do not ask the question.*

"The Rhine Institute is unhappy with me. Lundgren was the only controller they had who could handle Josie."

"I handled her with no problems. We have a good rapport."

"I just have to tell Rhine something."

"Try the truth. Tre killed him. Lundgren was dead when I got there."

"There are shades of truth. Do you think *he* was the leak in Durham?"

"The possibility crossed my mind, but I never had a chance to discuss it with him. The main thing is I didn't kill him."

"What about Doctor Gates?"

Raven shrugged.

"Gates' death has attracted major media interest. I authorized a low profile rescue OP. What I got was three dead bodies and unwanted attention."

"Four. You are forgetting the nurse. Four and a half, if you count the attempt on Josie. You told me 'low-profile,' and that is what we did. We extracted Josie. We got in and out without leaving tracks, and despite a hit-team on site."

"Gates was more of a political operative, but, okay. It just bothers me that the pieces don't fit."

"Sir?"

"Nothing fits. We have been turning over rocks and tapping all sources. I have even been calling in favors from foreign assets. Nothing makes sense. The trails don't lead to Iran, they lead to the UN."

"A false flag operation?"

"Or perhaps something more subtle. Even before Obama or Islamic *jihad*, NGOs and social organizations were major players on the world scene. A lot of arms trafficking has always been private. It's possible we're being played."

He is saying the threat may not be a nation state. An enemy we do not know. It was possible. Non-Government Organizations and private groups had access to missiles and weapons of mass destruction.

"Do you have any ideas?"

Raven shook his head. "I've been focused on Iran. Are you going to share or keep me in the dark?"

"Let's start with Tre. He and Gates were controlled out of the UN in New York."

"By an Iranian named Firouz. I listened to the intercepts. They were Iranian assets."

"Not Tre. We know Tre was a Russian asset with a long and twisted history."

"KGB?"

"Indirectly," Goldfarb said. "The *komitet gosudarstvennoy bezopasnosti* was disbanded in 1991, but he got some of their training. He originally came out of MININT, the Cuban Department of the Interior. He started with their National Revolutionary Police, but they moved him to the Department of General Intelligence after a few years."

"International espionage, spies. So he went to one of the KGB's charm schools for tradecraft?"

"There wasn't anything subtle or intellectual about the man. He was born in Jamaica to a Cuban father and an American mother. That proved to be useful."

"Citizenship...."

"Multiple citizenships. As a child, Tre had British and Cuban passports. After Carter relaxed the rules, he picked up US citizenship. Later he got one from Canada too. He hid out up there for years." Goldfarb pulled out a cloth and started wiping his glasses.

"How did Tre get connected with Iran?"

"That's the point. He did not, as far as we know. There's blood on his hands and open files at several Western intelligence agencies, but no Islamic connection we're aware of."

"I don't understand," Raven said.

"Have you ever worked against the Soviets?"

"You've seen my personnel folder."

"What I recall from your agency records was mostly from the sandbox, and a bit in South America. It was vague about who the targets were."

"I never worked much against the Soviets, except in Afghanistan."

"Here's a short history. Up through WW II, the Communist Party and Marxism had an open presence. It was fashionable for a time, but during the Cold War, and especially after the McCarthy Hearings in the 50s, Communism became illegal and went underground. The preferred refuge and cover was in labor unions."

Raven nodded.

"It changed again in the 60s. The unions had problems with corruption and organized crime, which was exactly the time when the United States hit a crossroads with Cuba."

"The missile crisis."

"That heightened public disapproval of Communists, and the unions were getting too hot for them as well. Bobby Kennedy was all over the unions, chasing corruption and foreign agents. Jimmy Hoffa was convicted and did prison time on several charges, first on bribing a juror, and later for fraud. The second conviction got Kennedy enough prestige to run successfully for the US Senate."

"When was this?"

"The mid-60s, just before Vietnam. Hoffa did jail time starting in 1964, and Kennedy was elected to the Senate that November."

"So the Unions were no longer a cozy place for Soviet or Cuban Agents," Raven said. "And Communism was still out."

"So far as the official Communist Party, but communism with a small 'c' was coming back. Che Guevara was an anti-capitalist folk hero. Still, by the late 70s, the preferred cover was in Green or Humanitarian Aid Organizations with missions like 'saving the planet' or 'social justice,' 'sustainability,' and the ever popular 'Global Warming'."

"Or cooling...."

"Yes. Climate alarmism. Saving the planet. They saved trees, whales, birds, screwed their brains out, and did drugs."

"Like the hippies in the 60s."

"Not really. Woodstock was history. Things became more organized and more violent. These were serious revolutionaries seeking money and power. Even the women were violent revolutionaries. Several groups dealt drugs and a few extended that to weapons."

"Sounds like humanitarian aid to me."

"Extreme Liberalism prevailed. Saul Alinsky was studied and taught by mainstream politicians. The major groups avoided being labeled as violent, or even as revolutionaries. The Communists officially distanced themselves, but left assets with plausible deniability in place. The high road was to become respectable to Western liberals and especially to our politicians."

"Respectable?"

"Absolutely. The radicals who had founded violent groups like SDS and Weather Underground moved over to organizations like Tides, which, as IRS approved non-profits, could collect tax-free money and route it to hundreds of other groups. Popular causes like the Humane Society used entities like Share Group for fundraising, which was founded by a Teamsters Union fundraiser.

Liberals in Hollywood helped them with PR. They developed think tanks to help their friends in Congress craft legislation, sometimes even to plan appointments and policy. They lobby Congress and give grants to have schools and social groups teach their propaganda."

"Is that legal?"

"It might not be if the Communist Party or a foreign intelligence service ran such operations, but they don't. It might not be if we were in formally declared wars, but we are not. The game is to use our own systems against us."

"Let me guess: The fundraisers keep most of the money and launder it. The foreign agents love the cover, contacts, money, recruiting opportunities, and the loose leash from their masters."

"Correct about the money. They have even been nailed on that a time or two. The foreign connections are murkier. Social justice and wealth redistribution are the key words. If you hear them, it's a red flag."

Raven nodded.

"It's basically a replay of the 30s – 'Workers of the World Unite' and all that. Radical Green is the new socialism. The new Communists are carbon communists, saving the planet."

Raven was getting impatient with the pedantic lecture. He cleared his throat. "I've got the idea: shape shifters, moles, corruption, and deep cover. So how does Tre fit in?"

"At the fringes and all over the place. He's an Alinskyite, not a party line Communist, so he fit right in."

"How so?"

"Saul Alinsky was an American. He was no orthodox Communist, but a new breed. He was much too independent to join the Party. Instead, he became the mentor to the new Radical Left that emerged in the Communist collapse. He preached things like 'the revolutionary's purpose is to undermine the system and then see what happens.' This is the new communism. The methods are sabotage and transformational change from inside, not direct attack. Instead of rock throwing and bombs, it's sit-ins, programs to feed prisoners, and wealth redistribution."

"Political versus paramilitary?"

Goldfarb shook his head. "Not 'versus' – in addition to. The Alinskyites prefer to tap other groups for their violence, and a number exist for that purpose. Even the old 'Communist Party USA' is back. There have been revolutionaries inside the White House at times, people like Van Jones, a self-avowed Communist and violent revolutionary, but when such assets are exposed, they are distanced. The Alinsky game is political cover and plausible denial."

"I remember that name. Van Jones: It was in the news a few years back. He died. Is that how he was distanced?"

"That's unclear. It was ruled to be a boating accident."

"Do we have a list of Alinsky groups?"

"It's not that easy. Alinsky, like Marx, is dead. There are no formal Alinsky groups, but most of the new-left groups employ his methods and espouse his philosophy. They embrace other political entities, either to destroy them or as symbiotes to mold into the Alinsky philosophy."

"Vampires. They suck blood and hide from the light."

Goldfarb smiled. "An interesting choice of words. If you wish: Vampires for communism. Alinskyites either change what they touch into themselves or suck it dry and kill it. It's hard for me to imagine them having loyalty to a state sponsor, or any nation state being able to trust them."

"I've never heard of Alinsky."

"I'll get you some background materials to read, including his book. He is the spiritual leader of the new communism, with a small 'c.' Vietnam War protestors used his methods."

"Did he have Islamic radical connections?"

"None known. Not for Tre either."

"Keep going."

"I can't."

Raven blinked.

"It stops there. We know Gates' control, Firouz, but he is untouchable and we do not have access. We suspect that Firouz has somehow tapped resources, probably through the UN, that resulted in the loan of Tre from the Earth Liberation Front. There are rumors of high-level people behind the scenes that work across all these groups, but no one knows."

"The old right wing wacko theories."

"Uh-huh. Soros, Bilderberg Group, and all the rest. Phantoms, shadowy figures connected to the centers of power at the highest levels."

"Soros was real. Scary guy."

"He was indeed. Even paranoids have real enemies."

"James Bond nailed it. Who knew?"

Goldfarb shook his head.

"It wasn't the Russians at all. It was SPECTRE, a private conspiracy of evil unknowns."

"Ian Fleming was before his time." Goldfarb sighed deeply. "Perhaps you're right. Back then it was all about the Russians. We weren't even thinking about terrorism or high crime."

"Red telephones and overkill. It sounds as if you miss it." "I miss the clarity."

Raven tried to think of something relevant to say, but couldn't. "How's the President?"

"Alive. No change."

"Josie wants to see him."

"Why?"

"Something came up in a remote viewing she did. Something that effects the President. She wants to discuss it with him. Privately."

"Um...."

"What have you got to lose? You're stuck, he's dying, our intelligence sucks, and our mission to Iran is possibly mis-targeted."

"Succinct and depressing, but accurate."

"If you can get her access, its possible Josie might be able to help him."

"No more OPs on US soil."

"Of course not," Raven said.

Goldfarb looked thoughtful.

"You know her powers. If she agrees, we can try. Do you have a better idea?"

"I need to keep the Iran connection in play. That's what's been authorized."

"Do what you need to do, but we'd be fully engaged elsewhere. Can you handle that?"

"I can call in some favors. If necessary, I can start it without you."

"What are the protocols?"

"No formal assignment and no contact with the agencies. You would be doing intelligence collection under the guise of scientific research. She should be used to that."

"I'll see if I can interest her and find out what she needs."

Goldfarb got his determined look. "I can give you a month to come up with something promising, no longer. What do you need?"

"For starters, transport and access to the President for Josie and myself. Full medical support for her viewings in case anything goes wrong. I'd prefer to base ourselves here for the time being if you can keep us under the radar."

"Just the two of you? Like in Durham?"

Raven nodded. "We'd start slow. She is still healing. I'll need weapons and back up to do anything operational, but that should be enough to get us started."

"I owe you an apology for Portland," Goldfarb reached into the console next to the table. He handed Raven his Sig, clip holster, and knife. "We've loosened the protocols for you. The President has cleared you to carry in his presence."

Raven popped out the magazine, checked it, and tucked it under his shirt.

"I need to get back to Washington so I can work some connections. I will make a call and see if the President's health permits a visit. When I get something set, I'll send the plane back for you."

"Works for me. Thank you, Sir."

"Try not to shoot anyone while I'm gone."

Raven smiled and touched the Sig under his shirt. "I'll do my best. You might want to get me some ammo and a long gun with a scope and suppressor."

"I thought you said no weapons until you went operational. Are you changing the rules?"

"Not at all. These are for training. An M-4 would be fine, with a dozen 30 round magazines. About 5,000 rounds for each weapon. When we go operational, you can hook me up with an armorer."

"Just keep a low profile."

"Absolutely."

"Let's try to avoid the public. There are private ranges here for both pistols and long guns. The facility is well guarded."

"That's comforting. Mostly, I need some target practice. It calms my nerves."

Goldfarb frowned.

"I'm still responsible for Josie's personal safety. Right?"

"Yes, of course."

"She works best without guards around close, and you'll want me better prepared than Durham." Raven could feel the energy in his voice.

"I'll get what you need and have the guards back off, but why are you so happy?"

"I must be getting mellow in my old age, Sir. Everything in life is a trade off. You gave me a choice between Josie and Iran. I picked her. I'm wrapping my mind around it."

"Don't wrap it too tight, you might hurt yourself."

Raven heard the sound of a car and looked out the window. "Here's our food. Tell you what. While we're having lunch, we can talk about rice, roast lamb, and camels."

"Spare me."

CHAPTER TWENTY
THE MAN WITH THE GOLD ROLEX

The UN Building, New York, UNICEF House, 2:35 PM

Firouz was getting angry, but he dared not leave the room. The call had come from the Secretary General's office. He was directed to go to this room alone, wait, and not communicate with anyone, especially not the Ambassador, his nominal boss. He had been waiting for thirty-five minutes.

The door swung open and a short round man with black slicked-back hair entered. Without a word, he settled into the chair at the end of the table facing the only door. Firouz looked him over. He was less than 5' 10" and at least 250 pounds, but the thing you noticed was his eyes. He had hawk-like eyes: Yellowish-brown, and intense.

"Thyāty," the man said. *Greetings*. Not *hello*.

"My native language is Farsi," Firouz said in English, "and your Arabic is deficient. Aside from your accent, which is Iraqi and offensive, 'greetings' is a term reserved for friends, and I don't know you."

"It's sufficient that I know you," the man said, showing him a UN ID. "You may call me Mr. Ricci."

"Why am I here?" Firouz was trying to place the accent. Mediterranean. Probably Italian.

"You are here because the Secretary General's office ordered you be here."

Firouz nodded.

"I got a similar call. My role is to provide an introduction. We are having this meeting outside the main complex because it does not involve official UN business, but has good security. This room is screened and swept for bugs."

"UNICEF deals with humanitarian aid," Firouz said. "I had nothing to do with the Gaza incident, nor did Iran."

"You talk too much, Mr. Firouz, and I care nothing of such matters. I said I was here to provide an introduction. You are here to listen."

"I'm listening." Firouz felt a chill.

"I'm afraid you've bungled into things that don't concern you. In a few minutes, a man will be here. You will probably recognize him. He's in the news frequently and is noted for his humanitarian nature and causes."

"Why do I care?"

"Your country is one of his causes. He has been very helpful with issues like sanctions, inspections, and arms embargos. His name is Dr. Claas Vogel. It will go better for you if you treat him with the utmost of discretion and respect."

Firouz did not speak. He recognized the name.

"Are you listening?"

"What have I done?" Firouz said.

Ricci waived a hand dismissingly. "That's not for me to say. For now, we wait."

Twenty-seven more minutes passed before Vogel entered. He shook his head, closed the door behind him, and eased himself into a seat.

He looked like an accountant, or maybe an undertaker, and nothing like his images on television. He was balding with a fringe of gray. He was pale and thin, with a beaklike nose. He wore a black suit, white shirt, and a pale blue tie. The suit looked expensive. Vogel was wearing a gold Rolex, heavy gold cufflinks, and a large ring, also gold, with what appeared to be a caret-sized diamond on his left hand. "You're Firouz?"

"Yes, Sir."

Vogel looked over at Ricci and sighed. "Vat are ve to do with dis one, Marco?"

Ricci gave one of those helplessly expressionistic shrugs the Italians are noted for. "I was directed to attend this meeting, but I'm not briefed."

"Not so far," Vogel agreed. He looked distastefully at Firouz. "You Arabs are your own vorst enemies. Vhy don't you just hang a neon light on your head and vear a name tag that says 'terrorist.' Do they let you ride on airplanes?"

"Sir?"

"I vas referring to your bushy black beard and Muslim garb, like a bad movie. Don't you think anyone might notice? Americans aren't total fools."

"I have rights."

"Due to a diplomatic passport. We have teams with lawyers tasked for political desensitization. Foolish gestures do not advance global governance. They cause problems and raise hackles."

"How dare you," Firouz snapped. "I'm a representative of the Islamic Republic of Iran."

Vogel stared at Firouz. His eyes were an intense blue, devoid of any trace of emotion. He shook his head. "It's best you do not waste my time. The reason you still live is due to a personal intervention by Ayatollah Golzari on the Assembly of Experts. You'd do well to close your mouth and answer my questions."

No one knew that name. Firouz fought to keep his composure. "What have I done?" He was ashamed at the quiver in his voice.

"Ja, vhat haff you done? Dat's vhat I will be asking you. Questions about vhat you have done and failed to do. The American President is still alive, and two of our best agents are dead. Do you know vhy?"

Firouz shook his head. "It's unclear...."

"The American FBI has recordings of your conversations with Gates. You are blown, Mr. Firouz, and that fact limits your usefulness to me or to the Islamic Revolution."

"That's not possible...."

"I've seen the transcripts."

How does he know these things? "You are sending me back to Iran?"

"Not me. The press release will say Iran is recalling you for routine consultations.

"I'm sure you'll be given the opportunity to explain how your mission was compromised. I was directed to tell you not to return to your home or to leave the UN complex except to go directly to the airport. It would be … inconvenient … if you were arrested."

Firouz bit his lips. "I'll need instructions from my government."

"And you shall have them," Vogel said. "Your diplomatic passport will get you through airport security. You will satisfactorily answer my questions, and I will give you an instruction letter and airline ticket when ve are finished. A limousine with darkened windows will be provided. You are booked on the 7 PM Aeroflot flight to Tehran tonight."

Firouz blinked. "Aeroflot?"

"Yes. An admittedly miserable travel experience, and the flight takes almost 24 hours, but that is what your government preferred. The flight arrives at 2 AM, but I assure you that you will be met when you arrive. Do you have any questions?"

"This is most irregular, I'd like to …"

"I want you out of the country tonight, and Iran agrees. I hope you have your passport with you. If not, we can…"

"I have it."

"Ja." Vogel glanced at his Rolex. "My questions will take some time, and your limo will be outside at 4:30. Would you like to call and confirm this?"

Firouz said, "That's not necessary, Sir."

"Then ve start now." Vogel pulled a small recorder out of his pocket. "Gott en Himmel, vhy would you use Gates as an assassin? Are you mad?"

"He'd done such assignments before…"

"Years ago. He was long retired from such work."

"He was a medical Doctor and available. It was a simple medical intervention in a hospital. Gates had unique qualifications for this job." Firouz said, trying to sound confident.

"Dr. Gates wasn't a field agent. He had irreplaceable contacts in Washington, contacts which are now lost to us."

"It was a low risk assignment…" Firouz cringed as Vogel and Ricci exchanged a look.

"Your primary mission involved the President. Why did you send a kill team to Portland? Who was the target?"

"I don't know, Sir."

Vogel groaned and closed his eyes.

"It was a 'Jane Doe,' an unidentified patient. A *jihad* cell leader in Ohio, Mallah Haj Rashid, targeted her. Rashid's actions left this woman injured and dying. I was assigned to finish the job."

"If you didn't know who she was, how did you find her?" The question came from Ricci.

Firouz took a deep breath, using the time to collect his thoughts. "It wasn't difficult. We followed the medical transport records. All it listed was the Jane Doe and her attending physician, a Dr. Lundgren, who had moved this patient to a hospital in Portland."

"Ach," Vogel said. "So we will ask Mr. Rashid and Dr. Lundgren, and it will become clear to me and your leaders why this matter was sufficiently important that it got two agents killed and diverted you from finishing the termination of the President of the United States. Is that vatt you tell me?"

"No, Sir."

Vogel took a gold pen and note pad out of his pocket. He started tapping the pen on the table. "Then vatt the hell do you tell me?"

"They're dead, Sir."

"The President and the girl?"

"Yes, Sir. Almost certainly. And the others as well."

"The President is *not* dead. There has been no announcement or transition of power."

"I said 'almost certainly,' Sir. The hospital records list the Jane Doe as deceased. Our last reports are the President is dying from a poison with no antidote. If he is not dead now, he will be soon. It's inevitable."

Ricci said, "I think he means...."

Vogel raised a hand. "Mr. Firouz will tell us what he means. Who's dead?"

"Lundgren and Mallah Haj Rashid. They are both dead. Dr. Lundgren was killed in Portland."

"Was Lundgren also a target?"

"No, Sir. Perhaps he interfered."

"Who killed him?"

"Most likely it was the domestic operative we borrowed, Tre. He liked to use a knife, and Lundgren's throat was cut."

"*Most likely. Almost Certainly.* Is there anything you know for certain?"

"Yes, Sir. Mallah Haj Rashid is dead, and so is Lundgren, with absolute certainty. Both left wives. There were public funerals."

Vogel took a deep breath. He passed a hand over his eyes. "Did Mallah Haj Rashid also die in Portland?"

"Rashid died some time ago. That's how I got the assignment."

"How?"

Firouz looked puzzled.

"How did Rashid die?"

"I can answer that one," Ricci said. "Mallah Haj Rashid died in Durham, North Carolina, over a month ago. It was in the news. He was killed by the police. There were Muslim protests."

"Yes," Firouz said, looking relieved. "That's how I was given the assignment. I'm telling you the truth."

"What happened in Durham?"

"I don't know," Firouz said. "There was an incident. All I know is what was in the media. I wasn't involved."

Vogel sighed. He picked up his pen and pad and put them back in his pocket. "They can finish your interrogation in Tehran about the Portland incident. He pushed the recorder closer to Firouz. "Now I want you to tell me in full detail everything you know about the operation involving the President, and especially what you know about his current medical status."

"Yes, Sir," Firouz said.

Vogel glanced at his watch again. "You have thirty minutes, no more, and God help you if you leave anything out or tell me anything that isn't precise truth."

Firouz started talking.

CHAPTER TWENTY-ONE
IT IS THE EYES

The Ranch, Mendocino, California

Raven sauntered up the steps to their suite. He felt better than he had in a long time. The little Sig stuck in his belt was like an old friend, comfortable, and his meeting with Goldfarb had not been the disaster he had feared. Best of all, Josie was back.

He paused, sniffing the air, and then grinned. *She is starting to relax.*

It was a good sign.

Raven gave the code knock – one then three, because the day of the month was odd. He had Josie practicing basic protocols, nothing extreme, just to get things working again. Not because this facility wasn't secure, to make her comfortable and get her used to it.

"Honey, I'm home."

It was their little joke, a line from old TV sitcoms that he had turned into an "all's well" code. If he had said, "I'm back" it would be an alert. Anything else would be a caution.

The door was locked. *Good.* He secured it behind him and set the latch. The patio slider was open, and the smell of marijuana mingled with the soft sea air and fragrance of blossoms on the deck.

Josie had added flowers in pots to personalize the place. Raven agreed, using them to conceal half a dozen wireless security cameras that linked to the laptop he had bought.

"Out here."

That was the "all clear." Raven ditched the gun, his shoes, and grabbed an IPA and a bottle of chilled chardonnay from the small fridge. "Want some wine?"

"Sure."

She was naked on the lounge, soaking up sun, a half smoked joint on the stand next to her. She stretched sensuously, rolled over, and smiled up at him. *God, she looked beautiful.* Her long hair was regaining its sheen.

Raven popped the cork, and handed her a glass.

Josie took a sip, licked her lips, nodded, and put a hand on his leg. "Yum." She ran an appreciating gaze over him and smiled. "You're getting hard."

"You're getting stoned."

"Not yet," Josie said softly. "I've been thinking. If we don't plan our future together, any road gets us there. Personally, I'd like to avoid some of those paths."

"Yeah. Me too."

"Today is a gift." Josie stood, turned her back, and demurely slipped into a robe. "This is a major milestone. I never thought I would do drugs again after that damned hospital. It freaked me out."

"Durham was bad...."

Josie eased herself down on the lounge, light as a feather, and met his eyes. "I've been thinking about that. It was my fault."

Raven shook his head and started to speak, but she cut him off. "You need to listen. Why are we accepting our taskings and assignments so uncritically?"

"It's what I do...."

"All your life, and it's a miracle you're still alive. We are Americans. Do we believe in central planning or freedom?"

"What are you saying?"

"You know my talents. We were ordered to focus on Iran's attack and Antarctica, so we did, exclusively. It was mistake. If I had targeted some viewings to protect us, the attack in Durham could never have happened. We'd have seen it coming."

"I'm not a mercenary or a rogue agent. All my life I've served my country."

"I know." Josie was silent for a long moment, gazing out across the sea. She sighed deeply. "Washington is *so* screwed up."

Raven nodded. "Yeah."

"We're a good team, my love, but we need to work smarter."

"I thought we were."

She shook her head, flipping the hair off her shoulders. "We were going to do one more assignment, retire, and spend our lives together. Instead we were almost killed because no one was covering our backs."

"Goldfarb tried. He sent Black with military backup…."

"Too little, too late, and you know it."

Raven was silent for a long moment. Finally, he said, "It was my fault. I should have…."

"Bullshit," Josie snapped. "Stop blaming yourself. Treat me as a partner. Let me help. Let me do my share."

Raven blinked and looked at her.

"If I'd tried, could I have seen that attack coming?"

"Most likely."

"Right. And we could have evaded it."

"Or thwarted it…."

"Yes. Do you know what I've been doing while I was waiting for you?"

Raven grinned. "Smoking dope and getting horny?"

"Before that."

He shook his head.

"I did two remote viewings." She paused at his concerned look. "I was careful…."

"You told me yourself you need a control and medical backup. I have arranged for both. You should have waited."

"I was careful. I stuck with easy and soft. I did not view Iran. I didn't look for military operations, avoided anything potentially violent, and didn't go deep."

There is a lot of violence around. "Where did you go?"

"I checked out this location for tonight. Before you got here, I knew exactly when you would be back, that you had gotten your personal gun back, and that you'd stash it under the pillow on the couch. Right?"

"What else?"

"That's the good part. We're safe."

"Not possible. I can get off the grid sometimes, but you are a national asset. You will always need protection. Not just because I care for you, not just because I gave my word, because it is part of my job. If I didn't take that on, someone else would have to."

"I know." Josie smiled softly. "But we're safe for tonight. I scanned events all the way through breakfast tomorrow. We are clear, my love. No violence. No threats. We can relax like normal human beings, just for a few minutes."

He wanted to believe it. He had seen her work. "Okay."

"Your world is a scary place. You are always hyper alert, tense. I can see it in your eyes, like a wild animal searching for threats."

Raven grinned. "Or looking for targets…."

"What?"

"When I first signed on at Langley, one of the trainers worked on that. She called me a commando type. She said that was bad, that you could spot commandos a mile away."

"How?"

"She said it was the eyes. She put me through classes to mask my alertness."

"They actually had classes?"

"Sure. Part of the training was to help you blend in as an agent. I guess it must have worn off some when I moved to paramilitary OPs."

"Did you sleep with her?"

Raven shrugged. There was no way to keep secrets from a paranormal. He was getting used to it.

"Well?"

"Once."

"Only once?"

"She kept asking me questions…."

"I can imagine." Josie laughed. "Maybe her training did you some good after all. I'm going to attempt to move you to the next level."

"Why do women always want to change men?"

"They don't." Josie looked serious. "It's a lot of trouble. But being close to someone, caring for them, changes you."

"It sure does. I fought all the way to the President to get to see you."

"I know. Now we are together and you can let down, at least sometimes. This is the best time we will get anytime soon. We can have lives, at least a little, if you'll let me do my part too."

"What's the other part?"

Josie frowned.

"You said you did *two* remote viewings."

Josie nodded.

"What was the other one?"

"The President."

Raven blinked.

"We're going to see him."

"Yes. I spoke with Goldfarb. Do you know who poisoned him?"

"I didn't dare go there. Not without you as a control and medical back up. That is too dark. I just tried to see future probabilities."

Raven knew how violence traumatized her. "What did you learn?"

"We're going to see the President three days from now."

"I'll arrange transport."

"We have to save him."

Raven had a gut feeling what was coming, something totally outside of his abilities and expertise. "The President has the best doctors possible."

"Did that help me?"

"No. What helped was my getting you out."

"What helped was your out-of-the-box approach."

"What are you saying?"

"You changed the probabilities. If we leave matters the way they are going, the President is going to die in eight days and a few hours. America goes downhill fast after that. No matter what we do in Iran, it goes downhill, and it takes us with it."

"How sure are you?"

"I'm never **sure**. You know by now how it works. It was a solid remote viewing. Every scenario I saw had him dying soon. The probability lines clustered at about eight days, three hours."

"What about our visit to him?"

"I didn't see any significant change after our visit, but I did sense it was a nexus point."

Raven did not have a clue what she was talking about. "The President knows he's dying. It's not our responsibility…."

"I'm not trying to save **him**. I am trying to save our world and us. If he dies, every probability line I saw leads to disaster."

"What's a nexus point?"

Josie frowned. "It's hard to describe. It is a center, a special place, a connected group of future events. A lot of probability lines wander through that particular point in time and space."

"Like when I was in the bomb vault at Natanz?" It was before they had met, and he had barely escaped with his life. He had later learned it was Josie who had saved him.

"I didn't dare look that deep, but, yes. It's basically the same phenomena."

"But different?"

"Yes." Josie nodded. "Different. It's hard to explain."

Raven smiled encouragement. He still did not understand, but there was no point in pressing her further. "What are you suggesting?"

"Tonight we relax a little. Tomorrow we have a good breakfast and you prepare me for a deep viewing. After that, I don't know what we do…"

"What are you hoping for?"

"When we see him, we can possibly intervene. I am trying to figure out how. I don't know what else to do."

"So we improvise." Raven took a sip of his beer. "We'll think of something."

CHAPTER TWENTY-TWO
TRINITY

Building 422, The Presidio of Monterey, California

The agent was nervous. She had picked up her instructions at the dead drop and decoded them using her one-time pad. She did not trust anything electronic, especially now.

The message at the drop was one word, "CALL," along with an unfamiliar New York City phone number, a time and three dates. Two had already passed. This was her last chance. She had delayed as long as she could.

Why would they insist she call?

Security was tight. They knew that. She had reported it.

Access to the base was restricted, only a short list of people were allowed into the clinic, and she was sure everything was being monitored. Her cell phone was in a drawer at home with the battery removed. It could be used to monitor and track her, and it was better to leave it than be questioned about the missing battery if she was searched.

The Secret Service was checking everyone and the gate guards had shut down civilian access except for a short list of contractors. The Presidio had turned into a small version of the Green Zone. It was worse than Iraq. She knew because she had been there. She once spent ten months in the Emerald City.

At least the contact time fit her work schedule and patterns. The trainers always emphasized it was the abnormal events that drew attention.

It was not uncommon for her to spend time on the beach before she went home, especially after a twelve-hour day.

She drove slowly, stopping at the gate for the inspection. It was not her day. This time they made her get out of the car and open the trunk. Everyone was checked coming in, but the outbound inspections were random.

The young Marine proceeded to do a full inspection under the watchful gaze of his partner, who was cradling a short-barreled pump shotgun. "You're clear."

"Did you find any nuclear weapons?"

He flashed a smile, shook his head, and handed her purse back. "No, ma'am."

"Good to know."

He stood back, waving her thorough, and she got in and slowly drove away. She turned right with the traffic and watched her mirrors. Detecting no surveillance, she sped up, and popped on to US 1 North, heading in exactly the wrong direction. There was a black SUV with tinted windows behind her. That was suspicious.

She slowed until it passed, watched the taillights disappear, then exited at 402B, and drove slowly on the small back streets, making many turns, and finally stopping in Del Monte at a convenience store, where she bought a cold bottle of lemonade and got two rolls of quarters in change. She returned to her car and sipped it slowly until the parking lot was empty.

Convinced she was clear, she cut West over to Del Monte Avenue which she took southbound, back past the Naval Postgraduate School. She finally exited on Park, near the public beach. Traffic was light.

Phone booths were long gone, of course, even in eccentric California. It was just one of those stupid kiosks, but at least it was dark. She dialed, dropped eight quarters, and waited. The phone was answered on the third ring. It was not the voice she had expected. "Doctor Lemon, please," she said. "I called to see how my mother-in-law is doing."

Yellow was caution.

"She's sleeping, and he's not here."

Sleeping. They were giving her a new control. She was counting seconds in her head. Six passed before she responded. "I'm worried about her."

"We all are," said the voice. "We must pray."

"Yes." They were setting up a meet.

"Trinity is close. Ask for Reverend Jones."

"You're sure?"

"On the peninsula." There was a click and the line went dead before she could object.

The call had taken twenty-one seconds.

The agent frowned. There was a cluster of churches down past the big hotels, out toward Pacific Grove. Trinity was a sanctuary for illegals. It was one of the Liberation Theology churches, mostly Black and Hispanic, angry men and women, waiting to turn the tables on their presumed oppressors and take over.

Kill the crackers, Reconquista, and a good place to avoid. Why don't they just hang a neon sign on my head?

When she pulled up, she saw it was an old Spanish style building with a courtyard. Guarding the massive wrought iron gate was a tall black man with a shaved head and a large revolver on his hip in an open holster.

The agent got out. "Is my car safe here?"

"I take care of it. We be expecting you, Sister."

CHAPTER TWENTY-THREE
THE VOID

The Ranch, Mendocino, California

Josie took deep breaths, feeling sensations coming back, feeling her body coming back. The paranormal trainers at the Rhine Institute insisted that was not right – they said her mind and body remained connected through remote viewings and just her perceptions shifted, but it was how she always felt at the end of a remote viewing. Like she was reconnecting.

She stretched, flexed her arms and legs and wiggled her fingers, careful not to move too swiftly. She smelled flowers. She felt sunlight on her skin and a cooling breeze. She sensed safety, a protective presence. Slowly her physical senses came back as her mind and body reconnected. The distant rumble of surf and the faint cries of sea birds helped. She was in a peaceful, safe environment.

When she opened her eyes, Raven was watching her.

"What time is it?"

"Late afternoon." He came over to her and wiped her face with a cold cloth. "After four. Are you okay?"

"I'm good."

He held out a bottle of water. She took it, sipped carefully, and nodded thanks. "What happened?"

"You tell me. You were gone for a long time."

"It was frustrating. Give me a notepad." She wrote tentatively, filled a few pages, and put the pad down.

Raven watched silently. He went to the refrigerator and got himself a beer.

"It was a busted session. Not your fault." Josie took small sips of water. She always came back from viewings dehydrated.

Raven handed her a fresh bottle. They had done several remote viewings together, with him acting as her control and safety line, but that was some time ago and she had never reacted like this. The standard protocol for Rhine Institute was to have a critical care unit on standby.

Several viewings involved violence. These had been traumatic for Josie. One was so bad it put her into intensive care. "Do you want a medical check?"

Josie shook her head.

"Talk to me."

"I don't need being fussed over by more doctors. I'm fine."

"Roger that." Raven dialed the number he had been given for the Fort Bragg ICU. When they answered, he gave a code number and said. "You can stand down. We're done for today."

Raven listened for a few minutes. "Yes, stand down the helo too. Just a minute." He put his hand over the phone. "They had a life flight on hot standby to cut response time if we'd called. Do you want to go again tomorrow?"

Josie shook her head. "We need to get better organized."

"Negative," Raven said into the phone. He frowned, listening. "I can't answer that. How about I call you in the morning?"

He listened for a moment, frowning. "I'll check. I do not have the authority to discuss it. Thank you."

He clicked the phone off. "They were faxed the Rhine Institute protocols, and they're not comfortable. They want more information."

"Rhine knows better than to discuss what we do. How was this set up?"

Goldfarb gave the hospital some kind of story about psychological experiments. Do you want me to call and ask him to instruct them to back off?"

Josie shook her head. "All that would do is raise curiosity."

"Should we move back to Durham?"

"No. We need to stay here."

He looked at her.

"I'm strong. My talents are working fine."

"Okay."

"I need to freshen up. I will take a shower. Then we can talk."

"Take your time. I will check in and find out what Goldfarb told them. He should have us access by now."

Raven had his feet up on the railing, watching the sunset on the water. His secure cell phone was on the table, alongside the little Sig .45, a box of ammo, and two magazines. "Hey, Babe."

"You know I don't like guns."

"Right." He turned the phone off, scooped up everything else, popped a mag in the Sig, and headed inside. "I was just cleaning up. A man's work is never done."

Josie smiled in spite of herself.

"White wine?" His voice floated back through the open patio door. "Cheese and crackers?"

"I'd love it. Thanks."

He returned with a bucket filled with ice, an open bottle in one hand, and two glasses. "Oregon this time. Duck Pond." A minute later, he returned with a tray of crackers and cheese. "You're making me civilized."

She took a sip. A Pinot Gris 2016 nicely chilled. It was smoother than a Chardonnay, a clean fruity taste, no oak. "Thanks."

"We got it straightened out. You're an expert on the behavior of intelligent aquatic mammals."

"Say what?"

"Intelligent aquatic mammals." He made swimming motions with his hands, then grinned and poured himself a glass of wine.

"Mermaids with large breasts and brains? You're going to test them?"

"Not me. Wrong species, too. You're the researcher, and the grays are running."

"I think I saw that movie. I was pretty stoned, but did not detect much intelligence. Gray space aliens, chasing scantily clad blondes with flippers."

"No mermaids. Whales. Seals, dolphins, and whales."

"This was Goldfarb's idea?"

"Uh huh." He took a sip of his wine, looked thoughtful, and picked up a slice of cheese and put it on a cracker. "Gray whales feed in the arctic, but they winter in Mexico, which is where they breed. They are heading back North now. Dolphins are out there too."

"If you say so…."

"That's our cover. Dolphins are still being trained by the Navy as part of the U.S. Navy Marine Mammal Program."

"Trained to do what?"

"The Navy says it's like Flipper, harmless and cute, but there were rumors, never verified, back during Vietnam that we were training them to kill. The Russian military is believed to have closed its marine mammal program in early 1990, but in 2000 the press reported that dolphins trained to kill by the Soviet Navy had been sold to Iran. You are doing psychic research on how to communicate with dolphins."

"Whales too?"

"Why not?"

"I need to do research on how to communicate with you." She held her glass over his head. "Would it help if I poured this on your head?"

"How do you feel about breeding in Mexico…?"

"You're lucky." Josie pulled the glass away and took a sip. "I'm not about to waste this."

Raven laughed. "This is serious damage control, Babe. The dolphin story has overtones of harmless wackiness."

"It sure does. It's a stupid story."

"It's a great story. We're using it as cover."

"To protect us from what?"

"Our own bureaucracy, of course."

"I don't understand."

"The good doctors in Fort Bragg, the ones we need for your medical support, were becoming afraid they were being sucked into a sinister government plot."

"Smart doctors." Josie finished her glass and held it out for a refill. "Maybe we can learn something here."

"Foolish doctors with no sense of adventure. They freaked out when they got a directive from Washington demanding support and ICU access without being told why. The guidelines they got from Rhine made it worse. We didn't want them calling around asking questions, so Goldfarb spun it into a Disney movie."

"He told them we were studying fish?"

"Friendly fish. Flipper, not the Creature from the Black Lagoon. Goldfarb calmed them down and de-escalated things. It's all cool now."

Working at Rhine was never like this.

"This time I want to keep us independent and further under the radar. All this was unnecessary. They had a helo on standby that could pick you up in fifteen minutes, but I can drive you to the hospital just as quick. The Fort Bragg hospital is only about 12 miles up Highway 1, the Shore Line highway. They don't have to do anything but keep an ICU open for when you're remote viewing."

"Works for me."

"Fort Bragg is just your average rural hospital, three on a scale of five. It is above average for orthopedic work, but the Emergency Room and ICU are basic. It is a trade off. We do not have the level of mission support we did before, but Bragg does not have a need to know what we are doing. What do you say?"

"I say you made a good call. This is not as if I am doing remote viewings into a slaughterhouse like the Mideast. I'll be fine."

Raven nodded.

"I made the same type of mistake you're talking about. Poor planning and mission support. We did not target my viewing. I got lost."

"Lost?"

"It's hard to explain. Remember how you gave me an object, and I tracked it across space and time?"

"The Noville notebook. You tracked the damned thing across half a century and half a world."

"It was a solid anchor. We call that 'outbound remote viewing.' What I wasted my time on today was 'coordinate remote viewing.' This time, all I had to work with is the location where the President is, the Presidio in Monterey. I found him okay. He's still alive."

"Did you discover who poisoned him?"

"He doesn't know, and I don't have a connection or a location that gives me any focus or traction. I went back to the dinner where he ate the poisoned mushrooms, but it did not help. I didn't see anything suspicious."

"Did you learn anything useful?"

"Not really. I spent most of my time viewing the future, looking for an option that ensures he will live. I went over it back and forth. I must have looked at a hundred probability lines.

"He's going to die in less than a week. I cut out before I viewed his death scenes, but went close enough to verify that his doctors had given up."

"Okay."

"Not okay. When the President dies, it gets scary. Evil takes over."

"How?"

"I'm not sure. There were not any clear probability lines. It was like a roiling black funnel cloud. I was terrified." Josie shivered and took a sip of wine. "I don't want to go there."

"Worse than your Mideast viewings?"

"Yes."

"Worse than the bad one?"

The one that almost killed me. Josie thought about it for a long moment and then nodded. "Maybe. I could not see any path. That has never happened before. If I went in there, I would never come out. I know it."

"Easy," Raven said.

"Don't make me go there."

"I won't, Babe. I promise."

"What do you want to do?"

"We need to figure this out. First off, I need to be sure I understand what you saw. The President dies. It all turns to shit, and then you hit a wall your powers can't penetrate."

"Basically. And no matter what we do or don't do, that black funnel is our future."

"It wasn't there before?"

"I don't think so. The last time I was just taking quick looks up to when the President got critical, and then backing down and coming in at a different angle. I do not think I could have missed something like that. It blocks everything."

"The funnel is death?"

"I'm not describing it well. In some ways, it is like a black curtain, but there is motion. It was roiling in time and space and it seemed to cover the whole planet. The only way I could stay clear was to back up in time.

I called it a funnel, but maelstrom would fit too. I do not know what it is. Life lines go into it and they vanish."

"So what made you say *funnel*?"

"I don't think it would look like a funnel in space, but it did in time. It started at a point, and spread in all directions as you moved forward in time. I was trained to make sketches of my remote viewings, but I don't know how to sketch this one. If you were standing on the planet without being able to shift through time, it would probably look like a huge cloud that swept toward you."

"Most of us can't shift through time, Josie."

"No."

"Do you think normal human senses could detect this?"

"No."

"You sound pretty sure."

"I watched it sweep over people. They did not seem to be aware of it. They did not flinch or try to run. They went about what they were doing until it hit them, and then they disappeared."

Raven's frown deepened. "Once upon a time, I was given training by some big dome atomic physicists. They talked about things like 'black holes' and 'quantum tunneling.' What I remember is that black holes ate everything – matter, energy, even light. No one had ever seen a black hole, and some scientists argued no one ever would. Nothing could escape them, not even light. If you shined light into them, it would not be reflected. It would just vanish."

"I think this effect was psychic, not physical."

"Why?"

"Trees didn't bend, grass didn't wave, birds didn't startle. One instant I could see things, and the next they would disappear. *Poof.*"

"Fade to black?"

"No." Josie shook her head. "Things didn't fade. It was as if someone threw a switch, like a blink. One instant objects would be sharp and clear, and the next I'd be viewing roiling blackness."

"We're learning things," Raven said. "Is there some place we can hide from this?"

"I doubt it. I shifted to several places in space, including here. There was only blackness. A black void. It spreads out from Monterey, and it was everywhere I looked. I did not dare get too close. The only way I could stay clear was to shift back in time or further away in space. But when I did the latter, it always got there."

"It starts in Monterey with the President's death?"

"There was a lag time, but yes. The edge of the cloud, the start of the funnel in time, was always after the President's death, and it was centered there."

"Has anything like this ever happened before?"

"Not to me. I have never heard of anything like it from the other paranormals either. I don't know what to do."

"Only one thing **to** do," Raven grinned. "I'd rather be sorry for something we did, than go down doing nothing."

"What are you saying?"

"We improvise. That's what I do, Babe."

"How?"

"One step at a time, and carefully. We do a recon. I say first we go to Rhine and see what their paranormals suggest. Maybe they have a talent who can see into or through the black funnel."

"Maybe they don't."

"Then we go to see the President and figure out what we can do to prevent this. Can you do that?"

"I think so."

"Do you have a better idea?"

Josie shook her head. "We only have a week."

"Right." Raven picked up his phone. "So we'll start tomorrow."

"What are you doing?"

"Calling Black. I think maybe he needs to steal us another airplane."

CHAPTER TWENTY-FOUR
IN THE BUBBLE

Building 422, The Presidio of Monterey, California

Jordan Harrington muttered a curse and lowered the phone from his ear. "I'll take the call."

He had enough problems. Only a threat to go over his head to the President's Chief of Staff made him take the call. He picked the phone up, checked the secure light, and spoke carefully. "I've been getting your messages. I'm sorry, but it's not possible."

Goldfarb said, "It's a simple request. We need access to the President. Now."

"You saw his condition."

"Yes."

"The President's ordered a total hold. I'm offended that you threatened to call Washington to start raising questions and demanding access."

"You didn't leave me much choice, Jordan. You refused to take my calls."

"You and your operative are two of only four people outside the lockdown who know what we are dealing with here. If you call the Chief of Staff or anyone in the White House, you are committing treason and defying a Presidential order. Is that clear?"

"I didn't call anyone except you. I am executing the mission orders the President gave us, orders that you are not privy to, and you are interfering with my performance of this duty. Do you want to talk about who's defying a Presidential order?"

"I do not."

There was a brief silence on the line, save for the hiss of the triply redundant RSA encryption. The military scramblers worked fine in combat, but got confused – lost sync – in quiet environments at times when conversation ceased. The technicians said something about putting white noise through pseudo-random protocols being computationally indeterminate. Harrington had no idea what that meant. Whatever it was, it was irritating as hell and could not be fixed.

"Look," Goldfarb said. "I'm not trying to cause you problems. I sense it is not going well, Jordan. I assure you that I have this on close hold. There will be no communications from me beyond what is absolutely necessary to perform our mission."

"What the hell does that mean?"

"I'm afraid you'll need to revise your need-to-know list. It's me plus two at this end."

"**What?**"

"In addition to myself and the senior agent who visited there with me, we have a technical specialist who is aware of the, ah, critical condition our nation is facing."

Harrington felt his teeth clenching. "On precisely whose authority did you take it upon yourself to start committing security breaches?"

"I've committed no breaches. She discovered this on her own."

Harrington did not try to keep the skepticism from his voice. "That's hard to believe."

"Ask the President."

"That's, ah, not practical at present."

"That's why this is so urgent."

"What are you saying?"

"I'm saying I believe you. The reasons you are reluctant to grant us access are precisely why she needs to see the President."

"For what purpose?"

"I can't say, not even over this link."

"You are asking a lot," Harrington said. "Under the circumstances even my own access is limited."

"You promised me access."

"Yes, I did. I specifically said 'alone,' if you will recall. And my offer was contingent on medical issues, which are now problematical."

"I don't have time to screw around. As it turns out, I know more about what's going on out there than you do."

"Not possible," Harrington said.

"I can give you a hint. Are you fully secure at your end?"

"As good as it gets. I am in a bubble. Just me. We don't even keep logs."

"Good," Goldfarb said. "It's game over in a week. You're out of time."

Harrington said, "No." *He knows the time of his death? His own doctors don't know that.*

"I'm sorry, Jordan. You're out of time and so is the President."

"You can't be sure of that."

"I'm sure enough. However, do not take my word for it. Call the Rhine Institute. They just lost two intelligence assets, and it affects you."

"How?"

"That will become obvious when you speak with them. Ask for Dr. Becker."

"What exactly does 'lost' mean?"

"It means **dead**. One is physically dead. The other is catatonic. We are not sure what caused it or how. It is something new. Rhine is calling it 'the Abyss,' maybe an energy field of some type. Whatever you call it, we believe it will be centered in Monterey a week from now, after the President expires."

"I don't have time to play games, Aaron."

"Correct. Barring an intervention, he dies in a week, the lid comes off, and the universe twists. I just lost two valuable assets having Rhine validate that."

"What kind of an intervention?"

"I can't say. That's why we need to see the President."

"Can't or won't?"

"Both. We're wasting time, and I doubt I'm telling you anything you didn't already expect."

"Maybe not. But you don't **know**, Ari."

"I **know**. There's just a difference between what we know, and what we can prove."

Harrington thought about that. *The existence of God and the outcome of future events were not provable. Intelligence findings fell into a dark corner of the same category. Pearl Harbor and 9-11 were obvious only after the fact. What seemed obvious before the fact – Saddam's nukes – was frequently wrong. There was no certainty.*

Goldfarb clearly believed what he was saying, but would never reveal his sources and methods. There was no point in asking. And even if he did ask, Goldfarb was right, there was no proof until after the fact, until too late. It got down to trust and competence. If you made the wrong call, you could spend the rest of your life second-guessing and maybe hating yourself.

Harrington listed to the hiss of the scrambled link and time passed. *Do I dare act on faith?* It was a difficult question. *Do I dare not act?* That one was easier.

Finally Goldfarb spoke, "Well?"

Harrington sighed. "You have a point."

"Thank you. Now I need to ask you something."

"Go ahead."

"The doctors have given up hope, haven't they?"

"They never give up hope...."

"Do you have any leads on who is involved in the assassination attempt?"

"You've been getting copies of the reports."

"I know what I've been getting. I'm asking you for the soft information, the rumors, the speculations and discussions that don't get written down."

Harrington did not respond.

"I'd prefer not to spend time arguing about this, Jordan. We don't have time, and I'm not sharing anything beyond my OPs team."

Harrington sighed. "We haven't come up with anything. No suspects. Nothing firm enough to be called a lead. While we are sharing, it has been rumored you are pursuing an Iran connection. What about that?"

"We're changing our view. I need you to get us objects associated with the assassination attempt."

"What kind of objects? I told you there are no leads. The CSI teams came up dry."

"We need anything that may have been physically touched by the assassins. Samples of the poisonous mushrooms and the sauce containers. Plates. Eating or cooking utensils. Things like that. Anything. Can you do that?"

"I suppose so, unofficially. The mushrooms are evidence, so they will certainly have been preserved. As for the rest, the common items, everything will have been cleaned and put away by now. They're of no use."

"I still want them."

"If you wish, but access to the President is still an issue. I cannot allow anything that increases his stress. It is beyond my authority. The doctors won't allow it."

"Can he talk?"

"Only for brief periods."

"That's sufficient. I need five minutes in private for two people."

"I'll do what I can. When?"

"What's the best time for access?"

"Early evenings, when it's quiet."

"We'll be there tomorrow night."

"I can't guarantee you access."

"Sure you can. Tell the doctors we may be his only hope. We just need five minutes alone with the President. If he doesn't agree, I won't bother you again."

"And if he does?"

"You will do as the President orders, of course."

"Yes," Harrington said. "What names do you want on the access list?"

"Same as before, plus one female."

"I can use your old paperwork for access, but anyone new gets checked. She'll need a valid ID, and it had better be squeaky clean."

"Not a problem. Is 19:00 good for the meet?"

"7 PM, for five minutes. I'll pick you up at the airport."

"Not needed. We will just come. Thanks, Jordan."

There was a click and the line went dead. Harrington pushed the button on the receiver a few times until a technician came on.

"Sir?"

"I need a secure line to the Rhine Institute in Durham, North Carolina. A Dr. Becker. He should be expecting my call."

"Yes, Sir. I'll call you back."

Harrington rubbed his eyes and slowly put the phone down. President Blager had been his friend for sixteen years. Blager was dying. The doctors knew it. He could see it in their eyes. Somehow, Goldfarb knew too. Goldfarb even had a timeline, and that made it worse.

Anyone who had thought it through was terrified over the political implications if the President died in office. The Secret Service guards were like zombies. No one smiled, and no one bantered.

America was weakened. The last thing the Republic needed was another leadership crisis, but one was coming and everyone knew it. The public trusted Blager and his policies. After a decade of corruption, that trust had been hard-won.

The President knew it better than anyone did, which was why he had locked things down. His mind was still sharp, but he tired quickly, and each day he was weaker.

There was not a damned thing Harrington could do now except pray. He had been doing that every night, and it did not seem to have helped. He was out of ideas.

CHAPTER TWENTY-FIVE
TWO DOWN

The Ranch, Mendocino, California

*M*en! Josie thought. She had wanted to walk the beach with Raven, just a quiet beautiful walk to help recharge for a remote viewing, but he passed. He was getting into his mission mode, worrying about details.

So she had walked alone. The sunrise was gorgeous, but it wasn't the same. When she got back, Raven was on the deck with a long gun, carefully fitting a cylinder to the barrel.

"Is that your new mistress?"

She melted when he smiled. "You're my mistress, Babe, and my lover. It's new to me. I'm still getting used to this relationship stuff."

She leaned down and kissed him. "Sunrises are beautiful."

"Nothing prettier than a backlit target or a ridgeline silhouette."

"Not what I meant, and you know it...."

"Your world is strange to me."

Tell me about it. What about yours, my love?

She stared at him. "Something scared you."

Raven shrugged.

He is trying to protect me from something. "What happened? What's with the gun?"

"We're going to see the President tonight. You and me."

"Someone's after us?"

"Not that I know of, but I need to sight in this rifle. I can handle the physical world, but you visit places I can't imagine, places where I can't protect you."

Something clicked in her mind. "Goldfarb called, didn't he?"

"Turns out Rhine already knows about your black funnel. They are calling it 'the Abyss' for some reason."

"Nietzsche…." Josie said. "Rhine Institute is into odd psychology and philosophy, and unanswerable questions. Friedrich Nietzsche personifies that. He was the 'God is Dead,' guy." Josie stared into his eyes. "I never asked you. Do you think he's right?"

"Absolutely not. America is a shining example that He is not dead. God has covered my ass, repeatedly. I do my best, and He helps make sure it is good enough. I think maybe He even helped us find each other."

"How do you know God has protected you?"

"I'm still alive, and a lot of good men and women aren't. Our nation is still free, against the odds, despite the blunders and bad leadership. How else can you account for that?"

"I can't. It's a miracle." She smiled softly.

"Every day is a miracle. We survived Durham alive and sane. Against the odds, together we survived. Think about it."

"I do. So what is this about an abyss? Did you report my viewing to Goldfarb?"

Raven nodded.

"Goldfarb told Rhine about the funnel cloud, and that's what they chose to call it. They like that sort of metaphysical mystical stuff. 'You gaze into the abyss…' Nietzsche said that."

"So I'm told. Yes, Goldfarb asked Rhine to try looking."

"This funnel is darker than a void, an empty abyss. It is soul sucking. I can sense it."

"You are right."

"Oh my God." Josie was staring at him with horror on her face. "I just figured it out. Rhine sent some of their young researchers into the black funnel, into the Abyss."

"Yes."

"What happened?"

"It's dangerous, just like you thought."

"Did someone get hurt?"

"Two down. They had Hispanic names."

"Alavarez?"

Raven nodded. "I think that's right. The male was Carlos."

"Carlos and Carmen Alavarez?

"Sounds right."

"I was at their wedding. He was a post Doc from Peru and she was the granddaughter of Cuban immigrants. She was only twenty-two. How are they?"

"Beyond help. They never came back from their viewings. Rhine has ruled the Abyss off limits. They are shut down so far as remote viewings."

Josie winced.

"I've got to do some prep. We are to be at the airport by 16:00, 4 PM. I will be back in plenty of time. We've got you a meeting with the President."

Goldfarb did not send the M-4 that he had requested. Instead, he had a local shop prepare him a Mini-14 ranch rifle along with a note that said, "Blend in. You're a civilian."

Raven had, as sophisticated shooters will, improved it. He had the shop's gunsmith bed the action to the stock, using an Accuracy Systems 3-point mount. He had changed out the stock trigger for a Jewell that gave the weapon a four-ounce pull without creep and overtravel. He had opted for a McGowan Medium barrel, certified, hand lapped, threaded, and custom fitted with a SureFire sound suppressor.

They had done a great job of getting it all together. Now it was his job to see how it worked. It took only four rounds to get it sighted in at 100 yards. From the start, he was shooting two-inch groups over open sights.

The scope was primitive technology compared to holographic sights, but he liked it. It was rugged and simple, used no batteries, and had plenty of light collecting power. It was the best they had at the local gun shop, and it would do fine. He had zeroed it at 200 yards, and after that was a no-brainer. You just clicked the T2 elevation adjustment for range, and it corrected for the -8.2 inch drop at 300 yards, or the +1.5 overage at 100.

Raven expected to do most of his shooting close, so that was his preset, the length of a football field.

The Ruger Mini-14 was a tactical carbine, not a heavy rifle. It was easy to swing, light, and reliable. The mini was better mannered and it could take an optical scope, which the M-4 could not. Even with the scope and suppressor, it was less than nine pounds. The problem that it shared with the M-4 was the 5.56 (.223) round, a tiny 55-grain full metal jacket bullet.

Raven solved that by using civilian ammo, not the UN-approved 5.56 rounds, but American-made, redneck's choice, kickass .223 rounds. The hottest loads they had at the gun shop were Hornady. He had bought up all they had: 60 gr. Hornady V-MAX polymer tipped hollow points, a hard-hitting explosive round that had low penetration for urban tactical use.

Overall, he was pleased. His tuned-up mini shot well. Best of all, the rig radiated "civilian," as Goldfarb had specified. A hunter might have something that looked similar. If a country sheriff noticed it in his trunk, they could have a friendly chat about shooting coyotes.

He would store it with the flush fitting five-round magazine. He had decided to standardize on 20-round mags for his normal use. It was not a full-auto rig. *If I can't get it done with 20 aimed shots, it just is not my day.*

The hard work was done. Now he was just putting a few hundred rounds through his new gun to practice handling and get used to it. The balance was good, even with the SureFire sound suppressor, which added 2.75 inches to the barrel length. One nice thing about the small round was that a small suppressor was adequate. To his surprise, he shot tighter groups with the suppressor.

The remaining problems were legal, not ballistic. Unless ATF/Treasury paperwork was filed, a sound suppressor was an illegal Class III device. With his custom-built flash suppressor of the same weight in its place, he was righteous, no questions asked.

Raven would store and transport the mini "legal," and shoot it suppressed when operationally prudent. The nice thing about a sound suppressor was the gun did not go *bang*, it went *ulch* or *groff*, or something like that, a lot less loud, but more importantly, the sound was dissipated to other points on the horizon and was less noticeable as a firearm report.

With the tedious work done, Raven was having fun. He removed the suppressor and put on an electronic headset that blanked the sound of his shots, but let the crystal *tink* of his rounds hitting the target downrange come through clearly. He leaned into the bench rest and squeezed off a full 20-round magazine.

Tink tink. Tink tink. Tink tink, as fast as he could pull the trigger, until he achieved slide lock back. Every round went home, well inside a two-inch circle at 100 yards.

Leaving the scope on, he did the same with two mags at 200 yards. *So far, so good.* That pattern fit inside a six-inch circle.

The target at 300 yards was next. *This is not a sniper rifle, it's an autoloader. I'll be happy with 8-inches.*

Raven's first two shots hit paper, but were outside. *That is what happens when you rush it.* Taking a deep breath, he flexed his fingers, and settled his thoughts. It was getting darker and he felt a breeze. He dialed in one click of windage adjustment.

His next magazine, rapid fire, was all on target. Then he did it again. All the rounds but two were inside a six-inch group.

CHAPTER TWENTY-SIX
MANA

The Ranch, Mendocino, California, 10:30 PM

"Honey, I'm home." Raven sounded cheerful. Josie smiled as he came in, toting his gear, the Sig on his hip showing because of his tucked in shirt, a gun bag heavy with ammo in one hand, and his rifle case in the other. "It's late. I almost went to look for you."

"It took longer than I thought."

"Problems?"

"Everything's fine."

"Did we have fun with our boy toys?"

"Let's just say I'm good to go on over watch. Chris Kyle would approve."

"I've got something to show you."

He dropped his gear by the door, came over and sat down next to her, smelling of sweat and cordite. "We don't have to be at the airport until four, right?"

He nodded.

She handed him a penciled sketch. It was an old building in the Spanish style, surrounded by a walled courtyard. Under it was a single word. *Trinity*.

"I got bored and did another remote viewing. I may have hit on something."

She saw concern in his eyes. "Don't go rogue on me, Babe. My job number one is to keep you safe."

"I'll use you as my control. Promise. But this one was safe and easy. I was careful."

Raven nodded, sighed, and studied her sketch. "Did you view any vegetation around it?"

"Flowers and shrubs. A lot of green with red flowers. I didn't recognize the type."

"No cactus, rocks, or sand?"

Josie shook her head. "I couldn't get a location fix either."

"It could be California or Mexico. The building is maybe early 20th century, but the gate is modern with an automatic opener. My guess is California, as the Mexicans do not like the peons to see what is behind the gates. They build their walls higher. What does Trinity mean?"

"I don't know. It just popped into my mind when I viewed that structure. I think it has some connection with the President. Can you check it out?"

"I'll pass it to Goldfarb. His sources and methods apparently don't do well at finding terrorists or assassins, but they can probably find a house. You've been doing more than looking at old houses, haven't you?"

"I have an idea. It's going to take some explaining...."

"Okay."

"Remember I told you I wanted to be a healer?"

"Uh huh."

"I studied Huna in Hawaii before I worked for Rhine. It's what got me started in parapsychology."

"Huna?"

Josie nodded.

"Never heard of it."

"Sure you have." Josie grinned. "The big Kahuna?"

"Surfing movies?"

"That's the modern usage, from riding the big surf off Hawaii, where the waves roll in from the northern Pacific unimpeded across thousands of miles of ocean. Oahu's North Shore has the best surfing in the world during winter. Surfing became a cult there, years ago, before it was a sport. Back then, surfing was almost a mystical experience, and the best surfer is still called the big Kahuna."

"So?"

"Rhine gave me a grant to go there and study after they tested me and found I had paranormal talents."

"It sounds like a boondoggle to me. A surfing holiday?"

Josie shook her head. "It was kind of like Harry Potter's magic school, but in a parallel universe. It taught strange things in strange ways, but, unlike Harry's, it was not preppie, not formal, and certainly not tainted by evil. There was an abundance of quiet and meditation, and no drama whatsoever.

"I studied Huna, seeking harmony and beauty. The intention, why Rhine funded me, was to open channels in my mind. The ancient practitioners of Huna, the Kahunas, were renowned for healing and levitation. My advisor was a high level Kahuna."

"I've never heard of 'Huna.' Why is that?"

"It's not much talked about or well understood. Western researchers gave up trying to understand it. I learned the precepts and some of the techniques, but I do not claim to understand it fully myself. I've never discussed their teachings with anyone."

"Not with Rhine?"

"No. The Huna consider their religion to be a private matter. There are several religions in America that feel that way, and the courts uphold it in contracts as a part of religious freedom and personal privacy."

"It's a religion?"

"Some say so." Josie shrugged. "The word 'Huna' means 'secret' in Hawaiian. The precepts overlap those of New Thought Religion in the West. Others say Huna is a form of metaphysics, with a focus on spiritual healing. Whatever it is, I found it fascinating. Have you ever heard of *mana*?"

"Manna from heaven?"

"Western words are poor tools for discussing Huna concepts." Josie frowned. "The kind I'm talking about, the Huna kind, is spelled M-A-N-A. In the Book of Exodus, manna has two Ns and is described as food from heaven, available six mornings a week. The concepts may be related: The notion that belief can affect physical reality. Maybe *Mana* produced Manna. Alternately, some say the ancient spelling may have been the same, with two Ns. I'm not sure."

"You lost me back at Exodus, Babe."

"*Mana* is the first of the seven precepts of Huna. It means all power comes from within. There are other precepts you will find familiar. *Aloha* is the basis for Western love. It means being happy with someone or something."

"Hmmm," Raven said noncommittally. "Did you ever levitate?"

Josie smiled at his bemused look. "A few times, but I was never really good at it. Mostly I had to be stoned, but the problem was when I got too stoned, I didn't care. I never thought levitation was useful, to be honest. Cars, boats, and airplanes do a better job, so far as I'm concerned."

"Okay...."

"My studies were focused on sensitivity and healing. In ancient times, shamans practiced Huna. Today it is more like an art, or maybe a myth, and, unfortunately, one that does not fit well into modern science. Nevertheless, a few concepts stuck. In the Hawaiian language, the term Kahuna is used for any expert."

"Including experts in healing?"

"Yes. Even today, Kahunas include experts in diagnosing illness, but many have MD degrees and cloak what they are doing with modern terminologies. That is passive healing, diagnosis, but another way to express the first precept of Huna is *ike* - **The world is what you think it is**. The second precept is *kala* - **There are no limits**."

"If I think the world is a certain way, it **is** that way?"

"No. Not think. Not suspect. You must **believe**." Josie smiled. "You, my love, sense your environment acutely, like a big cat prowling a hostile jungle, but you don't believe. You are always looking behind the masks, searching for evil in the shadows."

"I believe in **you**."

"I know." Josie's smile was radiant.

"You live on a higher plane than I do. I worry about that."

"Don't," she said. "You distrust and are wary. It is what has kept you alive in dangerous places. You sense evil, as a sheepdog does wolves. I feel safe around you."

"You said this Huna thing is 'without limits.' Do you mean that literally?"

"What is taught is there are no **natural** limits. The limits are in ourselves, but we can all change the world to one extent or the other. I trained myself to believe I can see across time and space, the universe grants me that, and so it is. Your gift is almost the opposite of mine."

"I have no powers."

"Of course you do. You fight monsters and confront evil. Ancient societies were protected by both warriors and priestesses, and for a reason. Evil is like kryptonite to sensitives. Those trained in Huna fear it and try to hide from it."

"Like Luke Skywalker and the dark side?"

"In a sense. With remote viewing the main danger evil poses is only our own self-destruction, but manipulating matter and energy is far more dangerous. Doing it at the subtle levels needed to bring about healing – the cellular, neural, molecular, and perhaps even the atomic – is the most dangerous of all. There are ancient legends of a war that shifted continents, caused the great flood, and almost destroyed the planet."

"Are you a Kahuna?"

Josie shook her head. "Not even close."

"You underestimate your abilities, Babe. Normal humans can't see across time and space."

"You're kind. At times, I felt like a dog that was being trained to form words. The natives, those raised and trained in Huna for tens of generations, are far beyond me.

"I got to where I could sense health or illness, but I wouldn't dare try to heal someone. I'd be as likely to harm as to heal."

"Your talents saved my life. Are you forgetting that?"

Though one may be overpowered, two can defend themselves. Josie smiled softly. "I'll never forget waking up in the hospital and seeing your black rose. Your talents saved me too. If we are healing each other, and I think we are, it is because of love. That's different."

"But some Kahunas can heal?"

Josie nodded slowly. "I've witnessed it, and, yes, that's where I'm going with this."

"You want us to get involved in **healing**? You and me?"

"I do."

"Why?"

"To shut down the black funnel cloud."

"The Abyss? The void? The one that eats remote viewers?"

"It won't eat anyone if it doesn't exist."

"Huh?"

"It's simple logic. The President's death initiates the Abyss, and we know the doctors can't save him. The only option I see is to keep him alive."

"This is impossible. You said yourself that all the probability lines lead to his death."

"Maybe the future can be changed."

"You didn't see any chance of that, did you?"

"No, but I'm way beyond anything I can imagine. I have never seen anything like the Abyss before either. You always say it's better to do something than nothing."

"What *can* be done?"

"You keep asking me questions I can't answer."

"Sorry." Raven smiled. "You stretch my brain, Babe."

Josie sighed deeply, venting frustration. "This is beyond my abilities, but my Kahuna, my adviser, was a healer. I would like to have him sense the President's infirmity. What do you think?"

Raven was silent for a time. Finally, he shook his head. "No way in hell."

"Why?"

"Goldfarb lacks the authority, even if we could persuade him. No one has the authority to authorize it, not even the President's personal physician. The closest held secret in the country right now is the President's condition. There would be assholes puckering from here to Washington if we brought in any outsider, much less some kind of hippy-dippy mystic."

"I thought you'd say that."

"Damn right. It is way beyond anything we could effect. Forget about it. No one would touch that with a pole. No one is going to allow any experimenting on the President."

"Unless they had to."

Raven blinked. "Huh?"

"I've researched you, my love. One of your tendencies is to run a bit loose with orders. I have viewed scenes where you told superiors it was 'better to ask forgiveness than to seek permission.' That is why the CIA called you 'Cowboy.' Right?"

"What's right is that I was fired with prejudice from the Agency."

"But you were right…."

"What's that got to do with it?"

"Everything. I've invited my Kahuna to visit Monterey, and said we'd pay his expenses."

"You told him about the President?"

"Of course not." Josie shook her head. "I wouldn't do that without your agreement. I told him I need his help, but he would have to come to the mainland, something he has never done. He values his solitude and serenity."

"You didn't ask me first?"

"I couldn't. You were off playing John Wayne, and we're running out of time."

"This guy is a recluse?"

"More like a hermit. Except for his students, and I'm honored to be one."

"He lives on a mountain top or something?"

"A hut on Kauai, actually. Way back in the rainforest. There's no road or power, and not even much of a trail."

"No phone?"

"There's no anything. He stays close to nature, and distant from modern civilization."

"He's not coming then."

"No, he's coming. I invited him."

"When?"

"Soon."

"How?" Raven's voice was strange. "You said he doesn't have a phone."

"I couldn't …. didn't …. use a phone. There are other ways sensitives can communicate if they've become attuned."

Raven was shaking his head.

"I think we can get him to Monterey tomorrow. We will need to have tickets in his name waiting at the airline counter there. You'll need to make his reservations and book him a room."

"Book him a flight?"

"Uh huh. He is doing me a big favor. He's never been on an airplane or driven a car."

Raven took a deep breath and let it out slowly. "Of course not. He probably levitates."

Josie finally recognized Raven's look. *Bemusement.* "He doesn't worry about things like that, but this trip will be stressful for him. I'd like you to book him first class and get him a quiet room with an ocean view."

"Your Kahuna knows about the President, doesn't he?"

"I didn't tell him."

"You didn't have to. If he has the half the powers you describe, he **knows**."

"The main thing is **we** didn't tell him. Are you with me on this?"

"The main thing is Goldfarb is going to shit bricks."

"No, he won't."

"Even with all your powers, I can't believe that."

"We're not going to tell him. If we don't, who will?"

"I don't know, but someone will. Rhine would for sure. Goldfarb approves paying their invoices."

"Rhine won't tell him anything. For one thing, they are shut down. For another, they will not know. My adviser has never revealed his presence to Rhine. He can block remote viewing when he chooses. He'll block any meetings we have with the President."

Raven stared at her.

"Think about it. Goldfarb lacks the power to do anything. If this doesn't work, nothing has changed. If it does, he'll be happy."

"This is the craziest idea you've ever had."

"Probably. Do you have a better idea?"

"No."

"Well?"

Raven said, "I'll book his flight and room."

CHAPTER TWENTY-SEVEN
OFF LIMITS

The Ranch, Mendocino, California, 8 AM, Next Day

*T*heir flight to Monterey was uneventful. They went alone, were met at the airport, and whisked through security with no problems whatsoever after they had emptied their pockets, removed their shoes, and had been scanned and all but strip-searched.

Harrington barely glanced at Josie's creds. He welcomed Raven, still using his Ron Browning identity, greeting him, only saying, "You are invited and expected. Be quick about it."

President Blager was alert. Their meeting with him took a total of four minutes and fifty seconds. Blager looked at Josie. His first words were, "You're the paranormal from Rhine."

So much for their false IDs. They were convenient fiction. The President knew.

Josie said, "Thank you for seeing us, Mr. President. Do you know why we are here?"

He gestured at the equipment that surrounded him. "I'm hoping for a miracle."

"We have two purposes. Part one, the most important, is saving your life. May I have permission to try? I would need brief periods of private access with you for healing therapies. I'm the only one who'd need access to you through security."

"What does that involve?"

"Sensing what's killing you. Stimulating your organs and natural defenses to cast it off. The closest description in our culture comes from the Bible and myth. I'd be putting my hands on you and praying silently."

He smiled faintly. "What do I have to lose?"

"We'll do our best. I can't guarantee…."

"I think my warrantee has about expired. What's your second purpose?"

Josie looked at Raven, who stepped forward. "America has enemies who have tried to assassinate you, Sir. We can help find them."

"I need you to be more explicit."

"We have some unconventional methods we can employ. We would work independently, informally, and covertly with the agencies you already have working on this. After we have the bad guys, we could help as needed with the interrogations."

"Then?"

"I'd ensure the threat is neutralized so there are no more attacks. I would report details and results to Doctor Goldfarb. It would not involve you directly in any way."

"Agreed. Goldfarb will be your control. I do not want to know. Neither does my successor, should Josie's healing efforts prove unsuccessful."

"Mr. President, you have my word on it."

"And mine," Josie said. "It is very important for your healing that you put such evil from your mind. Please hold positive thoughts."

"I'll work on it," The President said. "I'll issue instructions to ensure you have access to me without interruptions. Come back soon, please."

"I'll be back tomorrow night," Josie said. "Same time."

With that, the meeting ended, and they took their leave. They were back at the Monterey airport in 40 minutes and back at The Ranch and in bed before Midnight.

They were just finishing breakfast, when Raven's secure cell phone gave a triple beep.

"It's Goldfarb," he said.

She nodded.

He picked it up. "Raven. Correct. We got the greenlight. Josie's in."

Time passed as Josie sipped her coffee and stared out at the sea. Usually Goldfarb's calls were brief. Raven was silent, listening intently.

"Understood, but I want Black," he finally said, "He's part of my team and used to working with us. She's right here, and we're ready."

He listened for a moment. "Do you want my opinion, Sir? It sucks. Political correctness has turned the FBI into a bunch of pussies." Another long moment passed. "Roger that, Sir. I will not forget. Raven out."

He tossed it on the table. "We must be at the airport by four. They're going to do a hot pickup, and Goldfarb won't be with them."

"You sound irritated."

"His head is into the Iran OP, not helping us. He says that is his priority, the President wants to see us, and we can visit him on our own. We are relocating to Monterey. Goldfarb's gotten us a civilian aircraft for transport, Black is our pilot, and the FBI located your house."

"Trinity?"

Raven nodded. "The old Spanish one."

"All that would seem to be good news. What's wrong?"

"The house is in Monterey. It probably does have something to do with the attempted assassination of the President. What would be normal is a sneak and peek to check it out and put it under surveillance, but that's not going to happen."

"Why not?"

"Orders. The FBI says it's off limits."

"What does that mean?"

"We are not to offend political sensitivities or argue about the Bureau's law enforcement mentality. Goldfarb said he would 'have my ass' if I set foot in that church."

"I'm not allowed to do remote viewings?"

"We're allowed to do research, but no active OPs and no backup."

"Do you have a clue what's going on?"

"Goldfarb's power comes from the President. My guess is he is in a damage control mode. He expects the President is going to die. When that happens I expect we'll be re-tasked, and I'll be off to Iran."

"Why?"

"I think Goldfarb will want to do that for our own protection before our cover and support vaporizes. What do you think?"

Josie touched his arm softly. "I think we don't have much time. It might help if I knew **why** the Trinity house is off limits."

Raven gave a short laugh. "It's not a house, for one thing."

"It looked like a house to me."

"It used to be a house, a private villa owned by a movie producer, but it was purchased by an extremist religious group back during the Obama Administration. It's a church now, an icon for religious tolerance and social justice."

"Islamic?"

"No. That is another reason Goldfarb dismissed it. It is a church, not a mosque. There is not any connection to Iran or Islam. It's run by a black Liberation Theology minister, the brother of a well-connected California Congressman."

"I don't understand."

"It's about politics. Political Correctness. This is one of the 'God Damn America' churches. The minister has a chip on his shoulder the size of a timber. We enslaved his ancestors, you and I, including his great grandfather. In any case, Trinity is off limits."

Josie shook her head. It did not make any sense. "His grandfather is **our** fault? Yours and mine?"

"That's what Liberation Theology is about."

"About slavery?"

"It's about oppression. In the case of America and blacks, slavery is the hot button."

"Slaves came to the New World long before there **was** an America. They got here before the Pilgrims, back in the early 1600s, almost 200 years earlier."

"Who told you that?"

"Dr. Martin Luther King. A European ship brought slaves to Jamestown a year before the Mayflower and the Pilgrims. I studied religion, and I've never heard of Liberation Theology."

Raven shrugged.

"This is important. There is a connection between Trinity and the President, but I cannot target my viewings without something to anchor me. A person or an object would be best."

Raven spread his arms, palms up, signifying helplessness. "Goldfarb said Liberation Theology was 'Christianity meets Karl Marx.' It is new, as religions go. The Communists started it in South America, back around Vietnam.

"Che Guevara used it to subvert the Catholic Church and enrage the peasants, up until when the Bolivians killed his ass. The believers think the only way to gain salvation and go to heaven is to throw off the oppressor, by either killing them or taking their property in the name of social justice. In this case, the presumed oppressor is white America, and the oppressed are black. The same general notion led to the Black Panthers and the Weather Underground, also back in the 60s."

"That's clever...." Josie said musingly. "America clamped down hard on Communism, but we are big on religious freedom and tolerance. They found a loophole."

"It's a religion based on Marxist revolution, the way Goldfarb explained it. The *jihadists* want to kill or enslave the Infidels. Liberation Theology Christians want revolutions to kill the oppressors and achieve social justice."

"Jesus holds us guilty for the sins of our fathers? And the way to go to heaven is to steal from others and kill them?"

"Goldfarb termed it group salvation." Raven said.

"What is the difference between that and the Muslims killing *Kuffar* for the *Umma*?"

"I don't know, Babe. I do know America loses our wars at home and in the media. The things we worried most about in covert OPs were the bad guys, liberal reporters, and our own Congress. This is just one more example."

Josie waved her hands in frustration. "I'm trying to figure out what to do, and now you're telling me we're stuck with **nothing** to do except healing, which we don't know **how** to do. But we both know the doctors damned sure can't do it in the President's case, so we're the only hope."

"Actually, it is several levels deeper," Raven said glumly. "We don't know how to do healing, but Goldfarb thinks you might and that while you are here you can do some remote viewings of Trinity. Since he lacks the authority to take action in the first place, it is all academic. And if the President dies, it is game over and we are shut down anyway. He's grasping at straws."

"Doesn't it bother you that **nothing** we want to do is approved?"

"It sucks, but you get used to it."

"We are going to retire after this one, and move somewhere far away, right?"

"Uh huh." Raven nodded. "That's the plan."

"Keep telling me that. So what do we do now?"

"Improvise. I will work on a way to get an eyeball look at the house. You work on a way to save the President. How's your Kahuna doing?"

"He's coming. He'll be in Monterey tonight in time for our meeting with the President."

"What's his name?"

"Georgie."

Raven rolled his eyes. "Marvelous."

Trinity Church, Monterey, California

Ricci stared at the black minister. Reverend Dilbert Jones was a small man, perhaps five foot eight. He was thin, frail looking, and baldheaded, with long bony fingers. His face was distinctive with owlish eyes, protruding lips, and big teeth with a gap in front.

When Jones spoke, all that changed. You forgot what he looked like. He had a powerful resonant voice that captured attention, as did his dialect and choice of words. He spoke in an odd mix of East Los Angles jive, a relic of where Jones grew up in a troubled single-parent family, and the eloquent oratory that led him to the leadership of a major church.

Despite his charisma and stature, the man seemed incredibly dense, worse than the third world dolts Ricci worked with at the UN. He was losing his patience. "I need to move my assets in here temporarily, Reverend. It will only be for a few weeks."

"No way, no how. You must think I'm crazy. You get a bunch of camel jocks camping here, and we stand out like we is in a God Damn Klan meeting. This is a quiet neighborhood. The Bros notice, and someone is bound to talk."

"You've worked with Hamas before."

"Yo, down on the Arizona border, running weapons. Different time, different place. It was safe. No troops on the border. We stashed the bootie on BLM lands, where the cops and Border Patrol can't go. But this is a small town with a big military, and something at the Presidio got 'em locked down tighter than a tick. You know anything 'bout that?"

"Nothing that concerns you. It's my business, and you were directed to support me."

The Reverend finally nodded. "Fair enough. I don't want to know. You need men with guns, fine by me. But no Hamas. They are too visible, and all they want to do is blow things up. Whatever happens, win or lose, it would blow the cover for my church. We have a sweet deal here."

He has a point, Ricci thought. *Hamas is difficult to control.* "Have you ever worked with a man named Tre?"

"Yo. He's a Bro...."

"He's a dead Bro. He was a lunatic. He killed one of my best agents, a man who will be difficult to replace."

"He use da knife?"

Ricci nodded.

"Tre like to play with knives...."

"Not any more."

The two men looked at each other for a time. The New World Order was like that. Independent groups with disparate interests. The thing they had in common was a desire to bring down the advanced nations, the old order, especially America. They each had their own methods and assets.

Fortunately, it was easy to find people and weapons. There was a lot of hatred and resentment in the world. Each year, America and the West were weaker.

"Why don't you just tell me what you need?"

"Most likely, nothing. Not if you let Hamas base here."

Reverend Jones laughed, a deep rolling chuckle. "That's not why we talking, Bro, not why you want to put Hamas and weapons in my church."

"I may not need a thing, if you stick with the plan we had."

"Never mind the maybe. We talk about what you do, what you willing to pay money for."

"My project is going well, but I want some insurance in case my primary plan doesn't work. If you will not let me base Hamas here, I will put them elsewhere, but will need a backup team. I'll make the call as to which one we'll use."

"If it goes so damned well, how come you sitting here in front of me instead of sipping tea at the UN? You be one heavy dude for field work, Mr. Ricci."

"We don't want to take chances."

"You will have to be a bit more descriptive than that."

The jive talk was gone. Jones was studying Ricci. The Reverend's words were judiciously enunciated. They were delivered in the same resonant tone he used from the pulpit. Behind the religious garb and the trash talk, there was a shrewd mind.

He has been playing me, Ricci realized. "I have an agent inside the Presidio. If matters don't proceed as I desire, I will know."

Jones nodded.

"In that case, I will need a small team that can speak fluent English and pass as harmless. I can provide IDs that will get them through the gate and into the target building."

"How many?"

"One car with a pass for the base. Call it four people."

"That can be arranged. What is their mission?"

"The same as for Hamas. This would be a kill team. If this is handled properly, there will little resistance. We can get them inside a hospital unit before any alarm goes up."

"What weapons are preferred?"

"Inside the building, there are two guards with handguns. There will be a few doctors and nurses, plus a patient and possibly my agent. Handguns should be adequate. Perhaps some plastic explosive and a few grenades, but no long guns or rocket launchers."

"Just weapons that are easy to conceal."

"Exactly. Suppressed, if possible."

"And the mission, precisely?"

"I want everyone killed and the building burned. It would be a total of about six to ten people, most of them unarmed."

"What about your agent?"

"Everyone dies. There are to be no survivors."

"The Americans are soft targets. They don't allow their military to carry guns, except for the guards, who will, of course respond to the attack."

"Yes."

"The guards at the Presidio are United States Marines. They will be heavily armed, and they will block escape. This is a suicide mission."

"Correct. Your team will die fighting, just as Hamas would. Is that a problem for you?"

"No, it's your problem. It will cost you."

"That's not my question. The team will not be taken alive. They will take suicide pills if necessary."

"I know what your question is, Mr. Ricci. Yes, they will kill for the revolution. Yes, they will die for the cause. I can get you four people. Three men and a woman. They are all in good physical condition and skilled in small arms."

"Have they killed before?"

"Every one of them. Two of the team are cop killers."

Ricci nodded approvingly. It was like with the drug gangs. To reach the inner circles, you needed blood on your hands. It was a part of the initiation. "I can get you plans of the building we're targeting. I want your team to practice. I want to watch and be satisfied with their performance."

"Of course. We have a training facility back in the Redwoods. We can even do live fire if you wish. When do you need this resource, and how long will my team be committed?"

"I want them here now to start training. We have about a week before I'll know if your assets are needed."

"They are here already, but the fee will be substantial. These are the best people available."

"Yes, I expected that."

Ricci waited. He had indeed expected it. MS-13 had lowered the prices for violence in California. The going price for a drug hit in Watts or Oakland was about $100, and for $10 thousand – ten long, it was called – officials at any level were fair game. The Border States were getting to be like Mexico, one of the benefits of the Global Economy. Armed victims or heavily guarded targets cost more, but you could get a street cop killed for a thousand dollars.

Ricci had figured that an operation in Monterey and on a military base would be much more expensive. Still, the price did not really matter.

Terrorism and murder was so much less costly than war. It was bleeding the West dry.

"The main thing is we expect results."

"Of course, and you shall have them," the Reverend said. "Another reason why our fee is substantial."

"You will find my sponsors are quite generous."

"They will need to be," Jones said. "This will cost you a million dollars."

Despite himself, Ricci was shocked. He slowly shook his head. "That's ridiculous. Hamas will do the work I require free."

"I'm sorry, but our price isn't negotiable." Jones smiled, sucking air between his teeth. "It's your choice, Mr. Ricci, but I can't let you use Trinity as a base of operations for Hamas to start a war. We did not mind hosting a few private meetings for friends, but if you want an attack on a military base, you will put this church and our ministry at risk. If anything went wrong, there might be wide reaching consequences."

"That amount is absurd."

"I'm not going to use my own resources. Nothing will be traceable to Trinity. Where there is a need to assure results, we contract our hits to the Black Panthers. I will use one of their best kill teams."

He is not so dumb after all. And it is not my money. "That's still too much."

"It's cheap at twice the price, and you know it. As you said yourself, this is a suicide mission. The fee I quoted includes providing for the families of the team, and including false identities. You are paying for professionals. Nothing will be traceable."

"A million dollars in cash?"

Reverend Jones shook his head sadly. "I regret the US dollar is so unstable these days, and the Americans have proven to be diligent at tracking large sums coincident with terrorist incidents. I would need the fee in Swiss francs and put into a numbered account in Zurich. We could use the conversion rate effective the day of payment, if that's agreeable."

Ricci nodded. "There are a few minor details we must consider."

"Always...."

"I propose paying you more."

Jones smiled. "So far I like this negotiation."

"I will pay you $100 thousand when I'm satisfied with your team's performance. You will get another $100 thousand when the team is inside the target building. And when it is known the mission was successful and that everyone involved is dead – including everyone in the building and everyone who knew anything about this arrangement except you and me – you will get the rest of the $1 million you demand."

"What if you abort the mission? We'd need a fee."

"That's fair," Ricci said. "If we cancel, and I don't dispatch the team, I suggest $50 thousand to pay for your time, trouble, and eternal silence."

"That is acceptable," Jones said. "But you mentioned paying us more?"

"Yes." Ricci stared into the Reverend's eyes, seeing the greed. In the end, it always got down to money and power. "We both know it is essential this be a clean operation. In particular, there are to be no trails that lead to my organization or me. None whatsoever."

"Understood."

"That has to be crystal clear, as if your life depended on it."

"I said I understood."

"After a year has passed with no comebacks and no investigations that point to anyone actually involved – other than the sadly deceased team, of course, whichever one I choose – your church will be given a generous donation."

Jones murmured. "Anyone involved…?"

"There could be considerable, ah, official interest. If any suspicion comes your way, and we hope it does not, that will be entirely your problem. My organization will remain distant from all this, and you will have no further contact with me. If your organization draws suspicion, there will be no bonus. How you deal with any such matters is your problem as well. Deception, political action, and false trails are up to you."

"False trails…." The smile broadened. "False trails. I like that."

"The bonus money will be laundered so you can report it to the IRS. I think the sum of $200,000 should suffice."

"Indeed it would. We could add it to our World Peace ministry."

"Then we have a deal." Ricci smiled. "*Grazie*. It's a pleasure doing business with you."

CHAPTER TWENTY-EIGHT
INTERVENTION

Building 422, The Presidio of Monterey, California

The President looked worse. The big machine in the corner was making more noise. It sounded as if it was straining. Its whirring noise had turned into a whine.

President Blager was facing them, his bed cranked up. He still had a cannula in his nose and tubes attached his arms. Electrodes still led to machines that monitored his vital signs, but the traces were no longer all green. Some flickered yellow, prompting soft beeps.

He was pale, and his eyes were dull. The clear tubes connected to the machine in the corner and the President were still circulating blood, but the color of the fluids going through them had changed, dark brown in one tube and brownish red in the other.

The President was deteriorating. His organs were failing, and his life support systems were struggling to keep up.

"Thank you for seeing us, Sir," Raven said. "Dr. Goldfarb couldn't make it...."

The President made a weak gesture, glancing at Josie. "Ms. Lynch, right?"

"Please call me 'Josie.' They are only going to allow us a few minutes with you."

"Can you help?"

"We can try. May I speak freely, Sir? Some of what I say may be upsetting."

"I'm not a fool," Blager said. "Tell me the truth."

"Your Doctors are beyond their abilities. I have done remote viewings of the near future. You will die in a week if something can't be done."

"I believe you. Can you save me?"

"The honest answer is that we don't know. The mentor who helped me develop my talents is a healer. I'd like to have him take a look at you."

Raven said, "He's nearby, but he's not a Doctor. There is no way we're going to be able to get him a clearance to see you alone in the time remaining, much less approval to treat you."

Josie said, "He's not likely to pass a background check."

"Does he have medical credentials?"

"None that would be recognized," Josie said. "George is, ah, unconventional."

"If you think your associate can save me, let's give it a try." President Blager gave a soft laugh. "It's not like I have a lot to lose…."

Josie heaved a sigh of relief. "Thank you, Sir."

"It is I who should thank you," the President said, "and I do. "What do you need from me?"

Raven said. "Private access for short periods. Can you keep your room empty for a half hour at specified times?"

"Yes, providing the medical alarms don't go off. Getting your friend access to the base and this room might be difficult, though." Blager shook his head. "I'm still the President, but I'm not sure I can convince the Secret Service or the doctors to…."

"That's not a problem, Sir," Josie interrupted. "Would you like to meet him? He's aware of your condition, and he won't hurt you."

Blager laughed, but it turned into a cough. Josie grabbed a wipe from the table near the bed and dabbed his face. "I'm dying, Josie. What do you want me to do?"

"Just wait, Sir. It will become clear."

Raven turned, glanced at his watch, and blocked the door, bracing himself. "Two minutes, Babe. No more."

"Right," Josie said.

In the next instant, Raven heard a rustling and a gasp from the President. He did not look back. He was leaning against the door, blocking it.

Josie said, "We're good."

A new voice spoke, deeply resonant. "I'm *Kaimi*, Mr. President. May I touch you?"

When Raven glanced back, the big Hawaiian, well over six feet and 250 pounds, was towering over the bed, touching the President's face with the fingertips of both hands. Raven turned his attention back to the door.

"She calls you George," the President said.

"Since she was a young girl. It is our little joke. My English surname was *Keoki*, or 'George' in English. I've not used it for years."

"Can you help me?" the President asked.

"Time's up," Raven said. "Move it."

"Yes," came the deep voice. Then there was a whoosh of air, followed by a rap on the door.

"Not yet. We need another few minutes," the President called out.

"Sir, your Doctor needs...."

"Five minutes," there was a snap in the President's voice.

"Yes, Mr. President." The guard's voice was muted.

Raven turned to see a frozen tableau. Only Josie and the President, looking at each other.

"How did...?"

"I can't answer, and it doesn't matter, Sir," Josie said. "We need to arrange a time for George to visit you every night. The room must be empty with the door closed. Can you make that happen?"

The President nodded. "They get done feeding me by six, and the Doctors make their rounds before seven. How about 7:30 until 8? I will tell them I need time alone to pray, and that I want the door locked with no interruptions for any reason. They should allow it."

"That would be perfect."

"19:30 hours," Raven said.

Josie touched the President's hand. "Don't give up hope."

With that they both took their leave, not speaking until they reached the parking lot."

"Hope this works, Babe," Raven said.

"Yeah...."

Private Beach House, South of Monterey, California, the next morning

"This is nuts," Black said.

Raven grinned. They were sitting at the patio table, with photos, maps, and architectural diagrams spread out. "You're going to get some religion, son."

"I'm telling you, this is a bad idea. Really bad."

"Why?"

"For one thing, I'm Jewish, white, and a registered Democrat. Why would I be attending a radical black church?"

"This is America. You can attend any church you want to."

"I signed on for technical support, not to play James Bond with a Bible. I don't know what the hell I'm doing."

"Not to worry. We have got you covered. You won't be going in alone."

"A SEAL team?"

"No, but I brought you some toys." Raven reached into the bag by his leg. He pulled out a small earpiece and a cell phone.

"I've already got a phone."

"This one's special. It is a secure cell phone, but, if you push the right buttons, it converts to a secure, undetectable COM, and a weapon. It's an experimental unit made for us by Cybertech in Oregon. Not even NSA can break their encryption. In COM mode, it uses a spread-spectrum pseudo-random code that transmits below the ambient noise level. Scanners will not even notice it.

"The earpiece is a bone phone. You put it in your ear and stick the phone under your shirt when you are in COM mode. It is voice-actuated. It uses bone conduction technology and pairs with your phone and the other units our team will have. If you speak even softly, your teammates will hear you and vice-versa."

"What if two people are talking?"

"The first person who speaks owns the channel. Operational range is about a mile if there are no obstacles. Right now, we only have three of these units. One for you, one for me, and one for Josie."

Raven gave him a quick checkout on the special features. When he was finished, he handed it to Black. "Can you work it okay?"

"No problem. What's the mission?"

"All you'll have to do is get inside, look around, and come back and report. Do you want a weapon? I've got a hide-out .357 derringer."

Black took the weapon. "I'm going to stand out. Why would I even be there in the first place?"

"You're on a date."

"Say *what*?"

"Josie will here in a few minutes, and it all will become clear."

"Clear isn't the problem...."

Raven held up a hand, cutting him off in mid-sentence. "Just wait."

Black sighed, took a deep breath, and turned to studying the building plans.

There was a knock on the door, and Josie's voice. "Honey, I'm home."

"On the deck, Babe," Raven said.

"I brought a friend," Josie called as her key turned in the lock. She appeared with a statuesque black woman, built like an Amazon. The woman wore black Nikes, a short skirt, tee shirt, and heavy gold jewelry. She was not wearing a bra. "This is Moira."

Black stared.

"Up," Josie said.

"Huh?"

"Her eyes are located higher," Josie said. "Say hello, Mr. Black."

Moira smiled at him, folding her arms across her chest.

"Hello," Black said. "I'm sorry, you caught me off guard. Call me John."

"He doesn't get out much," Raven murmured. "You're going to take him to church."

Moira said, "Dr. Goldfarb briefed me."

"I'm Raven."

"So I hear." Her smile faded. "Why isn't the FBI covering this? The last I checked, we were in the States. Isn't this their turf?"

"Our friends at the Bureau have had an attack of political correctness." Raven looked at Black. "Moira will keep you from being embarrassed in church. She has a divinity degree."

Black said, "You don't **look** like a minister."

"That part of my career didn't work out. I went to school on an athletic scholarship, volleyball, George Fox Evangelical Seminary. It was a nice little town in Oregon, but they were Quaker. Not my cup of tea, but I appreciated the education."

Black stood up, met her eyes, and took her hand. She was an inch or two taller than he was. Maybe six three. "Hi. Sorry if I was…."

"A sexist male?" Josie murmured.

The two women exchanged a look and smiled.

Black looked at Raven. "Okay, so she's the right color, looks like a good spiker, and knows religion, but this is still nuts."

"That's why it's going to work. Moira did a tour in the Marines, served in Intel in Baghdad. She has more experience than you at ground combat."

"Is that true?"

"Which part?" Moira shrugged. It made her breasts jiggle. "I wasn't much of a spiker. Too short, and I was not as quick as the small girls. Mostly I was a splinter butt. I sat on the bench, but it paid my college."

"What about the Marines?"

"That part's true. I shot expert with the M-16, but carried my dad's Colt .45 for my primary weapon."

"You're into nostalgia?"

"I'm into what works and a long gun didn't. My kills were up close. Defensive shots. Semper Fi and all that shit. How about you?"

"All that shit, but I was a pilot, Air Force."

"Hauling toilet paper into remote places?"

"Fighters."

"You kids can get acquainted later," Raven said. He tapped the plans on the table. "This is Trinity church. They are holding services tonight at seven. I want you to take a look inside."

"Roger that," Black said.

Moira frowned.

"What?"

"This needs discussion."

"We're discussing it."

"Good. I am not sure I want to go in there with you. This is a Black Liberation Theology church. You were briefed on that, right?"

"Some."

"Liberation Theology is angry and violent. It is so far from Christianity you could not find it on a map. It replaces God with Karl Marx. One of the Popes called it demonic."

Raven said, "It's a wacky religion, no argument. Look at the bright side."

"Which would be?" Black asked encouragingly.

"They're not likely to behead you like the radical Islamists. All I want you to do is take a casual look at the place. If she's worried, I can give her a hide out weapon."

"No," Moira said. "I'm good."

"I think he's saying your dad's .45 would be a tad bit obvious." Black offered her the derringer.

"I'm not worried about a weapon, I'm worried about *you*. I can get in and out easy. You might get your white ass kicked. Or worse."

"So cover me then. Take the damned gun."

"Don't need it." Moira produced a small knife from under her blouse.

Raven and Black exchanged a look.

"*Muteki* Series # 204. Neck knife. I have several, but this is my favorite. Up close, it is better than a pistol. Saved my life once."

"Works for me," Black said.

"Good." Raven gestured at the plans and photos on the table. "There is a guard, but no indication of any sensors or metal detectors. It is a church, not a fortress. Right?"

Black nodded. It was obviously a church.

"I'm thinking more like a hornet's nest…." Moira said softly. "I'd fit in. He won't."

Black said, "Because I'm white?"

"Partially," Moira said. "Have you ever seen combat? Not from an airplane, but up close and personal?"

Raven said, "He helped us get Josie out of Portland. He led a covering force into Durham to extract us from a major *jihadist* attack. He's got balls."

"I'm asking him," Moira said. "If this turns bad, can you kill *jihadis* without hesitation? We don't have FACs that clear us to engage targets. No challenge, no discussion, no ROEs, no Geneva Convention, just 'bang' between the eyes? Hard kills. A tenth of a second is the difference between living and dying."

Josie looked at him. Raven shook his head and did not speak. *Black's inclination to go gentle was something he had intended to do some ass chewing about.*

Black said, "I'll be happy to demonstrate my skills. I am great in an airplane, good with a pistol, not worth a damn with a rifle, and marginal in hand-to-hand."

They all looked at Moira.

"It's your call," Black said. "What do you say?"

"I'm more worried about what's in your head than if you can punch holes in paper. If we are in a bad spot, I need to know you will shoot to kill and deal with the rest later. Unless you can, I want no part of this."

"I'm not going to let you down. You have my word. We can go do some drills together. No mission unless you think I'm up to it."

"Agreed," Moira said.

Raven said, "I can get you a combat range and a trainer this afternoon. I want you to do some multiple-threat drills as a team for confidence."

"Thank you," Moira said.

"Try not to shoot each other."

Black gave him the finger. Moira laughed. It broke the tension.

"Have we had anyone inside Trinity?" Black said.

"You'll be the first, and I want a team. One to look and one to distract. You're in charge."

"Then we do it her way. Innocent as lambs. I'll leave my derringer in the car."

Raven said, "Take the cell phone I gave you."

Moira smiled. "If you get into trouble you can call home or take their picture."

Black said, "This is just a recon, right?"

"That's the plan. I am your over watch. I'll cover you with a long gun from outside, just in case."

Black said, "Didn't President Obama get married in a Liberation Theology Church?"

"I have no idea."

"He definitely did," Moira said. "It's a great cover story. We're engaged and looking for a suitable place to get married."

"We go in soft and lovey-dovey, holding hands and looking for Jesus. If we encounter any resistance, we just leave."

"Like I said, it's your call," Raven said. "Do it however you wish."

Black looked at Moira. "Don't forget the soft and lovey-dovey...."

She smiled sweetly. "So where's my ring?"

"Ask me in the morning."

Raven said, "I love it when a plan comes together."

CHAPTER TWENTY-NINE
SAFE AS CHURCHES

Private Beach House, South of Monterey, California, 5 PM

R aven was getting his gear together, making final checks. He had his Sig locked and loaded in a paddle holster under his shirt, and four spare magazines loaded with six rounds of Hornady critical defense ammo in his cargo pockets, two on each side.

Screw the Geneva Convention, I am a civilian.

A black nylon fanny pack held six 20-round magazines for the Mini-14, a pair of Night Vision Goggles, and extra batteries. A COM paired to Black and Josie's units was in his left vest pocket. It fed the bone phone in his ear.

Raven dropped a grenade in his right pocket, an olive drab can with yellow bands and lettering on the side. He paused, frowned, and added one to his other pocket, similar but a white can with no bands.

Josie had an odd look on her face.

"What?"

"Hand grenades?"

"You never know."

"You said it was a church. Goldfarb and the FBI will have fits if you blow it up."

"Trinity *is* a church. Not to worry. These are non-lethal."

"Those kids are going in unarmed, and you're preparing for a war."

"Those are just M12s and M8s. Totally harmless."

"They don't look harmless."

"The olive drab one is a flash-bang, the other is white smoke. These are distraction and concealment devices. I am not taking tear gas or high output smoke grenades, M34s. Those are white phosphorus. They burn at about 6,000 degrees."

Josie continued to stare at him.

"I don't expect to use these. I'm not going to be working close."

"What about the guns?"

"Same thing: Just in case. I doubt they'll be needed."

"Talk to me. If you think it's dangerous why…?"

"The reason it's safe is because they are going in like innocent lambs. The girl was right. She can get in and out with minimal risk."

"Except you vetoed it."

"Our mission is to get Intel to help target your remote viewings. We'll only get one shot at it, and two people have a better chance than one."

Josie could sense his concern. "Are you okay?"

"I don't like being the leader. I'm off safe, while those kids go in."

"Do you want me to do another remote viewing? It will take me a bit of time to get into a meditative state."

"Not yet. Just give them an over watch starting at seven when they go in, just like you did for me at Natanz."

The first time she had remote viewed him. A terrible time.

Raven's mission had traumatic consequences. She had refused to take further assignments for Rhine, and Raven had gotten crosswise with the CIA. One thing led to another. They wound up working together, eventually becoming friends, and then lovers.

Life surely has odd turning points.

"If you sense anything bad, back out and call me on the COM. I'll be there."

"Where will you be?"

"Outside." He tapped the map. "There is a taller building on the south side of Trinity across an alley. It has a flat roof. I can cover the front from there."

"You're sure this is safe?"

"Absolutely. Like the Brits say. Safe as churches."

"What a **stupid** thing to say."

"If you are talking about gun-free zones, most of the shootings have been in schools...."

"I'm talking about your stupid quote. I find it offensive."

"Huh?"

"That quote is from Thomas Hardy, a British 19ᵗʰ Century novelist. One of his characters, a beautiful girl, Tess, got pregnant, had her unwanted baby in a field, and was ostracized. Her baby died, and she had to bury him at night in a cardboard box, secretly, in shame, and without ceremony. Hardy wrote that ugly girls were 'Safe as churches.' What a horrid quote."

"I'm sorry. I know how violence freaks you out."

"Don't you *ever* tell me something is safe when you know damned well it's not. Okay?"

"It was just an expression. I was trying to say something positive. *Nothing's* safe, Babe. You know that. America's safety went away after 9-11. Both parties screwed up, and the deal debacle with Iran made it worse."

Josie took a deep breath. He was right. "I'm sorry. I'm just edgy."

"I am, too. That is what you are noticing. In a sane world with a declaration of war, there would be an FBI penetration team going in hard with backup and a warrant. As it is, we have a dying President, a politically correct, legalistic government, CYA bureaucrats, and two green kids bending the rules. That is why I am going. That's why we're both doing over watch."

"I know that. Just don't bullshit me, okay?"

Raven leaned down and kissed her. "Sometimes I screw up."

"Because you care. It's part of why I love you."

He hefted his gear, but paused at the door and looked back. "I'll cover them."

"I know you will. Just be careful. We finish this and retire."

"Yes." Raven closed the door carefully. The click of the latch was loud in the stillness.

Trinity Church, Conference Room, 8:05 PM

Raven did his COM check, and Black said we were good. They had gotten in with no problems. So far, so good. All was peaceful, and the Minister had been welcoming.

What an odd little man, Moira thought, looking up from the pad where she was taking notes. *So fiery when preaching, and so folksy and courteous in private.* "Reverend Jones, your sermon was inspiring, but we don't want to join your church. We just want to get married."

"Why?" Jones' large, owlish eyes were intense.

Moira said, "We're in love and…."

"No. Why in my church?"

"It's my mama…."

"Is she coming to the wedding?"

"No, Reverend, but she wanted me to marry in a Black church. It will be a small wedding. Just us and a few friends…."

"White friends?"

"Some. Is that a problem?"

"Mixed marriages are not something I endorse, but we have a few white congregants."

"I saw one."

That earned her a sharp look. "Where?"

Moira gave her best puzzled look. "At the service, of course. There was a distinguished looking large man, Italian looking with black hair…."

"Well dressed?"

Moira nodded. "Is he a congregant?"

"No. That is what threw me off. There were no white members of our congregation at the service. We get grants from foundations. Mr. Ricci is here for liaison work."

"Oh," Moira said.

"Have you considered the problems resulting from mixed marriages?"

Moira frowned. "If we're going to discuss personal matters like that, I'd prefer my fiancé to be present."

"Your fiancé wanted to look around our compound. I thought it best to allow that. This is your wedding, but he's not a Bro." The Reverend put an emphasis on the last sentence.

Moira did not respond.

"You need to think this through, sister. The crackers have oppressed blacks throughout America's history. They made us slaves. The Man stole our freedom…."

This is not going well. Moira feigned a friendly smile. "Reverend, we love Monterey and your old church, but I don't want to discuss politics. I am here to arrange my wedding. Mom wants us to marry in a Black church."

"I have a responsibility to counsel you to prepare you for marriage, my child. For us to be saved, we must throw off the chains of the oppressors before we are called before God. It is our only salvation. To be married here, it's necessary that you understand our teachings."

Moira smiled to soften her words. "Reverend Jones, with all due respect, my faith is between me and my God. When the time comes that I'm called before Him, I will...."

There was a sharp rap at the door. Moira stopped in mid-sentence.

"Not now," Jones called out in a tone he had not used before. There was the snap of command in his voice, not the resonant tone he used for his sermons.

"We caught a cracker coming out of the atrium."

"I said **not now**," Jones said.

"He was in your office too...."

"You know about this?" The Reverend stared at Moira.

"Of course I know. You instructed my fiancé to look around while we talked. I presume he was doing as you instructed."

"You lie to me girl, and there be punishment. Thou shalt not lie."

Moira touched the small knife under her blouse. White steel and handmade, it was sharper than a scalpel. With a fixed blade, it was to be gripped firmly and pulled from its Kydex sheath with care.

One of the things she liked was how perfectly the shape of its Arizona Desert Ironwood haft fit her hand. If your hand slipped on a knife without a guard, you would be gripping a razor. That was why Marines and SEALs sometimes wrapped the hafts of their knives with tape.

She looked the Reverend in the eyes. "I asked you to allow John to participate in our conference. You refused. He was just doing what you wanted. What's the problem?"

Jones raised his voice. "Bring the cracker in!"

The door popped open and John Black was half-carried in between two large black men. One eye was blackened and there was blood on his face. They released him and he stood swaying.

Moira rose to her feet and stepped around the table behind the Reverend, staring at the Guards. "Your men beat him! Have you gone mad?"

The Reverend did not reply.

She looked at Black. "Are you all right?"

He spit out blood, swayed, and steadied himself. Then his head came up and his eyes focused. He looked at Moira and nodded.

"What happened?"

"There's an atrium. I was looking at the plants when these goons burst in and started hitting me."

One of the men, large, wearing a black beret, a black wife-beater tee shirt with the sleeves cut off, and a big revolver strapped to his hip raised a fist. Black cringed.

Moira recognized the image on the shirt, a black cat with fangs on a white circle, with the words "power to the people" emblazoned in red. Black Panthers. Violent thugs and agitators. Revolutionaries. "Are they going beat him again?"

Jones shook his head. "No need for that...."

The man stopped and lowered his fist at a gesture from the Reverend.

"They have guns! Why do you have men with guns in a church?"

"These are my security people."

"You run a strange church, Reverend Jones." Moira stood behind him glaring at the guards. "Why would you assault my future husband? If you didn't want us to marry here, all you had to do was say so."

"There's been a misunderstanding."

"There surely has been," Moira took a deep breath, figuring the odds. She could cut the minister's throat before his men could react, but they would never get out of this room. Could she use the minister as a shield, and get his men to drop their weapons? *Not likely.*

It got down to fight or flight. Neither was hopeful. Black was waiting, obviously willing to let her make the call. She could see him taking deep breaths, trying to clear his head.

How much could he help her? *Not much.* The men were both larger and stronger, and he had left his derringer in the car at her request. He would not be a match for them.

Moira made a decision. *Now or never. We are getting the hell out of here.*

CHAPTER THIRTY
IT IS A ROUGH RIDE

Private Beach House, South of Monterey, California, 8:27 PM

Josie forced herself out of the viewing before violence started. She had not gone deep. There was no one to tend her if she was traumatized. She blinked and took deep breaths, orienting herself. Then she screwed the bone phone in her ear. "We have a problem."

Raven was there. "Go."

"They're in trouble."

"Where are they?"

"The minister's office." Josie described the location and the situation. "Black hit pay dirt, but was caught. The guards beat him. He stuck to his cover, and they took him to the minister."

"How many bad guys?"

"At least four. Two are holding Black, big brutes, armed, plus the minister.

"Moira's stalling them, trying to talk her way out. Black is semiconscious, but was coming around. Trinity has gone to lock down. The church emptied out after the service, but there were two men at the front with long guns. They don't seem to mind if anyone notices."

Raven said, "Where are they?"

"Inside the front gate, behind the wall."

"I can't see them unless they come out."

"They seemed to have fixed positions. One on each side of the gate."

"There's a side door on the North wall, used for deliveries."

Josie glanced at the plans. "In the alley?"

"Yes."

"Correct," Josie said. "There's a double door. Heavy wood."

Raven was silent for too long. "What are you doing?" Josie asked.

"Working my way over there. I think I can get to the top of the wall and cover them, but they are going to have to get out of the building on their own. I can't raise him. Can you?"

"No. Black still has his phone, but I lost COM when he went inside. He took his bone phone out and put it in his pocket."

"Their car is parked on the NW corner of the Trinity wall, by the alley. If you get COM, tell them to head for it."

"Do you want me to call Goldfarb?"

"No. When everyone is well clear, call 911. Do it then, but make it an anonymous call. Put something over the phone to muffle your voice. Just tell them that there are gunshots at Trinity Church and hang up. Understand?"

"Yes," Josie said. "I'll see if I can do a viewing. What if they can't get clear?"

"Call Goldfarb. Tell him I'm going in to get them, and to send the Marines because we're in deep shit."

Trinity Church

"We're leaving," Moira said to the Reverend. "I'm taking John to a hospital and I'm calling my mama. You can explain yourself to her."

There was a long silence. Finally, Reverend Jones nodded. "Ms. King, I'm sorry there was a misunderstanding, but this church is private property. We have excellent lawyers and the right to defend ourselves."

"Against a couple who came wanting to pay you money to hold a wedding?"

"This was a misunderstanding."

"Please ask your men to step away from the door and away from my fiancée. They frighten me."

Reverend Jones nodded and made a gesture. The two goons stepped over to the wall.

"Just a minute," Black said.

They all looked at him. The big man put a hand on his revolver.

"Let's call your mother now. At least let her talk with the minister."

What is he up to? He has no idea how to contact mama and she has no idea I am here. Moira said, "Are you sure you want to do that?"

Black nodded.

Raven said you were the lead. I hope you know what you are doing. She looked down at the minister, using him to block the guards' view. Her right hand grasped the hilt of her knife. "Is that okay with you, Reverend?"

The big guard laughed. "Ain't no way your mama gonna accept this white trash for a husband. I maybe slap him around some more...."

A wave from Jones silenced him.

Black pulled out his phone. He held it up, gestured with it, and took two steps toward the big guard, pointing it at him as if to make a point. "We can talk this out...."

The guard started to say something, when there was a muted pop. A red spot appeared on the big man's temple, and he fell like a stone.

Moira was already moving. She jerked the Reverend's head back and pressed the point of her knife up under his chin. Blood flowed. Jones tilted his head back and stretched his neck, moving away from the pain.

She lifted him out of the chair to his feet, and pressed the flat of the blade hard against his throat. "Don't move. One twist and you are dead. I want your man flat on the floor by the time I count to three."

The Reverend made a strangled sound. She was choking him.

"One, two...." She pressed harder. There was blood running freely down the knife.

"Do it," the Reverend croaked.

The remaining guard looked at him.

Moira relaxed the pressure slightly. Jones gasped, sucking in air. "Do it. Hands on your head and down on the floor, like she said. Now, fool."

The guard did not move

Black had the pistol from the big man's holster. He thumbed the hammer back, and leveled it. ".44 Magnum," he said. "Do you feel lucky?"

The man hit the floor, face down.

Black nodded approvingly. He looked at Moira.

"Don't worry about the Reverend. Take care of the guards."

"Right." Black brought the gun butt down hard on the head of the man he'd shot. There was a sickening crunch. The body did not even twitch.

Black moved to a corner where he could cover the Minister and the man on the floor.

"Put your hands on your head and get down on the floor next to your man, Reverend."

Jones was leaning on the table gasping for air. "You're a murderer…"

Black took two quick steps and laid the gun barrel hard alongside the minister's head, backhanding him away from the table. Jones fell to his knees, blood still running freely from under his chin where Moira had cut him.

Black stepped behind the minister and gave him a push with his foot, laying him out flat. "Crawl over to your guard. I want you both spread-eagled or the last sound you hear will be this cannon."

The two men took the position.

"What now?" Moira said.

"See if you can find something to secure them and keep them quiet."

The dead guard had flex cuffs in a pouch on his belt, and a spare loader for the .44. Moira found a roll of silver duct tape in one of the cabinets.

Within seconds, they had the guard trussed up like a turkey. Black checked the cuffs, and then secured his feet and hands together, slapping tape over his mouth and rolling it around twice, leaving him face down on the carpet, with his knees bent back in an unnatural position. Black removed his gun, a smaller revolver, flex cuffs, and spare ammo.

He rolled the Reverend facedown and cuffed his wrists behind him. "What about this one? You think he'd make a good hostage to get us out?"

"Those guards are Black Panthers. They'd shoot right through him to get us."

Black winked at Moira. "My thought as well. Let's cut their throats and be done with it."

Right, Moira thought. *We will mess with their minds and see what happens.* "We got a plan, my man…."

Moira eased over to Reverend Jones and again laid the knife blade against his neck. "You want I should do it quick or slow? I could start with a little cut…."

The Reverend was sobbing. "Don't kill me. I'm a man of God."

"We know you had some Iranians here," Black lied. "Where are they?"

"Hamas. Crazy fuckers. It was part of our humanitarian aid efforts, but we had to send them home."

"I want names and descriptions." Black held his phone up to record the answer.

The Reverend reeled off three names and descriptions.

Moira was impressed. *The ploy actually worked.*

"They are out of the country now?"

"I don't know. They're not here."

"How many guards do you have here?"

"Four," Jones said.

"Do you believe him?" Black asked conversationally.

"Not for a minute."

"Me neither."

"Five," Jones blurted. A wet spot was spreading on the rug and Moira could smell urine. The minister was terrified. He had soiled himself. "I'm telling you the truth. Five guards at most. Reggie's one of the congregation, but I think he has gone home. There are four Black Panthers. They don't work for me. They work for Ricci."

"He's lying," Moira said.

"I believe you're right." Black nudged the minister with his toe. "Who's Ricci?"

"The Italian your fiancée saw at the service. He's with the UN."

"Details. I want his full name." The nudge turned into a kick.

"Marco Ricci. I don't know his title."

Black was staring at his cell phone. He held it up for Moira to see. It was a text message. No COM but text was getting through. "G R O. Guards at gate. Use N Side door. H A."

"The Panthers are here as assassins, aren't they?" Moira asked.

There was no answer, just sobs.

"I'm trying to save your life, Reverend."

Jones was nodding frantically.

Black and Moira exchanged a look. She mouthed words silently, pointing at the Panther facedown on the floor. *He is afraid.*

Black nodded agreement.

Moira pointed at the door.

Black nodded again. "To hell with it. It is bad luck to kill a minister. Truss him good."

"Right." Moira wrapped up Reverend Jones like the guard, putting tape over his mouth, and then looked at Black. "Are you okay?"

"I'll live."

"If we can get out of there. You want to keep the .44?"

"Sure. What's the other one?"

".357," Moira said.

"It's yours. Consider it a wedding present."

Moira grinned. "You ever shoot a .44?"

"No."

"That one's a Dirty Harry classic, the model twenty nine. Hang on tight. It's a rough ride, cowboy."

"Roger that."

There was no one in the hall. The minister and the remaining guard were locked in the utility closet.

Moira kicked the door. "Any noise and we're going put some bullets your way. Keep still, and someone will find you after we're gone."

There was silence.

They locked the office behind them. Black had a look of concentration on his battered face. "The exit on the North side opens into an alley. We go to the left."

"I know the way," Moira said. "What was the rest of that message? H A?"

"To get clear. Haul Ass. Raven must know we are in trouble. We're authorized for lethal force."

"You're sure?"

"Positive. G R O. Gloves are off."

"So, did you know that when you shot the big man?"

Black shook his head. "I knew we'd only get one chance. That phone only holds two little .22 longs. I was scared shitless."

"Me too."

"He was already dead when I bashed his skull in."

"You did fine."

"They are growing toxic mushrooms in the atrium. I got samples along with some pot. They're growing that too."

He handed her a baggie. Moira stuck it in her pants and carefully slid the knife back in its sheath. *Large Mushrooms. Death caps. They do look like a penis.* "This is what they used on the President?"

"I'd bet on it. We have to get these samples back."

Moira nodded.

"You need to get the baggie to Raven."

"Right. Let's move. I will take point.

"I should…."

"Ladies first. I'm less conspicuous than your white ass."

"You look better too."

Moira produced a scarf and draped it over her pistol. "We go out smooth and quiet. If I see anyone with a weapon, I am putting them down. Then we run like hell."

"Works for me. I got your rear. Figuratively."

Black gave a little grin. He unbuttoned his shirt, letting it hang loose. About all he could do was to hold the big Smith and Wesson under his shirt and try to look natural. With an 8-inch barrel, it was about as easy to conceal as an antiaircraft gun.

Moira examined Black more closely. The skin was turning purple around his eye, and the whole side of his face was badly bruised. "Can you move fast?"

"I had double vision, but it's cleared. My head hurts, but I can walk. The 'run like hell' part might be a problem. If it comes to that, leave me and get out with the evidence. "

No wonder he shot the bastard. "We're both going to get out of here. Hang back a little, but try to keep up, okay?"

"I'll be ten feet behind you."

Moira took off down the hall, moving soundlessly at a fast walk. Black followed.

CHAPTER THIRTY-ONE
BLOCKED

Private Beach House, South of Monterey, California

Trinity was blocked from Josie's remote viewing. A dark miasma of violence hung over the church. She dared not go there without Raven to help bring her back if she got into trouble.

All she could do was wait and hope. Raven was there. He would check in if they were in trouble.

She sent a silent prayer for help, and was relieved to feel a friendly mental contact. Kaimi. She signaled an invitation, and instantly he was there in the room with her.

"I need help."

The big Hawaiian said, "I sensed your confusion and stress."

"We have a mission running. My friends are…."

"I know," Kaimi said. "Evil gathers. They are safe for the time being, but there is a different problem. One we must discuss. I'll be brief."

"How is the President?"

"Alive. I would like to say he is getting better. He *is* getting better, but something strange is going on."

Josie waited. She knew better than to press her Kahuna. He would explain things in his own way and his own time. "I'm listening."

"I can sense that the President's body is healing. He is getting stronger. His organs are recovering from the toxins. I'm helping them regenerate."

"Good."

"Normally, yes," Kaimi said, "but it isn't this time. That is the strange part. When I sense the President's body and spirit, I can see wellness emerging and his lifeline getting stronger. When I leave him and look into the future, I see his life ending sooner."

"I don't understand."

"Check it yourself. The trend you reported continues despite my efforts. The more the President's health improves, the shorter his life span becomes."

"That doesn't make any sense."

"No, it does not. That's why I came."

"Should I attempt to view the President's death scene myself?"

"I think not. In my own viewings, I see his lifeline strong and getting stronger, but when I jump into the future, he is dead. Between there is a gap, a blind spot."

"Why?"

"Something abnormal happens."

"Are you able to view into the Abyss?"

"No. You were wise to avoid it. There is now a gap just before it, a dead zone, where my viewing is also blocked. Beyond that gap lies the Abyss, the void."

"That's what I saw too. The present. Then a dead zone. And finally that horrible black funnel."

"Yes. The Abyss."

Josie said, "What is the Abyss? Rhine doesn't know. I've never seen or heard of such a thing."

"I think of it like a psychic black hole, or perhaps a gateway to Hell. It is extremely dangerous. This phenomenon has been observed at least once before."

"How long ago?"

"Two millennia."

Josie said, "The death of Christ?"

"Correct. It occurred after Christ's death as the world was sliding into darkness. Today historians call it the Dark Ages. The light of civilization, even of intellect, was almost extinguished."

"I sense that the President's life line goes into the dead zone, something happens in there where we can't see, and then comes the Abyss."

"I see it the same."

"Is this something new?"

"Possibly. It is a gap. I can see and touch the dead zone, but I cannot see into it either. At first, it was only a few minutes, but it is growing. I cannot view the President's death. I dare not touch the Abyss. This entire segment of space time is somehow twisted."

Josie said, "It wasn't there yesterday. I could see The President's death by poison, then the Abyss. No gap."

"Correct. That universe has split. The gap appeared when my healing efforts started having positive results."

"What should I do?"

"I'm not sure. I just needed to report that my healing is working, but not helping. I don't know why."

"But you have suspicions...."

"Those you associate with fight evil. Powerful evil. Our paranormal powers are being overwhelmed by a flood of evil. Violence may be the only way to stop it."

"Where do you detect it? Is there a focus?"

"It's all around us. It is here in the physical world. Your Raven friend holds it at bay to an extent, but it is close, strong, and it is gaining power. It is why the President is dying in the first place. His death seems to be a nexus."

Josie sighed. "Do you want to go home?"

Kaimi shook his head. "I made you a promise. I will finish this for you, but we have only a few more days. My efforts are being thwarted. I am convinced that something else kills the President, but I can't see what."

"What do you suggest?"

"Tell Raven. He is a warrior and we are not. He knows more about fighting evil than we do."

"Yes, he does. This is not the first time our lifelines have intersected."

"I know that, and you both died."

"I would have died this time, but he saved me."

"Just as you saved him. Together you are strong. Persistent legends and writings, including the Bible, teach us that human evil has periodically destroyed whole civilizations. We are now in such a time, and with technologies that can literally unleash the fires of Hell. I wish I could do more...."

"We do what we can. Thank you for coming and thank you for your help."

"I must go now." Kaimi paused, "One more thing...."

Josie looked into his eyes, seeing sadness.

"Call the man named Goldfarb."

She started to speak, but stopped when her mentor raised a hand.

"Call him now. Ignore your instructions and call him."

"Why?"

"Because you have nothing to lose and neither do the rest of us. Our world is at risk."

Kaimi touched her face gently, smiled, and then he was gone.

CHAPTER THIRTY-TWO
MOIRA'S RUN

Trinity, Monterey, California, 9:12 PM

Moira stopped at the heavy side door. It was locked. She struggled for a long moment, but could not open it.

So much for the fire codes, Black thought.

Moira looked back at him, gesturing toward the front of the building.

Black shook his head. He approached, nudged her aside, and leveled the big .44.

"My magic wand opens doors for us."

"I'm more worried about attracting attention."

"So move fast and we'll be long gone. Okay?"

"Can you move fast and keep it up?"

"Watch me."

"I won't leave you."

"You won't have to. I'll keep up."

"Okay."

"Look away, hold your ears, and run like hell when I get this open."

The shot echoed down the corridor. The big slug shattered the door and left a gaping hole where the lock had been. A kick flung it open.

Moira said something as she dashed past him, but Black's ears were ringing, and he missed it. Later he would wonder what she said. She took off along the wall toward the car, moving like a gazelle.

Black struggled to keep up. His head and chest hurt. He felt dizzy. His breathing was not right. Maybe he had broken ribs.

Moira paused at the corner of the wall and he gained some ground. She was peering around the corner, looking for hostiles. She did not wait. She must have judged it clear, because she sprinted toward the car.

There was a shot. Moira stumbled. She was falling when she disappeared around the car.

Black moved right. He saw the shooter, clear in the moonlight. Another black beret, but this one was holding an AK. The man fired short bursts. *Kak kak, kak kak, kak kak.*

Black heard the rounds punching into their rental car. There was no return fire. It was long for a pistol shot, but he swung the big .44 and snapped off a shot. The gun kicked high, a clean miss.

The big magnum had a long, heavy trigger pull and was impossible to hold steady. His arm tingled from the recoil, his ears were ringing, and he felt dizzy. There was no way he could rapid-fire effectively.

It would have to be single shots and the next one had to count. He was not going to get another chance.

Black watched the AK swing toward him. The shooter popped in a new magazine.

He went to one knee to take up the two-hand supported, and laid the gun on high center mass. At least it had tritium dots on the sights.

Thumbing the hammer back, he braced the revolver with both hands. With the front sight bold and sharp as death in the notch of the rear, he squeezed.

Cocked, the trigger pull was better, short and crisp. The hand cannon boomed like the end of the world. This shot went home, dead center. Black saw it hit.

The big slug rocked the man back like a rag doll, but he was still on his feet.

Oh, shit. Body armor.

He would have to try for a head shot. He fought to pull the big gun back on target.

A fleet of 7.62s rocketed overhead, inches from ending it forever. Black dropped prone, seeking the ground for a calming influence to steady the heavy revolver. Again, he lined up the sights. Again, he thumbed the hammer back, knowing this was his last chance.

Where the hell is Raven? Why isn't Moira shooting?

Then the man's head exploded, and he was down.

CHAPTER THIRTY-THREE
THE PROMISE

Trinity, Monterey, California, 9:27 PM

Black was sitting on the ground by the car holding Moira in his arms. Raven approached carefully. His bone phone was working. He could get Josie, but not Black.

So much for low profile. Goldfarb is going to shit. Now all we need is a friendly fire incident. He sang out, "Coming in. Hold your fire."

Black said, "My hearing is coming back, but my ears are still ringing." He did not look up. He was breathing raggedly and there were tears running down his face.

"We are clear," Raven said. "Two dead guards at the front gate, plus the one out here. Let's get out of here."

"She's dead."

Raven pulled his shooting gloves off, leaned down, and gently touched Moira's throat. There was no pulse. Her face was serene, unmarked, but her blouse was stained dark with blood.

He took the body from Black and gently laid her on the ground. There was just the single wound, but the bullet hit major arteries. The entrance wound in her back was small, but her chest was ripped open. The round must have been tumbling.

Moira would have bled out quickly, if the shock did not kill her first. *There was no hope of surviving that much damage. She never had a chance.*

Black said, "Where were you?"

"Doing my job, same as you. Except for Durham, I have lost friends on my past three missions. Good friends."

"That doesn't fucking help!"

"Easy. It's over. Keep it down."

Black took deep breaths. "It doesn't help."

"No, but that's how it is."

"Do you ever get over it?"

"Not really. They told me I would, but they were wrong. I still have ghosts. They accumulate." Black was covered with blood, his face was bruised, and his eyes were wild in the moonlight. "You look like hell."

"They worked me over pretty good. Moira got me out."

"Did you find anything?"

"Yes," Black said. "She didn't die for nothing. I got a name, Marco Ricci, along with samples of the mushrooms that were probably used on the President. They are planning a follow-up attack. They had an Arab kill team at Trinity initially, but shifted to using Black Panthers."

Black extracted the baggie from where Moira had hidden it. He gently kissed her forehead, and then handed it to Raven.

"Ricci is running the kill team?"

"Either him or the minister, Reverend Dilbert Jones. There seems to be a leadership dispute."

"Where are they?"

"Jones is tied up in a store room in his office, along with a guard and the body of another one. Ricci bugged out, but he was at the church service tonight."

"Description?"

"Italian. Looks like a Mafia Don. Well dressed. About 5' 10," 250 pounds, black hair. Funny eyes: Yellow-brown, and intense. Like a bird or something."

"No one like that came out." Raven stood up and looked at the car. It was trashed. The 7.62 slugs had punched out most of the windows and flattened at least two tires. There were puddles of fluids under the car. He could smell gasoline.

"We'll have to leave it."

"I'm not leaving her!"

"Easy. We will take Moira's body, but I don't think that car is going anywhere. Is it clean?"

Black looked at him as if he was crazy. "What do you think? Look at it. The left rear fender and tire are smeared with her blood."

"The papers. Are the papers clean?"

"It's a rental. We used false ID."

"We'll burn it. I will get you to my vehicle. I want you to get Moira back to the Presidio, tell Goldfarb, and give what you found to Jordan Harrington personally. Can you walk?"

"One way to find out." Black struggled to his feet and stood swaying. "Where are you going to be?"

Raven handed him a set of keys. "I'll help you to my car and get my own transport back. I need to do some clean up."

"You're going to kill Ricci, aren't you?"

"I'm going to tidy up."

"That's not an answer."

"If I find him, we're going to have a talk. Maybe we can go waterboarding together. I liked Moira. She is dead. We have been under attack since Durham, and now they have tried to kill the President. I'd like it to stop."

"The ROEs said minimal force. You told me the FBI has declared the church off limits."

"The ROEs got Moira killed. Political correctness and legalistic prissiness. Do not talk to the FBI or Harrington, just to Goldfarb. Tell him what happened here is my responsibility. We used inadequate force."

"What's the body count?"

"I think five, so far, counting Moira." Raven looked at the big .44 in Black's hand. "You killed the guard you got that cannon from?"

"Yes."

"He was the one who beat you up?"

"Yeah. He was a scary guy."

"Not any more," Raven said.

"No...."

"You did the right thing. In the field, we do what needs doing."

"I don't think I'm cut out for fieldwork. It sucks."

Raven could see Black was close to cracking. "Right now you need to Cowboy up and finish the job. Fuck the protocols if it gets down to your life or your team. Take down the bad guys and blame it on me. Understand?"

"Yes, Sir."

"Good. Let's go."

Raven pointed at the alley across the street, and then helped Black gently lift Moira. "Are you sure you can carry her?"

Black gave a short laugh. There was no humor in it. "What's the choice?"

Raven held his Mini-14 out, barrel up. "I could carry, and you could cover me."

"No. You are the pro. You are better with personal weapons. Just cover my back."

"Roger that." With Raven's help, Black slung Moira's limp body over his shoulder. He took several deep breaths.

"You got her?"

"Yeah. I can do this."

He sounded like the little train. *I think I can, I think I can….* Raven handed him the .44 and picked up his Mini-14. "Are you sure?"

"I'm not going to leave her."

"Agreed, but if I start shooting, get down, and get to cover. If it turns to shit, I want you to get your ass out of here. Leave her, leave me, get to my car, and get your evidence back. You will not do either of us any good by hanging around. Can you do that?"

"Yes."

"When you get to the other end of the alley, hit the clicker and my car lights will flash. It is a gray Taurus. Drive slow and legal, but if you are taking fire, you punch it and run as if you have a rocket up your ass. The vehicle has some armor."

"Roger that."

With Black clear, Raven was heading back to Trinity when Josie checked in.

"We're clear, but it's a bad time. Can I call you back?"

"It's important." Josie said.

"Black is on his way back. They hit pay dirt."

"Good." There was a long pause. "What about Moira?"

"We lost her."

"Oh, my God."

"It's been a goat fuck out here. We had to shoot our way clear. Moira was hit, and Black is in bad shape."

"They were becoming close."

"That too, but the guards worked him over pretty bad. He needs medical care."

"How are you?"

"Pissed off. It is a bad time to talk. I'm going back to finish this."

"No," Josie said.

"Excuse me?"

"No, you're not. I spoke with Goldfarb. He is on his way here. He instructed me to give you some orders."

Oh, Shit. "I'm listening."

"I'll quote him. He said, 'Any Cowboy bullshit and I'll throw you to the wolves.' If we get a break and find the control – which you have – he wants them untouched."

"I'm not sure I heard you right."

"You heard me okay, and we both know it. Goldfarb says espionage depends on disinformation. He wants us to get ahead of this."

Raven was silent for a moment.

"Did you hear me?"

"Yes."

"Repeat it back."

"Untouched. Espionage. Disinformation, instead of force."

"There's more. I agree with Goldfarb."

"What?"

"I said, 'I agree with Goldfarb.' You need to listen to me."

Raven moved into the deep shadows and sat down. He needed to concentrate and finish the conversation. "I'm going back to tidy up."

"No. Don't do it. Follow your orders, for once."

"I have a good chance of getting the leader of the kill team."

"It doesn't matter. There will be another one. And another one after him."

"He can tell me who he works for."

"Maybe, but I can find that out too, with your help, and much more. The main thing is Goldfarb believes us. We are on the right track. This is not just about Iran. He's shifting his focus."

Raven said, "Iran is where it started. America is at risk as long as they have nukes. Their Constitution mandates it."

"Yes. That threat continues, as do counter OPS, but Goldfarb has Intel that Iran is out of the command loop. They are tools. This is higher level. This is a domestic threat. We have enemies within."

"Even so, I'm close. I can…."

"It doesn't matter. Tell me this: Are you running into any Arabs or Iranians out there?"

"No, domestics. Black Panthers and wacky religious nuts, but…."

"Think about it. **You promised me.** We are partners. We get to retire and have lives."

"Yes."

"I want us to end this, move on, and get out. They can throw killers at us endlessly, year after year. You mow them down, but they will keep coming. We almost lost our whole team in Durham, and now we've lost Moira and maybe Black."

"He's just a little battered around the edges."

"Don't change the subject."

Raven said, "Spell it out. What's next?"

"Iran's nuclear attack on America failed, so they shifted tactics. Our enemies are now trying to topple our government by killing our President. His death is the key event. It unleashes chaos."

Wheels within wheels. Layers of conspiracy. Puppet masters. "I've got a question."

"Go ahead."

"Who is **they**? If it's not Iran, then who is it."

"It is Iran, but this is planned, enabled, and empowered by people in Washington. Think about it. The deal to give Iran nukes came from Washington and the UN, not Tehran."

"It did. Who's selling us out now?"

"We don't know enough yet, but Goldfarb is convinced the threat comes from high-level insiders. The President thinks so too."

"The President is dying...."

"We must prevent that. The main thing is this. If you go rogue, you're not going to do Moira any good, you're not going to do America any good, and you're going to lose Goldfarb's support."

Raven sighed deeply. "This is a bad time...."

"It's the only time we have," Josie said. "There's more."

"Go ahead."

"If you don't come back in, you'll lose me too."

"You don't mean that."

"I *do* mean it. You are making a big mistake. Do not go Rambo on me. We can do better. Please come back."

Raven was silent for a long time.

"Are you still there?"

"I'm thinking...." *Women. Why do they make it so complicated?*

"I love you. Please come back in. We are a team. We can end this and be happy. Listen to me. Please."

Raven took several deep breaths. He stood up and set the safety on his carbine. The night was quiet, and the click seemed preternaturally loud in the stillness. "I trust you, Babe. Hell, I even trust Goldfarb. He might be right on this one."

"Are you coming back in now?"

"Affirmative. I just have a few details to attend to."

"No more killing. Okay?"

"Not even if they piss me off?"

"*No.* Self defense only. Just come back safe."

"Not to worry. I need to handle some transport issues. Black has my car. When you get Goldfarb, tell him I am coming in, that Black is on the way to the Presidio, and that he needs to keep the FBI off his ass. It would be best to have Harrington meet him at the gate. Most of the blood isn't his, but he could use some medical attention."

"Understood. I can reach Goldfarb. I'll be waiting for you."

"You did good, Babe."

"We're going to be okay."

"Roger that. I'm coming back."

CHAPTER THIRTY-FOUR
BETTER OR WORSE?

The Presidio, Monterey, California

Goldfarb had taken over Shapiro's office again. It was secure and close to the President. Josie and Raven were there to brief him.

Goldfarb said, "Do you have a good fix on this Ricci character? The Agencies do not have a thing, neither does Defense. He does have a UN file. He is an Italian national, an assistant undersecretary for some kind of obscure global coordination. He has a background with various social and environmental NGOs. Saving the world from things like Global Warming."

Raven said, "What's he doing in Monterey?"

"No idea."

Josie was studying the red file folder she had been given. "The photo will help, but physical objects are best for finding him. Can you grab me some personal items?"

Raven said, "He's running a kill team. Why not just grab him and save some time?"

Goldfarb frowned. "Forget about it. The Bureau already has a bad case of pucker over your church raid. Don't even think about rousting a UN official."

"It turned out well, considering. Nothing...."

Goldfarb held up a hand. "Stop. No interrogation. Is that clear?"

"We need something physical," Raven said. "She doesn't have enough to focus her viewings."

Josie pushed, "It would help a lot."

"We have no legal grounds for a search."

"It's not like we have a lot of time...."

"How about something from his desk at the UN? A sneak and peek. That would not take a Judge or a search warrant. It's not US soil."

"A physical object," Josie said. "Anything would help."

Goldfarb jotted notes on the pad in front of him. "I'll work on it."

"New topic. There is nothing in the news about Trinity, which seems to be a minor miracle given that you were leaving shell casings and bodies all over. And a burning car."

"The bodies and shell casings weren't ours. Black used a revolver, I policed my brass, and we brought Moira home."

"Why didn't the church report you killed their guards?"

"There are two possibilities. Either God smiled upon us, or we ran a superb covert OP and deserve kudos and accolades."

"You're not going to sell me on the second," Goldfarb said dryly.

"Maybe we got lucky. I'll take that."

Goldfarb shot him a dirty look.

"The car burning was to conceal evidence. It worked. We had an agent down and another injured, but we put out smoke, covered our tracks, and got clear. Black and Moira did not leave a trail. They were just an innocent couple looking to get married."

"I doubt they endeared themselves to the minister."

"You debriefed Black. What's your read on Reverend Jones?"

"He's a celebrity, politically connected, and runs a high-profile radical left church."

"Not the minister stuff. As an enemy operative how well did he handle this, ah, incident?"

"Poorly. He is clumsy at best, and incompetent at operational matters. His Panthers overreacted. They are thugs looking for trouble. He is using radicals with criminal records as paramilitaries, just as Hitler did with his Brown Shirts. That only works if you have a Supreme Leader to cover things up and control the courts, which he doesn't."

"Not yet. Not so long as President Blager is alive."

"Good point." Goldfarb took some notes. "Keep talking."

"It was in our best interest to keep the incident low profile. Apparently, the bad guys embraced the same logic. I expect the Reverend knows they screwed up. The Panthers initiated violence to intimidate. It spun out of control. Do you think he's happy about that?"

Goldfarb made more notes on the pad. "No."

Josie was watching the interplay, trying to assess what Goldfarb was thinking. Even with her sensitivity, she could not tell. *Raven is doing a lot of guessing.* "We need remote viewings to validate our assumptions."

Raven said, "There are important things we don't know. The Reverend said he was in charge. What he did reveal may have been false."

"Noted."

"We can learn all that and more with remote viewings. Reverend Jones does not want the police or media involved. I'd say understandably so, especially if Trinity is, or was, being used as a forward base to finish off the President, don't you think?"

"What do you think?" Josie said. "We could use some guidance here."

"I'm not sure what I think. What I **know** is that you have no evidence. You are just guessing. And Raven is trying to cover his ass for not staying clear of Trinity."

"I **did** stay clear. Two private citizens attended a peaceful church service and inquired about planning a wedding. They were attacked. I helped them get clear."

"Not Moira."

"No, but we brought her back. It's unlikely the bad guys know she's dead."

"We'll know more when I do my viewings," Josie interrupted. *That wasn't fair.*

"We know some things already. Ricci is gone, *poof*, and the good minister's still there preaching his gospel of hate, just like nothing happened."

"Which brings me back to my main point," Goldfarb said. "Why didn't Reverend Jones report something? What does he have to lose, with the Panthers and Ricci gone? You can bet his church is squeaky clean by now."

"He's afraid," Raven said.

"Of what?"

"Of us, maybe. He is maybe afraid of retaliation or legal action. Of the Panthers, for sure. They can't be happy over having their buddies killed. He may be afraid of Ricci, of his boss, or of Ricci's boss. Alternatively, of whoever is behind them. Who knows? The main thing is that he did not report anything. He doesn't want official attention or publicity."

"I'll grant you the last point. The rest is just guessing."

"The rest is informed professional opinion. It might be time to put an agent inside. Given what happened, and the stakes, maybe the FBI will wake up and do their job."

Josie said, "Surely, someone has reported this to law enforcement. Why would people ignore gunshots and burning cars?"

"Most people keep their heads down these days," Raven said. "We're on the way to becoming a third world nation."

Goldfarb said, "There were no police calls made, except for the car fire. There are over a million illegals in California, a million property crimes per year, and a quarter of a million vehicle thefts. There's lot of drug gang violence, most of it unreported. Gunshots are not uncommon in that neighborhood. There were riots when public benefits were cut."

"It's not like Oakland or East LA," Josie said. "This is an upscale town."

Raven said, "If you lived there and saw Black Panthers shooting at people, would you call the cops or get involved?"

"Perhaps not, but a brave woman was killed getting information. Why aren't we talking about Moira? Don't we owe it to her to continue this?"

"You can field that one, Doctor. We had no backup. Again."

"You had no approval, and this is a bad time for second guessing."

"Moira's dead, but the President is still alive. Support was late in Durham and nonexistent here. You may have to bend a few rules, but we need to get serious about killing the bad guys."

Goldfarb took off his glasses and started cleaning them. "I'm aware of what has been accomplished and the sacrifices made. We can grieve and honor Moira after we have finished our mission. Right now, there is a larger issue facing us. It's why I came back."

"The President," Raven and Josie chorused.

"Yes." Goldfarb put his glasses back on. "I've spoken with him. Are your paranormal methods actually healing him? He says yes, but will not discuss details or methods. He said I should speak with you."

"I wondered why I was here," Josie murmured.

"Well, now you know. Might he live?"

Josie was silent for a long moment. "It's complicated."

"I'm sure it is, but I require a simple 'yes' or 'no' answer. Will the President live?"

Josie shrugged.

"This is probably the most important question you'll ever be asked, and I need an answer. Our nation may depend on it. My course of action certainly does."

"Who lives or dies depends on God. Do not lay that on me. You know the limitations of paranormal viewing, Doctor. I can offer insights and glimpses, not proof, never guarantees."

Raven said, "Easy. There's no certainty, but tell him what you can."

Josie sighed, and then nodded. *Goldfarb is a pain in the ass, but he has the connections to help if he wanted to. The President trusts him. We need his support.*

"He may live. There is a chance, but the situation is baffling."

Goldfarb frowned. It obviously was not what he wanted to hear.

"Would it be more useful if I just said I didn't know? It's the truth."

"His doctors used to say he was dying. Now they say they don't know. You said he might live. That doesn't help me at all."

"Give him details," Raven said.

"Dr. Goldfarb demands assurance about outcomes. I don't have it."

"I'll take details," Goldfarb said.

Josie looked at him.

"Opinions. Details. Insights. Just tell me what you can."

"The President's organs are regenerating as a result of our interventions. His health is improving."

"Significantly?"

"Yes."

Goldfarb's said, "So he's going to live."

"No. I can't say that. I wish I could."

"Don't quibble," Goldfarb said. "You are telling me that he's likely to live."

"No, I'm not. His health is improved, but my viewings indicate that the President dies **sooner**."

Josie sighed. *He doesn't get it.* "If you push me for a yes or no, my answer would have to be 'he will die.' I'd have to tell you that we've failed and that he's dying sooner than if we'd done nothing."

"Sooner?"

"Yes. At present, our interventions have **shortened** the President's lifeline. In that sense, we've done harm, not good."

Goldfarb stared at her.

"Since Blager was poisoned, I have **never** remote viewed a future where the President didn't die soon. It now seems he'll die sooner and healthier."

"The better he gets, the sooner he dies?"

"That's what I'm seeing. I just get glimpses."

Goldfarb said, "That makes no sense whatsoever."

"The interventions work, but the more the President's health improves, the more compressed the probability space-time of his lifelines becomes. His health is improving, and his future is changing, but not for the good. Our efforts do not change the outcome. He dies sooner."

"And you don't know why."

"Correct. Not a clue."

"And this Abyss thing that kills viewers is still out there?"

"Yes. I am blind except for the near term. I can't see into or past the Abyss. I can't view the President's death. I don't know why."

"Tell me what you do know."

Josie started talking.

CHAPTER THIRTY-FIVE
MUSLIMS AND GLOBALISTS

The UN Building, New York, UNICEF House

Vogel glanced at his Gold Rolex and adjusted his cuffs to show a little more sleeve. "I have an important dinner scheduled tonight. I am going to be asked questions. Gott in Himmel, you haff a simple task to do in California, and show up back here. You call me on the way to New York, but tell me nossing. Why do you vaste my time?"

"The Americans are excellent at intercepting communications, Sir. I didn't want to talk on a phone, even if the call was supposedly secure."

"There hass been nothing on the news. Is Blager dead?"

"Yes, Sir. He is." Ricci squirmed uncomfortably as Vogel's eyes drilled into him.

"Then vy iss diss not on the news? The White House says he's on vacation."

"He still breathes, Sir, but he is dead. He remains on life support. He's dead, but they've not disconnected him and declared clinical death."

"How long can diss go on?"

"There have been cases where machines have kept dead people alive in a vegetable state for months, even years."

"Diss must not be one of them. Our plans cannot move forward until death is official and there is a transition of power. It is time to end this."

"Yes, Sir. May I ask a question?"

Vogel nodded.

"Why was the Black Minister put in charge instead of me?"

"In charge? He vass not in charge."

"Someone neglected to inform him of that. Who does he work for?"

"Vee are all part of the movement. He vorks for us."

Ricci frowned. "But not for you? Is that what you are saying?"

Vogel looked away. Ricci took a deep breath. "I was not told that."

"What happened?"

"The Muslims were running this, weren't they?"

"Before you, Ja. You know that. Firouz. You replaced him. It was deemed best to not have additional Iranian connections."

"The *jihadists* took exception to this?"

Vogel made a dismissing gesture. "The Muslims didn't like it, but our allies in Monterey were as unhappy with Firouz as you were. He got one of their assets killed. Reverend Jones was furious."

"The Black ecoterrorist."

"Correct," Vogel said. "Mister Tre."

"I doubt that was the reason. The Reverend is a racist. I think he hates Arabs, and I know he distrusts them."

"With reason, my fellow infidel." Vogel laughed. "Do you trust them?"

"No, of course not. But I can work with them."

"The Muslims are steeped in hatred and betrayal, but they are fierce fighters, good hosts, willing to die, and totally ruthless to our enemies. If you are their guest, you are safe. They are useful, but only a fool would trust them beyond narrow limits."

"Only a bigger fool would trust Reverend Jones. Islam has the Koran, but Liberation Theology knows only hatred for the presumed oppressor, which is anyone unlike them or more successful than them, which, of course, is everyone else, including us."

"The Reverend is successful. He's a celebrity with high level political connections."

"Who is also narcissistic, insecure, and prone to bad judgment. Everything that could go wrong did go wrong."

"Enough." Vogel made a dismissing gesture. "None of us is perfect. We have many disparate groups working to change the world. Even if what you say is true, and some of it is, what difference does it make? Tell me what happened."

"Firouz had a Hamas kill team lined up. Reverend Jones vetoed it. He removed Hamas. That is where it started to fall apart. That's what I was left to deal with."

"Firouz had a highly motivated team," Vogel said. "How could Jones interfere? Muslims would never take orders from the Reverend."

"It's not about orders. It is about access. Jones refused them access to Trinity, his church, our OPs base. He ordered them to leave."

"How did he justify diss?"

"He said they were too visible. He said the ability to employ Hamas effectively is limited. The place where Blager chose to die is inside a heavily guarded military facility. It would have been difficult to get a Muslim kill team with weapons and bombs inside."

"Difficult, yes, but not impossible. We have assets inside."

"We do, Sir. They argued against using Hamas."

"Argued this to you personally?" Vogel demanded.

"Yes, Sir."

"On what basis?"

"The leader said the President was dying anyway. She said there was no need to take more risk."

"What risk? Hamas would die in the attempt. That is how they work. They die for Allah, joyously. No loose ends."

"Not for them, but it would leave local assets, including her, exposed. The Reverend thought that just having Hamas there put his church at risk."

"Why didn't this come up before?"

"Firouz and the Iranians have a different agenda than we do."

"Do not force me to ask questions," Vogel said. "Are you saying they are traitors to their own Revolution? Death to America is core to the Islamic Republic of Iran. It was built into their Constitution in 1979."

"Sir, we all want the President dead and a transition of power. That is the plan, agreed to by all. The difference is that Firouz, Hamas, and the Iranians prefer violence. They want an event that would exceed 9-11, a major terrorist attack that kills the President while he is protected by his Secret Service and in the middle of a heavily guarded green zone."

"And then to use the event for recruiting."

"Yes."

"A major symbolic attack. Yes, Islamists do prefer such things, especially the Iranians. They celebrate victories, and put monuments and mosques on their sites. They would happily overkill America and Israel with nuclear weapons, just to make their point and spread fear. Next to that, I expect they'd prefer to behead Blager and make a video."

"Exactly right, Sir. Jones wanted him dead, but with less collateral damage."

"So what happened?"

"Reverend Jones replaced the Hamas team with American citizens, Black Panthers. His argument was that he ran a Black church and that they would fit in. They did blend in, but they do not fit our needs. They do not have a military mind set. They are street thugs. I could not control them. He didn't try."

"And…."

"For cover, the Panthers were tasked with providing security for his church, Trinity. Without authorization, they set upon a young couple, outsiders who'd come in to arrange a wedding."

"Why?"

"I don't know. Only one of them survived, and his story made no sense. The woman was Black, but her planned husband was white. It offended the senior Panther, who beat the man badly. Somehow the couple turned the tables, killed the team leader, and escaped."

"Vhat do you mean, escaped? It wass a church. How did zay escape? They just walked out and went home. Is that what you tell me?"

"No, Sir. Trinity is a walled complex. The Panthers were guarding it. Those at the gate had automatic weapons. There was a shoot out, a firefight. The Panthers died in the mêlée, plus one of the normal Trinity church guards."

"This young couple fought their way past a team of heavily armed guards? That does not seem plausible."

"I don't know, Sir. The minister and the last remaining Black Panther were tied up and locked in a utility closet. I found them and set them free, but by then it was all over. For all I know, the fools shot each other. I didn't stick around."

"So you just left?"

Ricci nodded.

"Then what happened?"

"You would have to ask the Reverend. There has been nothing in the news. I assume he cleaned everything up, disposed of the bodies, and went back to waiting for President Blager to die."

"What about the Hamas team?"

"The team is intact. We're getting them a new safe house, Sir."

"This is not all your fault. I am sending you back to Monterey. Do what you need to do, but get this done."

"Yes, Sir."

"This is taking too long. I don't want to hear again that President Blager is dying, when the fact is that he lives."

"No, Sir, but…."

"Go on, but no excuses."

"It might be better if he just succumbed. He will die soon. It is only the machines that are keeping him alive."

"You have a week. That is all. Do you understand me?"

"We can get a kill team in, but not back out. There is no need…."

"That's not your concern."

"You put me in an impossible position. The Black Panthers would not take orders from me. The Hamas team would not take orders from either me or the Reverend."

"I will see that Iran gives emphatic and specific orders that Hamas will accept your targeting. They will obey such an order. You will be able to direct the Hamas team as you wish and supply them such weapons as you deem appropriate.

"Your job is to get them to the target. They will kill the President and die in the process. Does that address your concerns?"

"Yes, Sir."

"Understand me, *I want Blager dead*. I do not in the least care how he dies, I just want him dead as soon as possible. Unplug him if you wish. Smother him with a pillow. Shoot him in the head. Or blow up the building. Only the result matters. If this is bungled, I assure you that you will wish you had gone in with the Hamas team and perished with them. Much depends on this."

"Yes, Sir."

"Good. One more thing. This couple that fled the church. I want them identified and located. It would be best if they met unfortunate accidents. Whatever resources you need will be supplied."

Ricci said, "Some misdirection would be useful. Even with diplomatic immunity, I'd prefer not to have the Americans looking for me."

"What kind of diversion?"

"I was thinking of perhaps leaving some false trails to the Reverend."

"Do what you need to do," Vogel said. "Just don't leave any tracks that lead back here, or to our superiors."

"How much does Reverend Jones know about our plans?"

"His knowledge stops with you and Firouz, nothing more." Vogel laughed. "We agree on more than you know, Mr. Ricci."

"Sir?"

"I don't trust him either."

CHAPTER THIRTY-SIX
PARANORMAL PARADOX

The Presidio, Monterey, California

Josie had been over the same ground several times and was getting exasperated. "That's just how it works, Doctor. Some think the human race, long ago, was more adept with paranormal powers then we are today. Racial myths would so indicate. Why do you think it might be that this talent faded?"

Goldfarb said, "No idea. Do I care?"

"You do. Back during the Cold War, when paranormal viewings were a big deal, when Stanford and Rhine Institute and Congress were not embarrassed by the subjective nature of the art, what was it about the viewings that justified the investment? What were their taskings?"

"The difficult ones, of course."

"No. If it was merely difficult, the Agencies still used conventional intelligence methods. Paranormal talents were reserved for the *impossible* taskings. That is what justified us.

"The signature cases that justified funding for paranormal viewings were *all* quests for what was impossible to know. Curiosities like Ingo Swann's famous viewing of a ring around Jupiter in the early '70s, tactical near successes like identifying where the Iran Embassy hostages were being held, but especially the strategic breakthroughs like identifying the Russians' Typhoon class SSBN missile sub. All the legendary paranormal successes were like that."

"I know the stories," Goldfarb said.

"The issue is informing action. Getting people to do something. Let me refresh your memory. One of our viewers described a new type of large Soviet submarine with eighteen to twenty missile tubes being constructed in secret at their Severodvinsk facility in a remote, land-locked building. This source described the *future* construction – I stress the construction had not yet even started – of a canal to launch the vessel, and provided a time frame for the launching."

"I recall the incident. It was a long time ago."

"Good. Recall then, that our paranormal, impossible-to-obtain information wasn't trusted and wasn't deemed actionable."

"Correct," Goldfarb said. "But in this case the National Security Council was sufficiently interested to retask our KH-9 satellites to cover that time window continuously. As a result, we got two good pictures."

"A year or so later. And in the case of Ingo Swann's viewing of Jupiter's rings, no one believed him until years later when NASA validated his viewing. Need I go on?"

"What's your point?"

"It's simple, but important. Our leaders believe in the wizardry of technology, but dismiss or neglect the more powerful wizardry of the human mind. Don't you find that odd, Doctor?"

"Not at all." Goldfarb shook his head. "Think of the Cuban Missile crisis. The intelligence community knew about those missiles for months, but it was only when the Navy did an illegal low-level over-flight and got Kennedy pictures that America acted and initiated the blockade. When the stakes are high, it's easier to convince politicians of truth in pictures, than of truth in some vision or sketch drawn by a mystic."

"You are mistaken. It is not about *truth*. It's about human bias."

"You're splitting hairs."

"No, she's not," Raven said. "Remote viewers are a way to know the unknowable, even if through a glass darkly. You need to understand that if you are to employ Josie's talents effectively. You need to stop worrying how Congress would giggle if it ever leaked that we trusted paranormals."

"I'm not worrying. Nothing is going to leak. What we do stops at the President."

"Stops **with** the President, who is dying," Josie said. "Paranormal methods are our last, best hope to save him, but pointless if you are not willing to act on what we learn."

Raven said, "Even more important, you need to understand your viewpoint is outdated. Photos are no longer actionable proof, and you know it."

"I do?"

"Sure. What if I had brought high-quality photos back from inside Iran's nuclear weapons vault at Natanz? Would any preemptive action by America have resulted? Not bloody likely. Look at the Obama/Kerry deal debacle."

"I'd prefer not to," Goldfarb said.

"The only way I got out of Natanz was as a result of Josie's viewings, Sir. That is about as actionable as it gets. She saved my ass. I took action without proof, based on what I saw with my own eyes."

"You're posing hypotheticals. I need information that is actionable by outsiders."

Josie said, "Nothing I do will ever be actionable by outsiders. Not unless you and the President, through your own power, choose to make the inexplicable actionable."

"She's right, and you ignore that at our peril," Raven said. "The term 'our,' in this case, being inclusive of the President's life and our nation's security."

"Trusting photos is no better than trusting remote viewings," Josie spoke, keeping the focus of Goldfarb's attention on her. "I'm the last person to lecture you about technology, but even I know that any teenager with a computer can doctor photos to make them look real."

"You exaggerate and overstate." Goldfarb waved an arm dismissingly. "There are forensic photo analysts who testify to support images. They can't do that for your viewings."

"That's bullshit, Sir," Raven interjected. "It's also a circular argument."

Goldfarb glowered. Josie suppressed a smile.

"Have you ever been through the details of all the crap they put into digital forensics these days, now that we're supposed to play nice and give terrorist killers civilian trials?"

Goldfarb shook his head.

"There *is* no proof, Doctor. Reality and fiction overlap. There is at least as much truth in thriller novels as in network news or Intel reports. Both parties voted by large majorities to approve the Iraq war, which later proved to be an unwise strategy.

"The main thing was that as soon as the war became unpopular who had approved it and led the charge – leaders of both parties – was forgotten. The result was dead Americans, a Vietnam style bugout, and a political blame game that continues to this day."

"Your point is?"

"It gets down to who you choose to believe. I once had to listen to two days of testimony from FBI experts. We had a high-res photo of a terrorist whom I helped nab toting a bomb into a subway. It showed his face clearly, but he got off."

"Why?"

"What the forensics experts do is track something called fractal discrepancies. They look at images under electron microscopes, infrared scanners, and sometimes even break it down to sound waves and look for noise. It costs a fortune, takes a long time, and still seems generally useless for legal proof. At least that is what I gleaned from the judge's acquittal.

"The image of the terrorist was clear. One expert argued the frame contained discrepancies, two said it did not. The judge found reasonable doubt and dismissed the case."

"So now you're a photo expert?"

"No, but we had the right guy. The defense argued the photo was bogus, and that knuckle-dragging Muslim haters were framing his client. The question the judge parsed to decide was simple. Was the photo 'authentic' or 'inauthentic?' There was no clear answer."

"How can there not be an answer?"

"What the experts look for is smoothness of images, patterns of relationship between pixels, the length of shadows, color consistency, lighting intensity across various parts of the photos, and a dozen or more other things like 'clone-stamped' areas. It's very technical."

"Right," Goldfarb said. "And, in the end, it turns photo evidence into proof."

"No, it does not. The FBI forensics people told me that there is no answer to 'authentic,' that the best you can do is to prove a lack of evidence of photos being doctored. In this case, the testimony was 'no indication of the presence of fractal discrepancies which would suggest photo manipulation techniques had been employed.' It's all subjective."

Josie said, "Absence of evidence is not evidence of absence."

"You're splitting hairs again. What comes out of all this is legal proof that the picture is authentic, that no one doctored the photo."

Raven shook his head. "No first-rate expert would ever so testify. The best he or she would say, with a string of weasel words about the level of detail the lab can detect and so forth, is 'no tangible evidence of fractal discrepancy.' That's as good as it gets."

"It would be good enough for me."

"But it's entirely subjective. In the end, you just trust an expert opinion."

Goldfarb frowned at him.

"A futurist named Toffler, back in the 90s, said, 'The sophistication of deception is increasing at a greater rate than the technology for verification.' He argued that it meant 'the end of truth,' and he was right. Josie's viewings have as much truth as does photographic evidence."

Goldfarb's frown deepened.

"You've worked in intelligence all your life, Doctor. Was there ever any certainty?"

"Of course not." Goldfarb said, "But I do miss the Cold War. There was more clarity."

"Was there ever any proof? Even back then?"

Goldfarb sighed. "Not much. Just the photos."

Josie said, "It might save us all some time, if it gets down to subjective expert opinion anyway, to trusting your experts in the first place. In this case, that would be me."

Goldfarb stared at her.

"Alternately, if you don't trust her, send us home and get someone you do trust."

"There is no such person."

"Then we have a problem," Josie said softly. "It gets down to faith, and I think you need to decide what you choose to believe if anything is to go forward."

Goldfarb was silent for a long time. Finally, he said, "Keep talking."

"Allow me to summarize," Raven said.

Josie nodded at him and smiled. *Thank you.*

"We keep bumping into two hard truths that you seem to think are mutually exclusive." Raven held up one finger. "The President's health is improving, as result of paranormal intervention." He held up a second finger. "The President is dying sooner, also as a result of the same paranormal intervention."

"I absolutely agree," Goldfarb said. "Now you tell me how that helps."

"What if **both** of those facts are totally, absolutely true?" Josie said. "Why don't you assume that, believe that, cling to that truth, and see where it leads you?"

Goldfarb was frowning.

Raven is getting through to him, Josie thought. *He needs to figure this out himself. If we tell him, he will be skeptical.*

Finally, Goldfarb said, "Where I get to is this: President Blager's death isn't caused by health."

"Yes."

Goldfarb looked at Raven, who said, "Keep going."

"Something else kills him."

"That's what we think. Not the results of the mushrooms."

"It's the only possibility I can think of," Raven said.

"So go investigate it. Do one of your viewings."

"A viewing you've admitted you will distrust because it isn't proof? We'll do a viewing, of course, but we'd like you to employ some deduction of your own first."

Raven said, "We agree it gets down to faith, Doctor. What does your judgment tell you?"

"Someone else kills the President."

"Correct," Raven said. "This is good news, because it's actionable."

Goldfarb said, "Access to the President is highly restricted. It has to be someone close enough to get access with something lethal."

"More," Josie said. "It would likely be someone who would know for a certainty that taking extreme risk to kill the President was necessary."

Raven said, "They would have to know for sure that he was recovering, that he'd survive the poisoning attempt. Otherwise they'd just wait and let him die from the previous attack."

"The more he recovered, the more urgency they'd feel to mount a second assassination attempt," Goldfarb said. "That's why Blager's lifeline gets shorter."

"It wouldn't be an attempt. It would be action, quick, violent, and certain."

"That's our logic," Josie said. "What do you think?"

"The logic is sound," Goldfarb said thoughtfully. "This would be a short list of suspects. Everyone who has access to the President has been thoroughly vetted. They are all impeccable."

Raven said, "If you shoot at a King, you'd better kill him."

"What are you saying?"

"They wouldn't take a chance on a single assassin. It would likely be a redundant attack."

"Is that what you'd do?" Goldfarb said.

"I've never assassinated a head of state. If I did, it would probably be from a distance, or through others, given that I prefer living."

"A remote kill device, a long gun, or a suicide team," Goldfarb said. "Not one of those is probable."

"Improbable doesn't mean impossible. What else?"

Goldfarb said, "The only people with good access are the Secret Service and the Medical Staff. People deeply inside."

Josie nodded. "As you said, impeccable. Who watches the watchers? Since my local viewings are blocked, you need to be fully alert."

Goldfarb said, "I should trust you, get out of the way, and let you do your job. You should continue with viewings to find the kill team, and in aiding the President's recovery."

Raven said, "Here's the key thing. Finding them is not enough. We will not get legal proof. Do not expect us to. Are you willing to issue a blanket kill order if we find the terrorist team and its control, based on paranormal evidence?"

"I am. Unless the President overrules me."

"That's what we need. I would keep this discussion on a close hold, Sir. Just you and him."

"I'll advise the President that I've given you a greenlight and let you know."

"Let's confirm it tomorrow," Raven said. "Not here. Breakfast at our place?"

"Agreed." Goldfarb looked at Josie, "Thanks...."

CHAPTER THIRTY-SEVEN
WHO BENEFITS?

Private Beach House, South of Monterey, California

"He's early," Raven said. They were sitting on the patio, sipping coffee, and watching the security cameras on the laptop he had set up. They watched a dark car come up the long driveway in a cloud of dust. It stopped at the front door, and Goldfarb got out. Alone.

He looked around, searching the grounds, and started towards the front door.

"He looks nervous," Josie said.

"We had some upset when Goldfarb snuck in on me back at the Ranch. I stuck a gun in his ear."

"Nothing like building confidence and working relationships."

"I was a bit twitchy. He startled me."

"Are you going to be on your good behavior?"

"Like a choirboy, Babe. If you'll make some more coffee, I'll go fetch him."

"Behind you…"

Goldfarb, about to knock on the door, jumped, and then turned. "Jesus."

"We're off the grid here, so I put up some security cameras and motion sensors in the woods. I didn't want you to think I was getting sloppy again."

Goldfarb eyed the Mini-14, hanging loosely, muzzle down. "Furthest thing from my mind."

"Were you followed?"

"Not that I could tell. I ran CSRs. I doubled back several times, and stopped to watch the ocean in a place where I could see my back trail. Your roads are so sparsely traveled out here it's easy to check for tails." He looked at his dust-covered car. "I burned half a tank of gas getting here. Where'd you find this place?"

"We got it from a private owner, a reclusive novelist who likes to keep homes in remote places. We rented it under an alias." Raven gestured at the door. "Go on in. Josie is making coffee, and we have bagels. If you'll let me borrow your keys, I'll be right behind you."

Raven checked the vehicle for bugs and tracers. It was clean. The car did not have a built-in GPS, which was good. Then he started the engine and checked it again.

When he came in, Josie and Goldfarb were watching the monitor. "Did you find anything?"

"No. It's clean."

"You're paranoid. I haven't forgotten my tradecraft."

"Nothing personal, Sir. I am trying to keep this as a safe house. Other than you, no one knows we're staying here."

"What about Black and Moira? Tell me they weren't here when you probed that Black church, Trinity."

"She's dead and he won't talk. We are getting near the end game. Do you blame me?"

Goldfarb took a sip of coffee. "Actually, I don't. If the President's security has been penetrated, we're all at risk."

"An isolated small team. Targets on our backs. No covering force."

"Thank you," Josie said. "For taking our warnings seriously."

"Harrington is having independent background checks made. We have doubled the security. No one sees the President alone and no weapons in his presence."

"Except for that pistol you've got in the clamshell holster under your shirt...."

"Does it show?"

"There's a body scanner and other sensors in the doorway. It is amazing the goodies you can pick up on the civilian market these days. I'll be sending you a bill."

Goldfarb said, "Harrington is packing too. He said he'd not carried a personal weapon for fifteen years."

Raven safetied his rifle, leaned it against the wall, and poured a cup of coffee. He sipped it and smiled thanks at Josie. "Any progress?"

"We're still keeping a lid on about Black and Moira, but her parents will have to be told. Black has a concussion and is on medical leave. We are going to arrange a private funeral for Moira, a closed casket with no announcement. The President wants to see she gets a medal and her mother is informed when all this goes public."

Raven raised an eyebrow. "President Blager's active and involved?"

"There's been a conspiracy to keep it concealed how well he's been doing. He no longer uses the machines except when others are in the room. Only his personal physician is allowed to monitor his vitals. He is only to keep paper notes and sworn to secrecy."

"We got his greenlight to proceed?"

"Yes." Goldfarb glanced sharply at Josie.

She smiled at him, the picture of innocence.

"What about the Secret Service? Are they running security checks?"

"Constantly, along with surveillance. Nothing abnormal so far. Harrington is having the FBI do it again under the directive of cover of a counterterrorism exercise. All with access to the President are under surveillance when off Presidio grounds. What else do you need?"

"What about the church?"

"Trinity is under surveillance. Nothing is happening. No Black Panthers. No Hamas. Nothing on the news about an incident there. We have taps and bugs in place, and are working on getting an agent inside."

"I want us to see the files, logs, summaries, and analysis. I'd prefer that you be our only contact."

"Agreed. I will get you updates daily. What else?"

"I presume everyone with access to the President is staying on the base?"

"Except for special out-of-town visitors like you, yes."

"Can you keep us off the grid?"

"We can try. Harrington says he'll do what he can."

"No logs for us, of course. I want copies of the logs for every time people with access were checked in and out of the gates, into that building, or into his room."

"The Secret Service has all that. There are no logs for you and Josie, except for your original visit under the Ron Browning identity. The protocols you wanted are in place."

Raven took several deep breaths, thinking. He looked at Josie, then back at Goldfarb. "Good. Now let's talk about the unmentionable."

Goldfarb frowned.

"You're an old Cold Warrior, Sir. What was the highest state of alert the United States has ever reached?"

"DEFCON 2, during the Cuban Missile Crisis." Goldfarb had a haunted look in his eyes. "I'll never forget that one. DEFCON 2 has only been used twice, thank god. SAC was all the way to DEFCON 2, but the rest of the country was at DEFCON 3. It was one of only six times in history that DEFCON 3 has ever been used."

"There is a precedent then, for putting some forces on high alert, but not others?"

"Yes," Goldfarb said. "Contrary to the movies and videogames, it's hopeful theory. Brave men pray that such contingencies are never needed."

"What about 9-11?"

"It was the fifth time for DEFCON 3. The sixth was the squabble over Iran's nukes after Israel, Egypt, Jordan, and Saudi Arabia hit them."

"I'd like you to privately float an idea to the President to start thinking about."

"Go ahead."

"Does he have the authority to order FAST PACE for his local environment? Not nation-wide, just enough to ensure his personal security. Can he declare that?"

"How did you know FAST PACE was DEFCON 2?"

"Sources and methods, Doctor, are never discussed. It does not matter how I know, but I would like us, including Josie and the President, to discuss that scenario. You didn't mention it, but the Joint Chiefs briefly took some forces to DEFCON 2 at the beginning of Operation Desert Storm."

"They did indeed. Oddly, the President made a similar suggestion to me."

Goldfarb looked at Josie. "With your powers, you could find out anyway. FAST PACE is a code word. It moves the nation to DEFCON 2, but by using that nomenclature, it can serve as a warning to the military that this is only an exercise with weapons hot. In fact, neither of the previous two uses of DEFCON 2 was worldwide."

Josie shivered. "Is this justified?"

"For the President's assured survival as Commander-in-Chief in a high-risk environment? Hell, yes."

Goldfarb nodded. "That or the threat of a hot war or WMD attack is justification. We went to DEFCON 3 over an axe murder incident at Panmunjom, Korea on August 18, 1976."

Josie said, "We're discussing truly horrific events."

Raven said, "We're trying to prevent them."

Goldfarb said, "It's a precaution. There is much we do not yet know. We will work on multiple levels to learn these items. We need to know who was involved in the first attempt to assassinate President Blager, and who is planning and staging for the next one.

"A higher alert status would prevent danger, not increase it. We prepare and plan to ensure nothing horrific can happen. Whatever the Abyss is, we don't want it. What we are talking about is one way to help prevent another attack, but you remain our best hope."

Josie said, "I'll do a viewing."

"Some things can be known. He can help you target your viewing."

"He's right," Goldfarb said. "When investigating crimes, the police have sayings like, 'Follow the money.' It serves as a methodology to help them focus on suspects."

"*Cherchez la femme.* Look for the woman." Raven said. "In France they always suspect sex as a motive. Women so easily lead men astray."

Josie said, "Only because men are so easily crazy as loons."

Goldfarb said, "The key concept here is, *Who benefits?*"

"Right," Raven said. "If the President dies, who comes to power?"

"Oh," Josie said.

"Indeed. We need you to search for who benefits during your viewings."

"Yes, Sir."

Raven nodded. "We will need you and the President to consider exceptional methods. We need solutions for how to best protect him if the normal systems break down."

"Methods assuming that it may not be possible to trust our own security forces?"

"You get my drift, Sir. Will you do that?"

"No." Goldfarb shook his head.

They both blinked and stared at him.

"You don't get to pass this one off, Raven, so you can go do your lone wolf thing. We are into a place where there can be no mistakes or misunderstandings," Goldfarb said. "It's best that we *all* sit down and discuss this with the President before you start breaking the rules. I need both of you as part of that discussion. Is that clear?"

Josie and Raven exchanged a look. She nodded.

Raven said, "Crystal."

"Good." Goldfarb stood up and held his hand out for his car keys.

"Thank you, Sir," Josie said.

Goldfarb managed a grim smile. "The President and I appreciate what you have done. We are sorry about Moira, but I need you to get on with your viewings. Can you do that?"

"I'm good. We'll start as soon as you leave."

He looked at Raven. "I've got to get back. Help is coming. You have a greenlight for action as you deem appropriate, but we need to find you targets."

"I'll walk you to the car, Sir. Thank you for your support."

CHAPTER THIRTY-EIGHT
CONFUSION AND ADJUSTMENT

Building 422, The Presidio, Monterey, California, Two days later

They did not log in. Harrington escorted Josie and Raven to the President's room. He rapped on the door. "They're here."

"Two minutes." It was Goldfarb's voice.

Harrington turned to the young Secret Service agents. "Who is in charge of security?"

"Here in the building, Secret Service handles it because of the President's presence. On the base and at the gates, it is the Marines. They have tanks and Humvees with .50 Cals to back up the perimeter guards. A squadron of Army Apache helicopters is on call for air support."

"What instructions were you given?"

"To guard this door in pairs, four-hour shifts. Access for you, plus two unnamed guests you personally vouch for, and Doctor Goldfarb."

"No one else?"

"Not unless the President specifically authorizes it."

"What about the medical staff?"

"His personal doctor is cleared. Otherwise, access only in pairs and with your permission, Dr. Goldfarb's or the President's, Sir."

"What else?"

"You saw our two agents in the lobby?"

Harrington nodded. They were hard to miss, with MP-5s openly displayed, dark suits, and radios in their ears. They had done identity checks, checked photos, made him and Raven display their weapons, and verified their signed carry approvals with the President's signature.

"There are two more at the rear door, and six on stand by. There is a Marine squad on the perimeter behind the concrete barricades that surround the building. No vehicles except for ambulances are allowed in the parking lot, and those are searched."

Harrington looked at Raven. "What do you think?"

Raven looked at the agents. "How do you know we're the same people who were checked through up front?"

"It's a short access list, Sir. We have your descriptions and photos memorized. Plus you were tracked on video all the way from the lobby to this room."

Raven looked at the younger agent. "That so?"

The agent nodded and tapped his earpiece. "I'm on that channel, Sir. Any sign of a switch and they give me an alert.

"There are other protocols as well. You were videoed at the gate, and we know the normal travel time between there and this building. If there are anomalies…."

"That's enough detail," Raven said. He looked at Harrington. "Is this for real?"

"I'm not sure I understand you."

"Do they have live ammo, or is this like Beirut?"

In 1996, despite early warnings and a high state of alert, the guards for the barracks at Khobar Towers were not issued live ammunition. Their weapons were unloaded. A suicide bomber in a fuel truck loaded with a ton and a half of explosives had crashed the gates. The explosion brought the 8-story building down, killing nineteen and wounding 372.

It was an embarrassing Islamic terrorist victory. The terrorist at Khobar Towers was trained and funded by Iran. American Rules of Engagement, both on and off the battlefield, had been a troublesome issue ever since, especially after 9-11. In 2010, General Stanley McCrystal was fired, his distinguished career ended, for publicly objecting to self-imposed ROEs that prevented defensive airstrikes or artillery if there were civilians in the area. It was the first time in over half a century that a top combat general was dismissed in wartime.

*It was madness. Terrorists were **all** civilians. They were illegal combatants who did not wear uniforms or follow any laws of war. They used women and children for human shields.*

"Live ammo. Here, on the perimeter, and at the gates."

The Secret Service agents nodded. "With one in the pipe."

"May I see your weapon?" Raven held his hand out to the senior agent.

"We have a protocol for that as well, Sir. It involves leveling hot weapons at you. Do you wish to proceed?"

Raven nodded.

The younger agent pulled his sidearm from a shoulder holster, stood back about six feet, centered his weapon on Raven, and assumed a combat stance. "Ready."

The senior agent drew his pistol, a Springfield XDM, popped the magazine out, ejected a round, and locked the action back. He handed Raven the weapon butt first.

The round was a half-jacketed hollow point. There was nothing politically correct about being hit with one of those.

"You like the .45?"

"I do, Sir. It's got authority."

Raven handed it back. "It only holds 13 rounds."

"Thirteen plus one, Sir. If that won't get it done, it's just not my day."

Raven smiled. "What level of force is authorized?"

"Lethal force after one challenge within this building. Outside it's a matter of command judgment. Immediate lethal force is authorized if an intruder runs a check point or fails to stop."

The older agent racked the slide and holstered his weapon. He looked at his assistant. "You can stand down, Tim. The Marines shot the tires out on a delivery van yesterday. No injuries, but it got everyone's attention."

"How do you get supplies in and out of this building?"

"Push carts, Sir. The Marines help us with that."

Raven said, "It looks good to me."

"I hope so," Harrington said. "Goldfarb didn't want heavy weapons inside the building. We can go in now."

Masjid Abu Bakr Mosque, Fort Ord, CA

Ricci preferred furniture, but he was sitting on a rug with his feet tucked under him, sipping spiced tea. He eyed Kamal, the Hamas team leader, a small man, with a beard, olive skin, and a scar on his left cheek. "I apologize. There was some confusion, but it's sorted out now."

Kamal shook his head. "I think you do not adequately understand operational matters. Little about this is satisfactory. Our last location was much superior."

Ricci wondered why a Palestinian would have a British accent. The man sounded like a Cambridge Don. "How so?"

"Trinity Church was a walled complex. It was in a neighborhood where there was little police presence, and was quite private. We had easy access to the Presidio. Here we have a long drive with many eyes. This building is small, open, and almost a tourist site. There are people with cameras everywhere. Americans are racists. They hate Muslims and tend to notice us."

"Trinity Church is not available." *Best not to mention the firefight.* "Among other things, the minister objected to your presence."

"He is a problem?"

"Not at present. He has been."

"I warned of this. Reverend Jones is political, weak, and a fool. He never wanted our presence, only your money. I spent time in Somalia and Kenya. The Blacks are backwards in their thinking. Why do Americans tolerate them?"

"I'm not an American, so I can't really say." Ricci did not want to argue. He had served under Kofi Atta Annan of Ghana when he was UN Secretary-General, and greatly expanded its powers and funding. He had seen what the man from Kenya had done to change America, to curb its pride, arrogance, and false sense of exceptionalism.

"I discuss my operational imperatives." Kamal's dark eyes flashed. "Surely there are other churches, other Mosques. Many places shelter illegals. We should seek them out."

Ricci said. "None that are available are close, and this topic wastes our time. You must adapt to reality. You are here for a contingency that may not even happen.

"Our sources report that President Blager is dying. Most likely, you are here to spend a few days in a pleasant spot. Then you get to go home, having served Allah. You will return richer, and better for the experience."

"You are certain of that?"

"No man can be certain of the future, but, yes, I'd say it's likely."

"If Allah is willing...."

"There is no cure for the President's condition. We have good sources inside. They report the President will be dead in hours. That is the best outcome. We should let events transpire."

"The best outcome is a victory for *jihad*. One that would humble the Great Satan." Kamal smiled. "Picture photos of President Blager's severed head on the Internet, or images of his death in a fiery explosion. It would help our recruiting. *Allahu Akbar*."

"You are here under my orders. Your leaders in Hamas have cautioned you that this is a sensitive matter. Much is at stake, and you will not jeopardize it for a recruiting video. Results are needed, not propaganda."

"I know my orders," Kamal said. "My men and I have been respecting our mission constraints. *Come to America and train.* We did. *Leave America like thieves in the night.* We did that as well. Now we are back, as ordered."

"You get to issue the order to activate us, but, after that, I am in charge operationally. I accept your command and your constraints, but I get to choose the means we employ after you issue the kill order. Once released, we are an arrow in flight: There will be no interference or second-guessing. Is that agreed?"

"It is. So long as it does not jeopardize the mission."

"I'm afraid you have already jeopardized my mission, Mr. Ricci. We have no weapons, explosives, or equipment. When we left they were abandoned."

"I jeopardized nothing. Reverend Jones ordered you out because you made him nervous. He preferred other means, perhaps because of your own conduct.

"You make me nervous as well. The **only** mission requirement – I cannot stress this enough – is that the President is dead in no more than six days. How he dies is irrelevant to our cause, what matters is that he dies."

"I understand my mission orders," Kamal said. "We argue needlessly. Control your discomfort and get our weapons back so we can do our job."

"I shall, Mr. Kamal. Give me a list. If I cannot retrieve your weapons from Reverend Jones, we can get what you need from the drug gangs in LA. Just give me a shopping list."

"If we are to perform in six days, I will require our weapons in three, and a place to practice with live fire exercises. This tiny mosque isn't suitable."

"I'll do better than that," Ricci said. "We have a secondary objective for you, a soft target, a young couple who upset the Reverend's plans and caused us inconvenience. You can practice on them."

"A young couple? What happened?"

"To be honest, no one is certain. Reverend Jones replaced your force with Black Panthers."

"Street thugs. He is a fool."

"A young couple came to Trinity asking to hold a wedding, one black, one white. His Panthers beat the man, the couple retaliated, and they escaped."

"The man was white?"

Ricci nodded.

"How did the couple escape?"

"That's not clear. Apparently, the woman had a knife. At least one of the Panthers was shot with his own weapon. The Reverend is unwilling to discuss it."

"Hamas would not tolerate such incompetence."

"Whatever happened, all but one of Reverend Jones' Panthers were killed. That one was left tied up with the Reverend. Neither of them saw the escape."

"Incredible. How can this be?"

"I don't know. They may have shot each other. The good news is that this did not attract attention from the police or the media. We need to keep it that way. I'm to conduct a clean up."

"By killing the couple?"

"Yes, of course."

"How about the Minister?"

"No. That is definitely **not** authorized."

"As you wish." Kamal barked a short laugh, and rose to his feet. "What you ask shouldn't pose any difficulty. It will be good practice for my men.

Just get me our weapons, photos of the targets, transport, and their location."

Ricci stood, and then bowed slightly. He knew the Muslims preferred that to handshakes. "It's a pleasure working with a professional, Mr. Kamal."

CHAPTER THIRTY-NINE
REMEMBER WHO WE ARE

Building 422, The Presidio, Monterey, California

Harrington did not enter himself. He let them in and closed the door behind them.

The room was even more crowded than last time. In addition to the medical machines, there was a small desk next to the bed, and folding chairs.

The President was out of bed, off the machines, and seated at the desk. He looked good and was holding a yellow folder. "I've reviewed your viewings. They are remarkable."

Josie smiled. "Thank you, Sir. I hope they're useful."

Goldfarb said, "We're identifying the players, and validating your sketches." He proceeded to fill them in about Marco Ricci and his past connections. He finished with saying, "Ricci is back in town. He visited Trinity Church. We got good photos last night and a tape of a meeting with the pastor. Apparently, before the Black Panthers, there was a Hamas team based there."

"Before?" Raven said.

Goldfarb nodded. "They were ordered out by the Reverend, apparently, not long before the incident. He thought they might attract attention. It is why Ricci dropped in. They left weapons that he wants back."

"Do we have a list?"

"We do. AKs. RPGs. Grenades. A lot of Ammo. Ricci did an inventory."

"Where are they now?"

"We don't know."

"Where's Ricci?"

"Same answer. We don't know."

Raven said, "You're kidding, right?"

"It's my fault," President Blager said. "Josie's viewings are not legal evidence. On my orders, we did not share that information. The church is only being watched."

Goldfarb looked at Josie. "Now that we have the photos and tapes and talks of weapons, we can ask the FBI to put Ricci under surveillance. It would help if you could do a viewing to find him before we set them on the trail. We think he's in the area."

"Yes, Sir," Josie said.

"Along with a Hamas kill team?" Raven said.

Goldfarb said, "Why else would he want the weapons?"

"Marvelous," Raven said.

Josie put a hand on his arm. *Easy, my love.*

"You were briefed on our heightened security?" the President asked.

"Yes, Sir."

"What do you think?" Goldfarb asked. "The FBI, Secret Service, and military think it's adequate to stop a kill team."

"It seems robust, but I'm not an expert in executive protection."

"Do you have any comments on other aspects of my viewings?" Josie asked. "There was a lot I didn't understand. A lot of loose ends."

"The content was remarkable," Goldfarb said. "We know the person Ricci meets with at the UN, the one you sketched with the big Rolex, Dr. Claas Vogel. He is a Swiss National, a multi-billionaire. Some call him the new Soros, but he keeps a low profile and has not crashed any currencies that we're aware of."

Goldfarb handed Josie an eight-by-ten black and white photo, and she passed it to Raven. It was the man she had sketched.

Raven examined it, nodded, and passed it back to her. "Vogel works for the UN?"

"With the UN, actually, not for it. Vogel made his money in natural resources, including oil. Now he has become altruistic and serves as Chairman of the World Economic Forum."

"I know him," President Blager said. "Not well, but we've met."

"Here's another," Goldfarb handed Raven a photo of a woman. "She's of more immediate interest."

This one was a four by six, in color. "Who is she?"

"One of my doctors," President Blager said.

"Dr. Susan Stein," Goldfarb said. "She's American and has been on staff for some time. Her husband works for the State Department. They met in Iraq, when she was working for the World Health Organization. The rules at State now prevent husbands and wives from serving at the same station, so on his last assignment, she decided to stay here...."

"Where's her husband?"

"You don't watch the news much, do you?" Goldfarb said.

Raven shook his head.

"Her husband's name is Ira, Ambassador Ira Stein. Does that ring any bells?"

"No."

"Ira Stein is a unique asset," President Blager said. "He's been missing for several months. His last assignment was working for me."

"What makes him unique, Sir?"

"I'll take that one," Goldfarb said. "Stein is fluent in several mid-East languages, including Arabic, Hebrew, and Farsi. He has dual citizenship, US and Israeli. His father served under and was trained by Henry Kissinger. Ira has served under both parties as roving Ambassador to the Mid East. He disappeared from Southern Iraq sixty-seven days ago. His driver was killed, and he vanished. No one has taken credit for the act."

"What city?"

"Basra."

"Down near Iran, and a seaport where they could easily extract him." Raven said. "Does the wife still have access to the President?"

"Restricted access, about once a week" Goldfarb said. "Either Harrington or I make it a point to be present during her visits."

"How many red flags do you need?"

"I've known the Steins for years," President Blager interrupted. "I was at their wedding. They both have top clearances. I trust them implicitly."

"What's her specialty?" Raven said, looking at Goldfarb.

"Disease pathology."

"I presume you're aware this is a security nightmare?"

Josie put a hand on his arm.

"As you've admitted, executive protection is not your expertise," Goldfarb said. "You've seen our security arrangements. What more could be done to protect him?"

"We can get the President the hell out of here, for one thing," Raven snapped.

"What are you suggesting?" Blager asked.

Josie cleared her throat. "Before we get to that, there are a few other details about my viewings that you might want to review first."

There was silence in the room for a long moment. Finally, Blager said. "Proceed."

"Do you recall my notes about what I couldn't see?"

"The Abyss thing?" Blager said.

"Yes. In addition, I now cannot view the end of your lifeline, which is soon, about three to five days if I had to guess. There's a gap between that and the beginning of the Abyss."

President Blager nodded.

"We talked about that," Goldfarb said. "It's on my list of things to discuss. What's the significance?"

"I don't know. I have never seen anything like it. Neither has Rhine. But, whatever it is, I think it's dangerous."

"That's why I want us to get the President out of here," Raven said.

"Raven has a theory," Josie said.

"But no paranormal ability," Goldfarb said.

"I'd listen to him. I really think you should."

"Go ahead," President Blager said.

"When we first looked at this, the end of the President's life line was clear. It preceded the initiation of this Abyss."

Heads nodded.

Josie said, "The common thought was that the President's death initiated, or was timed to coincide with, some monumental, cataclysmic outside event. Right?

"Yes," Goldfarb said.

"Do we all agree?"

Heads nodded.

"I didn't hear any other explanations that made sense," Blager said.

"Good," Josie said. "Here's the key point. The end of your life and the Abyss used to be sequential. When we started healing you, the two events separated. The Abyss did not move in time – it seems fixed – but your lifeline has shortened. Now there is a gap between its end and the Abyss. The gap has been growing. It has now become a dead zone that blocks my viewing."

The President nodded. "Can you say more about that?"

"I'm sorry. My paranormal senses are blind. I dare not view the Abyss closely, and I cannot view the end of your lifeline. It gets…. blurry. I just can't see."

"Dr. Goldfarb told me that. Is there anything you *can* tell us?"

"I wish I could, Sir."

"I can, Mr. President," Raven said. "There's one small problem with your current security procedures."

President Blager raised an eyebrow. "Small?"

"Tiny. I almost hesitate to mention it."

"Please do."

Raven said, "Your procedures do not work. You are going to die soon, somewhere inside this dead zone where she cannot see. That's what her viewings are telling us."

"Is that what it means?" The President was looking at Josie.

"I don't know. It could be."

Blager stared at her intently.

"This is something new. I am seeing a blur when I try to view the future. I can no longer see the end of your lifeline, your death. What I see is your lifeline becoming a blur. Another way to say it is that your lifeline splits into myriad possibilities, a gray fog of indeterminate probabilities, after which comes the Abyss."

"It looks like death to me. What else could it be? That's why I want to get you out of here, Sir."

"Spell it out, Raven," the President said. "What are you suggesting?"

"I've spent a lot of my life off the grid with powerful enemies looking for me. One thing I know: If they can't find you, they can't kill you."

"You want me to run and hide?"

"I want you to live, Sir."

President Blager and Goldfarb exchanged a long look. "What do you suggest, Aaron?"

"Sir, I can't advise you in this. It's terrifying to think that our best efforts wouldn't be able to protect you, but…."

"Go on," the President prodded. "Say it."

"You know how I feel about Vice President Dunbar. With every fiber of my being, I think it would do great and lasting harm to our nation if you died in office and he replaced you.

"For all I know, when we speak of the Abyss, we unknowingly speak of Dunbar and his actions in the future. You are my Commander in Chief, and I serve you and our Constitution, but I do not know what to recommend. I'm sorry, I just don't know. It's your call."

"There's no evidence for this, other than remote viewings?"

"No, Sir. None."

Josie shook her head. "Just the viewings. Other remote viewers glimpse this future as well, but none of us knows what it means. The Abyss is so dangerous that Rhine has shut down its viewings."

A long time seemed to pass. The room was totally still. Josie could hear her own breathing. She could feel her heart beating. Finally, the President shook his head. "No."

He looked at Raven. "I can't do that. I was elected to serve the American people. I am not going to run and hide from the responsibility of my office. It is not about me, it is about the Office. I am not leading America if I am off hiding under my bed. I must say no."

Raven said, "Your mind is firm about this?"

"It is."

"There may be another way, Sir."

"Go ahead."

"Time is running out. We are not sure how you will be assassinated. We do not even know who was behind the first attempt. We are getting closer to learning where the evil is, but the future outcome is unchanged. There is an intelligence and purpose working against us."

"That's just a theory," Goldfarb said.

"Yes," Raven said. "But it's all we've got."

Goldfarb looked at Josie. "You're the paranormal. What do you say?"

Josie said, "My viewings are blind. Raven's theory fits the facts as we know them, but that's still a long way from knowledge or certainty."

"What's your other way, Raven?" Blager demanded. "I get the feeling everyone here knows what's coming but me. Stop pussyfooting around, people. Let's get this over with."

"It's simple but ugly, Sir," Raven said. "We start eliminating the likely suspects, and see how the future changes. My vote would be to start with Vice President Dunbar."

"You mean, kill him?"

"If the gap and the Abyss vanish, we'll have gotten the right man."

Goldfarb said, "Or maybe not, if the kill team – the one we can't find – is already activated and does its job anyway."

"True."

Surprisingly, the President laughed. "It seems you don't like Duncan either. There are many people in my administration who share that feeling."

"It's not personal, Sir. If I went around killing all the assholes in Washington, there would be no end to it. The reason Dunbar is a key disconnect point is simple. With him gone, few, if any, of our enemies would consider assassinating you."

"He has a point," Goldfarb said. "Speaker Ross is seen as a bit of a right wing Hawk, Mr. President."

The President stopped smiling. His face was somber. "Thank you for your loyalty, but I've got to say no to this option as well. Running and hiding would destroy my personal honor and perhaps besmirch the office of the President, but a cold-blooded murder, even if deemed preemptive, would destroy our nation's honor. If I'm to die, it won't be as a coward or a traitor."

President Blager looked at Raven. "We need to be clear on this."

"Yes, Sir."

"Don't misunderstand me. This is not about plausible denial. It is about our integrity, yours, our nation's, and mine. There has to be a bright and shining line between good and evil, between us and the bad guys. You know that. If we ever lose that, we lose the America we love."

"I understand you, Sir. Duty, Honor, Country. I took that oath myself a long time ago. It is not necessary that we kill Dunbar. We could just take him out of circulation and see if your lifeline probabilities extend."

"It might…." Goldfarb started to speak, but the President cut him off with a gesture.

"My answer is still no. Once we start down that path, it's a slippery slope," the President said. "I distrust the bastard myself. He is certainly the one who benefits most if I die in office, and we all know it. But it does not matter. I do not want him killed out of hand. Or even taken off to interrogate."

"I understand, Sir. Tell me what you want us to do."

"I think we should pray, Raven. That's what I've been doing."

"Yes, Sir."

"Bring my Administration evidence that the Vice President is a traitor and we can have an impeachment and, if convicted, perhaps hang him."

"I'm not good at arresting people, Sir."

"We have others who are. Just get me proof."

"I can work on that, Sir," Josie said. "No proof, but trails that lead us to proof."

"So can I," Goldfarb said. "There are strong connections between Claas Vogel and Vice President Dunbar. Among other things, Vogel helped fund his campaign. They meet every few weeks. I'd like those meetings monitored, along with their phones and computers."

"Do it legally. I'll sign what's necessary."

"Legally, we'd have to initiate an investigation and get a judge's approval."

"Do it. I am supposed to be dead soon. It's now or never, Ari."

Goldfarb said, "I'll give it to the FBI. They have purview."

Josie stood up, holding the photos. "If there's nothing more, I have a lot of work to do."

"Please check in daily," President Blager said.

Raven stood too, and looked at Goldfarb. "Can you keep him safe?"

"I can try…."

CHAPTER FORTY
TELL ME THAT ISN'T TORTURE

The Presidio, Monterey, California

Goldfarb and Harrington were sitting in Shapiro's office sipping coffee when Goldfarb's phone rang. He looked at it. "That's odd."

"The President?"

Goldfarb shook his head and pushed the button. It took several seconds for the secure light to come on. "You're supposed to be doing a viewing."

"Oh," he said. Then after a pause, "What?"'

Harrington tensed at the alarm in Goldfarb's voice, and started to stand. Goldfarb shook his head and waved him down. He took a pen and jotted some notes on a pad. An address.

"Right. I understand. No sirens, nothing official. Twenty minutes. Damned right he can explain then." Goldfarb punched the phone off and heaved a deep sigh.

Harrington said, "Is this some kind of an emergency?"

"No."

"What then…?"

Goldfarb was shaking his head. Finally, he looked up, and sighed again. "It's not an emergency, at least not yet. It's more like a loose cannon on the deck."

"I presume that was your Mr. Browning."

It took a second for Goldfarb to realize that Harrington was using Raven's cover name. That was on the base roster, Inspector Ron Browning, EPA. *What a tangled web we weave.... Too many cutouts. Too much bureaucracy. Too many layers. Too many agendas. Too many people with overlapping authority.*

Goldfarb sighed deeply. It was times like this when he most missed the clarity of the Cold War. He had once taken a Yale course on decision theory. There were times when consensus was best – major wars, abstract technical matters, or unknowable economic policy. There were other times when you just had to fucking do it – like when on the bridge of a warship in a Typhoon, or when dealing with terrorist killers. This was one of those times.

Harrington was the insider, the Chairman of the Working Group that oversaw Special Paramilitary OPs, and a Special Assistant to the National Security Advisor. He provided their access to the President and they were longtime friends, but his loyalty was to Washington protocols, not to the needs of running a Field OP. Harrington usually came to the right decisions, but as with Durham, sometimes too slowly. Time was too short for explanations and consensus.

Harrington was technically in charge, but he was not one of the few cleared for remote viewing access. When Goldfarb had set up the Browning legend, he thought it would be for just for one short visit, and that Raven would soon be off to Iran. *I am getting too old for this shit....*

Harrington was looking at him strangely, and he realized that he had spoken aloud. He was rattled. "**Shit.**" Goldfarb said again, putting emphasis on the word.

"Are we having a minor administrative problem?" Harrington asked dryly.

Goldfarb shrugged. He realized Harrington was still waiting for an answer to his previous question. "That was Browning's assistant, Josie. She'd borrowed his phone, and, yes, they are here on the base." He held up the address. "Is this close?"

"Temporary Quarters for visiting officers. Sure, ten minutes, we can almost walk. What are they doing there? If it is on the Presidio, it's my responsibility."

I do not think so, Goldfarb thought. "They are with your Dr. Stein."

"She's not mine," Harrington said, and then he stopped, realizing the implication, a shocked expression on his face. "She is one of the suspects with access that you wanted under surveillance. Those orders haven't gone out to the FBI yet."

"She's a person of interest, Jordan, not a suspect."

"What are your people doing here on the base in her housing unit? Arresting her?"

"No. We'd have the FBI do that."

"Questioning her?"

"Possibly."

"You know how badly an improper interview can screw up a legal prosecution. Can you say GITMO? All those 9-11 *jihadists* that couldn't be convicted because their civil rights had allegedly been abused?"

"I'm fully aware of our penchant for legalistic pettifoggery."

"So what the hell are your people doing over there?"

"Talking with her."

"Talking?"

"I think 'interrogating' may have been the operative concept."

"Jesus," Harrington said. "Tell me that doesn't translate into torture. Waterboarding?"

Goldfarb shrugged. He had no idea. Raven was not noted for political sensitivity.

"The last thing we need is more problems, Aaron. This could be a political nightmare. There are laws and the last thing we need is a media circus that could involve the President."

"Dr. Stein has revealed something important about the President's attempted assassination."

There was anger in Harrington's eyes. "That's not what I'm asking you. Was she harmed?"

"I'll let you know when I see her. I do know that she is alive."

"Are you sure?"

"Of course I'm sure. I could hear her – I presume it was she – sobbing in the background. They want me to hear her testimony firsthand. Josie asked me to come over, but to allow twenty minutes for Dr. Stein to calm down."

"I'm going with you."

"Good. That will save us time, something we are very short of, but no sirens, no drama, and no official presence. Just the two of us."

Harrington frowned at him.

"Let's not get into an argument over this, Jordan. If needed, we can bother the President to adjudicate the situation later. For now, we will just quietly drive over and see what is going on. No FBI, no Marines. A quiet little drive and some conversation. Is that acceptable to you?"

Harrington pulled out his pistol and checked the chamber. "Sure."

Goldfarb rapped on the door.

"Who is it?" Raven called.

"Me. Let us in."

The door swung open and Goldfarb entered. Raven was standing well to one side, with his Mini-14 leveled. "Are you alone?"

Goldfarb shook his head. "Harrington is with me."

"Invite him in."

"Not yet. Where's Dr. Stein?"

"With Josie."

"Is she harmed?"

"Yeah. You could say that."

"I guess now is when I have to order you to put that weapon down."

Raven shrugged, set the safety, and leaned it against the wall. "Not by me. The bastards sent her one of her husband's fingers. She's a basket case."

"I want to speak with Dr. Stein alone."

"No problem. First bedroom down the hall. Knock first." He called out, "Honey, I'm home."

Goldfarb looked at him.

"I didn't want Josie to be worried. It is clear. Go on in. Just knock first, like I said."

Goldfarb looked subdued when he came down the hall. "What a mess."

"Did she confirm what we told you?"

Goldfarb nodded. "Wait here. I'll get Harrington." He went to the door and called out.

Within seconds, Harrington pushed his way into the room. He had a Model 1911 Colt in his hand and a grim look on his face. He started to swing it toward Raven.

"Bad idea." Goldberg stepped in front of Harrington. "Put that away."

Harrington blinked and looked at him.

Make my day, Raven thought, touching his concealed Sig. *Point that weapon at me, and I will stick it up your ass.*

"Put the fucking gun away, Jordan. On my responsibility." Goldfarb waited as Harrington complied, then looked at Raven. "I'm going to let Jordan hear her story firsthand, just so there's no confusion."

"Sure."

Goldfarb and Harrington had somber looks on their faces when they returned. Goldfarb heaved a deep sigh and seated himself on the couch.

"I need a drink," Harrington said.

Raven shrugged. "There's water in the kitchen."

"That won't help."

Goldfarb looked at Josie. "We're canceling the FBI alert on her, but will keep the surveillance in place for her own protection."

"Good," Raven said.

Josie said, "Dr. Stein killed the assassin, the head chef, with his own mushrooms when she caught on to what was at stake. She's been stalling the Minister and Ricci ever since, telling them the President was terminal."

"She procured the mushrooms," Harrington said, "and did not inform us."

"She didn't know. She was just a courier," Josie said. "She was playing along trying to keep her husband alive, but she is not a traitor. She was afraid to tell anyone. She would never intentionally hurt the President."

Goldfarb nodded. "That's what she said."

Raven had never seen such a determined look on Josie's face. "I can't be mistaken about that. She was so alone. She delivered a package, but she had no knowledge of the mushrooms or that the chef was to kill the President until after he'd been poisoned."

Harrington said, "What did she think was in the package?"

Josie shrugged. "Some pot. Grass. Marijuana. No big deal."

Raven nailed Goldfarb with a look. "You heard Dr. Stein, and you hear us. Now it gets down to deciding and acting. Do you believe us or not?"

Goldfarb said, "I believe you."

"How about you?" Raven looked at Harrington.

"Why didn't she come to us in the first place?"

"Why do you think? She was afraid if she exposed them, it would get her husband killed. Either they'd kill him outright, or we'd get him killed in some half-assed, bungled rescue attempt."

"We haven't done well at rescues," Harrington admitted. "Her husband's probably dead by now anyway."

Goldfarb sighed. "Dr. Stein is traumatized and pretty worn out. She took some sleeping pills. I don't want her left unprotected."

"Right," Raven said.

"I'll see Marines are dispatched to guard this building," Harrington said. "Yes, I believe you. I admit our war on Islamic terror has been a bit spotty."

"We can count on your support?"

Harrington said, "Yes. The hell of it is that Dr. Stein is right. There's little chance we could get her husband back, especially if he's been moved into Iran."

"That's a secondary issue," Raven said. "Right now we have only a day or two to save the President."

Josie said, "He's right."

Goldfarb said, "We'll get to that, Jordan. Right now, I need my team back at work on more urgent problems. We are operating on the assumption that we only have a few days to save the President's life."

"That's what he said. Am I permitted to know why we believe that?"

Raven and Josie exchanged a look. Raven gestured, a slight motion of his hand. *Let Goldfarb handle this.*

"You don't want to know, Jordan," Goldfarb said.

Harrington's eyes narrowed.

"Sources and methods. If you have concerns, you'll have to take them up with President Blager."

"I did."

"Good. Then, I suggest we should all follow our orders. My first priority is to defend the President. There's a Hamas kill team in the area." He looked at Raven. "Have we located them?"

"Not yet. We have started. The way we identified Dr. Stein was a meeting she had with Ricci at the Trinity Church.

"She knew about Ricci and the chef, but thought the Hamas team had been recalled. Before Ricci, her control was an Iranian named Firouz. He was replaced a week or two ago, about the time when the Hamas team was recalled.

"After the shootout at Trinity, they're back, looking for weapons." He looked at Harrington. "That was an action item for you and the FBI."

"I'm working on it."

Raven said, "Stein thinks there is at least one other terrorist agent inside of the Presidio, but that she was the only one with access to the President."

Goldfarb said, "You've done well. I want you and Josie to stay focused on the kill team. Find them. Find Ricci. Look into threats to the President's life. That is the priority. After he's safe, we can worry about Stein and her husband."

"Yes, Sir."

"Jordan, do you need help prodding the FBI to get fully active? I want surveillance on anyone who might be involved. I want phones tapped, people followed, and briefings daily."

"We're doing it now. Trinity Church was the only lead."

"Ricci is controlled out of the UN," Goldfarb said. "We could use some of your clout."

Harrington sighed. "That one is going to be a tough nut to crack. He has diplomatic immunity. We're working on it."

"While you're cracking nuts, the other connections are to Claas Vogel, the billionaire, and Vice President Dunbar."

"We have started the process. Various approvals are required and...."

"We can discuss the details later. The main thing is that you're on it."

"We are."

"Good." Goldfarb looked at Josie and Raven. "Let's roll. Why are you still here?"

Right on. Hallelujah, and praise the Lord. Raven stood up and looked at Josie. She smiled encouragement. "We're on it. Thank you for the support. We'll keep you informed."

"You've done well. Dr. Stein could become a significant resource for us. It's the first break we've had."

"Yes, Sir," Raven said. They made their exit.

CHAPTER FORTY-ONE
A DUSTY TRAIL

Masjid Abu Bakr Mosque, Fort Ord, CA

Ricci glared at Kamal. "I got your weapons back. You should be happy. You did not tell me you had RPGs and a .50 Caliber Machine gun. These would have been hard to procure without attracting attention."

"The weapons are satisfactory, but I have learned there is a Monterey Mosque, the *Masjid At-Taqwa*. It is closer to our target."

Ricci shook his head.

"It would be better for us to base there."

"It's not available."

"Allah provides. Muslims stand united against the Infidels. *Those who bear the **power** and those around Him celebrate the praise of their Lord and believe in Him and ask protection for those who believe.*"

He quotes the Koran to me, a socialist? Ricci shook his head, forcing control. "Those at the Monterey Mosque are not part of our network. This mission is my responsibility. America is not subject to Sharia Law and not all Muslims practice *jihad*."

"Nor do they need to. That is my glorious privilege and duty. To serve Allah and die in his service. Our brothers at the Monterey Mosque will stand with us. If they do not they are heretics."

"I begin to see why Reverend Jones sent you away, Kamal. You put our mission at risk. If you do not accept my orders, I will be forced to do the same."

Kamal said, "To send us back?"

"I am close to making that decision. You can die in Allah's service somewhere else. My responsibility is ensuring that President Blager is dead in the next three days. If you and your men achieve that result, we have common objectives. If not, you are of no use to me. The result I care about is the President's death. Only that."

Kamal said, "If you send us back, your mission will fail. There is no time to get another team in place."

"I fear it could, and ask you to consider wisely. When you are called before Allah, do you wish to explain to him how you had a chance to kill the President of America, the ruler of the Great Satan? To tell him you failed because of your arrogance. Do you wish to explain to your superiors why you refused to accept my orders, and why you quibble about minor details? I need you to serve Allah, do your duty, and complete our mission."

Kamal's eyes flashed. He produced a black American K-bar combat knife and laid it on the table, the blade pointing at Ricci. "You dare to lecture me about duty?"

"We are all accountable. Your actions and desires put our mission at risk."

"My heart wants me to kill the Jews who defile my homeland, but I'm called here with my team for a greater purpose. I have come halfway around the world to a country I loathe for this duty to Allah. If you fail, I will kill you myself."

"The President will die, Kamal. I need to know if you are the proper weapon for that task. Ricci stared into Kamal's eyes and placed his hands on the table. "Only I can get you to the President. If you use that knife, you sin against Allah."

"It is no sin to kill an Infidel. It is the way to heaven."

"You were ordered to obey me, both by your leaders and by your Imams. Iran's Ayatollah Golzari himself has blessed this and issued a *fatwa*."

"How do you know this?"

"Your commander was Firouz."

Kamal nodded.

"The Ayatollah ordered Firouz recalled. I was the replacement chosen. Bigger things are at stake here than your martyrdom or selfish interests."

A long moment passed, with the men frozen in place. Ricci waited, studying Kamal closely. Despite his intelligence and refined British accent, under the skin he was a primitive beast from an earlier century, one bred and trained only for violence. Some day, the Iranians would have to deal with Hamas, just as Hitler had to kill his own Brown Shirts on the Night of the Long Knives, because, despite their loyalty, they had become a danger.

This one likes killing too much. Next to the North Koreans, the *jihadists* were one of the most difficult groups to work with. *All they know in Palestine is hatred and the Koran. Hatred seeps out of the sand and rocks. I need to end this.*

Ricci slapped the table. "Our time is short. Either use that knife, or obey my orders."

"I will obey. It is Allah's will." Kamal slipped the knife into a sheath on his leg.

"I do not wish to have this argument again."

Kamal gave a bow of submission. "You are in command."

"We have three sources inside the Presidio. Only one has access to the President. She reports he is on a deathwatch, and that security procedures have been greatly tightened. The other two sources corroborate what she says about security. The building that holds the President is off limits."

"Your sources are suspected?"

Ricci shook his head. "It's a new protocol. Even our inside agent is searched when she enters that building. She is only allowed to see him with an escort. Vehicles are not allowed to park close to the building."

"I wish to speak with her."

"That's not possible. She is followed if she leaves the complex. I dare not risk this asset until after the President is dead."

"Can she be trusted?"

"She's our best source. Everything she has told us has checked out, and it was she who enabled the President's poisoning. It was costly to, ah, develop her cooperation, but we're pleased with the results."

"The Americans are soft. There must be a weakness."

"Yes," Ricci said. "A man named Goldfarb, a professor of some type, an advisor, drives a green Lincoln. He is not followed or escorted when he leaves the Presidio. Each day at mid-morning, he visits the President's room. Sometimes he is late and in a rush. He rolls down a window, and they wave him through the gates at speed and without inspections."

"And they let him park next to the building. Americans are fools."

"Do not assume that. We presume Goldfarb is armed, the car is armored, and that he has ways of communicating. He will not be a soft target. This is not as easy as killing, you must take him alive. Dare I trust you with this?"

"I obey your orders. There have been times when my team took Israeli hostages in the Gaza Strip. We've done it before."

Ricci handed Kamal two pictures. One was of a large green car with tinted windows. It was quite distinctive. The second showed the same vehicle, but covered in dirt to where its color was hard to discern.

"It looks as if it's crossed a desert," Kamal said.

"No one knows where he goes. There is no desert close by. None of the local beaches has sand that color. Every time Goldfarb leaves the Presidio, his car is clean. When it comes back a few hours later, his car is dirty, covered with the thick layer of yellow-brown dust you see.

"We have tried to follow him. He uses good tradecraft and our efforts have not been successful. I ordered them stopped. We don't want to alarm him."

"Perhaps a broken down vehicle to block the road? That is useful in Iraq."

"We must do better than 'perhaps,' and this is not Iraq." Ricci shook his head. "We will only get one chance at this, and a damaged vehicle or a dead hostage would do us no good. In addition, those in security are racist bigots and tend to notice people from the Mideast. Your men would stand out."

"You have a plan?"

"What is the Americans' greatest weakness?"

"Stupidity. Americans are fools, soft and politically correct. It is child's play getting across their borders. They cannot imagine how much they are hated, and how many of us want to kill them. They have no suspicion at all. The Israelis are more difficult."

"It's true Americans are naive, but their greatest weakness is greed. I have agents going around with pictures of that car, and a story of a child molester and a deeply concerned family. We have offered a reward to learn where that car goes every day, the place with the dusty roads or driveway. I expect for money the locals can provide us with the information we seek."

"Excellent. When you find the lair, we can go in at night, take that place, and then take the professor hostage when he visits and walks in unsuspecting."

"Exactly," Ricci said. "That vehicle will provide you access. I will let you know when we find where Goldfarb goes. Take him alive, but kill everyone else."

CHAPTER FORTY-TWO
LIKE A WET DOG

**Private Beach House, South of Monterey, California,
Early Afternoon**

Raven looked down at Josie, and adjusted the sheet. Soft music was playing and there were candles spread around the room. "How are you doing?"

"I'm good. My viewing of Dr. Stein turned out well. Do you want me to pick up where we left off?"

"Can you latch on to Ricci? From where he met with Stein?"

"Easily. I set a mental bookmark. Where do I follow him?"

Nowhere traumatic, Raven thought. *Not yet. She has been through a lot.* "Let's avoid the wet work for now."

"Huh?"

"I want you to stay clear of the kill teams."

"They wanted me to...."

"Not yet," Raven said. "The FBI is on it, the President is well protected, and we have a few days. Let's start with the peaceful places. Maybe Ricci's planning meetings with Hamas?"

"Not a lot happens in the ones I've viewed. Ricci's a suit."

"Say again? What's a suit?"

Josie smiled. "Ever notice how hard it is to communicate these days? If I said "apple," would you think of a fruit or a computer?"

"Neither. I would think of sex. It's your fault."

"Me?" Josie's smile turned demure and innocent.

"It's a power you have over me. You got me all hot when you said 'apple.' All that stuff about Eve...."

"Hopeless." Josie gave a little flick of her eyes. "We have work to do."

"Darn."

"A suit is middle management. Ricci does not set policy. He is just a cog in the machine. He supports operational teams and passes along orders, but he stays clear himself. He doesn't get involved in operational details."

"Like the guy who used to run the gas chambers? 'Just doing my job for the Fatherland.....' I'm not responsible."

"Uh Huh. Ricci seems to be the cutout for the gold Rolex guy."

"Vogel." Raven thought about it, and then nodded. "Good idea. Let's snoop around those in power and see what crawls out. You found Vogel and Ricci meeting at the UN."

Josie nodded.

"I'd like to know if either of them have connections with Vice President Dunbar. Start with Vogel, as he is higher level and more likely. Can you do that?"

"What exactly am I looking for?"

Good question. "Let's go high concept."

"Find the head of the beast?"

"Exactly. Let's start with a look at intersections of Dunbar to Vogel or Ricci. Assume the goal of this tasking is establishing links, direct or indirect, between Islamic leaders and Vice President Dunbar: That would be high treason."

"Intersections?"

"Face-to-face meetings, for a start. I want policy-level stuff to take back for Goldfarb and the President. I want the top leaders, not the counselors or spooks. Let's see where that leads."

"Such senior people are well shielded. There will be many levels to search through. Could this include heads of state?"

"Maybe."

"This could take a long time."

"Start with the Vogel/Dunbar intersections. I think that would be the most appropriate level of contact. If you come up dry, then look for Ricci/Dunbar. Can you search that way?"

Josie nodded.

"It's a huge win if we find something. Imagine if Bush had located and whacked bin Laden instead of invading Iraq? Game over."

"I'll need to be back and oriented before Kaimi shows up for dinner. If I'm not back by four, touch me and get my attention."

Raven frowned. "You sure? I thought interrupting you was something to avoid."

"Just be soft and gentle, like I showed you. It's okay."

"No raucous sex?"

Josie rolled her eyes. "Just whisper in my ear, like I showed you."

"Okay, Babe. Can do."

Josie took deep breaths. "I need to relax. Can you get me a glass of white wine?"

Raven did, a chilled Sauvignon Blanc, and she took several sips. "That's good. Dry, not sweet. Thanks." She slipped the sheet off, removed her dress – no underwear. Then she lay down on her back, pulling the sheet up under her chin.

Raven was silent. This was the tricky part. He needed to protect Josie from interruptions, bring her back if needed, and get her to an ICU if something went badly wrong and her systems started to shut down.

Above all, he had to be careful not to distract or defocus her viewing. Disturbing Josie during a viewing could cause permanent damage. He had only done that once, to save her life. It had worked, but they had been lucky.

The phones and alarms were off. Raven seated himself in a comfortable chair with a view down the long driveway, and settled in. He had a file on VP Dunbar to help pass the time.

He watched closely as Josie started her trance. She looked beautiful, like a goddess. She was serene when she dropped into her viewings, and her body was coming back from the trauma of Durham. The sheen and silkiness was back in her long brown hair, now spread loosely over the pillow. He could see her heavy breasts and nipples through the thin cloth.

Raven tried to concentrate on her eyes. Brown. Alert. Staring at the ceiling.

Her breathing slowed as she moved into a meditative state. Her body became relaxed. Her eyes stayed open, but now with a vacant gaze. Josie's body was still there, but her mind was off moving down a time-space corridor to places Raven could not imagine.

Some were dangerous. He hoped wherever he had sent her was well clear of the Abyss, but there was no way to know. She was in a place where he could not protect her.

Josie had come back from her the viewing at 3:30 with no problems, a half hour early. She was smiling. "Bingo," she said, holding her hand out.

Raven handed her the sketchpad without speaking. He had been through this enough that he knew better to distract her while she was trying to recapture the images she had seen.

She made two quick pencil sketches. One was of Vogel in an office with Vice President Duncan. There was an American Flag behind the desk, and a recognizable picture of the VP shaking hands with President Blager on the wall. The other was of Vogel and Duncan in a dimly lit room with dark wood. They were sitting in a booth, and Vogel was passing an envelope across the table.

Josie stopped sketching and looked up. There was a faint sheen of perspiration on her face and arms. Raven expected that. Josie got chilled when viewing, but had hot flashes when she returned. Doctor Lundgren once told her it had something to do with sensory deprivation.

Raven gave her a towel. She wiped her face and flashed him a smile, looking pleased with herself.

"Want a beer?"

She touched her wine glass.

"I can get you some that's chilled."

"Just water. Ice water." Josie blinked her eyes and looked around the room. It always took her a little time to reconnect when she got back. Her body remained in the room during remote viewings, but her mind and senses were elsewhere. Raven could not imagine how it must feel to be that vulnerable.

He brought her back a tall glass of water. Just two cubes, so it would not be too cold to drink quickly. She did, draining the glass. Raven took it and went to fetch another. When he returned, she was sitting up with her dress back on.

"It was a good viewing. Let me give you the highlights." Josie touched the sketches.

"Go."

"That one is VP Dunbar's office in the West Wing of The White House. He and Vogel meet there every few weeks. The room is secure, they talk freely, and neither takes any notes."

"Always alone? No other participants?"

"Always alone. I viewed seventeen such meetings over the last six months. There is a clock on the wall. The longest meeting was almost an hour. The shortest was fifteen minutes. Twice Dunbar made phone calls."

"Sounds like a good place to bug. Can you revisit and get the phone numbers he called?"

"I can. The other sketch is in some kind of a bar or restaurant. It is dimly lit with dark wood. It is a short drive from the White House. They dine, do not talk much, and pass things. The envelope depicted contained money. These meetings are less frequent. They had seven over the same time period."

"Vogel wouldn't take anything incriminating into the White House, there are searches and logs. Did the Secret Service accompany Dunbar to the restaurant?"

Josie shrugged. "I wasn't looking for that. I do not think so. If they did, they didn't come inside."

"Okay. Next time, drop back and check that."

"There were five meetings between them in the two-week period before the President was poisoned. Two were in the restaurant. The last one is what I depicted in the sketch."

"They actually passed an envelope across the table? That seems sloppy."

"That was the only time. Usually they come with identical brown leather attaché cases, which they swap. They put them by their feet, and each leaves with the other's case. That meeting seemed rushed. They did not have the cases that time. They were only there for one drink, ten minutes or less."

Raven nodded and looked at his watch. "You did well. I think that is enough to get some taps and cameras put in place. We still have a few minutes before your friend arrives. Anything else unusual?"

"One of the meetings in the Restaurant did involve a third party, Ricci. He came in with Vogel, got introduced, and then left."

Dunbar and Ricci. Interesting. Maybe he is more than a suit. "Was there a gap after that meeting?"

"Yes. They didn't meet again for several weeks, if that's what you mean."

"What about Dunbar's other offices?"

Josie looked puzzled. "What other offices?"

"He has at least two more. Small official meetings are usually held at his residence. He has an office there. It is located on the grounds of the United States Naval Observatory (USNO), a mansion built in 1893. You don't hear much about that in the media."

"Sure don't. Get me an address, and I'll check next time...."

"The VP has a ceremonial office too."

"Three offices? The taxpayers are generous."

"I doubt they know. I did not until Goldfarb told me. The imperial aspects of the Executive Branch are not much publicized, for obvious reasons. In any case, the ceremonial office is traditionally used for press interviews, which Dunbar seldom holds."

"Why not?"

"President Blager is old school. Goldfarb says that he agrees the office of the VP is as useful as a bucket of warm spit."

"Blager said that?"

"I doubt he did, actually." Raven shrugged. "Goldfarb is a professor at heart and it's apparently a famous quote. Cactus Jack."

"You're making this up."

"Nope. Cactus Jack was what they called Vice President John Nance Garner. He was from Texas, and reportedly both colorful and powerful."

"I've never heard of him."

"I'm not just a knuckle dragger with a gun, Babe. I've been doing research on Vice Presidents and the office." Raven's tone turned pedantic. "Garner served two terms as VP under FDR, and he is most noted for saying the Vice Presidency is not worth a bucket of warm spit. He and

FDR had a major falling out about the time when Roosevelt chose to run for a third term. Garner ran against FDR, lost in 1940, and disappeared into the sands of history.

"A lot of our history is missing or wrong, especially the parts where progressives like FDR were playing loose with the Constitution. He was more like an emperor, and the only President who did more than two terms. After him they passed the term limit law, the one Obama challenged."

"Okay, enough. I believe you. Are you saying Blager and Dunbar don't get along well?"

"They are cordial. The issue is a lack of trust, according to Goldfarb. Blager keeps Dunbar on a short leash. The VP's ceremonial office is in the Eisenhower Executive Office Building (EEOB), located next to the West Wing on the White House premises. It isn't used much."

"I'll check that one too. Like I said, this is going to take a lot of time."

"Vogel went to some trouble to introduce Dunbar and Ricci. Could the two of them have met alone?"

"They could have, certainly. I didn't look for that either."

"Let's do that next time, and also get the dates of the meetings."

Josie said, "Make a list, and we'll talk more later. I need to take a shower before Kaimi arrives. I feel sticky. Do I smell sweaty?"

He leaned close and sniffed. "Not really. More like a wet dog."

She stuck her tongue out. "For that, you get to fix dinner."

"I thought we'd go out."

Josie stood up and shook her head. "No way. Kaimi is not a 'go out' kind of guy. This is his first time to the mainland. He is freaking out about all the people around. He says there are too many people in California."

"Most would agree with him. We're in deep shit if he gets to meet the California crazies."

"I'm worried about him meeting *you*."

Raven smiled.

"Seriously, do be careful what you say. Kaimi wants to go back to Hawaii. Unless you develop a knack for psychic healing, I'd be nice to him."

"You respect him a lot, don't you?"

"I do. He is almost like an uncle to me. It was kind of him to come over and help."

"I'll be good. I can even cook on a grill. Do we have any dead red meat?"

"Beats me." Josie smiled, turned, and took her exit, taking care to make a few sensuous wiggles on the way out, the thin dress accenting her curves. Her voice came floating back. "You might want to sniff his butt and see if he smells like a wet dog...."

CHAPTER FORTY-THREE
BASHING GATORS

Private Beach House, South of Monterey, California

K aimi showed up with a fresh-caught fish and a small cooler. The fish was ready to cook, and the grill was warming up. He and Raven were sitting on the patio.

Kaimi reached into the cooler, pulled out an IPA, and offered it to Raven. *My favorite.* "Josie must have told you about my epiphany."

Kaimi's bushy white eyebrows went up. He smiled, shaking his head slowly.

"British friends taught me to enjoy India Pale Ale. Would you like one?"

"It is for you. Alcohol and drugs disrupt my meditation."

Raven raised his bottle in a toast. "I'm surprised she didn't tell you."

"She doesn't often talk about personal things, even to me. I did some viewings and made a guess."

Sure he did. Raven was getting used to being around clairvoyants. *It was not a guess.*

"IPA is an excellent choice. It will go well with the fish."

Kaimi tapped his head. "The beer was for you, but the fish is for me. There is too much noise, too many people, here in California."

Other than the soft breeze, the evening was utterly quiet. "Noise?"

Kaimi tapped again. "Noise in my head. It's distracting."

OMG. This is the guy we are depending on to save the President? Raven kept his tone neutral. "You hear voices?"

Kaimi smiled, shook his head, and his eyes twinkled. "Background noise. I am sensitive to peoples' thoughts and feelings, especially intense ones like passion and violence. I could not stand to live on the mainland, but I need to stay long enough to finish what I have promised. I've been spending a lot of time out on the ocean where it's quiet."

"Do you enjoy fishing?"

"I enjoy serenity. Back in Hawaii, I live alone in the jungle and meditate. Here, I fish, as far offshore as possible. Fishing passes the time and quiets the noise in my head. It helps me meditate and focus my powers."

Raven nodded.

"This is a California yellowtail. He was lost and cold. Normally they do not come this far north, but a variety is common off Hawaii. They make excellent sushi, but I filleted this one.

"I brought fresh limes. Josie prefers it grilled lightly with lime." Kaimi hesitated. "I do need to ask something of you."

"Sure."

"Is she comfortable with that weapon under your shirt?"

"To an extent. She does not freak anymore. It's there to protect her, and has."

"The two of you have adapted to fit together. For me, your weapon creates darkness."

"Oh," Raven said. "No problem. I can put it in a drawer."

"Yes, please," Kaimi said. "Could you also unload it? To you, it is a tool, but to me violence is…. disruptive. I know you're now a part of Josie's life, but I must confess it surprised me at first."

"Yeah." Raven popped the magazine out and put the Sig in the knife drawer. "Better?"

"Much, thank you. Humans are a violent race, are they not?"

Raven nodded.

"Violence is your job, I know. I understand you are good at it."

"I have to be." *It keeps me alive.*

"Yes, but how do you feel about it?"

"It's what I do."

"Why?"

"People sleep peaceably in their beds at night only because rough men stand ready to do violence on their behalf."

"Orwell. A prescient man, but his most bleak visions, and worse, have come to pass. With modern technology, evil is so powerful that it overpowers basic humanity."

"It can, if we let it," Raven acknowledged. "Are you familiar with our General Patton?"

Kaimi nodded. "A violent man, but a good one. He helped free Europe from the Nazi darkness. For a time, he was the only General the Nazi Military respected and feared."

"You know your history."

"I know that history quite well. I went back several times and watched as it unfolded."

"Why would you do that?"

"I couldn't believe horrific events like the holocaust and the killing fields were purposely planned. I didn't think civilized people could willingly embrace such evil."

"So you looked yourself."

"I did. It was frightening that normal people can be induced to commit genocide. I needed to see it myself."

"Why?"

Kaimi looked into Raven's eyes. "To better understand why people like you exist."

Raven blinked. *Say what?*

"Patton called the endless rows of tombstones in France 'monuments to the pacifists.' He argued ignoring or tolerating evil was as bad as the evil itself. Is that what you were going to tell me?"

Paranormals know. He reads me like a book. "Yeah, pretty much. Something like that."

"Josie was my best student, but she chose to become a seer rather than a healer. She sought beauty in the world, but there is so much darkness on the land that it led her to discover her gift."

Raven frowned and shook his head. "I don't understand."

"You don't know much about paranormals. Have you met others?"

"Only Josie, and, of course, the legends I've heard from her about paranormal Cold War successes. Your profession has fallen into disfavor with our political class."

"Josie is the only one of the Huna who ever chose this path. We do not view our powers as a profession. We generally prefer private lives, as distant as possible from industrial civilization. What we do is an art and a way of life.

"It was surprising to me when Josie chose to leave us for the mainland. To be honest, I almost tried to discourage her, but to do so is against what we believe. God is divine, and each of us must be free to choose our path."

"Life, Liberty and the Pursuit of Happiness. Is that why she came to America?"

Kaimi smiled. "Actually Josie came to us *from* America. She had a grant to study in Hawaii, but returned to the mainland when it ran out. They were most eager to get her back and give her accreditation. The Rhine Institute wanted her as a sex therapist, a career that has many trappings, including money and status. Americans are obsessed with sex."

"So what happened?"

Kaimi shrugged. "Josie found drug-addled sex shallow, along with people desperately clinging to their youth, versus maturing, gaining wisdom, and learning to love. She sought other uses for her talents and eventually lost interest in acquiring formal academic credentials."

"That led her to the intelligence community?"

"In truth, it was the reverse. It led them to her because of her powers and their need." Kaimi shrugged. "She stayed because the work gave her a purpose."

"What purpose?"

Kaimi looked into Raven's eyes intently. "Life."

Raven shook his head.

"Josie chose the highest possible purpose, saving advanced civilization so that people may live free, safe, and in comfort. Most Huna focus on the quest for an eventual Nirvana as humankind finds peace and perfection, but she chose to deal with the near term."

"Josie saved my life. Is that what you mean?"

"She has saved lives, including your own, but what I speak of is a broader concept. Josie's calling is preventing evil. It surprised me at first when I discovered the two of you had bonded, but now I understand."

Raven took a sip of his beer and waited.

"Your soul is tired. I sense that."

"Yes. We are going to retire together, Josie and me. That's our dream."

"Why do you continue?"

"What I do is needed."

"As long as evil exists, it will always be needed. You know that."

"Yes. So it seems."

"So how do you decide when to retire?"

I wish I could answer that, Raven thought. "If good men do nothing, evil wins. Isn't the purpose of life to leave the world better than when you arrived?"

"Have you accomplished that?"

"I don't think so. Evil is ascendant, despite my efforts. The Abyss you sense being one example. Josie senses that it hides a horrific future, a new Dark Age. It frightens her that even her powers are blind."

"It frightens me as well," Kaimi said. "What you do is needed, but you pay a high price, and so does she. That is why I came. I'll help if I can."

"Please tell me more," Raven said.

"Josie finds evil using her talents, but can do little about it when she does. You kill evil as the mongoose does the snake, as Beowulf killed Grendel. Alone and in darkness."

"When we first met, Josie told me the same. She said I want to save the tribe, even at the sacrifice of myself."

"Josie gives you vision. Evil hides in darkness and fears the light. Evil does not change, but it is clever at masking itself, and expert at deception. You are not alone, Raven. This will end, and you'll find redemption."

Raven gazed at Kaimi for a long moment. "It's been a long time since I've trusted anyone, Sir."

"But you trust Josie and she trusts you."

"I do trust her. I hope she does trust me. I almost got her killed, you know."

"You must not think that. The truth is that you saved her and she saved you. Evildoers are often hard to find until too late. They hide their presence and intentions.

"Josie can find them for you, whether they hide in plain sight, or in darkness half a world away. We are near a crisis point, a nexus. If the two of you prevail, this will get better."

"Eventually."

"Yes. God never said it would be easy. You need to believe in yourself. The battle between good and evil is eternal, but light is more powerful than darkness."

"I'm tired and Josie is scared. If I make a mistake, if I even hesitate at the wrong time, I'll get her killed."

"Perhaps, but the reverse is also true. Alone, you are each doomed. Together, you are formidable."

"Josie is a gentle spirit. My journey has been one of paranoia and vigilance, and the end is always red, raw violence. Then it repeats. Must this continue? I don't know a better way."

Kaimi said, "Nor do I. I am coming to believe that is because there is none, yet. Nonetheless, we must continue the quest. Someday humankind will find an answer."

"How or where, Sir?"

"Throughout human history, for every God, there is a Lucifer. For every Christ, there is an Antichrist. We hope that humankind can evolve beyond this condition. That is my purpose, but it is people like you who protect us. You buy us the time we need. You keep us alive so we can continue trying."

"How do you know that?"

"Have you ever heard of the Fermi paradox?"

Raven shook his head.

"Enrico Fermi was one of your leading scientists of the 20th Century, the father of atomic energy. He saw limitless energy as helpful to advancing mankind, but, unfortunately, we've not done much with that gift except to boil water and make bombs."

"So what's this paradox thing?"

"It's a logic exercise he conceived after Hiroshima. The number of stars is essentially infinite, and some of them must have planets with life, just as ours does. Of these myriad planets with life, some races must be much more advanced than our own."

"Okay."

"The problem is we've never encountered any other intelligent life in the universe, even though simple mathematics and logic would indicate it should be teeming with such life.

"Fermi's paradox is this: In a universe that must have almost infinitely numerous highly advanced civilizations, we've never detected a trace of even one, save our own. How can this be? Why are we alone?"

"No idea," Raven said.

"Perhaps intelligence isn't a survival trait, Raven. What if when God grants beings intelligence and free will, that greed and evil always triumph, disaster results, and darkness reigns? What does this portend? What can we learn?"

Armageddon. Scary thought. "And you think this Abyss thing you and Josie speak of is such an outcome?"

"I don't know, and can't know, but that's my fear."

"What's the answer?"

"That good men and women do what we can with the gifts the Almighty has granted us. The Huna seek a higher path for humanity. That is our quest, my quest. In the meantime, we need people like you to keep us alive by slaying the dragons and monsters."

"By killing...."

"It is difficult for me to speak such words and maintain the inner peace I require to function. Let me just say that with Josie's help you can find the roots of evil and hack them off."

"Sometimes," Raven said, thinking of Durham.

"What you two can do together is needed. It helps."

Raven took a deep breath and let it out slowly. "Only for a time...."

"You speak wisdom," Kaimi said. "This is true, and Gandhi said it as well. 'Violence can do good, but only for a time.' However, in these times, humankind needs all the time it can get, and all the chances it can get. The time you provide is needed."

"We are to bash the alligators so you can figure out how to drain the swamp?"

"I don't see another way," Kaimi said. "My powers are all but useless. In a little under three days, the only future I see is the Abyss, a black void.

"I'm healing the President, but it isn't helping, and I don't know why. But when Josie does a viewing, there are ripples through time and space. The Abyss shifts slightly. It… trembles. Whatever the two of you are doing, it has an impact."

"We'll continue," Raven said.

"I bless you both for what you are doing. Did Josie tell you about the Huna?"

Raven nodded.

"Our powers are great, but this may have happened before. Long ago, something went very wrong. We do not know what, but the dark side took over and it almost destroyed our planet. All our powers failed to prevent disaster. Did she tell you that?"

"Some," Raven said.

"Josie is something new. She can remote view and sense events closer to violence and death than any other seer of whom I am aware. She provides vision into dark places to assist those with other talents. I now understand your affinity for each other."

"In Durham we almost destroyed each other."

"But you did not…."

"No, not quite. What I need to know is this: Do I put her at risk?"

"To live and love is to risk." Kaimi gave a small shrug and spread his hands. "You put her at risk, and you keep her safe. She does the same for you. The warrior and the priestess were effective pairings in the old times, the times of legend."

"Did those times ever really exist?"

"Yes, but the memories have been lost. The Garden of Eden is remembered, but not the dark times. I think the history of man has been one of episodic crisis. I do not know why, but I seek to learn. In dark times, in the iron years, people like you are needed."

"This happens repeatedly?"

"There have been many such cycles, but we forget. Ying and Yang, darkness and light."

"We remember the Holocaust, and our World Wars," Raven said.

"Some people do." Kaimi smiled softly. "Only dimly, and these were conflicts that you won. Consider this: The greatest spoil of war is that the victors can get to write the history. Heroic myths matter.

"America failed to do that after Vietnam. You let the losers write the history, and it started a downward slide. It enabled evil."

Raven blinked. "I never thought of that...."

"Did Josie ever tell you that in a previous life she was a Celtic priestess, the temple prophet for The Great Queen?"

"She said that when we first met. Is it true?"

"I believe so. She died in 56 BC when Roman soldiers under Gaius Julius Caesar destroyed her temple. It was a time not unlike what your Republic and the Western Democracies are now experiencing with Radical Islam, a clash of civilizations.

"In the end, the Celtic culture was lost except to myth. Our viewings are cloudy into that time, but, at her core, Josie remembers. The two of you think that you met by accident, but I believe it was destined."

Raven rubbed his hands down his face and took some deep breaths. These were heavy concepts. He did not know what to say, so he waited for Kaimi to continue.

"I came here to help my student, but also to prevent a dark age. If your President dies and the Abyss forms, I fear the dark history will repeat. What did she tell you about me?"

"You're her *sensei*, her mentor, and a healer. She shared what you are doing to help us. About the President...."

"We must discuss that more, but not now, please." Kaimi nodded toward the door, and Josie appeared, her smile radiant.

CHAPTER FORTY-FOUR
AGREEMENTS

Masjid Abu Bakr Mosque, Fort Ord, CA

Ricci was coming to hate this assignment. The Arabs were lazy and single minded. *In sh'allah. Why bother to plan when it was all up to Allah anyway?*

They wanted to kill and die for Allah. They did not care about mission objectives. They wanted dead infidels and a glorious afterlife.

Ricci managed to arrange an office with a door, but Kamal had the manners of a goat and the persistence of a tax collector. He interrupted daily with the same questions: "Is the President still alive? Can we attack now?"

He was like a child on a car trip repeating, "Are we there yet?" endlessly. No wonder the Reverend wanted him and Hamas as far away as possible.

Operationally, nothing had changed. President Blager was dying, and an attack was premature. Ricci still had almost three days left on Vogel's timeline for the kill. With any luck, nature would take its course and the bastard would just die. Then he could go home. For now, all he could do was wait.

There was a knock on the door. Ricci suppressed a curse. He took two deep breaths, reached into his desk, pulled out the silver brandy flask and took a swallow. The fiery liquor warmed him. "Come in," he shouted, not bothering to hide his irritation.

Kamal was carrying an AK. He was wearing tan Camo fatigues and black combat boots. His eyes locked on the flask and his nostrils flared in anger. "Allah forbids alcohol. You are in a mosque."

Ricci did not bother to reply.

Kamal pulled over a folding chair, leaned the gun against Ricci's desk, and seated himself. "You will burn in the fires of Hell, Mr. Ricci. I will enjoy watching your skin char and fall off."

Ricci sighed, dropped the flask into a drawer, and pushed it closed. "This isn't – as you complain yourself – a real mosque. In effect, you are a guest in my house, Mr. Kamal, eating the food I have provided. Respect would be appreciated."

Ricci had no idea if it was a real mosque or not, but the fact that Kamal said that it was not left room to argue. There were prohibitions against alcohol in mosques, but killing each other in mosques was forbidden too and it did not stop them from doing so.

Kamal did not speak.

Apparently, I won that round. Ricci eyed the Hamas operative critically. "Did you locate the wedding couple we're seeking?"

Kamal shook his head. "There's been no sign of them since they left Trinity Church. The registration for the car led nowhere. They did not leave by air or bus. They just vanished. Perhaps the Reverend's guards killed them and disposed of the bodies. All it takes is a boat and some weights out here, and no traces would ever be found."

"I'm not interested in theories, just let me know when you find them." Ricci gestured dismissingly. He did not care about the missing couple, but gave Kamal the job to keep him occupied. "I hope you and your men are not wandering the streets of Monterey showing weapons? In would be, ah, somewhat awkward if you were to be arrested."

Kamal flashed his teeth. It was not a smile. "We're deploying on a mission tonight. I thought you might want to know."

"Action against the President is not yet authorized. Do we need to review who is in charge here?" *Again.*

"That's not the mission I refer to. The rewards we posted worked. We know where this professor Goldfarb – the man who controls access to the President – goes every day. There is a remote house on a private road south of Point Lobos. The dirt on this road matches the dust of Goldfarb's car. He has been observed entering the road."

Ricci's eyes narrowed. "What do you plan?"

"We have the road intersection under observation. Late tonight we will go in and capture or kill the occupants of the house. In the process, I expect we'll learn more about the President."

"Continue."

"When Goldfarb visits tomorrow, he is ours. If the President is dead, that ends it. We kill our hostages and leave. If the President still lives, we take Goldfarb, gain access, and finish the job our predecessors bungled."

"I was handling this...."

"Too slowly, I think. You were given a timeline to finish this matter with the President, one that has almost expired. I decided to help."

Ricci felt a tinge of fear. *He has been talking to his command in Hamas, or perhaps to Vogel.* He nodded slowly. "That is acceptable."

"It's settled then." Kamal's eyes were cold, but it was definitely a smile this time. "We'll finish this matter by the time the sun sets tomorrow, *In sh'allah.*"

After Kamal left, Ricci pondered the situation for a few minutes. Kamal was a hothead and the President was dying anyway, but the last thing Ricci needed was a perception that he was not following Vogel's orders. He finally sighed, stood and headed off for the local Internet café.

Once there, he ordered a 16-ounce latte, and sipped it slowly. After he was convinced no one was paying attention to him, he logged into a private Gmail account, using the username and password he had memorized.

Ricci was careful to use only the draft folder. There was already an email in the folder, directed to someone called "papa bear." He opened it and read the text, something innocuous about cupcakes. It did not matter. This email would never be sent. The Americans and their NSA were good at intercepting messages, but even they could not intercept a note that was never sent.

Ricci deleted the text and added his own. Three sentences: "Most important you put the cat out tonight. Do it by the morning if you don't want a mess."

Vogel's agent in the Presidio checked this folder twice a day. This was the kill order. Whatever Kamal did, this note ensured the President would be dead by morning.

It made no difference to Ricci who got credit for the kill. If Kamal and his men arrived late and died while trying to assassinate a dead man, it was not his problem. Ricci doubted Hamas would care, even if they found out, which was unlikely.

If the President was still alive and Vogel's agent missed him, it was not Ricci's fault. In that case, Kamal and his team could still die as martyrs for Allah while killing Infidels, including the President. They would be heroes and he would be rid of them.

Ricci smiled to himself and savored his latte. *The best strategy is one where all paths lead to success.*

Private Beach House, South of Monterey, California

Josie and Raven watched Kaimi leave. He stopped on the porch, looked back at them, smiled, and faded out of existence. The general effect looked like the transporters on Star Trek, but without any shimmering or sound. Kaimi faded into transparency and then was gone. The last thing they saw was his broad grin, like the Cheshire cat.

"Holy shit," Raven said. "Can you do that?"

"Not a chance. George is more advanced in that art than I am."

"Did he talk with you about warriors and priestesses?"

"He says we need to be careful. History has not been kind to such pairings, at least not the ones he mentions."

"The ones he discusses are from dark times. Like now." Raven put his hand under her chin, tilted her face up gently, and kissed her.

"I like it, but what was that for?"

"An apology. I love you, Babe. I screwed up big time and got you hurt."

"Durham was my fault. I panicked."

"No, it was my fault. You did exactly what I told you to do. I got in your line of fire. I think we need ground rules."

"Rules of Engagement? You had a dispute with the CIA over that, as I recall." *They fired you, my dear, and with prejudice.*

"Yeah. Screw 'em and their ROEs. I was thinking of rules *for* engagement, just some simple things to ensure we survive as a couple, when we're so different."

"What exactly do you have in mind?"

"We need it clear who's in charge at various times. Remote viewings and paranormal Intel is you. Direct action is me, especially if we're blown and have to defend ourselves."

"You mean violence?"

Raven nodded. "I do."

"I thought that's what we **were** doing."

"We are, but let's make it explicit. My keeping you safe is job # 1. If you are at risk, you defend yourself as needed, and we sort it out later. Kaimi told me that Huna philosophy allows for self-defense."

"It does." Josie nodded. "That *is* what we're doing, I thought."

"Right, but I need you to do something more for me. First off, if I get my ass shot while you are defending your own life, we agree it is my own damn fault. You do not blame yourself. Goldfarb thinks guilt over me put you into a coma. Can you promise to do that?"

"I can try. You said, 'first off.' What else?"

"The rest is to prearrange who is in control. If the shit hits the fan, and I yell 'down,' I need you to get your ass down. No discussion, no reflection, you just dive for cover."

"No problem. You know how much I abhor violence."

"Then you need to **stay** down and out of the line of fire until I sing out 'clear' and the shooting stops. If we had done it that way in Durham, I could have handled Rashid, and any damage done to him or me would have been on my conscience."

"You did handle Rashid, my love."

"I don't understand."

"Rashid wasn't on my conscience. I did not take his life, you did. I shot him to defend Black and myself, but gunshot wounds were not what killed him. Your knife did."

"I got him? Are you sure?"

Josie nodded. "I went back, did a viewing, and checked. You slashed him from ear to ear. His death was instantaneous. With no blood to his brain, Rashid never felt anything. Certainly not the bullets I put into him."

"Then why…?"

"I fell apart because I felt **your** pain, not his. I shot Rashid, and my bullets went through him into you. It was like shooting myself. It was awful. I was certain I'd killed you."

"Well, you didn't." Raven said. "What else?"

"I was afraid that my being a killer would strip me of my powers. It did not. If anything, they are stronger."

"Because you were not a killer?"

"That's what I thought, after I did my viewing and learned I wasn't. Kaimi convinced me it was more fundamental. He says the laws of God and the universe allow killing to defend life or prevent evil. The gurus know this, but few in today's paranormal community have tested it. He says I am the first one in several hundred years. There is an entire body of literature on this."

"Really?"

"Augustine of Hippo. *Jus bellum iustum.*"

"Huh?"

"Kaimi says my actions are justified by St. Augustine's 'Just War Theory' from 400 AD, the time when the Roman Empire was collapsing. Rome had been sacked. Christians were being slaughtered, until he came up with the notion of 'just wars.' Some say Cicero had the same concept before Christianity existed, and others say Saint Augustine was only expanding on what was in the Bible, but Augustine of Hippo is the one given credit.

"Augustine's thesis depicts the history of the world as universal warfare between God and the Devil. Nine hundred years later, during the Crusades, Thomas Aquinas expanded upon it. Bush One used this to justify the Gulf War. He got the approval of Congress and most religious leaders, even the Muslims."

"I think we need to talk more."

"Good idea. I want us to spend the rest of our lives doing that."

"I don't want us to screw up this warrior/priestess thing, Babe. Too many have in the past, including you, at least once. It usually gets them killed."

"Including us, almost. Those are the cases Kaimi talks about. What he omits is that in the dark times, entire populations die off. Two thousand years ago, most of the Celts died from violence or starvation. The fact that I was temple priestess made it personal, but the result might have been the same if I had been a peasant girl. We faced Roman genocide."

"Now we face *jihad*, terrorists with missiles and nukes."

"Potential Islamic genocide. A generational war."

Raven took a deep breath and let it out slowly. "Exactly. Not on the other side of the planet, but where we live. There is no place to run. No place to hide."

"Yes. We have to win. We can. Good is more powerful than evil."

"I believe that too. You have great powers, Josie. If we work together we can win."

"You want something. What should we change?"

"What we can. Better focus, more trust, less hesitation. We need to make life **safer** for each other, not more dangerous. It is like calling in an air strike. We do not want any more casualties from friendly fire. No more Durhams. That tore us both apart. Each of us believed we had harmed the other. I could not live with that."

"Me either." Josie smiled radiantly.

"What?"

"You have the oddest way of showing affection. Do you love me...?"

Raven gave a crooked little grin. "You're the paranormal. Don't you know that?

"I know, but a girl needs to hear it."

"So do we have a deal?" Raven persisted. "I need a promise from you. When I say 'down,' you drop like a stone, stay down, and let me handle it. When it is done, I will call **Clear**." When we are in a hot zone and fully engaged, I have the lead. Okay?"

"Gladly, but I need a promise from you too. When I tell you we need to back off, like when you wanted to rampage through Trinity to avenge Moira after the bad guys bugged out, you do it. Here's why: *Paranormals know shit we can't explain.*"

"I did back off, and I still want to get the team leader who killed Moira."

"Barely, and you can't."

"Why not?"

"You blew his head off. He's the one you shot when you saved Black."

"Oh," Raven said. "What else do you know?"

"I think you just proposed to me. Are you going to make an honest woman of me?"

"You're the most honest woman I've ever met, Babe. Yeah, I want to marry you."

Josie smiled. "Are you going to kiss me?"

"Uh huh."

And he did.

CHAPTER FORTY-FIVE
NIGHTFALL

Building 422, The Presidio of Monterey, California, early evening

Harrington and Goldfarb exchanged a look. Goldfarb shrugged. They looked at the President.

President Blager said, "You are telling me I'm not safe here?"

"We are compromised." Harrington said. "As you know, we've been debriefing the agent who participated, albeit unknowingly, in your poisoning."

"Dr. Stein."

"Yes, Sir," Harrington said. "Everything she's told us that can be checked out has been checked out. I'm convinced that she did not and would not have knowingly harmed you."

"I concur," Goldfarb said.

"How are rescue plans for her husband progressing?"

"Nothing new, Sir. Right now, protecting you is our priority."

"I'm not leaving here and going into hiding," The President said.

Goldfarb cleared his throat. "Actually, that's the problem, Sir."

"What?"

"You're almost over the poisoning, but still at risk, Sir. We still expect that you will be dead in 24 to 48 hours."

"And exactly how do you know this?"

"Harrington shared the opinions of your personal physician with me."

The President nodded. "He'll be releasing me in a day or two. I do not dispute that. What about the rest?"

"That's softer information, Sir."

"How…." The President stopped. Harrington was not cleared for remote viewing intelligence. He cleared his throat. "Oh."

"Yes, Sir."

The President sighed and looked at Harrington. "Dr. Goldfarb will be discussing Special Intelligence, Jordan, from a source that doesn't concern you. It is best that you step outside and forget what you heard when you leave this room."

"Understood, Sir," Harrington said. "I'm not privy to his sources and methods. Nor do I wish to be."

Harrington took his exit. When the door had closed and latched, the President said, "Continue."

"Josie reported, correctly, that the interventions to improve your health were successful. Her viewings of the future remain unchanged. She thinks your death triggers the onset of what we are calling the Abyss, a black void. This is death. It is now less than 48 hours away."

"I need more details."

"I wish we had them, Sir. Josie's viewings are blocked. All she can sense is a gray zone, a void that turns dark and then is followed by the Abyss. She can't view your death directly."

"Then you tell me nothing new."

"What's new is that this disaster is imminent. Time is running out. Josie cannot see inside the void, but she can still sense when the Abyss starts. It is close."

"Keep talking," the President said.

"We are looking at a window of uncertainty about twenty four hours long which starts as early as tomorrow evening. Somewhere inside that gray window of uncertainty is your death. The time coordinates are uncertain to the extent I mentioned, but Josie is confident this location is ground zero. Whatever happens, it starts here, in this room, and soon."

"I need something actionable, Ari."

"That's why we're here. Until this risk is past, I want myself or Harrington to stay here to protect you. We'll be the last line of defense."

The President smiled and looked around his room. "Here? You mean that literally?"

"Yes, Mr. President. Anyone who enters has to get by one of us. We think you will die in hours, even healthy, and despite increased security."

"That assumption is based only on remote viewings," President Blager said, "of an event that you admit yourself can't be seen or sensed directly."

"Do you accept that's Josie's viewings have a good record of success?"

"An excellent record. Over 80% as I recall."

"Better, actually," Goldfarb said. "Here's where the logic comes in."

"Go ahead."

"We've already made a number of changes to improve your health and security, but none delayed or prevented your death. Why?"

"Why do you think?"

"The most likely possibility I can see, Sir, is that a kill team can somehow get past your fully alerted military and Secret Service protection. My people are working that one as a top priority. Josie reports there is a Hamas team in the area, controlled by one Marco Ricci, and not run out of Trinity Church. Her viewings are partially blocked, but she is convinced there is a small team still out there."

"How small?"

"The Black Panther team we disrupted was run out of Trinity. It had four operatives, three male and one female. We think the Hamas team is the same size."

"Based on what?"

"Operational considerations. That is how many adults can fit in a normal car, and how many bunks there were at Trinity. We are assuming they brought back the same Hamas team that was there before."

"You've not located them yet?"

"No, Sir."

"The Secret Service says I'm safe."

"They don't have access to our information," Goldfarb said.

"No."

"It's a matter of attitudes, Sir. Your security forces think the crisis is past. Raven's team believes the greatest risk is yet to come. Josie has been right about everything so far, from the kill team operating out of Trinity

John D Trudel

Church, to the fact that some people close to you were aiding the terrorists. In both cases, our interventions neutralized these threats."

The President nodded slowly.

"We're not saying the Secret Service and Military don't do a good job at protecting you. Their efforts are helpful. If we combine what they are doing with what Josie is seeing, it gives me more confidence we can stop this."

"I need you to speak more specifically, Ari. I don't understand."

"What's interesting to me is that as we've hardened your security, extended the perimeter, disrupted the opposition, improved your health, and blocked threats, the outcome did not change."

"When you say, 'outcome,' you mean my death?"

"Yes, Mr. President. Our actions to prevent this outcome have not been effective. That tends to make me want to look for something else."

"You are saying someone else tries to kill me? Someone on the inside?"

"That's one possibility. Dr. Stein says they do have another agent inside. She suspects it might be someone on your staff or security team."

"On the Secret Service?"

"We have no idea, Sir. As soon as the kill team is located and neutralized, we will shift Josie's focus to looking for another mole. She has already checked everyone with access to you."

"I won't leave," the President said.

"Yes, Sir. I respectfully request that at all times, for the next 48 hours, either Harrington or myself be here in your room. By then, we'll know more."

"In this room? Can't you guard me from outside?"

"That would defeat our purpose, Sir. There is already a guard outside, one quicker, stronger, and more adept with weapons than we are. We plan to deal with any threats that get past him."

"How?"

"We're armed, Sir." Goldfarb displayed his .45.

"Do you know how to use that, Ari?"

"I used to, Sir."

The President groaned, but he was smiling. "Okay, enough. I will do as you wish for God and country. However, get me a weapon so I can defend myself, and bring in a sleeping bag. I would prefer a Colt 1911 as well. That was my personal sidearm in the military."

"You can have mine, Sir. I have a spare in my car. I will get it and my sleeping bag. I have to be somewhere for breakfast, so I will take the first shift. Harrington can relieve me at 05:00."

"That works," the President said. "When you get settled, I want you to lock the door, but to keep the space in front of it clear."

"Why?"

"We have another little secret to share. Josie has a paranormal friend who looks in on me at 19:00 each evening. A healer. He wants the door locked. It does not inhibit him. Should I try to warn him that you're here?"

Goldfarb smiled. "I don't think so. If he's a paranormal who can ghost into a secure facility through locked doors, he'll probably figure it out himself..."

Spindrift Road, South of Point Lobo, California

When they left Highway 1, Kamal had started wishing they had a four-wheel drive vehicle. American cars were toys, worthless in the desert or rough terrain.

Spindrift road was paved, but when he killed the lights and turned off onto the soft dirt private drive, they got stuck.

Kamal cursed. He unsnapped the dome light, removed the bulb, and made everyone get out. With him at the wheel, they carefully pushed the car back off the road into the bushes, put branches under the wheels, and checked to make sure it was free to move by starting the engine and rocking it back and forth a few times. By the time they were done, his team was breathing hard and covered with sweat.

He ordered a break. He had them drink water to hydrate. He made them wait a few minutes to get familiar with the night sounds, to give their eyes time to adapt to the dark, and to focus on the mission.

The night was dark with only a few stars. Kamal looked back towards Highway 1, now about half a mile away. They were screened by trees and well out of sight. He could hear occasional traffic out on the highway, but could not see any headlights. The two houses they had passed on Spindrift had been dark. They were rentals and showed as vacant on the web site for their listing service.

Kamal knelt behind the car and got his hand-made map out. He had made copies at the local Kinko's, and each member of the team had reviewed it. He gestured for them to cluster around, and, using his small flashlight with the red lens, he illuminated the map and marked their current location. "We're here. Mark it."

They did.

Mohammad was their point man. He was al-Qaeda trained as a sniper and scout. Kamal tapped his shoulder. "How long do you need to get into position without being detected?"

"Forty-five minutes, no more."

"We'll allow an hour. No lights. No talking, and stay about ten meters apart. Take prisoners if possible, but if any resist, kill them."

That got nods. They had already been briefed, but it was good to go over it again.

"There are people around," Kamal said. "Do you hear the traffic on the highway?"

His men nodded, except for Hani, the kid. Kamal cuffed him. "Did you hear the traffic?"

"I think so."

"Pay attention. Did you hear it or not?"

"I hear the traffic."

"Good." Kamal turned his attention to the others. "Make sure no one escapes to get help, but no noise. You are to use knives and suppressed weapons only."

The men screwed silencers on their pistols. Regrettably, only Mohammad had one for his AK.

Kamal said, "Ahmed, you stay with the car. If anyone tries to leave, stop them. If anything goes wrong, get clear. We'll hide our weapons and regroup at the Carmel River Inn."

"I remember the briefing," Ahmed said. "No problem."

He was a big man, but clumsy. He typically made as much noise as the entire rest of the team when moving about. Ahmed was strong as a bear and good at interrogation, but terrible where stealth was involved.

He bumped things, as if he expected them to move out of his way. At the mosque, he had already pulled a doorknob off and broken a chair.

Those who knew him and saw him coming stepped aside. Kamal had watched him break necks with one hand. He beheaded infidels with a casual stroke of his combat knife.

Ahmed's English was excellent. He was a U.S. citizen who grew up in LA. He knew the local mannerisms and slang, had ID including a California driver's license, was gregarious, and should not attract attention.

"When we secure the house, I'll send Mohammad back. You bring the car, and we will hide it in the garage. Stay on the drive and be careful not to get stuck again."

Ahmed nodded.

"Any questions?"

There were none. The men were ready.

"*Allahu Akbar.* Let's go."

CHAPTER FORTY-SIX
A USEFUL RELIC

Building 422, The Presidio of Monterey, California, 10 PM

Goldfarb was in deep sleep, having disturbing dreams of fleeing enormous woodpeckers with jackhammers through a dark forest. He was running, but making little progress. They were gaining on him. He knew if they caught him, he would be hammered and pecked. He woke in a cold sweat, disoriented, and confused.

He heard a soft, persistent rapping on the door, and a louder noise. Goldfarb recognized it. *Snoring. Sonorous snoring.*

He forced his eyes open. He was on the floor of a dimly lit room. The President's hospital room. *Right. Ad hoc guard duty.*

It is the details that get you, Goldfarb thought. The President had neglected to mention he snored like a bull moose. The floor was hard. He should have brought a pad, an air mattress, or, better, a cot.

Goldfarb was stiff and his back hurt. He forced himself to raise his head and look around. A quick glance assured him the President was sleeping peacefully. The tapping on the door continued. "Coming," he called softly.

Goldfarb struggled with the sleeping bag. The damned zipper was stuck. There was another rap. "Wait. I'm coming."

He could not find his glasses. He did not feel rested at all. His brain was muzzy. He wanted to splash cold water on his face, but none was available.

Goldfarb finally escaped the clutches of his bag, sliding out onto the cold tile floor. He stood up, shivering in his Jockey shorts and T-shirt. *Why do they have to keep hospitals so bloody cold? You could hang meat in here.*

Memory came back. The glasses, along with his pipe, the one he never smoked, were in the vest pocket of his tweed jacket, hanging on the chair. He slipped the jacket on, immediately grateful for its warmth.

He started for the door, and then remembered his gun. *Damn.*

Where did I put it? Goldfarb thought back on the evening, trying to remember. He had not toted a gun in the field since training. For decades, personal weapons were forbidden on domestic bases.

"Just a minute," he called again in a harsh whisper. *However unlikely it is that I will need a weapon in this multilayered bubble of security, I had better get it.*

The snoring stopped. The President was starting to stir.

He finally remembered. The presence of weapons had upset Kaimi, Josie's mystic mentor. He had asked Goldfarb to put his pistol somewhere safe and out of sight during his visit.

Kaimi went on and on about it. He threatened to leave if the gun was not secured and removed from ready access. He waxed eloquent about how weapons disturbed the harmonious state of mind he needed to access his paranormal abilities and tend the President. In the end, Goldfarb gave up and put his gun in the dresser across the room.

The rapping came again, louder. The damned fool was going to wake the President.

"What in the hell is going on?" the President mumbled.

Son of a bitch, Goldfarb thought. He gave up, hit the room lights, moved to the dresser, yanked the drawer open, and got his gun.

The President hit the button to crank his bed up, blinking in the light. He was looking at Goldfarb with an irritated expression.

"I'm sorry, Sir," he said to the President. He turned to the door, raised his voice, and did not bother to hide his own irritation. "Wait a minute. I'm coming."

Holding his .45 in his right hand, Goldfarb reached down for the latch. It snapped open with a loud click. Before he could move, the door flew open with great force.

It clipped his left shoulder, spinning him around, and into the wall with a crash that shook the room. Goldfarb's gun went flying from his fist.

He fell to his knees in time to receive a kick that lifted him and moved him clear of the doorway.

Goldfarb felt ribs crack and his vision narrowed. A man he had never seen before wearing green medical scrubs burst into the room. The pistol in his hand swung away from Goldfarb, centering on the President.

Goldfarb's left arm was not working. He reached hard with his right, stretched, grabbed the man's balls with clawed fingers, and did his best to rip them off.

The man screamed in agony, and curled to a fetal position. The scream cut off, and the man took a deep breath, and straightened.

An incredible pain tolerance. I am in trouble.

He was turning, the muzzle of his weapon swinging back toward Goldfarb.

Goldfarb twisted, pulled as hard as he could, and swung a sidekick at the man's ankles, cutting his feet out from under him. Screaming again, the man fell like a tree, forward.

Goldfarb had to let go or risk a broken wrist. He held the grip anyway, shouting, "Shoot the bastard."

The President fired twice as the man fell. His big .45 boomed like a cannon, the noise deafening in the small space. The shots went high. Holes appeared in the wall and plaster dust showered down.

The man's fall saved him, but his head slammed into the rail at the bottom of the President's bed. He dropped his weapon and hit the floor with a thud.

Goldfarb took a deep breath. He flicked the gun away with his foot, pulled his right leg back, and kicked the man in the head.

He felt something snap in his foot and a flash of pain. *Bad idea. No shoes.*

Goldfarb's mind was racing. He remembered a long-ago class where a sergeant had recruits practice self-defense with sticks. *Jab at the soft, strike at the hard.*

It was worth a try. Goldfarb jammed his other heel into the man's balls, feeling it connect solidly. That prompted another scream.

Goldfarb struggled to his feet. It hurt like hell, but he made it. He stood there, swaying, breathing hard.

The man staggered to his feet. He was still in the fight.

"Nail his ass," Goldfarb shouted, taking a step back. "Finish it."

The President fired again, but missed high as the man dove for the floor.

Goldfarb's ears were ringing, but he could hear alarms sounding in the distance and footsteps pounding down the hall. The cavalry was coming.

The man heard it too. He was prone at the bottom of the President's bed, out of the line of fire. The man scrambled frantically across the floor like a wounded crab, slipping on the tile, crawling, reaching for his gun.

The President was starting to get out of bed, shifting to where he had a clear shot. It seemed like he was moving in slow motion.

The man touched his weapon.

I need to end this. Goldfarb scooped his pipe out of his jacket pocket right-handed. He hobbled forward as quickly as he could, ignoring the pain.

Goldfarb leaned down, pressed his pipe stem to the man's ear, and squeezed.

The pipe was a relic from his Cold War days in the field, a James Bond gadget that one of the technicians at the Agency had concocted. It fired a single .22 round. It was a generally worthless weapon, and there were better suicide devices, so it never caught on.

There was a faint pop and the man went limp. Goldfarb had carried it around for fifty years as a memento, and it had finally proven to be useful. You just never knew.

The President struggled to his feet. He took the two-hand grip, like on a range, and put two carefully aimed shots, center mass, into the body.

Goldfarb dropped his pipe and took a step back. He put his hand on the bed rail to steady himself. His ears were ringing, he felt dizzy, his left arm hung limp, and he could not put any weight on his right foot.

There was a short burst of gunfire behind him from an automatic weapon. More slugs shredded the prone body, and suddenly the room was full of Marines in body armor with M-4 carbines.

One of them caught Goldfarb as he collapsed, and then everything went black.

An annoying beeping noise filtered into Goldfarb's awareness. He came drifting up from a dark, warm, comfortable place and opened his eyes. The light was blinding.

He felt no pain, but when he tried to move, he could not.

"Easy."

He knew that voice. "Mr. President. Are you all right?"

"I'm fine, Ari. You protected me like a mama bear with cubs. How do you feel?"

Goldfarb blinked. His vision cleared. The President was sitting in a chair next to his bed. Goldfarb was strapped down, had leads taped to his body, a drip in his arm, a cannula in his nose, and there was one of those monitors with the green lines beeping on the table on his left side. Goldfarb's left leg was elevated in a cast, hanging from a cable, and his right arm, in a cast, stuck out straight from his body, also supported by cables.

"I can't move."

"You're not supposed to. There are 26 bones in the human foot. You managed to break six of them, including two toes. In addition, you have a broken collar bone, and four broken ribs."

Goldfarb's chest felt odd, but he could breathe. He could wiggle the fingers on both hands and the toes on his left foot. "I don't hurt."

"You will when the drugs wear off, but the doctors say you'll be fine."

"Good to know."

"If you're going to have the shit beat out of you, it's handy to already be in an ICU."

"Why are you here tending me, Sir?"

"I couldn't sleep. Too much adrenaline. I also want to ask you some questions if you're up to it."

Goldfarb managed to move his head so he could see the President's eyes. "Go ahead."

"When was the last time you carried a weapon in the line of duty?"

"That would be never, Sir. I did the weapons training, but even when I was in CIA's OPs division I had embassy cover. I ran agents and the Russians PNGed me once, but, unlike Hollywood, we didn't carry weapons in the field."

The President frowned. "P and G?"

"*Persona Non Grata*: They threw me out. The Cold War was ugly, but at least we had rules. We didn't kill KGB agents, and they tried not to kill us."

"What about the agent you were running?"

"They executed him, a GRU Colonel I'd come to like. For years, I wondered if it was my fault…."

"Yes, I can imagine."

"It was a long time ago. I came back to the States, rehabbed, and got my PhD. You probably know the rest of my career. My cover as a field agent was blown, so I became a professor and moved to policy level."

"How old are you, Ari?"

"I'll be seventy two on July 18th, Sir."

"How did you and Jordan come up with the insane notion of putting your bodies in front of me? I went along to humor you, but never believed it would get down to that. It damn near got you killed, Ari…."

"Josie and Raven kept saying how the things she's been viewing didn't make sense. It was a long shot, but we were out of ideas and needed to do something."

"You were right, and we were lucky."

"I'll take lucky, Sir. God protects fools and Americans."

"You saved my life."

Goldfarb closed his eyes, relaxed, and slumped back into the bed. "You're supposed to be the patient, Sir, not taking care of me."

"I've lost patience with being a patient. They are going to release me tomorrow. They moved me to another room with a better décor – no bullet holes in the wall. I'll unstrap you if you promise to be good and not struggle."

"Mr. President, I don't have the strength right now to struggle with a kitten."

The President leaned over and loosened the restraints. "Would you like some water?"

"Please."

"Small sips." The President held a glass with a straw for him.

"You're a good nurse, Sir."

"No, I'm a grateful President."

"Who was that guy, and how did he get in here?"

"*Taqiyya.*"

"Islamic deception?" Goldfarb blinked. "He was a Muslim?"

"He was indeed. The Muslims have been planting spies and assassins for 2,000 years. The use of deception to serve Allah is morally authorized. It is built into Islam. Yasser Arafat was a master of exploiting that gap, a terrorist who won the Nobel Peace Prize. Hitler almost got one too, you know. Hard to believe."

"What's hard to believe is that assassins have now penetrated your security twice, Sir."

"I don't intend to allow a third time. I have instructed the drafting of an Executive Order to ensure less political correctness in our security procedures. It may result in a law, and, if so, I want to put your name on it."

Goldfarb said, "Tell me more about this attack."

"There were no red flags. Like the chef who put the poisonous mushrooms in my pasta, he was a Westernized Muslim who fit into our society perfectly. He was well liked and everyone's best friend, but the FBI found *jihad* materials on his computer. His dream was killing *Kafir*, which is to say, me. He was eager to do that and die for Allah."

"What was his name, and what was he doing here?"

"He went by 'Barry.' His real name was Abdul Baari Mubarak. His family came from Egypt. He is distantly related to President Mubarak. He was a hospital orderly, and earned extra money by working night shifts."

"He's an American?"

President Blager nodded. "Second generation, and with a Secret Level clearance. His mother is a High School teacher, and his father is one of the instructors on staff at the Language Institute here. They went to college in the US. The parents claim to be surprised and distraught, as does the Imam at Monterey Mosque."

"Claim to be...?"

The President's face was grim. "It's hard to know where *Taqiyya* ends. The parents — young Barry was living at home — are in custody and being questioned. Barry killed the Secret Service guard outside and took his gun. He had befriended the guard. They played on the same soccer team."

"Nice guy...." *And damned Sloppy security.*

"Do you know what Abdul Baari means?"

Goldfarb managed a headshake. It was the easiest part of his body to move.

"Abdul Baari means 'Servant of the Creator.' If you spell it 'Bari,' as is on his birth certificate, it means 'Slave of the Creator.' Either way, Barry seems to have been on a mission from Allah. He was not America's friend, he was a *jihadist*."

"Do we know who was running him? Or was he an independent?"

"Not yet. The right people are working on it. I will see you get a copy of the report. The only thing I am certain of now is this: We need policy changes. We've been at war with Radical Islam for thirty years, and we're not winning."

"Yes, Sir."

"Heal and rest, Ari. I will see to it that you are not, um, disturbed again. As for me, I'm going get some sleep." The President stood up. "I'll see you at a more civilized hour, after the sun comes up."

After the President left, Goldfarb lay staring at the bullet holes and shattered plaster. His last thought as he drifted off was that he needed to call Raven in the morning. One thing was sure. He was not going to make their breakfast meeting.

CHAPTER FORTY-SEVEN
THE DARK WOODS

Private Beach House, South of Monterey, California, early morning

R aven came awake when his computer beeped. One of the security sensors had tripped. He got out of bed and tapped a key to wake the computer. It was the sensor out by the road, lucky number 13.

There were no alarms from other sensors, and this one did not have a camera. He had them set to trip for medium sized animals. Maybe setting them that high had been a mistake. Anything larger than a cat or small dog would trip his sensors.

There was a lot of wildlife around. Yesterday he had seen three deer, a buck and two doe. Josie had seen a large pig, up by the house. *I should have put in more cameras.*

"Murph…?" Josie mumbled. It was dark outside. No moon and only a few stars. Raven saw the dim shadow as she sat up.

"We got a security alarm, Babe. Not close, out by the road. It might have been a deer."

"Uh huh." She pulled the covers up around her.

Raven waited. Almost a minute passed, and then the sensor tripped again. Raven frowned. *A second deer? Maybe it doubled back?*

That had not happened before. Raven kept hunting clothes on the floor next to the bed. Not military, that was too sinister. Just a civilian hunting rig he had ordered from Cabelas off the web: Scent-Lok lightweight

Savanna, in the "all-purpose" Realtree pattern. It blended well with the local vegetation and was comfortable.

Raven slipped the coveralls on, dropped his little Sig into the right side cargo pocket, and put two magazines and a TAC light into the left. He snapped the pockets closed, and put on his socks and boots. Then he waited.

Sensor # 13 tripped again. *Three deer, well spaced, and moving slowly?*

Then two more sensors tripped, # 11, the next one in towards the house, and # 9, off to the South, but also closer to the house. Still no video or images.

Three large animals might be converging on the house. Deer would not likely do that, coyotes or pigs might, and a kill team certainly would.

Raven's training and experience kicked in. "I'm going to go look around."

He stood up and slipped on his matching shooter's gloves. He grabbed his camo head cover and Mini-14, filling his vest pockets with 20-round mags. Then he powered up his phone, careful to put it on 'silent,' and set it to monitor the remote sensors.

Nothing had changed. There were no new alarms, and still no video images.

Josie was dressing silently in the darkness. Dark clothes. A black sweater and jeans. He saw her pull the hammerless .357 magnum out from the drawer in her end table. "What is it?"

"I'm not sure. Maybe just some animals moving around. Can you sense anything?"

"No. It's too late to ask me that now."

Raven froze. "Why?"

"That dead zone I told you about has arrived. It has now reached our present. It is like a thick fog, still and peaceful, but I cannot see through it. My paranormal senses are useless."

"Are you okay?"

"I'm fine. I'm not scared. Fear and violence shuts down my paranormal senses, but this is different. It feels calming and serene. My powers are strong, but I cannot see anything except with my eyes. The dead zone was an appropriate name. My ESP senses gray all around us, a blanketing fog of probabilistic uncertainty. We knew it was coming. Now it's here."

"Yes. I will go check things out. It is probably nothing."

"We can run," Josie said. "If we relocate spatially, I might be able to get clear of the dead zone and do the remote viewing I promised you. The viewings you want are all set in the past, but, in this physical location, the edge of the dead zone is also in our past. It blinds me. I cannot see out of it. If we relocate in space, we might be able to get clear of it."

"Bad plan. That won't work for several reasons."

"Why not?"

"First off, most likely, it's nothing. If it is wildlife that is tripping the sensors, we will be running from nothing. I've been getting trips because of deer."

"What else?"

"Secondly, if it is a kill team, the way out is already blocked and we would be running into a trap. We are better off to make a stand here and call for help. Finally, we may not be able to get clear of this dead zone. Right?"

Josie said, "I didn't spend time studying it, but it did spread fast."

"Goldfarb will be here soon. He may have located the kill team by now. I think we should stay close. We have about run out of time. If the President dies, it is game over."

"Yes. What do you want me to do?"

"Stay safe. Do you remember what we discussed?"

"I'm to lock down, go to cover, assume anyone who breaks in is a lethal threat, and shoot them. You're going to sing out loud before you come back in."

"Yes," Raven said. "No mistakes this time."

"No mistakes this time." Josie's voice was steady. "If I hear shooting, I call the base for backup and tell them we're under attack."

"Exactly right, but it's probably nothing." Raven kissed Josie on the lips and said, "Lock the door behind me. You'll be safe here."

Then he was gone, fading off into the night like a ghost. Darkness was his element. Raven took a few steps and seemed to blend into the forest. *Poof.*

There were three primary ways into the house. The front door was made of solid wood and dead-bolted. The patio, double-pane tempered glass, and off a raised deck, had a locking bar. The door to the garage, again solid wood with a deadbolt, was less of a threat. She had disabled the garage door opener.

From inside the fireplace, Josie could see all three doors, and she had cover. That is where she nestled down. She seated herself, put a pillow behind her back – the brick was rough and hard – and set the .357 next to her right hand along with a box of shells, and a flashlight and water bottle by her left. Her cell phone was on, charged, and in her pocket.

Windows could be broken, but Josie would hear that and be prepared. And at the first shots, she knew Raven would be coming to help.

Josie made herself as comfortable as possible, and waited, trying to stay calm, trying not to think of Durham. She was good until morning.

Raven knew the ground. He moved to the predetermined spot he had chosen to defend the house. Here he had a good view of anything coming in from the road, a good field of fire, and cover to move around and reposition.

He pulled out his phone set to the screen with a map of the security sensors. The ones with no alarms were green, and those with trips in the last hour were yellow. There had been already been two more alarms, these were red. One was sensor # 10 – finally one with a camera.

Raven clicked on it to pull up the image. What he saw was not what he expected: pigs with tusks. The camera caught two clear images before they disappeared into the underbrush. One of the pigs was huge – twice the size of the others.

After Josie's sighting yesterday, Raven had checked and learned pigs were a game animal in California and quite common. They were found in 56 of the state's 58 counties, mostly on private lands, and could be hunted with game tags. They had been there since the early 1700s, but in the 1920s a Monterey landowner had introduced European Wild Boar, which bred with the domestic pigs, resulting in wild boar / feral domestic pig hybrids.

About what you would expect of California. There were probably liberal activist groups to protect feral pigs.

Pigs had poor eyesight, but good hearing and an excellent sense of smell. The boars could grow to 500 pounds, about three feet tall, and up to six feet long. They had razor sharp tusks, typically about 3-5 inches, but sometimes as long as nine inches. Of more interest was that they were territorial, could run at 30 miles per hour, as fast as a horse, and would attack if threatened.

Like humans, they could breed at any time of the year. Boars were aggressive when sows were in heat. Wild pigs and boars were opportunistic omnivores. They ate most anything, including meat. They were territorial and tended to stay close to home, ranging over a few square miles if left alone. In safe areas with ample food, family groups might form "sounders" of 50 or more pigs. *Not a good thing to run into in the dark.*

Raven doubted the little .223 rounds in his Mini-14 would stop a charging boar. They might just make him mad. He slung his rifle, and drew his Sig.

Even that wasn't much comfort. His best bet might be to climb a tree if he ran across wild boar. *How many were out there? Maybe quite a few.* He had seen tracks, but thought they were deer.

Maybe he had been mistaking pig tracks for deer. The imprints were similar. Hunters examined scat and looked for places where pigs had been rooting or rubbing. Unfortunately, Raven had not thought of that. It was time to start using his brain.

Pigs were smart. When hunted, they shifted behavior. Moderate hunting caused them to bed down at daybreak, and become active in the late afternoon. During heavy hunting, feral pigs moved only at night. If hunting was light or nonexistent, they foraged openly in the daytime, like the one Josie had seen up near the house. It had been well fed and nonthreatening.

The local pigs were obviously not used to being hunted. This was their turf.

Something has spooked them, Raven thought. They had sensed something threatening. The possibilities were limited: Bears, mountain lions, and people.

Until tonight, there had been no alarms other than what he had thought were occasional deer. Something had changed. Raven strained his senses, but the night was totally still.

The lack of night sounds was a danger signal. Somewhere out there, a predator was hunting.

Raven waited, intently aware, perfectly still, and well concealed. *Let it come to me.*

Mohammad peered at a world his Night Vision Goggles turned into shades of green. He moved rapidly and silently through the brush, his senses fully alert, holding his suppressed AK at the ready. His every move was confident. He wanted action and was hoping that the infidels would put up resistance.

Many yards behind him, and losing ground with every step, young Hani brushed away tears and struggled to keep up. The night was dark and he kept running into branches. He could taste blood running down his face. His feet hurt and he was out of breath. Hani grew up in the city, had never been in a forest before, and was scared.

He was only 17. Unlike the others, he had not been through the training camps. He knew the reason he had been sent to America was to do the jobs no one else wanted, and because of his good English and innocent look. Kamal said Americans liked children.

America gave him hope. Life was cheap in Gaza. It offered little beyond the Koran and learning to hate.

Hani volunteered to go to America. It wasn't like he had a lot of other choices. It was either this or volunteering to be a suicide bomber.

If the mission was successful, Kamal promised to leave him in America with some money. Kamal assured him illegals were welcome there, and said he would be given papers, free schooling, and health care. That had been four months ago.

Things had changed. When they got to America, the mission bogged down and nerves were frayed. Mohammad ignored him, Kamal cursed him, and he was afraid to be alone with Ahmed. He didn't like the way Ahmed looked at him, or his remarks about succulent young boys who looked like girls.

They had been pulled out once. Hani rejoiced when they left, but then, before they got home, they were directed back. He was told that the team of Americans – Black Panthers, trained fighting men – that replaced them was dead. They were no longer welcome at the church that sheltered them.

Hani wanted to ask about it, but didn't. All they would do is laugh at him. Kamal might cuff him. Whatever had happened, no one talked about it.

When they came back to California, it was worse. Hani's world was being hidden in a small mosque with violent people who terrified him, eating unfamiliar food that upset his stomach. The refugee camps were squalid and unchanging, but there was television and they fed you regularly if you sang your daily prayers, memorized the Koran, and participated in the demonstrations. At least you could go outside and walk around.

California was like being in prison. There was nothing to do, and no one bothered to tell him what was going on, until today when they were ordered to move out.

Hani expected something like Gaza. They would kill infidels and blow up military buildings, but instead, he found himself out in the woods attacking some kind of a farmhouse in the middle of the night. It did not make any sense to him. He had no chance of keeping up with Mohammad, but if he did not, he knew he would be punished.

This forest was a nightmare. Hani was thinking it might be better to be throwing rocks at Israelis than running into trees, running towards an enemy that even Kamal seemed to fear.

There was a sudden noise. Hani froze. The bushes in front of him were moving. He was in a small clearing, there was enough light to see. There was something large in the bushes.

Terrified, Hani started backing away. There were sounds. Some kind of animal. There was a snuffling, like large beasts smacking their lips. Kamal said there were bears and mountain lions in California. Hani wasn't sure what a mountain lion was, but knew it had claws and teeth.

Hani brushed blood and sweat from his face and unslung his AK. It was the only weapon he had other than a knife. Kamal said not to make noise, but a knife didn't seem useful against lions and bears.

Hani backed up, turning slowly back and forth, his gun leveled. His heart was pounding.

There was sudden noise behind him. Hani spun. He saw eyes. They looked red in the starlight. Several pairs of eyes were coming at him, dark low creatures, moving fast.

Hani screamed and clamped the trigger down, a long ragged burst. The AK almost tore loose from his hands, but he'd hit at least one. There were squeals of pain.

The eyes were still coming. One beast was down, but it was still crawling toward him. Two more were coming fast. Hani fought to level his gun and aim.

Something hit him from behind, tearing his leg, and Hani was falling. Then he was down. He rolled frantically, trying to bring his gun up.

There was sudden pain as fangs ripped into his stomach. One beast had its head buried in his belly. It was ripping him open. Blood spurted.

The creature was too close, inside the muzzle arc of his weapon. He could not bring his gun to bear on it. Hani kicked frantically, knocked the beast free, stuck the gun muzzle against it, and fired. The rounds ripped into the creature, it fell back, and then his gun clicked empty.

Another beast landed on him and started ripping at his intestines. The ones he'd hit were still alive, crawling toward him. More were coming.

The last thing Hani heard were grunts and squeals of triumph.

The stillness of the night was shattered by a long ripping blast from a fully automatic weapon. Someone was holding the trigger down and spraying bullets. The shooter was close, perhaps only few hundred yards, and certainly no more than a quarter mile.

Raven strained his ears. The shots came from the direction of the road. Concentrating, he could hear faint screams, followed by an even longer burst of fire, then silence.

The sound was unmistakable: the weapon was an AK, being wielded poorly – by someone untrained, in a total panic, or both. Arab *jihadis* shot like that, spraying fire everywhere. He had seen it often, twelve year olds with AKs spreading terror and killing unarmed civilians.

Such sloppiness did not do well against armed, trained enemies. It made a lot of racket, but was not effective.

It did not matter to Islamic leaders. Arab kids from the *madrasas* were cannon fodder, throwaways that were easily replaced. Aimed shots and fire discipline were not a priority. Weapons were cheap, and there was a limitless supply of fanatics eager to die for Allah.

A jihadi just died out there, Raven thought.

He stayed still, watching and listening. A minute passed, and then he heard a shout, followed by something large crashing through the brush, running toward the gunfire. An animal would not do that, it had to be a man. He'd been close.

Too damned close, Raven thought. *This one is dangerous. He's had sniper or scout training. He made it within easy range of the house without being detected. If I had moved, he would have had me.*

Raven thought for a moment, considering options, but he knew what he had to do. He remembered the words of an old SPEC OPs weapons sergeant in a long-ago training class. *Seize the opportunity, asshole. God just smiled on you.*

Raven came to his feet and took off at a jog. It was getting brighter. There was no moon, but the clouds were clearing, and there were a few stars.

When he found the scout's back trail, Raven moved faster. After about two hundred yards, he stopped, stilled his breathing, and listened. *Nothing.*

Raven moved another 50 yards, more slowly now, following broken branches, and tried again. *Nothing.*

Raven was getting the hang of it. He was following a well-traveled game trail. Down low, it was obvious where many animals – almost certainly pigs – had broken branches and rubbed against trees. Higher up, above about three feet, there were signs that a man had come through at a run, someone who was not worried about making noise or leaving sign.

He moved another 25 yards. This time he heard voices. Two people were arguing in Arabic. *Bingo,* Raven thought. He was no longer worried about pigs or animals, they would be long gone. The most deadly predator was man.

Raven pocketed the Sig and unslung his suppressed Mini-14. Putting one glove over the action to muffle the sound, he clicked the safety off. Then, using maximum stealth, he moved closer.

Raven wanted to see what was going on.

The voices grew louder. He was close. Peering through the bushes, he saw two men standing in a clearing. One was angry, waving his arms. The other was taller and had his back to Raven.

That one held a suppressed AK. Raven could see the long cylinder on the end of the muzzle. There was something strapped to his head. Raven strained to see. *Oh shit.*

Bad news. That is the scout, and he has NVGs. All he has to do is turn around, pop them on, and I am like a deer in the headlights.

Hamas sent their first-string team. They just lost a rookie, but this guy is a pro. He would be deadly inside about 100 yards. The other one is an officer. He had never encountered a suppressed AK in the field, and the bad guys did not usually carry Night Vision Goggles.

Decision time, Raven thought. *I can drop them. Do I take the shot?*

He was the only thing between these men and Josie. *How the hell did they find us?*

Raven did not fire. Josie was a strategic asset, worth any risk. She would be totally exposed if he went down. He was looking at one element of a larger kill team, and he knew his own backup was a half-hour or more away.

I need to take them all out.

Raven needed to know more. He started working his way off the trail, moving silently, careful not to leave any sign. After a few yards, he found a sturdy tree.

The voices were clear now. He was close, very close. He could hear every word. They were arguing about moving a body. The arm waver was giving orders. The scout was refusing, quoting something from the Koran about pigs.

Raven reached down, found some dirt, and rubbed it carefully on the parts of his face that showed through his headgear to blacken it. Slowly, silently, he pressed close to the trunk and peered around the tree.

The *jihadists* were ten feet away, arguing heatedly.

CHAPTER FORTY-EIGHT
REDEMPTION

Private Beach House, South of Monterey, California, early morning

J osie was dozing, but came instantly awake when she heard the distant shooting. She remembered her promise to call for backup if she heard gunfire.

It was gunfire, but it was not close. Her special senses were still blocked, but the gray fog seemed thinner in places. She could feel Raven's presence out there. He was okay.

We should have been more specific. Should I call the police? The military?

Josie frowned. Neither seemed a good idea. The shooting had stopped.

In Durham, the police responded to 911 calls, but they never had a chance. They had been shot down in the street by an Islamic paramilitary force with overwhelming firepower.

The military, stuck waiting for orders, talked young John Black into volunteering. They sent him ahead – alone – to help Josie and Raven. Black was overwhelmed and shot down, just like the police.

Everyone did their best, but it had been a debacle. Raven called it a cluster fuck. They were still recovering from that, still emotionally raw.

She had promised Raven to call for backup if she heard gunfire, but they had also agreed "No more Durhams." Distant gunfire was unanticipated.

Josie was unsure of what she should do. Last time, when she acted, it got Raven hurt. What would he want her to do now?

It came to her: *Goldfarb. He is our control.*

She dialed Goldfarb's number. The call went to voice mail. That was not surprising: It was four AM.

Josie identified herself, reported the distant gunfire, described the situation, and left a voicemail. She said Raven would call in to report when he got back. She marked her message private and urgent, and then played it back to be certain she had been clear.

Satisfied she had done her job as promised, Josie relaxed back against the fireplace. Goldfarb would know what to do.

There was no more gunfire. The night was still, even peaceful. The shots had been a long way off, the house was safe, and so was she. Whatever was going on, it did not seem threatening. Unlike Durham, she had no sense of foreboding. Raven would be back soon.

Josie started meditating, seeking harmony. Eventually, after she had regained her inner peace, she relaxed and dozed.

Raven waited by the game trail to the house, every sense alert. He had heard the *jihadis'* plans. The team leader was going back for reinforcements, but the scout would be returning to his position near the house. That could not be allowed.

No mistakes. This one is dangerous.

Raven had scattered some small dry branches along the trail. They would make noise, but, in this case, it was not necessary. He heard the man coming, moving fast through the brush.

He was moving faster than Raven could. It had clouded up again and the *jihadi* would have his NVGs on, giving him an advantage. Raven would only get one chance as the man came by, and then he would be at a disadvantage.

A severe disadvantage, once the scout realized Raven was there. He would be outgunned.

The AK fired a much heavier round. It was probably full auto, a machine gun. A solid hit anywhere would disable Raven and his adversary could see in the dark. The odds would be against him in a gunfight. His best hope was surprise and a quick kill.

Raven hid his Mini-14 in the brush. He took a firm grasp on his eight-inch Gerber fixed-blade black combat knife. It was not his preferred weapon, but it was deadly.

Raven was tense and sweating, but he had wrapped the hilt with black hockey tape so his hand would not slip. Both the upper and lower edges of the blade were serrated, designed to maximize the damage after the knife's initial plunge.

Never take a knife to a gunfight. Raven smiled grimly, recalling the old saying, but the Gerber was his best bet. *Fear is a motivator. I need to cowboy up and get this done.*

The man flashed by Raven's tree, running like a deer through the brush and over the broken ground, moving improbably fast. *Damn.*

Raven almost missed him. He took one long running step, and then made a desperate leap with all his strength. The man sensed him, hesitated, and that slight pause made the difference.

He clutched the man's forehead with his left hand and slashed his combat blade in a ferocious line across his throat, once, twice, and then stabbed him through the ribs and up into his heart. Without a sound, the man went limp.

Raven stepped back and the *jihadi* crumpled to the ground. Raven stood over the body, shaking in reaction. He was sweating profusely. He took a deep breath and wiped the blood off his knife on the man's shirt. He had to use both hands to put it back in its sheath.

The Gerber had done its job. Raven leaned against his tree, and eased himself to the ground. He took several deep breaths to still his racing heart. He pulled out a water bottle, and sipped it slowly. He pulled off his camouflage head cover, wet his handkerchief, and wiped his face. The cool water felt good.

Raven sat quietly for several minutes, breathing deeply, giving his body a chance to recover. He sighed deeply and rose to his feet.

He had plucked the NVGs off the man's head as he collapsed and tossed them clear. Raven studied the goggles in the dim light. They seemed intact.

He recognized them, a set of PVS-7 third-generation night vision goggles. The goggles were tan in color, not black. Original US military issue and expensive, not the cheap clones from a Chinese toymaker.

Raven nodded approval. *First-rate equipment. He probably took them off a dead American soldier in the sandbox.*

He slipped them on, adjusted the straps, and checked them out. The night came alive in green shades around him. *That is much better*, Raven thought.

Then Raven grabbed his Mini-14 and started back up the trail, moving away from the house. He had more work to do this night.

Raven scouted all the way back out to the access road. The NVGs helped a lot.

He had no problem finding his targets. Their transport, a 4-door Ford, was parked in the brush off the start of the dirt driveway into the house. There were ruts leading from where they had gotten stuck and had to push it into the brush.

The *jihadis* did not seem to be in any hurry. There were only two of them. The leader was standing next to the car, arguing with a large bearded man.

Raven crept close enough to hear what they were saying. It was the same argument, about retrieving the body versus the Koran's stated uncleanness of touching pig blood.

They were coming to an agreement. He waited, thinking furiously.

So far, this force, whoever they were, had been one-step ahead of him. His team in Durham had all taken casualties. Out here, Black had been injured, again, and was out of action. Moira was dead.

The bad guys were winning. They were lethal, aggressive, and persistent. They had gotten to the President through the tightest security in the world, and they kept getting too close to Josie. He could kill these two, but those running the OP would just send more.

They needed better intelligence. People at high levels were running this. The bad guys had been so effective that he and Josie were convinced they must have sources on the inside.

This shit has got to stop. He would set up a kill zone that he controlled, take down the muscle, and capture the leader for some heavy-duty interrogation.

The trick was to do it in a way that did not attract official notice. If he did it himself, Goldfarb could have the bastard out of the country and into rendition without anyone catching wise. In a country plagued with leaks, liberal bleeding hearts, and legalist process, it was the best chance at getting ahead of things.

Raven knew just the place.

Silently, he faded back into the brush, moving back up the trail. He scouted his chosen location and found a perfect shooting spot. He had excellent cover and a good field of fire. He could see them coming at a fair distance, and he could prevent egress.

Raven found a good tree, pissed like a racehorse, stretched his muscles, and flexed. There were two *jihadis* left, but neither was as formidable as the scout was. Mostly, they seemed to be arguing with each other. That was fine with him.

Then he settled into his blind and made himself comfortable. It was getting lighter in the East. He slipped off his NVGs, propped the Mini-14 on a good shooting rest, laid out a spare magazine, looked through the riflescope, set the lighting on the reticule, and got ready to kick ass.

Then he waited as the night softened into pre-dawn twilight. He would take them down at 50 yards. It was impossible to miss at that range.

Raven heard them coming a long way off. The big one sounded like an elephant crashing through the brush. The leader kept talking in Arabic, urging quiet.

Confusion to our enemies, and God Bless America.

The two men he had seen at the car were just entering the clearing, the one with the pigs and the other dead *jihadi*, the kid who had blown their cover by opening up with his AK.

That one did not look good. Most of his face was gone, his intestines had been pulled out, and a large pig had collapsed across him. There was a lot of blood on the ground, and insects were gathering. It would get worse when the sun rose and the day heated up.

The *jihadi* leader was pointing at the body, and the two were arguing again.

50 yards.

Raven let them get closer.

The two men separated when they reached the body, and he had a perfect shot. *It does not get any better.*

Raven put two suppressed shots into the big man, high center mass.

The rounds were on target. Raven saw them hit. The expanding bullets would make small holes on entrance, but the rest was not pretty. Raven swung right to the leader.

He was looking confused, staring at his buddy. He finally figured it out. He started to bring his AK up, pointing it in Raven's general direction.

"Drop it or die," Raven shouted.

The gun kept swinging.

Raven put a single round into the leader's right shoulder. The man staggered and dropped his AK.

Raven looked left, back at the big *jihadi.*

Incredibly, the big man was still on his feet, swaying, his chest covered with blood, his weapon coming up, centering on Raven. He must have seen the muzzle flash.

A double tap to the head fixed that. The man dropped like a pole axed steer.

Raven swung back to the leader. The man was on his knees, reaching for his weapon.

Raven put a round into the AK, shattering the stock. The man yanked his hand away.

Raven stood up and ran toward him. He kicked the AK away and stood looking down at his enemy. The blood had started to flow in earnest from the *jihadi's* shoulder.

"I believe your name is Kamal," Raven said quietly. He had heard him called that by the scout.

The leader's eyes narrowed as he lay there on the ground. His left hand suddenly shot up towards his mouth.

Raven tapped him hard on the temple with the butt of his Mini-14, stomping his boot on the man's arm, keeping it from the leader's mouth. When the man went limp, he knelt atop the Arab's chest.

Raven drew his Gerber knife from his leg sheath, and inserted the blade into the terrorist's mouth, vertically, so the sharp part of the blade was against his tongue, and the serrated razor teeth of the upper blade were against the roof of his mouth.

Kamal groaned. Blood streamed from his fresh cut lip and tongue, but the Arab's mouth was now propped open by the knife. He could not close it if he tried, and any attempt would cause further damage.

Raven reached carefully inside Kama's open mouth, and felt the molars. The top right one popped loose, and Raven removed it. Inside he saw a small white pill. Cyanide.

"You'll die soon enough, Kamal. Don't be in a rush."

Raven pulled his knife out of Kamal's mouth. He wiped the blood off by sliding the flat of the blade across Kamal's belly twice, and then sheathed it.

He gave Kamal a quick pat down and found the K-bar combat knife in its leg sheath. Still holding him down, Raven removed the K-bar. It had a US Marines logo on its hilt.

"Nice knife. Did you kill its rightful owner?"

Raven could see the answer in Kamal's eyes.

Raven leaned on his throat, used the K-bar to cut Kamal's shirt open, and checked his pockets and pouches. He found some magazines for the AK, several flex-cuffs, and a roll of duct tape. Kamal had been planning to take hostages, apparently.

Raven released the pressure on Kamal's neck and stood back. He pulled out his new NVGs and displayed them. "Your scout died badly, I'm afraid."

Kamal's eyes flashed. He tried to spit, but choked on his own blood.

"We can do this easy or hard, Kamal." Raven bent, dipped Kamal's knife in pig blood, and held it out. "Would you like me to wipe your wound with this?"

Fear crossed Kamal's face for the first time. "Please don't."

"Who do you report to?" Raven asked softly.

There was a hesitation. "Reverend Jones."

"You need to try harder, Kamal. You report to a man named Ricci."

Kamal's fear turned to panic. It showed in his eyes. "Yes, Ricci. I used to report to Reverend Jones. Now I report to Marco Ricci."

"Where is he?"

"I don't know."

Raven nodded slowly. It was possibly true. "Think about it. I'm sure you can come up with a better answer than that."

"What are you going to do with me?" Kamal asked.

It was a good question. Raven thought about it. It would be best to turn Kamal's interrogation over to specialists. "This is your lucky day."

Kamal was staring at him.

"I'll wrap your shoulder. Allah must not want you to die yet."

"American's don't kill prisoners...."

"I wouldn't be too eager to test that, if I were you."

Raven rolled Kamal over and flex-cuffed his wrists behind his back. He had plenty, so he used two pair. Then he wound duct tape over Kamal's wound to contain the bleeding, dragged him to his feet, and then over to a small tree.

"Down."

Kamal kneeled. He was acting docile.

"Sit. Straddle the tree with your feet."

"Good." Raven flex-cuffed Kamal's ankles together, again using two pair of cuffs, then put another pair on his wrists, and taped his mouth and fingers. Then he stood back and studied his work.

"That should hold you. I should be back before the pigs return."

Raven picked up his Mini-14 and slung it. Then he collected the rest of the weapons from around the clearing. Three AKs including the one with the shattered stock, three combat knives, a pistol, and a large pile of magazines. The big man even had a pair of fragmentation grenades.

Too much to carry. He smiled at Kamal. "Don't go away."

Raven popped the magazines out, checked the guns – Kamal's, the broken one, was hot, so he racked the action and pocketed the shell – and left them on the trail. He carried the magazines and grenades up the trail, found a burrow some animal had dug, and tossed them inside.

He was back in less than ten minutes. Kamal had not moved, but was watching him closely. His eyes were wild.

"No pigs yet," Raven said cheerfully. "I will try to get back before they show up. You might want to be as quiet as possible when they come for the blood, but it's up to you."

With that, he turned and started up the trail for the house. Raven did not look back. The sun was coming up over the horizon, and the clouds were clearing. It looked like it was going to be a beautiful day.

CHAPTER FORTY-NINE
MORNING

Private Beach House, South of Monterey, California, early morning

Josie recognized Raven's "all clear" call as he bounded up the steps and rapped on the door. "Honey, I'm home."

She heaved a deep sigh of relief. All was well.

"Just a minute." She had dead-bolted the door and put a chair in front of it. She pulled the door open, blinked, and felt her jaw drop in surprise. "What happened?"

"Long story, Babe."

Raven looked tired. He had dark stains soaking his left sleeve, and his rifle slung over his right shoulder. He smelled of sweat. His arms were out in front of him, palms up, supporting a small arsenal of machine guns.

"I'm glad you're back. I want to kiss you, but you'll need to put those weapons down."

"I'm about to do that if you'll let me in."

He entered. Josie closed and locked the door behind him.

Josie watched as he laid his collection of assault rifles down on the floor. She suppressed a shudder and refrained from saying anything. She sensed a dark miasma emanating from these guns. They had a crude appearance, a cheap, brutal look.

Josie disliked weapons, but she conceded a few of legend – Excalibur, and the Colt Peacemaker – had good karma. These were associated with freedom and noble causes. Raven's weapons had saved her life in Durham, and here as well.

These guns radiated evil. They were butcher's tools.

Raven opened the door to the small coat closet, and started carefully leaning the guns, butts down, against the back wall. The last one was broken, its stock splintered. It did not want to stand up until he moved it to the corner. When he was done, Raven stepped back, studying them critically for a long moment.

Josie said, "I heard the gunfire."

"Yeah."

He does not want to talk about it, Josie thought. *People died out there.* She suppressed a shiver and shut the closet door, pushing it until its latch clicked, as if walling off monsters. "I don't want those around. They reek of evil."

"They're not loaded and we won't be keeping them."

Josie said, "It's okay with the closet door closed."

"I just didn't want to leave them lying around."

I guess not. Josie was staring at him. She forced a smile. "Are you okay?"

"There was a problem, but we're safe now."

"Is that blood on your sleeve?"

Raven glanced down. "It's not mine."

"You're okay?"

Raven nodded and took a deep breath. He let it out slowly, visibly relaxing. Then he leaned down and kissed her.

It felt good. Josie pushed dark thoughts away. *No demons. They are locked in the closet, at least for now.*

"I could sure use a cup of hot coffee."

"I made some." *How did he get so much blood on his sleeve?*

Josie went to the kitchen and poured two cups. He followed her in and leaned his Mini-14 in the corner. "This is loaded. Is it okay to leave it there?"

"It's fine. No problem." Strangely, that was true. Raven and his weapons were protective, not threatening. Josie smiled and shook her head. *I must be acclimating.*

"Good." Raven eased himself into the chair with the window view.

"I need to know something. Am I losing my touch?"

Raven took a sip of coffee, and smiled his appreciation. "Don't think so. You look good to me...."

"What happened? I did not detect a threat. I was dozing when I heard the shots...."

"There were some bad guys, but it turned out okay. We just located and neutralized the Hamas kill team that's been after the President."

*No, they located **us**.* Josie blinked and stared at him. *Like in Durham.*

"Not like Durham," Raven said, reading her mind. "They never got close. We're safe."

"You're sure?"

Raven nodded. "Absolutely."

"Good. I called for help."

"Back when you heard the shots?"

"Uh huh."

"That was over two hours ago. So where's our backup?"

"I don't know. I did not want to overreact. The shots sounded a long way off."

"Most of a mile."

"I didn't sense that the house was under attack, or that I was at risk. I called Goldfarb, not the Presidio or 911."

"What did he say?"

"Nothing."

Raven's eyes narrowed. "***Nothing?***"

"He didn't answer. I left him a voicemail."

"That's sloppy." A flash of irritation shown in Raven's eyes. "How does Goldfarb get to be unavailable? He's our control."

"Did I do something wrong?"

"Not you." Raven smiled and shook his head. "You did fine, Babe. I just can't understand why he didn't answer and why we don't have backup." He pulled out his cell phone and glanced at it. "No calls."

Josie checked the clock on the stove. "Goldfarb should be here for breakfast in a few minutes. Do you want me to start fixing things?"

"Not yet," Raven said. "There's no rush now. I'll give him a call."

Goldfarb picked up on the first ring. "I was about to call you...."

"Where the hell have you been? Did you get Josie's message?"

"I said I was about to call. I'm not going to make our breakfast for one thing....."

"What....."

Goldfarb cut him off. "We were hit early this morning. I am strapped down in a hospital bed, trussed up like a turkey. My limbs are in casts, the facility is on full lock-down, and the doctors won't release me until they run more tests."

"Oh," Raven said.

"Forgive me all to hell, but you're not the only one with issues. Yes, I picked up Josie's message. Is everything secure out there?"

"Affirmative, but we were hit too," Raven said. "Is the...?"

"They had another sleeper agent inside the Presidio. The President's fine, but we took one KIA, plus myself injured. Not critically, but I'm out of action."

"Are you...?" Raven said.

'We can chit chat and make smiley faces later." Goldfarb was clearly not in a good mood. "Give me a status report."

"Yes, Sir." Raven proceeded to fill him in. There was a long pause as Goldfarb absorbed the information.

"You're certain this was the Hamas team we're looking for?"

"It wasn't Santa and the elves, Sir. Four *jihadis* with AKs, speaking Arabic. The leader's name is Kamal."

"Let me ask again. There are over a billion Muslims, and about a hundred million of them embrace radical Islam and *jihad*. What makes you think this was the group targeting the President?"

"You suggest there's more than one *jihadi* kill team in the area?"

"I'm just asking."

"Even the fucking FBI isn't that incompetent or politically correct, Sir. If anyone doubts this is the team, I suggest it is an excellent topic to bring up when we interrogate Kamal."

Goldfarb sighed into the phone. "The FiBI's were a bit embarrassed by our, ah, security lapse here. They generated a report on our current security status. It finds no evidence to support the theory of a Hamas kill team in the area."

"I'm sure that's comforting, Sir," Raven said dryly. "That must be the answer. Maybe I imagined the whole thing. Yeah, that must be it."

"Do you have to be a smart ass? The Military is pissed, the Secret Service lost an agent, and I'm flat on my back in the middle of this mess."

Raven took several deep breaths before he responded. "The FiBIs ought to be fucking embarrassed, and so should the Secret Service. The President and you should be kicking some asses. I have been up all night. I am covered with blood, our safe house is blown, and I have weapons and bodies all over the place.

"Those are the facts. You can come look yourself if you wish. Here's an opinion: Our OPSEC sucks and it seems the President's is no better."

"Your opinions are noted. Do you have anything actionable?"

"Yes. Two things come to mind. I'd like to know how we were blown, and I want us out of here by tonight."

"Understood. The President's security is first, but I agree. What else?"

"How many agents?"

"How many agents what?"

"How many FiBIs did it take to generate the report you speak of? A hundred?"

"Maybe," Goldfarb admitted. "A bunch and they are highly spooled up."

"Here's another action item: If you're not coming for our arranged meet, I need other black transport for my package. Now would be good."

"Bad idea," Goldfarb said.

"I thought you wanted action items."

"Yes, I do. Continue."

"The team leader, Kamal, is still alive. I want him removed, moved off the grid, and intensively interrogated. That needs to happen before the FiBIs come around and start talking about law enforcement and civil rights. As soon as Kamal's gone, I need cleaners."

"Rendition and cleaners," Goldfarb said.

"Affirmative. After that is done, and after we are long gone, do what you want. The FiBIs are welcome to what is left. A full Hamas kill team, with AKs, ammo, and even a few grenades. They can tape the crime scene, take pictures, and write another report.

"Hell, they can bring in TSA to grope them if they want to. This kill team has been moving across our borders and through our security like smoke. Not once. Several times."

The only answer was a grunt.

"Are you trying to speak, Doctor? Because that's not English."

"I'm thinking...."

"Okay." Raven waited.

"My answer is still no," Goldfarb finally said. "It's still a bad idea. R and T is forbidden. It is a bright line. We do **not** go there, on or off the reservation. There's a directive."

Rendering and Torture, Raven thought. "Let me say it phonetically, Doctor. Hotel Victor Tango. High Value Target. Do you understand me? We just got a break. If our counterterrorism people cannot understand that, they need miner's helmets with little lights, because they have their heads up their asses. If that's where we are, the fucking terrorists have won."

Goldfarb was silent for a long moment. "How do you know he's high value?"

Yeah, that is the key question, Raven thought. "Sir, I don't **know**. It is my judgment.

What I know is the package is dented a bit from handling, and we do not have a lot of time to discuss this. You will need to pick him up in the next hour or so."

"Damaged goods? That's less worth the risk."

"He'll live if you send an EMT with the extraction team, and do it quickly."

"Describe the damage."

Raven said, "I spoke unkindly to him about Islam. What do you think?"

"We're on a secure line," Goldfarb said. "I need specifics."

"I shot him. He was bleeding out, so I wrapped his wound in duct tape."

"Is that all?"

Josie was watching and listening intently. Raven made a "hold your ears" sign, putting his palms to his head.

Josie shook her head emphatically. Her signal was clear. "No."

Raven said, "You do not want the FiBIs to arrest him or take statements."

"I need details," Goldfarb said. "I'm not going to ask you again."

Raven spoke carefully into the phone. "I stuck a combat knife in his mouth. He's tied to a tree waiting for some feral pigs to come back and eat him for dessert after they get finished with his dead buddies."

There was a long pause. It was not easy to surprise Goldfarb, but apparently Raven had succeeded. Finally, he said, "You did **what**?"

"The details are tedious, Sir. You can have your rendition team take pictures when they pick him up. We're wasting time that we don't have," Raven said. "This isn't your common *jihadi*. He is high value. To an extent, he is being cooperative. He told me Ricci was his control."

"We already knew that," Goldfarb said.

"We *suspected* it. He verified it. Ricci is the connection to Dunbar."

"You raise a good point."

"This is a judgment call, but I'm calling it good Intel. There is something else unusual. He had a suicide pill concealed in a false tooth. Probably cyanide."

"No shit?" Goldfarb said.

"None whatsoever. That's how it went down."

"The pill. That's why you used the knife in his mouth?"

"Affirmative."

"You're sure it was cyanide?"

"No, but I've got the tooth and the pill. It's white, and I doubt it's aspirin. We can go around this all day, Sir. There's no proof. It's a judgment call."

Goldfarb sighed. "I'm inclined to back you, but transport is a problem for detainees. Everyone agrees, though I don't know why, that official government transport can't be used."

"I think it's the smell of brimstone." Raven said, mostly to signal how pissed off he was at the insanity of fighting a war for survival against an implacable foe, while entangled in legalistic and moral niceties. War was about killing the enemy, not about justice, and that was troublesome for enlightened nations.

It was an old argument. Free nations had problems fighting undeclared wars.

Rome had faced the problem for centuries. By the time it fell, it was no longer a Republic and had lost any semblance of freedom. To this day, historians debated whether it fell from conquest or from within.

It was a stupid argument. The obvious answer was, "Both."

Congress and the public did not get it. We are our own worst enemies. Putting Kamal into rendition caused endless problems, in many areas and at many levels.

Since 2006, American Presidents, including Blager, had been testifying that we no longer held detainees incommunicado.

Technically, they were not even lying. Technically, Kamal would be on his way to Guantanamo, or some unknown location, and his stay at some offshore interrogation center would merely be a stopover for "processing."

When Kamal arrived at GITMO, or worse, in a US court, he would be given lawyers at taxpayer expense, who would demand to know where he had been. They would also demand proof that his "rights" had been respected. It was not just a PR, moral, or legal question, it meant grave political, operational, and career risk to any who had touched him along the way, as well as to any covert assets or allies who had intersected with them. The downside risk was huge.

Most likely Kamal could never be released. The United States was in no position to answer the questions that would be posed.

Kamal was the leader of a team tasked with killing Josie and the President himself. Kamal deserved killing, but he also had key information and was part of a chain of conspiracy that reached at least as high as the Vice President. What Kamal knew, though unlikely to be admissible in court, could be the key to proving high treason. It could prevent future attacks.

Or not. There was no way to know without letting events play out.

The system sucked. Because of the rules, self-imposed rules, there were no good choices. Even though detainment cost more than a luxury hotel, the best outcome for the U.S. taxpayer was to give Kamal a comfortable room, free health care, a cot, and three hots for life.

There were still a few jihadis floating around in the system who had been ghosts since before Gulf War I. For one reason or another, they could never return to the world of the living.

In World War II, if you caught a spy or saboteur, you could just take him out and shoot him in the head. Summarily executing illegal combatants by hanging or firing squad had more moral clarity and historical precedent than eternal detainment. It was probably more humane, and arguably more effective at preventing future threats.

In the Pacific, neither side took prisoners, legal combatants or not. Americans left it to the local commanders. The Imperial Japanese Empire, with a few exceptions, did it out of policy.

In the 17th Century, we hung pirates without trials. An infant United States under Thomas Jefferson sent Marines to the shores of Tripoli and prevailed.

No longer. International Law had inexorably shifted from protecting the rights of sovereign nation-states, to promoting Global Governance and so-called "human rights." The UN Human Rights Commission was dominated by the third world, with its members including such totalitarian "bastions of freedom" as Argentina, Cuba, Libya, Uganda, and China.

So much for progress.

Raven waited. Pressing his lips together. Determined not to speak.

A long time passed before Goldfarb spoke. "I'll back you. A clean up team will come by to pick up your package by noon."

"Someone I know. Someone you trust."

He did not want to take any chances either. Not with his cover, and not with Josie's life.

"Agreed," Goldfarb said. "Your package is toxic and has a short shelf life. It will be off your hands by noon. If not, you are to do what you think is best."

Kill him. "Understood, Sir. Thank you."

CHAPTER FIFTY
A PERSONNEL CONFLICT

Conference Room, The Presidio of Monterey, California, Three Days Later.

R aven rapped on the door and pulled it open. "I came as fast as I could." He looked at the man seated at the table, letting his memory float back, trying to remember. The man stood up and held out his hand. "It's been a long time, Cowboy."

The man's light brown hair had mostly turned white and he was favoring his left leg, but it was the same man, General Mike Mickelson. Twenty Mike was a legend.

"Good to see you again, General. I am surprised you remember me. I was just getting started with the Agency back then."

Mike grinned. "The bastards fired you with prejudice, I heard, for unkind acts to our enemies, or something. Good for you."

"Or Something…. They call me Raven these days. Cowboy was erased. I've been sheep dipped."

"So I hear. I am a civilian now. Do you know about TSG?"

Raven grasped Mike's hand and shook it warmly. "A little. Transnational Security Group. A crazy notion for desperate times. I hope you can pull it off. Goldfarb said you might be working with us."

"Yes. I am trying to get TSG running and we have a problem. He's not coming?"

Raven shook his head. "Goldfarb is incapacitated. He called and directed that I meet with you, so here I am. He said we have an urgent mutual problem, but didn't give details."

"How is he?"

"He's damned lucky to be alive, but expected to recover fully. He tried to outmuscle a young *jihadi* assassin. The President put him on medical leave, not to be disturbed. I was surprised to get his call."

Mike said, "I want to hear more about that when we have time. Sit down, please. Do you want some coffee?"

"No, Sir. I'm good." Raven seated himself.

"Let's hear about your problem first. Goldfarb said your #2 wants out and you would like to keep him. What happened?"

"We're talking about John Black?"

"We are. How did you get him?"

Raven shrugged. "We're razor thin on the ground, Mike. You know the situation. Noah's Flood compromised everyone with a DOD clearance, the military and CIA were gutted, Washington is still PC, and on and on it goes."

"That is where I live too. It sucks. Tell me about Black."

"He is a good man and a patriot. He was a hotshot fighter pilot, but was busted out on a medical. We sheep dipped him for cover, and I took him on for technical support. He has engineering degrees. We got into shit and he had to come out in the field to bail us out."

"Durham. Colonel Marston told me about that one himself. Your covering force was stuck politically, so Marston improvised. He gave a civilian a borrowed handgun, a radio, a rental car, and sent him in as an advance scout. There was a kerfuffle when the Army came in hot to save him, but it settled out. They gave Marston a medal rather than a Court Martial."

"Something like that. Black was wounded in Durham. He recovered, stayed on, and came back. The kid did well. If not for him, I wouldn't be sitting here."

"Now he wants out. What happened?"

"I used him to probe a Black Power church that was hosting *jihadi* kill teams. He is green, but all I had. I trust him. He was the lead. I was outside to provide cover. It was a church. Supposed to be peaceful."

"But it wasn't?"

"No. They had to shoot their way out. He went in with a Black girl, an ex-Marine."

"Moira King. She did Intel and interrogations over in the sand box."

Raven said, "You know her?"

Mike nodded. "I do. Was Black wounded again?"

"Yeah. He got a beat down from some Black Panthers. Suffered a concussion. He seems over that, but it messed up his head and he wants out. The girl was killed and he blames himself. I am going to lose him. Goldfarb and I are crosswise about it."

"Why?"

"Long story. The short version is it leaves a hole that will be hard to fill. Maybe impossible. I have come to trust John Black. The longer version is that we cannot keep playing like little boys with our fingers in the dike. That's why Goldfarb told me about TSG."

"To give you hope. Is Black here?"

"He is. Goldfarb said to bring him. He's waiting outside."

"Good. What did Goldfarb tell you to do?"

"The call was only a few seconds. He said we had similar personnel problems. Said we should work them out ourselves. Said it was between us, and he'd support whatever we came up with so long as it didn't embarrass the President."

"Did he brief you in on TSG? Transnational Services Group? The company I've started?"

"No, he did not. Not really. As I said, he mentioned TSG in concept a few weeks ago. He said help was coming. I have not seen any yet. We could have used some. Is TSG real?"

"It's a long story. We are staffing up and I am running into the same things you have with Noah's Flood, Political Correctness, and years of bad policy. Bottom line is this: TSG lives or dies by money. Large, tricky, financial transactions. My # 2 is a young Black man named George Washington Jones. Ever hear of him?"

Raven shook his head. "Can't say I have."

"His PhD thesis changed the field of economics. He looks like a Black Einstein with glasses, hair and all. A bit quirky, but I was lucky to get him."

Raven was frowning. "OK, but what does this have to do with me?"

"Jones has been the key in putting together our financial plans. TSG will be the shell that covers and supports what you have been doing for Goldfarb. We'll be off the books, and as distant as we can get from political Washington."

"OK, but, again, what does this have to do with me?"

"Goldfarb briefed us in on the debacle at Trinity Church, including the fact that your OP saved President Blager's life. Without him in power, there will be no TSG. Even Blager has reservations about what we are doing. Officially he knows nothing, of course."

"Understood. So what is the problem? As you know, Blager survived."

"Jones has just turned in his resignation to me. He wants out unless your man, John Black, is charged with murder."

Raven sat for a long instant. He felt his mouth hanging open. He closed it and looked at Twenty Mike. "Did you say what I think you just said?"

Mike nodded.

"This whole situation with the President's near assassination is so far off the grid and beyond Top Secret that it must never see the light of day. Are you aware of that?"

"I am. Very much so."

"Good. I suggest you just shoot the son-of-a-bitch and we cut this conversation short."

"He's not threatening to talk. I trust him. George will not talk. However, he will quit, and, if he does, for all practical purposes that is the end of TSG. We do NOT have a Plan B. We do not even really have a Plan A. We are winging it."

Raven took a deep breath and let it out slowly. "Shit."

"Deep. Did Goldfarb or the President suggest any limits on what we can do to fix this?"

"Not to me."

"Nor to me," Mike said.

"We are on our own then. Why does Jones feel so strongly about this?"

"Moira was his cousin."

"No shit?"

"She was like his little sister. George's parents were killed in a home invasion back when he was in high school. Alveda King, Moira's mother, raised him. He feels we just got Moira killed in a half-assed, incompetent, illegal field OP right here in the Homeland. He said that his continuing at TSG would be to betray her."

"The kid's got backbone, General."

"Yeah. It is part of why I hired him. Do you have any ideas?"

"I do. We're screwed."

"Other than that."

"Is Jones here?"

"Yes. He's outside too."

"Are you thinking the same thing that I'm thinking?"

"That we should bring them in and put them together?"

"Why?

"It can't get any worse, can it? It might get better."

"How?"

"If Black quits, he's gone and Jones might continue with you. Either way, I am probably going to lose Black. If so, I am ready to retire anyway. TSG will go on, but I am done. Goldfarb can find someone else for the Covert OPS. Even if they kill each other, we are no worse off than we are now. What is your thinking?"

"Pretty much the same. Let's get it over with."

They assembled ten minutes later. Mike sat on one side of the table with Jones at his side. Raven and Black sat across from them. There were water glasses on the table.

It was Mike's meeting. He offered coffee, everyone refused, and then he gave a short summary of the situation. "Is that a fair assessment of where we are?"

Raven said, "I think so."

Jones said, "Yes." He was not trying to conceal his anger.

Black looked miserable. He said, "Pretty much."

Mike said, "Does anyone have anything to add, or any questions?"

Jones raised his hand, looking at Black. "I do have some questions."

"Go ahead," Mike said.

"For him."

Black said, "Go ahead."

"You didn't even come to Moira's funeral."

"I sent flowers."

"Do you think that is adequate?"

"No, I do not."

Raven said, "May I speak?"

Mike said, "Go ahead."

"Black was wounded in the recent OP. Moira was shot while leading him out. I was there, but too late. The reason he was not at the funeral was that he was in the hospital with a concussion. Today is the first time I've seen him since that night."

"You got my cousin killed."

Black dropped his eyes. "Yes, I did. I was the lead. I am responsible. If it makes any difference, I was coming here to resign. I'm sorry."

Jones blinked. "That's all?"

Black shrugged. "What else is there? It was a cluster fuck. I am sorry. I am proud to have known Moira and I will miss her. She deserves a medal."

Jones was silent.

Finally, Raven spoke. "A few things. Mr. Black: The President plans to give Moira a medal. The award will probably be classified and in a private ceremony. You will be invited. The information you acquired that she was bringing out had extreme value. Mr. Jones: I will give Mike a copy of my after action report. It will be highly classified, but if you still have your clearances I will ask him to share it with you before he burns it."

Black said, "Thank you, Sir."

Jones said, "Were you there?"

"Yes. It was my OP. I was in command, but outside, providing over watch. Just me. We had no covering force. We had no back up. I did not even have a spotter. Two people inside. Me outside. That's all."

Mike said, "That sucks."

"It does. I am responsible. This OP was not approved, but I deemed it necessary. Black and Moira volunteered. Both of them deserve medals. In my opinion they were heroes."

Mike looked at Black, "Have you ever lost anyone in your command before?"

"No, Sir. When I flew fighters, I was only responsible for myself. Moira had more ground combat experience. She wanted to go in alone, but was overruled. So that's how it worked out."

Jones said, "Can you summarize with happened?"

Raven said, "Shit happened, Mr. Jones. In covert OPs, that is how it goes down, all too often. It is a dark and dirty business. I've lost too many friends."

Mike said, "I think he wants the details."

Raven looked at Jones, "Do you? Or are you just here to blame someone for your cousin's death?"

"I want the details. The truth."

Raven looked at Mike. "Is he aware how classified this is? And the penalties for discussing it anywhere outside this room?"

"Yes. He is cleared and briefed in. For TSG to work, he has to be able to handle such things."

"We sent a small team, two people, into a church that was deemed to be safe. They split up. Black got what we were after, but was caught and badly beaten.

"Semi-conscious, they dragged him back to where they had Moira. The two of them managed to escape. After he was wounded, Black killed one terrorist. He gave Moira the take and told her to get out."

Jones said, "Moira was leading and Black was following?"

"Yes."

"I could not keep up," Black said. "I ordered her to leave me. She would not."

Raven said, "There was one *jihadi* guard left. He had body armor and an AK. The first I saw them Black was engaging him with a revolver he took off the guard he had killed, a .44. I saw his muzzle flash. He nailed the *jihadi* over the heart at about 50 yards with an unfamiliar pistol. I finished it with a long-range head shot. When I got there Black was holding Moira's body crying."

"That's enough," Black said.

"Is it?" Mike asked.

Jones was silent.

Raven said, "So that's it, Mike. We have to start over. Both of them quit."

"No," Jones said.

Black looked at him, but said nothing.

"What do you want?" Mike said.

"Justice."

Mike said, "You won't get it. This is combat. There are just wars, but there is no justice in war. Just living and dying. You do it as honorably as you can. To me, it seems like your cousin died well."

"Who pays for Moira's death?" Jones said. "I want to know."

Raven said, "That discussion has some possibilities, Mike. Should we go there?"

Mike looked surprised. "It does?"

"I want the person who killed my cousin," Jones said.

"You're too late," Black said. "Raven blew his head off. What's next on your list?"

"Oh," Jones said.

"What are the possibilities?" Mike asked.

Raven said, "There were two kill teams active. No survivors. There is one leader still out there, a HVT at the UN that we cannot touch yet, because the plan is to toss him. The attack on the President reached to very high levels."

Mike said, "How high?"

"There is no proof, but I'm personally convinced that the objective of this attack was to kill the President and replace him with Vice President Dunbar."

Mike said, "Dunwood Duncan Dunbar III, the socialist?"

"That's the one."

"Say more."

"I wanted to take him out. President Blager gave us a hard no, for the reasons you would expect: The Constitution, precedents, and there being a bright line between good and evil."

Mike said, "But...."

"I've been reliably informed that Dunbar will be announcing his resignation in the next week or so. He will then be a private citizen."

"But still a traitor."

Raven nodded, "In my opinion, Yes."

"Does his change of status cancel the Presidential order? Or just make it irrelevant?"

"No idea," Raven said. "It is murder or worse in any case, and best not to be caught, but if your lad wants someone to pay, I, for one, would not miss Dunbar."

Black and Jones looked at each other. Mike was silent.

"No," Black said. "I can't. I don't want to go there."

"Me either," said Jones. "Mr. Black, now that you are up to it, I'd like you to meet my Aunt Alveda. I'd like you to tell her how Moira died."

Black said. "I'd be honored."

"Are we done here?" Mike said.

"I am," Jones said.

"I need to talk with Raven alone," Black said.

"Yes, we do need to talk," Raven said, "First, I would like a few minutes with Mike alone. And then a few with Black if you'd loan us this room."

Mike said, "That works. We are fighting time zones and I need to be back in New York for a meeting. George, would you please call the airport and have our pilot get a flight plan in for New York, departing in forty-five minutes?"

"Yes, Sir," Jones said.

Mike thanked them for coming. Black and Jones left, closing the door behind them.

Raven eased into his seat. "I'll take that coffee now. We seem to have resolved your personnel issue."

"Miracles still happen. Thank you. What can I do for you?"

"You ever watch any old war movies?"

"Sure."

"I mean *really* old. Like World War I when the new replacements for pilots would come in every night, and half of them would be dead the next morning after the dawn patrol. Or World War II, where a few Marines would be cut off on a squalid jungle for months fighting against overwhelming odds without support or resupply."

"Guadalcanal. I grew up on those movies. Pork Chop Hill in Korea. The Frozen Chosin, cut off, forty below zero, with a million Chinese coming at you in waves. What's your point?"

"We've come full circle, Mike. America is weak. There are some old farts like us, but these new kids do not have a chance. We need back up and support we can trust. We need support infrastructure that won't betray us."

"That is our purpose. It's what TSG is trying to do."

"We need more than back up and support. I pull in the best we can find, kids like Black and Moira, and we then put them into impossible situations. Moira lasted less than one day. Black was almost killed his first time in ground combat."

Mike said, "I got it. What do you need?"

"I need secure first-rate training off-the-books for people like them. Something like the Farm the CIA had. Something like our elite military units have, but I need it to be completely separate from government. No Geneva Convention, no lawyering up terrorists, no giving them rights and using civil justice. Just killing terrorists and winning. I want this training to be an urgent priority, not a get-to-it-someday wet dream."

"Why?"

"Because no matter how many battles we win, America is in a generational war. Radical Islam has been a problem for 1,000 years. Today we face 10th century barbarians with 21st century weapons. I want to die knowing our children and grandchildren are going to win, and that our Western civilization will prevail."

Mike nodded. "I agree with you. I will do what I can. You have my word."

"Thank you."

"Thank you, and one more question. Where did you get Moira?"

Raven frowned. "I don't know. Goldfarb vetted her. She just showed up. Why do you ask?"

"Doesn't it seem odd to you that she'd appear as a walk-in to join a small covert unit that is totally black and off the grid? And that this would involve one of my key people at TSG?"

"What are you saying?"

"What do you think the odds are that this could happen by accident?"

"Low. Very low."

"Near zero. I think Jones tipped her off and she came and volunteered. I think that is why he has been so angry. He feels guilty, and was looking for someone else to blame for her death."

"Could be. If so, have him get us some funding for training so it doesn't happen again."

"I will. Good luck, Raven."

"Good luck, Marine."

CHAPTER FIFTY-ONE
THE BLAGER CODICIL

The Ranch, Mendocino, California, Two Weeks Later

Raven rapped sharply on the door.
"Come in." It was Goldfarb's voice. "It's not locked."
Raven hesitated and looked at Josie oddly. His expression was troubled.
"What?"
"This room, Babe. It's where they put me to recover after Durham."
"You were shot up and I was comatose. So much has changed...."
"Yeah." Raven yanked the door open, looked around, and called, "Where are you?"
"Out here. On the deck...."
Goldfarb was sitting in the sun with a stack of newspapers on the table by his chair. He had a cane next to him, leaning against the table, and a half cast on his leg. They had taken the cast off his shoulder, but his arm was wrapped and in a sling.
Raven glanced at the pipe in the ashtray. "That's what you used to save the President's life, back when you were playing John Wayne?"
Goldfarb gave a little snort. "Read the papers. Watch television. Get with the program. The President defended himself with a borrowed Army .45. It has been the top news story for a week. There's no way you could miss that."
"Come to think of it, maybe I did hear something...."

Right, and you said it was all bullshit, Josie thought, though she admitted the cover story was more plausible than the notion of a five foot eight, seventy-two year old academic prevailing in hand-to-hand conflict against an Islamic assassin.

"Hollywood plans to make a movie about it."

Raven said, "Are they going to include the part about how you opened the door without a countersign?"

Goldfarb rolled his eyes. "I expect they'll leave that part out, along with the fact that I was there. We did have the Secret Service controlling access to the building and the room. They are somewhat embarrassed about it."

Not to say about their dead agent, Raven thought.

"Well that settles it, then," Josie said. "What really matters is this: Is the President in good health now?"

Goldfarb said, "You're the psychic. Don't you know?"

"I think he's recovered – Kaimi said he has – but we blew out of Monterey so fast that I wanted to get the official version."

"Have you now regained your full ability to do remote viewings?"

"I have. You know how clear the air seems after a big storm?"

"Like you can see forever...."

"It's like that, like when you can see each individual blade of grass, and perceive distant objects sharply. The Abyss is gone as if it never existed. I've done three successful viewings since Monterey, but none were focused on the President."

"Walter Reed checked him out when he got back to Washington. He passed with flying colors. They used words like 'miraculous recovery.' The whole world knows about the assassination attempts and that he is in good health."

Raven shrugged. They had added an extra chair on the deck since his stay. He pulled it over for Josie, and slid the other one to his favorite position, where he could put his back to the wall, watch Goldfarb, and still have a good view of the ocean.

He relaxed into it and fixed his gaze on Goldfarb, who had an odd look on his face. "Have you seen today's news?"

"No, Sir."

Goldfarb held up a copy of the **Washington Times**. Its headline, in 48-point type, screamed, "Dunbar resigns." The lead for the *New York Times* was even larger.

"Do I care? The son-of-a-bitch….."

"Of course you care." Josie shot Raven a look. "Dunbar is linked to Ricci, Vogel, and Iran. I have seen it in my viewings. *He is a traitor.*"

Goldfarb said, "Exactly right. It is not what the media says, that is mere theater. This is huge."

"I'm not good at figuring out Washington or the media, Sir," Raven said. "Your message said Kamal was cooperating. I presume you get the take from his interrogations?"

"We'll get to that. Let's stick with the big picture for now. President Blager's popularity rating is 83% and rising. He is golden. It's a whole new ball game."

"So?"

"You don't watch the news, do you? Everyone in Washington keeps Fox and CNN news feeds in little windows on their computers."

"I don't, and we're not in Washington. Like Mark Twain said, why bother?"

Goldfarb frowned.

"Those who don't read newspapers are uninformed. Those who do are misinformed. Either way, we're screwed."

"Samuel Clemens did say that," Josie murmured, "long before radio, television, and the Internet. That is why you need people like us these days, Doctor. The media is Orwellian."

They both looked at her. Goldfarb chuckled and said, "Yes."

Good, Josie thought.

Raven was about to argue that most in CIA never left the building, the media spread disinformation and rumor, the fact checkers were corrupted and co-opted, and that Congress was disconnected from reality. Her interests were narrower.

Raven is right, but it is beyond our ability to fix that. If the President is okay now, we can finish this assignment and retire.

Josie wanted **out**. She wanted a life with Raven.

She held up a paper bag. "I brought bagels, lox, and cream cheese. How about we have these with coffee and you tell us what's been transpiring in the outside world."

"I'd like that," Goldfarb said.

"If I get to ask one question first," Raven said.

"It was the pigs." Goldfarb looked smug. "That's the answer."

"You haven't heard my question yet."

"Shush," Josie said. She got up to fix the bagels.

Goldfarb finished his coffee and smiled. "So, for the first time in a long time, the world news is good. President Blager is a hero. America is once again seen as the shining beacon of freedom, his own party is finally supporting him, and Europe is ecstatic – even the French – about finding a way to curtail radical Islam."

"Blager will get another term?" Raven asked. "We get more time to deal with the Iran threat?"

"Absolutely."

"Does this mean we can turn Iran into a parking lot?"

"It means we may not have to. The first meeting to negotiate a new Mideast understanding starts next Sunday. It is being held under the auspices of the United States, hosted by Egypt, and supported by the Arab countries, save Iran. Even Syria is interested."

"Do I get to ask my question now?"

Goldfarb said, "Sure."

"You get the take from Kamal's interrogations?"

"Yes."

"Iranian intelligence has targeted Josie. They almost got her in Durham, and again in Portland. The assignment we agreed on was for me to end that threat."

"Yes. What's your question?"

"Was Josie the target again? This would make the third time. Was she the bait to catch the President's assassins?"

Goldfarb said, "No."

"I'm not sure I believe you, Doctor. Once again, you left Josie exposed, hanging out like a tethered goat. A kill team shows up at our safe house in the middle of the night, and suddenly you're not taking our calls?"

"They didn't even know who was there."

"Say it again, Doctor. Tell me she was not the target. Because they were sure as hell coming either to kill or capture."

Goldfarb met Raven's eyes. "Kamal's team didn't know or care who was at the safe house. Josie wasn't the target, but, yes, they would have killed her."

"And me," Raven said.

"Yes."

"We were blown. How did they find us?"

"Easy," Josie put a hand on Raven's arm. "Let him talk."

Raven took a deep breath. Then another. "Go on...."

"It was my fault. You are correct about that."

Raven looked at Josie. She mouthed the word, "Wait."

"I was the target," Goldfarb said. "Understand this. Me. I was the target."

"You weren't even there...." Raven spoke slowly, keeping his tone neutral.

Josie thought, *He is less angry.* She waited for Goldfarb to answer.

"Kamal's team was to take the house. When I showed up for breakfast, they were going to take me and use me and my vehicle to get access to the President. That was the plan."

"You are scaring me, Doctor. Your tradecraft was so sloppy you let them follow you? You led them to us? That's how they found us?"

"No."

"You're sure?"

"Positive. They did not follow me. One of their assets inside the Presidio noticed the pattern of my visits to the President. I would leave the base early with a clean car, but return in time to make my meeting with him in a dusty car."

"So?"

"My patterned behavior and time schedule triggered a sequence of other errors. I was often late, and the guards developed a practice of waving me through. I usually parked in the lot next to Building 422."

"Where the President was housed. Inside the green zone and in violation of your own security procedures."

"Yes."

"How did they find our safe house?"

"The dust on the car was identifiably from that region. Ricci put out a cover story and paid the locals to watch for a green car at that time of day. Eventually, despite my counter-surveillance, they found out where I was going. The terrain is operationally difficult. There's only one major road along the coast."

"The source for this information is Kamal?"

"It is. I am sorry. Indirectly, it was my fault."

"What about the agent inside. Did he validate this?"

"No." Goldfarb shook his head. "The inside agent was one Abdul Baari Mubarak, known locally as 'Barry.' He's the one we killed in the President's room."

"The one who busted you up?"

"Correct. The operation was compartmentalized. Kamal was never told who the inside agents were."

"Then you're speculating about how we were blown," Raven said.

"The only loose end is who first tipped Kamal's team about tracking my car. Ricci probably knows. He showed Kamal a photo of my car, and said he got it from an inside source. Ricci implied it was Dr. Susan Stein, but she was used unwittingly and is on our side. She says she did not. She passed a polygraph about that."

"So it was Mubarak who fingered us?"

"Most likely. We will need Josie to do a viewing. The FBI has a preliminary folder on him. I will get you a copy. We are getting a lot of help with Mubarak since the President killed him."

"Since you killed him," Josie said.

"Leave it be, both of you. The President gets credit for that kill."

Josie sighed. *Layer after layer of deception.*

Paradoxically, Raven relaxed visibly. It did not bother him. He was used to it. "Tell me this. Would Kamal's plan have worked?"

"If his team didn't run into you?" Goldfarb said. "Good question. It has been the subject of some discussion. We need to discuss what happened...."

"We need to finish this first. Would it have worked? Could the kill team have gotten to the President?"

"That's difficult to know. Kamal was getting a lot of pressure from his control. Not just Ricci, from higher. The plan was a desperation move."

"What do our security people say?" Raven persisted.

"The Military and Secret Service say 'no.' The FBI CT center gives the plan maybe a 25% chance. They all would have died, of course."

"That is what terrorists do, Doctor. They die."

"Yes," Goldfarb agreed. "The thing is that in every scenario CT ran, I wound up dead. Josie was not a tethered goat. I was the stalking horse to get access. Me. You saved my life."

Josie said, "You didn't even show up that day."

"True," Goldfarb said. "Circumstances intervened. But if the plan had worked, I'd be dead."

"We'd all be dead if the plan had worked."

"All but the President," Josie corrected him. "He was well protected. You said the President had a 75% chance."

"The FBI said that, not me." Goldfarb said.

"Or maybe the FiBIs are just wrong, as inconceivable as that may be," Raven said.

"Screw the hypotheticals. I'm still going to credit you with saving my life."

Raven smiled. "If we credit the President with taking down the inside assassin."

"Yes." Goldfarb was obviously finished with the discussion. He looked directly into Raven's eyes. "I answered your question. Now I have some things I need to ask you."

"Go ahead."

"What the hell happened out there? The report the President showed me read like something out of a horror movie. Eviscerated bodies. Throats torn out. Blager had the distribution restricted to principals only, so I can't even show you a copy."

Raven shrugged.

"I need to know," Goldfarb said.

"What happened? *I redeemed myself.*"

"That's all?"

"The bad guys died, Josie is safe, the President is alive, and a Hamas kill team is no more. A happy ending. God Bless America."

Goldfarb looked at Josie. "Do you want to say anything?"

She shook her head.

He looked back at Raven. "Nothing to add?"

"No."

"You left out a few crucial details. What about the pigs? Kamal insists you were going to dip him in pig blood and kill him in cold blood."

Raven said, "I did not kill him."

"Perhaps not, but you did leave him gagged, bleeding, and tied up. He had to watch as his friends were eaten by wild pigs."

"They never laid a snout on him, Doctor. You and I had our talk, you made a high level decision, and I delivered Kamal intact."

Goldfarb rolled his eyes. "Intact?"

"Okay, yeah, I shot him. Not quite intact, but delivered as promised. You really need to get over this pig thing."

"I can't. It seems that the President has picked up on it."

Raven and Josie exchanged looks. She shook her head.

Raven said, "We have no idea what you are talking about."

"It will be announced by the White House next week," Goldfarb said. "The bodies of the Hamas kill team, along with several dead pigs and the corpse of the late Abdul Baari Mubarak are going to be buried in a special plot at the Presidio."

Raven blinked. "Are you serious?"

"The President is."

"The Muslims are going to go ape shit."

"Some will," Goldfarb agreed. "The ceremony and interment will be held inside the security perimeter. It will be attended by the President, the Secretary of State, prominent Islamic clerics, and a delegation of Heads of State from the Mideast."

"I don't understand," Josie said. "You are going to have to explain that to me."

Goldfarb said, "It will be in the news next week. The short answer is that after thirty years of unrelenting attacks from Radical Islam, the President has reached his limit. The precedent he mentioned involves Black Jack Pershing."

Josie shook her head. "I'm sorry…."

"I know the story," Raven said.

They both stared at him.

"Tell her," Goldfarb ordered. "I need her to know I'm not making his up."

"Shortly before World War I, the United States was having problems with Islamic terrorists. The local commander was General Black Jack Pershing….." Raven looked at Goldfarb. "Is that what we're talking about?"

"Correct. The place was the Philippines and the year was 1911. Do continue."

"It goes like this. There were a number of terrorist attacks against the United States and its interests by Muslim extremists.

"General Pershing captured 50 of the terrorists and had them tied to posts execution style. He had his men bring in two pigs and slaughter them in front of the terrorists. The soldiers then soaked their bullets in pig's blood in full view of their captives. Using those bullets, they proceeded to execute 49 of the terrorists by firing squad, dug a big hole, dumped in the bodies, covered them in pig blood and entrails, and filled the hole."

"I don't get it," Josie said. "What's the point of that?"

"Simply that it worked. They let the 50th man go. And for the next 42 years, there was not a single attack by a Muslim fanatic anywhere in the world."

"I still don't get it," Josie said. "Why not?"

"The Muslims abhor pigs, which they see as filthy animals. Some simply refuse to eat pork, while others will not touch pigs at all, nor any of their by-products. To these, eating or touching a pig, its meat, its blood, is to be instantly barred from paradise and doomed to Hell."

Goldfarb said, "That's roughly the same as what the President told me."

"Is it true? Muslims who touch pigs go to Hell?"

"It's controversial. Some say it is urban legend. Still, there are at least four passages in the Quran that forbid association with pigs or eating pork." Raven shrugged. "I've spent a lot of time in the Mideast. I've never seen a pig there, but I sure have gotten tired of lamb and rice."

"Islamic religious experts disagree about the 'doomed to Hell' part, but it is clear there is a strong Islamic revulsion to pigs," Goldfarb said.

"A few years back **London Times** reported the Brits had to withdraw 'The Three Little Pigs' from a literary contest because Muslims found the book offensive."

Josie shivered. "This is grotesque. Why are we talking about it?"

"The Muslims are going along with it," Goldfarb said.

Raven looked startled. "What?"

"Even for the Muslims, repeated assassination attempts on the President by *jihadists* are the last straw. The world is in flames. Most who are being killed by radical Islamists are Muslim themselves, and the rulers in the Mideast have also had enough."

"It's in the Koran," Raven said. "The part about pork being forbidden. And martyrdom is allowed by *fatwa*."

"True, but irrelevant. The Koran forbids suicide, but Iran's Islamic clerics found a loophole back during the Iran/Iraq war. They issued *fatwas* allowing martyrdom, promising heaven to those who suicide in the Name of Allah."

"That's my point," Raven said. "Those *fatwas* came from the highest level Iranian clerics. They cannot be overruled. Neither can the Koran."

"No one is trying to revoke them, at least not yet. What will happen is selective. There will be *fatwas* issued by clerics allowing punitive burials for those who target high officials with suicide OPs, to be conducted at the option of the nations whose officials are targeted or killed. These new *fatwas* will be announced at the interment ceremony."

Josie said, "That might work for the Hamas team, but the Barry guy wasn't a suicide OP, so far as I know. Wasn't he an American citizen?"

Goldfarb made a vague wave of his hand. "Citizenship isn't an issue for this policy, and it was a suicide OP for all practical purposes. Barry is dead and would have been under any likely scenario. His parents have approved of the burial and will attend. They are Muslim, but their view on this is mild, that only eating pork is forbidden. If some good can result from their son's death, they are in favor of it."

"Are they seeking something higher?" Josie asked. "Instead of being remembered as the failed assassin who attempted to kill our President, their son's legacy will be having made one small step toward an end to Radical Islamic violence."

"So I'm told...."

"I like it."

"What else?" Raven said.

"President Blager is going to embed this codicil into our foreign policy. It will be a part of all our treaty commitments in the Mideast, though initially applying only to attempted assassinations of high government or State Department officials. If you want U.S. aid, you sign the treaty. Israel, Egypt, Jordan, Kuwait, and Saudi Arabia have already agreed. They plan to embed the policy into their treaties as well. Europe is expected to go along."

"I like it," Raven said. "This is huge. President Blager has just changed the rules."

"So much for the big picture," Josie said. "What about us? What about now?"

"It's never going to be mentioned officially, but the President knows what happened and is grateful. No one is looking for you, as far as we know. You were not a target this time."

Raven said, "What about our mission?"

"Obviously, we don't want to mount aggressive OPs against Iran while things are shaking out in the Mideast. Me, I am going to heal for a time and do nothing.

"The President is back in the saddle. He has instructed me to take a few months off, and said he'd get back to me."

"We're done?" Josie said. *It sounded too good to believe.*

"That call is beyond my authority," Goldfarb said. "I'm not in a position right now to issue you specific orders or cancel OPs, but I'm open to any suggestions you have."

Josie and Raven exchanged a look. She nodded and gestured at him. *You take it.*

Raven looked at Goldfarb. "We've already started remote viewings to learn more about the hidden players who've been troubling us. We can continue these."

Goldfarb nodded. "Ricci?"

"As a primary. We have a short list: Claas Vogel, Firouz, and our old favorite, Akbar Safdari, who we suspect was behind the failed attack in Durham."

"Add Dunbar."

"Okay, no problem."

"They are parties of interest. What do you propose?"

"Light duty, research only, expenses, full pay, we pick the location, and we keep a maximum distance from Washington and Langley. We specifically want to get away from any official contacts."

"A working vacation? No bodies and no burning towns?"

"Right." Raven looked at Josie. She smiled and nodded.

"How do I contact you?"

"You don't. You will provide us false identities, including several non-US passports. We will check in from time to time. We will come back in three months, meet with you and the President, and then we will jointly decide what is next. Part of that discussion will involve our retirement."

Goldfarb nodded slowly. "That's within my authority."

Raven looked questioningly at Josie. She nodded, smiled, and put a hand on Goldfarb's good arm.

"What?"

"Thank you, Doctor. We'll do our best to avoid excitement and let you heal in peace."

"You have a deal," Raven said. "We agree."

EPILOGUE

Valle, Arizona, a Week Later

J osie peered down the empty road and shook her head. She looked at
Raven. "We need to communicate. Tell me why you picked this place."

He smiled and pointed behind her. "I was nostalgic for the sand box,
now that we've stood down from active duty. Tell me what you see."

Josie turned, blinked, did a double take, and then said, calmly, "I think
I'm losing my mind. I see pyramids."

"No camels?"

"Just pyramids. Two of them. Are they real?"

"Far as I can tell. Does it make you feel at home?"

"Not the first thought that crossed my mind. Hallucinogenic, maybe.
Disassociated, perhaps. But, No. 'At home' isn't coming up on my 'feelings'
list. What am I looking at?"

"Let's go see...."

To Josie's astonishment, it was a hardware store. Their false IDs
included Arizona driver's licenses, so Raven picked up concealed carry
permits for them both, along with several other items, including a large
roll of silver duct tape.

"What's that for?" she asked.

"Never can tell." Raven grinned. "Duct tape is handy. It might help
improve our relationship...."

The skinny old man behind the counter chortled, but it turned into a
choking sound when he saw the look on Josie's face.

"What's the other pyramid for?" Josie demanded.

The old man, Harry, turned out to be friendly and willing to talk about the history of the place. The rear pyramid was used for storage, and, oddly, a greenhouse and fishpond. It turned out the pyramid structures had been hand-built as a New Age shop by a long-gone hippie couple in the 60s. The one in the rear had a lap pool and grow lights.

At one time, there were dreams of communes and a local economy, but all that was left now was a subdivision with platted but undeveloped lots, no utilities, and a few trailers where owners had decided to camp.

The pyramids did not meet code, but they did have power and water. They were situated at the crossing of Highways 64 and 180, the only paved roads for miles. The county had granted Harry permission to occupy, so long as he agreed to bring them up to code. The project proved to be more extensive than either party had anticipated.

Eventually, rather than hauling supplies endlessly from Flagstaff, Harry set up a hardware store. He worked on improvements as his time, motivation, and finances permitted, which turned out to be sporadically. Ten years had passed, but that was still Harry's plan.

He was breaking even, he said. The two local gas stations did well, as they were halfway between the Grand Canyon and anywhere. He had recently converted the rear pyramid back to a marijuana grow operation.

"Really?" Josie said. Harry suddenly had her full attention. "Tell me more…."

"It's a 2010 law. If the patient lives more than 25 miles from the nearest dispensary, the patient or caregiver may cultivate up to 12 marijuana plants in an enclosed, locked facility." The man smiled. "Ain't nothing that isn't 25 miles away. I'm cool, long as I keep it locked."

"Will you sell me some?"

"You gotta have a permit."

"How do I get one?"

"I sell them."

Josie pulled out her Arizona license. The address was Sedona. She handed it over. "Will this do?"

"No problem. More than twenty-five." Harry nodded. "Got some good weed. You want a sample?"

Josie smiled radiantly. "Just put it on the bill. I'll buy an ounce of your best."

The man handed her a small bag and a permit, which she put in her purse. "Thanks."

Raven seemed to be enjoying himself. He bought a mix of ammo, mostly buckshot and rifled slugs for the 12-guage that came with their jeep, along with a tow chain and a big Maglite 4-cell flashlight with spare batteries.

The jeep was tan, with local plates and registration. It was somewhere between rented and borrowed. A SPEC OPS friend of Raven's overseas kept it stored at the local airport. It had huge tires, winches front and back, extra fuel tanks, and an engine that almost launched it into orbit as they left the airport.

Raven paid in cash. Josie passed on Harry's suggestion to visit Bedrock City, an adjacent 1960s theme park based on the old Flintstones TV series. She had seen it on the way in – rundown and overdone in gaudy, faded plastic. *Ugh.*

Harry looked disappointed.

"We're on our second honeymoon," she explained sweetly.

"Sorry." Raven shrugged.

Josie gave Harry a twenty and told him to split it with the park. She took Raven gently by an earlobe and started leading him out. The old man's laughter followed behind them until the door closed.

"*This* is our vacation spot?"

"Just passing though, Babe. Best to fit in with the locals."

"Seriously, tell me why you picked it."

"I wanted to be alone with your warm pink body…."

"What else?"

"It's off the grid, an empty, unincorporated area. You do a Google map and all you see is empty desert. Valle is not even on most roadmaps, and anyone but locals and eccentrics will stand out as if they have a neon sign on their heads. If any strangers show up at the airport, I will know it. We'll hang around for a week or so to see if anyone is following us."

"I was hoping for romantic."

"That too. You got it, Babe. Tonight, we watch the sun set over Grand Canyon, one of the best views on the planet. You will not believe how the colors soften and change, there is nothing like it. Then we get some big steaks, drink good wine, and sit in front of a fire. After which I ravish you in a king-sized bed."

"Yum." Josie smiled. "Hot showers and indoor plumbing?"

"Bet your ass."

"I think I just did," Josie said softly. "But I still want to know about the plumbing."

"Guaranteed. Toilets, soap, and the whole nine yards."

"You take a shower first?"

"It's a desert. We do it together and save water. Then we hang for a while, walk the rim, enjoy the views, and see the sights. After it checks out clear locally, you do your mental thing and contact Kaimi. When he has got it set up on that end, we move on to Hawaii and get in some beach time. He is lining up a house on a lagoon where we can snorkel. How's that sound?"

"I love you." Josie reached up, put her arms around his neck, and kissed him. It lasted a long time.

He smiled into her eyes. "Is that a Yes?"

"Do I get to drive the jeep?"

"Fucking-A," Raven said. "Yee-haw."

The wheels spun all the way until she hit pavement.

The End

FACTOIDS AND FANTASIES

L ong ago and far away (metaphorically), my nonfiction book *Engines of Prosperity* included a prescient mid-90s quote from Dr. Alvin Toffler, the futurist, *"The sophistication for deception is increasing at a greater rate than the technology for verification. This means the end of truth."*

In today's world, there is a lot of truth in fiction, and a lot of fiction in truth. These days, it is hard to discern which is which, and even harder to verify. There are still First Amendment rights, but truth becomes buried under spin, propaganda and plausible lies. Orwell warned us of this.

Raven's Run, featuring terrorists with Iranian nukes, came out before the Obama/Kerry "Iran Deal." It gave Iran a path to nuclear weapons and massive funding (~ $150 Billion) for terrorism. Iran is still chanting "Death to America," a goal which is embedded in their Constitution.

Privacy Wars predicted the NSA and IRS scandals, and I am not the only novelist to have done so. These days, people are going back and reading books like *1984*. *Soft Target* had the notion of a virtual Congress, and several pundits have since suggested that America might be better off with an "iCongress" than the one located in Washington. [**Note:** This has nothing to do with repealing any Amendments. The notion was that a return to how Congress worked in the early years – spending most of its time at home with constituents, versus inside the beltway with lobbyists – worked a lot better. Cyber technology could allow this and make us safer.]

My "Freedom Writers" blog, http://blog.johntrudel.com has facts, research, history, and guest posts. If you search for the phrase "is it real" you will find posts about how my novels touch unfolding reality. For the one about the Iran Deal, see http://blog.johntrudel.com/?p=2499

My author's page, www.johntrudel.com, is about novels. Here you will find interviews, reviews, and samples.

My view is that the best fiction is NOT reality, but it is an image of reality. Consider books like 1984, or any of the works from major authors like Tom Clancy, Brad Thor, Michael Crichton, and Vince Flynn, among others. Their novels resonate with truth.

In a world where news resembles propaganda, novelists are again becoming the canaries in the coalmine. History tends to repeat. The names Rushdie, Solzhenitsyn, and Lorca come to mind.

Recall the disastrous Neville Chamberlin "Peace in our time" treaty with Hitler. Can anyone think a "Deal" that allows *jihadists* nuclear weapons and delivery systems is a good thing? The media and the current administration say that it is. Kerry might win a Nobel Prize. Hitler almost did too, and he did make the cover of *Time*.

The Iran Deal was opposed by 71% of the public and most of Congress. A minority partisan block of 42 Senators voted NOT to disapprove. A few even gave warning speeches about the dangers of the Deal <u>before</u> they voted. Without disapproval, the deal stood. Iran got nukes.

Islam is Ascendant

The world is in flames. The Arab Spring has become the Islamic Winter.

Islam is now expanding as rapidly as when it started and quickly conquered two thirds of the world. There are more refugees than at any time since World War II. From Fort Hood to Boston and from Ramadi to Roseburg, *jihadist* attacks are increasing.

The FBI says there are now ISIS cells in every state. There are three Islamic groups working to establish Caliphates, all well financed, with modern weapons and political support. Despite this evidence, Obama said, *"The future must not belong to those who slander the Prophet of Islam."*

Obama's wars have "accidentally" advanced radical Islam. http://blog.johntrudel.com/?p=1523

Global *jihad* has not yet been "declared." Instead, we see terrorism and migration *jihad* — *Hijra*.

Jihad is acknowledged as an obligation at least as important as the Five Pillars of Islam. There is however, a moral obligation to tell your enemy that you intend to attack, when you have decided to do so.

The Greater *Jihad* (*Jihad al-Akbar*) is self-criticism aimed at self-perfection, similar to Ben Franklin's project described in his diary, or to the Christian examination of conscience. The Lesser *Jihad* (*Jihad al-Asghar*) is the requirement to defend and extend Islam until the entire world acknowledges the rule of Allah. Today we see the lesser. It is working.

Corollaries, supported by texts in the Qur'an and the Hadiths, are that non-believers who are exposed to the Truth and fail to comply must be eliminated, but temporary measures include *dhimmitude* (paying the *jizya*, stepping off the sidewalk to allow a Muslim to pass) and enslavement.

This Lesser *Jihad* is **not** less important than the Greater. It is the offensive game. It need not require military action. It can be practiced not only by the arm, but also by the tongue, the heart, and the purse. But slaying an infidel does guarantee you a place in Paradise, and a higher level with larger numbers of infidels killed. A famous Turkish massacre was marked by the extraction of the living fetus from pregnant women so that there could be credit for two infidels killed.

The astonishing spread of Islam in its first century was due to the sword. There was a hiatus after the defeat at Vienna when Western technology (more advanced weapons) made battle inadvisable. The nuclear weapon will be the great Equalizer, and allow *jihad* to proceed. The only option the West has to derail this juggernaut is to demonstrate that the Allah of Islam is powerless. That will be difficult, since Islam has had so many successes in the recent decades.

Remote Viewing

The Intelligence Community had a number of active remote viewing programs during the Cold War, including *Grill Flame,* which was probably the most famous. These programs were officially terminated some time ago, and some of their relevant materials declassified.

There is (or was) a declassified 1986 Defense Intelligence Agency (DIA) Training Manual for Remote Viewing available on the Internet. Joseph McMoneagle wrote a book, **Mind Trek**, and there is an interesting Marine War College Thesis, *Unconventional Human Intelligence Support: Transcendent and Asymmetric Warfare Implications of Remote Viewing*, submitted by Commander L. R. Bremseth not long before 9-11.

An entertaining look at the program's history is **The Men Who Stare at Goats**, by Jon Ronson.

Iran and the Mideast

Mark Steyn and others have written widely on the increasing conflict between Western nation-states and fundamentalist Islam. Steyn's **America Alone** and Samuel P. Huntington's earlier **The Clash of Civilizations** discuss this. **The Secret War with Iran**, by Ronen Bergman, is also recommended.

Before Jimmy Carter, Iran was one of our best allies in the region. Now the Islamic Republic of Iran (though not its people) is an implacable enemy of America, a growing power, and a deadly threat.

EMP Weapons

The Wall Street Journal ran an editorial, *The EMP Threat*, on August 9, 2008 which presented declassified portions from a July 2008 Congressional Committee Report chaired by William Graham. The physics discussed in my novel are accurate and derived from open sources.

Starfish (a nuclear test mentioned in **Raven's Run**) was real. Iran is publishing strategy papers about using EMP weapons. It is also developing intercontinental missiles and buying sophisticated air defenses from Russia.

America's Achilles' Heel

An attack that disabled America's power grid would be devastating. This weakness has been warned of for years, but the Media and Congress keep the lid on. In early 2014, *The Wall Street Journal* ran several articles on this, prompted by a professionally executed shooting attack, a dress rehearsal that disabled a key Silicon Valley substation in April 2013, leaving behind only fingerprint free shell casings and small piles of rocks that marked the best shooting positions.

Experts were unanimous that this was not a "failed attempt," but rather a "dry run." There are reports of other "unusual outages," but the attack on the Metcalf substation is the only one to make the national news (so far) and that only because of *The Wall Street Journal*. Sources in the power industry say, "No one will cover this (the risk of a grid shut down)."

The Senate did hold hearings about the Metcalf attack in 2014. Its focus was NOT on protecting the power grid, but to discuss concerns that the attack had gotten public notice. http://blog.johntrudel.com/?p=678

What are the consequences of even a "limited" nuclear attack that takes down the entire grid? Let us just say it is NOT good. Tens of millions of people would die.

Not with a Bang, but a Whimper?

I have worked in the Mideast. Muslims are the best hosts in the world. They live in a harsh land, and they treat their guests well. The book *Lone Survivor* is an incredible testimonial to this.

With that said, the history of Islam is one of conquest. The Lesser *Jihad* is constant against outsiders. Islam is a religion of the sword. It is built on conquest, beheadings, and enslavement. ISIS with its brutal beheadings and atrocities is using the old methods. It is as relentless, bloody, and horrific as were the conquerors of 700 AD.

Islam is an ideology of conquest, a total system of government and law with a religious component. It is a form of Theocratic Socialism, just as the Nazis were National socialists; Communists are International socialists, etc. Few Western leaders have understood that, with Thomas Jefferson and Churchill being exceptions.

Fundamental to Islam is Sharia Law, a belief that takes precedence over freedom and laws, national constitutions, and certainly over the Judeo Christian ethic and absolute codes of conduct like the Ten Commandments.

The senior Bush seems to have understood that. His son missed the lesson. Obama and the Arab Spring erased Bush II's gains in Iraq, and this unleashed the violent, radical Islam that had long been suppressed. Ancient evil has returned. The monster is out of its cage and gathering strength.

Western leaders say it is harmless. I wish they were not lying.

Islam rolled out of the Holy Land in the 8th Century and quickly conquered two thirds of the world. It took the West some 400 years to fight back — longer than the United States has existed. We seem to be in the process of repeating this bloody cycle.

The Crusades to push Islam back did **not**, and could not, come from inside the conquered territories. It came from the bloody edge of what remained and was at risk. One Spanish woman played a key role. An interesting, well-researched book on this is ***Isabella: Warrior Queen. Thomas Jefferson and the Barbary Pirates*** is also recommended.

In ***Raven's Run***, my characters thwarted a state-sponsored nuclear EMP attack. In ***Raven's Redemption*** that huge threat remains, but offstage. In both novels, they fight the Lesser *Jihad*.

ABOUT THE AUTHOR

John D Trudel has authored two nonfiction books and four Thriller novels: *God's House*, *Privacy Wars*, *Soft Target*, *Raven's Run*, and *Raven's Redemption*. He graduated from Georgia Tech and Kansas State, had a long career in high-technology, wrote columns for several national magazines, and lives in Oregon and Arizona.

http://www.johntrudel.com/

As an inventor and an instrument rated multiengine pilot, he has long loved aviation and technology. John had a pilot's license before he had a driver's license. He built and flew his own radio-controlled aircraft before they were called "drones" and programmed computers before PCs existed.

His popular "Freedom Writers" blog was selected by a Radio Host as one of the "top 8 in the Northwest." It has a mix of information about both real world events and novels.

http://blog.johntrudel.com

John's first four novels all won National awards. Two were finalists for the prestigious Eric Hoffer award. *Privacy Wars* predicted the NSA and IRS scandals, winning three Awards in the process and gleaning many media interviews.

Details, links, interviews, and video trailers are posted on John's website. The first chapters of his novels are there too, free.

Dr. Jerry Pournelle, the world famous SF writer and Star Wars scientist, described **Raven's Run** as a "Thriller on the bleeding edge of reality." If you like John's books, the most helpful thing you can do is to recommend them to your friends and post a review on Amazon.

THANK YOU ALL FOR YOUR INTEREST AND SUPPORT.